A Clear Destiny

A Clear Destiny

A Revelation Of Long Hidden
Ancient Scrolls Begins The
Greatest Adventure Of Them All

Callie McFarlane

Library of Congress Control Number:		2011901600
ISBN:	Hardcover	978-1-4568-6183-4
	Softcover	978-1-4568-6182-7
	Ebook	978-1-4568-6184-1

To order additional copies of this book, contact:
Xlibris Corporation
1-888-795-4274
www.Xlibris.com
Orders@Xlibris.com
92675

Dedication

To my husband in heaven, the love of my life, whose understanding and encouragement made me reach beyond myself—my enduring love and thanks. Eternity is too short.

June 2011

Nancy Z

Years pass for us all, and for some it means separation, but from the outset, we've had a special connection which has thrived. So it is that I wish you smiles, excitement and release from your heavy schedule as you walk with the characters in ACD. I can see you smiling now...

Much affection,
blah blah blah!

Me

Contents

The Beginning

West Bank of the Dead Sea, Judean Desert 1950

The heat radiated from the desert sand, wafting against the rugged wadi in iridescent waves. The limestone and granite cave cluster and southern cliffs called Ein Feshka lay along a 2.75 km stretch south of Wadi Qumran and extended south for another few kilometers ending at Ras Feshka. Hillel Naphtali Penuel Har-Ish leaned heavily on his staff, tucking the end of his *kaffia* more tightly across his face, squinting his eyes. He was just able to pick out three camels approaching at a hurried lope, their riders hunched forward, mercilessly urging their animals to outrun the following storm that loomed dark in the distance.

Scuttling back toward the cave, Hillel swung the pot filled with coffee and water over the goat dung fire. The shelter for the camels—meager as it was—abutted a curve in the wadi and had been readied with ample water, grass, tender shoots, and browse collected from the spring of Ein Feshka. With their bellies full, the animals would hunker down to wait out the storm, tightly closing their double row of eyelashes, and sleep for hours to dull their exhaustion. The travelers, too, would welcome the shelter of the cave and Har-Ish's hospitality after their arduous journey. After so many months in seclusion, he was eager for the sound of their voices and the news they would bring.

He stroked the young goat that, just having nursed, nuzzled his hand. But for this one curious kid, his small herd contentedly huddled in the rear of the cave, the bucks vying for the least dry fodder and the does chewing their cuds while they nursed. As he had recited many times previous, Har-Ish whispered religious intonations to the kid.

"Mizmor l'David, Adonai ro'i lo echsar. Bin'ot desheh ya'arvitseyni al mey m'nuchot y'nahaleyni. Naf-shi y'shovev, yan'cheyni b'maglei tsedek l'ma'an Sh'mo. Gam ki eileich, b'gey tsalmavet, lo ira-rah ki Atah imadi, shivtecha umishantecha heyma y'nachamuni. Ta'aroch l'fanai shuchan neged tsor'rai; di-shanta bashemen roshi, kosi r'vaya. Ach tov vachesed yirdeyfuni kol y'mey chayai v'shavti b'veit Adonai l'orech yamim."[1]

On and on he reverently chanted, the ancient Hebrew words of the 23d Psalm rolling from the tongue of his childhood memory. He glanced to the pile of stones covering the sack with the leather bound antiquity inside. "It will keep us safe, little one." The braying of the camels and commotion sounds of arrival drew his attention. Husein Al-Dhib and Hillel's cousin, Chalafta ben Haim ben Arach, entered the cave, the third man remaining outside to bed the camels.

"*Shalom*, Chalafta. *Shalom,* very pleasant to finally meet you, Husein ibn Al-Dhib." Hillel bowed his head deferentially, spreading his arms to welcome the visitors to his humble cave dwelling.

"*Toda, shukran*,[2] Har-Ish. Do you have what we seek? We have come far. I would see them." The dusty and weary Al-Dhib spoke in a flat tone, removing his traveling garments.

"Yes, yes, all is here. Please, rest yourself. I have coffee," affirmed Hillel, pouring a cup of the steaming, thick brew into a metal cup. Al-Dhib took the cup, his eyes levelly appraising Har-Ish. Sipping noisily to Hillel's compliment and pleasure, he nodded his head, his eyes never breaking his gaze.

"The package." Al-Dhib commanded. Hillel nodded and bowed, crossing to the stone pile at the side of the cave.

"It is . . . as you said it should be, honored one. These long months . . . I have protected them . . . until your visit." His speech halting, Hillel struggled with conversation, despite that he had rehearsed the lines of his negotiation many times.

"Protected it? Ha! From what? The stinking goats?" Al-Dhib's retort and tone indicated his disdain of the man and his surroundings. "I would see them now!"

Hillel hurriedly removed the last of the stones, retrieving the sack. Cradling it in his arms, he presented it to Al-Dhib. He glanced at Chalafta for some sign of encouragement, as this visit was not proceeding as he had anticipated. Chalafta remained stone-faced, staring at the sack as Al-Dhib gently unwrapped it, gingerly withdrawing what looked like a leather-bound roll.

"*Alhamdulillah!*"[3] whispered Al-Dhib in exclamation as he approvingly evaluated the scrolls within the leather bindings. "They are perfect!"

Hillel intoned, "It is as the word I have sent to you, honored Al-Dhib, is it not? If you will forgive me, we should speak about my promised payment. Then we can break bread together, yes?" Hillel Naphtali Penuel Har-Ish knelt deferentially, his eyes gleaming with the knowledge that his 'find' was greater than he imagined. The third man entered the cave and sat opposite Chalafta by the fire, helping himself to coffee.

Al-Dhib said to him, "Our friends have delivered on their promises, Ali. Do you not think it is time that we delivered on ours?" Al-Dhib smiled at Har-Ish and his cousin in turn. The deadly aim of Ali's pistol found its marks, instantly toppling the two Israelis where they sat. The goats scurried in frenzied circles and bleated with the gun's report, huddling deeper against the rear of the cave wall.

As he rewrapped the antiquities in their leather bindings, Al-Dhib said to Ali, "Remove this filth well away from the cave. The coming storm will have its way with them."

A lone and curious kid ventured toward his prone master, sniffing and bleating softly. Al-Dhib snorted. "And Ali," he said, pointing to the kid, "see to it that we have more than bread and dates to eat. The storm will keep us here for awhile."

Ali grinned as he inclined his head.

Chapter 1

Coastal Maine 1993

Along the rocky shoreline, the river was a dark gray with breaking whitecaps against the deep green of the pines. Marcy knew that the ocean at the mouth of the estuary would be roiling with three-foot waves. With rain pummeling her face, she raced to the welcoming warmth of the barn. As soon as the door creaked with her arrival, the horses whinnied a greeting.

"Hi, guys, looks like a true Nor'easter brewing up out there. Hmm, is anyone hungry?" Marcy giggled with delight, unable to escape nuzzles and nickers, as she threw hay flakes and scooped grain into feed troughs. This was one of her favorite times of each day. The unconditional love expressed by the horses when she came to feed, clean, and groom made her heart full, and she felt with surety that all was right with the world . . . at least while she was in the barn!

Her mother, Elizabeth, flipped the pancakes and poured juice into glasses on the table, smiling a welcome to her husband, Jeremy, as he clumped into the kitchen with the twins—each wrapped around a leg, heads tucked into their pajama shirts in a ghost parody.

"Can't seem to find the boys this morning, Liz," he said. "Seems they've made themselves invisible. At least that's what must have happened, since they didn't show up to brush their teeth when I roused them out of bed a while ago. Just vanished into thin air; what do you think about that?"

"Hmm," said their mother, "guess we'll have to feed these hotcakes to the dogs, since invisible boys can't eat visible food, can they?" The matched pair of Irish Setters wagged their tails at her remark, seeming to know its meaning. They immediately sat in concert, tongues lolling out of their mouths, tails thumping the floor in enthusiasm.

Giggling, the twins tumbled from their father's legs onto the floor, popping their heads out of their shirts with exclamations, "Here I am!" "We were here all the time!" "I'm hungry!" Scurrying to their places at the table jostling each other to gain the first seat, the twins were the epitome of happy, healthy six-year old boys.

"Okay, you two. Settle down and get ready to say prayers. Luke, take your elbows off the table and Matthew, take your napkin off your head." Elizabeth spoke with her usual tolerance tinged with humor, and the three of her "men" present smiled at her with adoration.

"Mom, do we have to wait for Marcy? The pancakes will get all cold and yucky!" intoned Luke. "Yeah," chimed in Matthew, "she'll probably be in the barn for hours and hours and . . ."

"Never mind boys," said Jeremy, "she'll be along in a minute. Then, after you're dressed, you can help her sort the barn before we go into town. That is, *after* you brush your teeth and brush those mops you call hair."

"Aw, Dad," said Matthew, just as Marcy burst into the kitchen bringing the smell of hay and fresh rain with her.

"You'll never catch yourself a man looking like that!" said Andrew as he plucked a hay wisp from his sister's hair, followed by a kiss on her head. Her older brother, as tall as their father and possessed of the same broad-shouldered torso atop slim hips and muscular legs, joined them at the breakfast table. Father and son grinned at each other as Marcy blushed, raking her fingers through her wavy auburn hair. All the men in the family were blonde and blue-eyed; the women had flowing reddish waves framing serious, deep-set brown eyes.

"At least Marcy was up in time to complete some chores before breakfast unlike some others I could mention," said their mother. "You didn't leave my cloakroom all muddy, did you? I'm having the Garden Club luncheon here today, so you're all on warning: muddy boots stay on the porch."

The others all looked at each other, the boys rolling their eyes, as Jeremy chided, "You all heard your mother. Behave yourselves . . . at least until the Holy Garden Club Ladies leave, okay?" The twins giggled, Marcy and Andy whispered about the day's plans, and Jeremy supervised the passing of breakfast platters. Elizabeth looked at her family with pride and love. She and Jeremy had four great blessings in front of them, coupled with many other of life's blessings. Sensing the moment, Jeremy looked up with humorous eyes turning soft and held out his hand.

"Liz, why don't you give thanks this morning?" They all held hands as Elizabeth began to pray, a tear slipping down her cheek.

Late summer, Maine 2005

Their mother served cool drinks on the porch as the family gathered to say their goodbyes. The twins looked at Andy with glances alternating from hero worship to uncertainty. The tight-knit family was feeling the imminence of life without Andrew Vale Stanton. The silence of these last few moments together was deafening.

Andy looked at his brothers and moved to gather them in a bear hug. "I love you guys. Take care of Mom for me, okay? And no getting into more trouble than I did, or I'll have to come home and whip your butts. College is great and you're going to love it, just don't forget you're there for an education," he said. With a serious face belied by twinkling eyes, he continued, "And I mean the kind that you find in books." The three Stanton boys clasped hands and knocked fists, grinning at each other.

Turning to Jeremy, Andy said, "Dad, thanks for backing me up on this. I know it's been difficult, particularly with Frick and Frack here leaving for college. I love you for that, and much, much more. Try not to worry." Andy grinned at Luke and Matthew, nodding his head at them, "Besides, I have a feeling they'll keep you plenty busy."

Jeremy held his eldest child around the shoulders and said in somber tones, "I have faith in you, son, and I trust that your decisions will be good ones. Whatever comes, wherever you are, know that you'll always be in our hearts and that we love you." Father and son, much like mirror reflections, looked at each other quietly, then hugged deeply and shook hands.

Elizabeth rose to kiss and hug her son. She was such a beautiful woman, regal in bearing, her fiery hair always slightly wild framing a heart-shaped face of milky skin from which burned her dark, passionate eyes. "I love you, Andrew. Come back to us safe and sound, and never forget who you are, not for one minute. Now, everyone take a bag and let's get Andy's things into the car before he misses his train. Boys, Marcy, ready?"

As they moved down the broad porch steps toward Marcy's Jeep, the horses came cantering over to the fence, their neighs a fitting adieu. The commotion broke the tension, and the family all looked at each other and laughed. It was a special moment none would forget.

Marcy had remained silent as her family shared those last moments together. She was to take Andy to the train station, and preferred that she and her brother have privacy to say goodbye to each other. The train station was unusually quiet with only swirling eddies of dust distracting their private thoughts. Marcy looked at Andy and saw a brother who had shared her life from moments of sorrow to giddy laughter, now a man about to embark on a journey that would lead him to challenges, accomplishments, and change. Would this inevitable separation change their relationship also? Would they be able to remain close with the demands of new lives pressing for their attention and time? Now, sitting together on the bench in the sunshine awaiting the boarding call, she felt desolate.

"Oh, Andy," sobbed Marcy as she put her arms around him. "I'm going to miss you so much. It feels as if part of me is being ripped away. I can't stand the thought of anything happening to you. You better keep in touch with me, or I'll have a nervous breakdown and it'll be all your fault." The boarding call resounded and the twins looked at each other apprehensively.

"Well, this is it, sweetie," said Andy.

"Go, and give them hell, okay? Remember, the CIA's never had to deal with a Stanton before." He picked up his bag and Marcy held his face in her hands. "You big lug, a whole lot of love goes with you, you know. Stay safe and come back here, okay?"

"Deal, sister mine," he said walking backward toward the track. "Forever," he called out.

"Forever," she called back. Waving through her tears, Marcy turned for the parking lot and the security of Windward Farm.

ChAPTER 2

White Birches Farm, Maine, September 2007

Tommy blistered around the course on the black stallion, clearing all the obstacles with room to spare. Both horse and rider glistened with a fine sheen of sweat from the thrill and exertion. 'What a team they have become,' Marcy thought with pride. Obsidian had suffered a third degree lameness earlier in the season that had threatened to compromise his show career, and Marcy had been key to his recovery and return to fitness. Tommy Brandon, Obsidian's owner and rider, had faithfully come to the clinic daily to check on his progress and spend "partnering" time with Obsidian during his long recovery. The two trotted over to Marcy—the horse blowing in triumph, the rider grinning from ear to ear.

"Marcy, me love, we've never gone better, thanks to you." Tommy was the darling of the show circuit: tall and lean, with looks and bearing borne of generations of fine English stock. His family maintained an estate not far from Windward Farm in addition to their manor house in the Hampshire countryside, and large flat in London. Tommy followed the international show circuit, leaving a trail of blue ribbons and broken hearts everywhere he went. For the remainder of the month, he would be in town until the trials were completed. He and Marcy had been seeing each other socially, brought together by her care and treatment of Obsidian, as well as a previous long but casual friendship.

"So, what do you hear from that brother of yours?" Tommy had a maddening way of asking about things directly and out of context. She had not mentioned Andy to him for weeks, but she had been harboring feelings of concern, not having heard a bleep from him in over two months. Andy had shared with her that he had taken the precaution of penning several short letters to their parents in advance, the envelopes to be posted by an associate in just such an event. Marcy had kept the covenant with Andy, feigning excitement when her parents read one of his brief messages aloud to the family after dinner.

"Nothing much of any account," she said, hating the deception. "Are you up to dinner at Windward? Mother said to invite you and your parents while they're visiting, if you're all available."

"Absolutely, my pet! One would have to be daft to pass up an invitation to sample another of your mum's meals. I'm certain Lord and Lady Brandon will accept with pleasure, but I shall ring you to confirm by 1700, if that's all right with you?"

"Perfect," she said, "talk to you then." With a quick wave goodbye, Marcy made her way to the Jeep, thinking how nicely the britches clung to the muscles of Tommy's thighs.

Everyone thought that Marcy was head-over-heels in love with Trevois Hattingley Swift, the Washingtonian Navy Commander Marcy had been dating for the last year. Tre was due to arrive later in the weekend for several days' visit. It seemed obvious that Tre was gearing up for something more definitive in terms of their relationship, if all the phone calls, gifts, and cards were any indication. The family had endlessly teased Marcy that this visit was predestined to usher forth a formal proposal of marriage.

"Darling," said her mother as she iced the top of the beautiful gateau she had prepared for dinner, "you know, you're going to have to sort things out in your mind sooner rather than later."

She was referring, of course, to Tre's upcoming visit versus Marcy's relationship with Tommy, which had been laced with frequent outings in the last several weeks. The meaningful look Elizabeth cast her daughter revealed her awareness of Marcy's conflict. Wasn't the vernacular expression 'sooner *or* later,' thought Marcy? Her mother's deliberate choice of 'rather than' made plain the inferred urgency.

"Mom, I'm just not ready to make a life-altering decision about anything right now. Just because all my friends are either married or engaged, shouldn't mean that I have to be. I like things just the way they are. And besides, where is it written that just because someone falls in love with you that you have to love them back?"

"Of course not, sweetie. I'm sure you know that Tre loves you, just as I'm sure you know that his feelings are not to be treated lightly, whether or not you reciprocate. Tommy is a dear and has been a delightful distraction, and it seems he, too, is attracted to you. And why not? My daughter is bright, beautiful, independent, and a woman of fine reputation. It's just that if you're not careful, one of those two fine young men is bound to have his heart broken, and break yours in the process. That wouldn't be fair to anyone, now would it?"

Marcy looked glumly through the windows that made up one wall of the homey but vast kitchen. On the one hand, Tre was the epitome of what any woman could want: sweet, intelligent, handsome, and oh-so-striking in his uniform, with a solid future. Tommy, on the other hand, was a playboy with nary a concern for his future. Where Tre was blonde and tanned with Northeastern granite features that suited any sailor, Tommy had dark, curly hair and a perpetual aura of mischief surrounding his fine-featured Hollywood face. Tre would carry on his family's Navy tradition; Tommy would do likewise in the tradition of his family, except that his life likely would be steeped in politics and the swirl of an upper crust social life. Both men had chosen their ultimate futures with consistent nudges of great expectations from their families.

How very different from the way in which her parents approached their roles in their children's lives. Each Stanton child had been encouraged to experience a host of things from cultural pursuits to sports to appreciation of the natural world to academics. Each had ultimately discovered those things that held allure, preference, synergy, or innate ability. Each was supported in the pursuit of their individual dreams, determining their own path, and the choice of their life course. Jeremy and Elizabeth had consciously chosen lovingly to guide their children with comforting arms, dependable structure, and sound advice. Their style of parenting gave their children the wings to fly away on the winds of their individual destinies.

The most stringent demand they ever made was that their children remember who they were in their heart of hearts, what they had learned, from whence they had come, and to say their prayers. Marcy could not help but smile, recalling that last admonition so consistently called out each time she left the farm to go back to university or grad school.

She, Andy, Luke, and Matthew were lucky indeed. Her folks had never placed their children under pressure, but merely wanted them to be true to themselves.

"If you base your life on what you know to be good, true, and beautiful," her mother had said countless times, "then you'll be surrounded by goodness, truth, and beauty, and all the bounty of God's world and His protection will infuse your life. Now, please take your clean laundry up to your room." Marcy laughed aloud in recollection. Her mother always seemed to dole out little philosophical gems paired with a behavioral reminder: muddy boots on the porch, feet off the couch, dishes in the sink, pick up, put away, do, and do not do. Somehow, that poignant life lesson made the medicine go down easier, because they all knew that every word was an expression of their mother's love for them.

Andy's amazing understanding of numbers, science, and puzzles won him math and science scholarships to college and beyond. He effortlessly floated through every accelerated course in all categories of study, achieving enviable scores on examinations and theses. Coupled with his natural athleticism, ability to learn and speak other languages, and personal strength of character, it was no wonder that the government took notice of such a shining star with genius potential they wished to sequester and employ for their aims. The private sector had made several bids for Andrew's attention, but his sense of patriotism and love of his fellow man had made his choice a simple one. He would work for the government in a secretive capacity thwarting the "bad guys" to make the world a safer place for everyone. Neither Marcy nor her family much liked the idea, but all of them supported Andy's choice, despite their concerns for his safety and desire to know more about what it was that he would be doing. It was so typical of Andy's idealism.

Marcy had an uncanny affinity for animals, indeed, all living things. The children had all grown up with horses, but Marcy had been the true equestrian. Her innate understanding of their needs led her to pursue a career as a veterinarian, underwritten by her love of science and natural-born desire to be a healer. Had she lived among the early American Indians, she would surely have been a medicine woman. She mused at her mother's patience over the years in view of all manner of wounded animal or bird that Marcy had brought home for care.

She had turned down several lucrative and prestigious offers from large clinics following various internships. She longed for the peace of Windward Farm after a long and exhausting day. Dr. Rawlings' offer came at just the right time in her life. Her qualifications more than sufficed for the equine demands of his practice, and their long relationship made her the ideal candidate to take over when he retired. His proposal intrigued Marcy and, although she had ample time to consider all the ramifications of such a commitment, the timing of Dr. Rawlings' proposition loomed attractively in the background as she considered her current dilemma.

Luke and Matthew had chosen to apply to the same university. They were both accepted, and so began the march to their own drummers. Identical to everyone but their family members, they continued their habit of practical jokes on everyone by "switching places" when it suited them. The two clowns had led the girls a merry chase, and still managed to excel academically like Andy and Marcy before them. They had been a handful growing up, but both were well-liked, well-balanced, sensible young men, if a bit mischievous. Each was an integral part of the other in virtually every way, as is often the case with identical twins. Neither was shy about their passionate love of family, and both young Stantons had earned their parents' justifiable pride. Marcy adored them.

"There! That's finished. Honey, you've been so distracted lately. Why don't you go up and take a nice, hot bath before the Brandons arrive? And while you're soaking, have a think about what I said, okay? I'm just trying to save you some heartache. I know you'd hate yourself for hurting one of them, and clarifying things now will prevent that. You'll know the right thing to do, and the right way in which to do it. Now go take that bath, and relax a bit," said Elizabeth, as she walked Marcy to the back stairs, an affectionately hugging arm around her shoulders.

"Marcy?" called her mother as she just rounded the first landing. "You might wear that pretty blue sun-dress instead of slacks. And perhaps Gram's pearls? It's going to be a warm night, and your hair would look lovely pulled back and up. It would be so much cooler. You can set the table on the porch for drinks and appetizers when you come down. Everything else is done, so enjoy your bath, honey, and just let your mind settle. I'll give you a heads up when time is getting short."

Typical mother, organizing everything and everyone to perfection. Marcy knew she was right and just trying to be helpful, but the problem was that no one could help. She was in a pickle and worse, she was not sure how to get out of it.

Chapter 3

Windward Farm, Maine 2007

"Good evening, Mrs. Stanton. May I present my parents, Lord and Lady Brandon. Father, Mother, this is Marcy's mother, Elizabeth Anne Vale Stanton." Elizabeth shook hands warmly with Tommy's parents, accepting a kiss on both cheeks from his father. "Ah, here comes Mr. Stanton with the twins," said Tommy, stepping across the room extending his hand to Jeremy.

Marcy watched as Tommy deftly handled the remaining introductions. Her mother's warmth put everyone at ease, and even the twins behaved with decorum. Leaving the window, she took a deep breath and walked through to the broad porch. With candles suspended from the soffits over the railings, her mother's potted plants artfully gracing seating areas, and the table presenting a scrumptious array of appetizers glistening below the candelabra, the scene could have been a clip from Martha Stewart's LIVING magazine.

"There you are, Marcy," greeted Tommy as he walked toward her to shepherd her toward his parents. Lady Brandon was selecting delicacies from the table under her father's guidance. Lord Brandon was discussing the punch with her mother seemingly enrapt by her every word, less by the choice of spirits to spike the punch, than by her mother's beauty and charisma. Marcy was unworried about meeting Tommy's parents, but she could not quell her concerns about making subconscious comparisons between Tommy, his family, and his circumstances to Trevois—his counterpart—whose arrival loomed heavily on her mind.

"Ah, the beautiful Marcia!" Lord Brandon smiled broadly, raising his eyebrows. "Thomas, your descriptions were accurate, my boy. She

24

is an uncommon beauty!" He lightly kissed Marcy's presented hand to her blush.

"Father, we *are* in the States, remember. A handshake is more normal here. Can't have you turning all the ladies' heads with your European flourishes, now can we?" Tommy grinned at his gray haired, distinguished father.

"But, Thomas, surely a mere handshake is not befitting a woman of Marcia's obvious caliber. The women of this family show distinction. Come, my dear, you must tell me all about what my rogue of a son has been getting up to these last months." Lord Brandon whisked Marcy toward the table to fill a punch cup for her. As Tommy followed the twins toward the pasture, Lady Brandon glanced up at Marcy as she and Tommy's father approached.

"Well, my dear, finally we get to meet. Thomas has regaled us with stories of you for months. I can now see just *why* his attention has been drawn. Beauty and brains—an unusual combination these days. How do you do . . . and please, my dear, let's drop the 'Lord and Lady,' shall we? You may address me as Madeline. William *do* try those smoked salmon rolls."

Redirecting herself to Marcy, she whispered, "William adores smoked salmon, so your Mother's choices are a real treat. Now, tell me about yourself, Marcia. I prefer getting my information from 'the horse's mouth' so to speak." She laughed jovially. "Wouldn't Thomas be pleased at my use of that expression?" Marcy smiled, nodding. Madeline continued smiling genuinely at her attempted humor, but her eyes probed Marcy's face.

"How do you do, Lady Br, I mean, Madeline. Sorry," Marcy flushed, "Tommy refers to you both as Lord and Lady so often, that's how I think of you. I'm pleased you were able to come to Windward Farm and join us for the evening. My parents know Tommy rather well, and enjoy him immensely. It's nice to be able to meet his parents. How long will you be in town?"

"Yes, that fits the description we've had of you, my dear. Well bred, direct, no nonsense, but utterly charming! Now, now, don't look so flustered. We shall be here only until the Wednesday, and then we fly on to California to meet up with old friends before returning to the U.K. A bit of a loop, but there you are. Thomas has told us that you are the assigned veterinarian for the trials again this week. So, perhaps we might have the pleasure of your company again. Shall we say, Monday? Is dinner or lunch better for you?"

"Well, yes, that is, *yes, I am* the assigned vet again this week, but as for lunch or dinner . . ." Her father's buoyant voice disrupted, announcing that dinner would be served in ten minutes.

"Marcy," Tommy called to her, rejoining the group, "that filly is fabulous. She is really coming on a treat. Have you been on her yet? Blimey, I can't believe you haven't told me how much she's grown. Trying to hide her from me in the 'back forty', eh? Father, you *must h*ave a look before we leave. You, too, Mummy, she's just your type—full of herself."

Tommy's enthusiasm brought smiles to his parents' faces. It seemed he dominated every situation with the force of his presence and his natural exuberance, thought Marcy. He came to her taking her arm in his, turning to his parents saying, "She's a cracker, isn't she? She breeds them, she fixes them, and rides like the wind. I reckon she'd take England by storm."

"She's a bonnie lass, Thomas, but I think she would remind the English of a fair Scottish lass from the old days, not one of our English lilies. What say you, Jeremy?" said Lord Brandon.

"Do Scottish women have red hair and tempers?" asked Luke, to everyone's amusement. Matthew punched Luke's arm, and said, "It's not temper, it's spirit, right, Dad? She's just like Mom and Gram before her . . . full of spirit." Marcy shot Matthew a grateful look just as her mother appeared in the doorway.

"Young man," said Madeline, "you are clearly meant for the Diplomatic Corps! Perhaps one day you will be an ambassador. What do you say, Matthew, does that strike a chord?"

"No, Mam, I mean, not just yet. One of us working for the government is enough for the Stanton family right now, I think. But thank you for the compliment." At everyone's good-natured laughter, he whispered to Luke, "It was a compliment, wasn't it?"

Luke shrugged, replying, "Who the heck knows, bro. Anyway, I can't imagine you in that sort of job. Although on second thought, you've always had a way with the ladies. *Old* ones, I mean, like Tommy's mother," he said snickering. Matthew muscled into Luke intending to deliver another veiled punch. "Mrs., uh, I mean, Lady Brandon," said Luke skirting away, "maybe Matt and I could stop in to see you and Lord

Brandon next year. We were sort of planning to backpack the summer around the British Isles."

"Why, we'd be delighted if you boys were to visit. We could show you around London and perhaps you could sit in on an open session of Parliament in the Visitor's Gallery. Would you like that?" Lady Brandon frowned. "Oh dear me, forgive me boys. You did say 'backpack,' did you not? I don't expect you would have suitable clothing with you for such an occasion, now would you?"

"What's this about a backpack junket?" asked Jeremy with upraised eyebrows. "This is the first I've heard about it." Luke and Matthew looked at each other, swallowing noticeably.

"I hope you're all hungry. It would be a shame to let this dinner cool to leftovers." As the Brandons were escorted to the dining room by Jeremy, Luke looked at Marcy and rolled his eyes. Marcy flicked his head and told him to behave at dinner for their mother's sake, taking each boy's arm to escort her to the table. "Saved by the bell, hmm?" she said with a wicked smile.

"This is for the birds," whispered Luke. "I feel like I'm marching down the aisle, for Pete's sake." Luke looked absolutely embarrassed and squirmed under Marcy's firm grip.

"Get used to it, brother mine. Some day you're going to have to do just that." Marcy grinned at him and then stuck out her tongue. "Now, suck it up, and be a refined gentleman for once. It won't kill you."

As they entered the dining room, Tommy leapt to Marcy's chair. The twins looked at each other and burst into repressed giggles. Elizabeth gave them a stern look as Jeremy pushed in her chair. Their father cleared his throat conspicuously, and remained standing until the twins took their seats. "Let us bow our heads together to give thanks," he began.

Later, while their parents chatted amicably over coffee and brandy, Tommy and Marcy walked toward the barn to the horses' greetings. Marcy felt more confused than ever. She always felt so at ease with Tommy. They shared a deep love and reverence for horses. He admired and respected her work. They knew many of the same people, at least stateside. His parents were wonderful people, despite their titles and obvious difference in lifestyle. She particularly enjoyed his mother's forthrightness. Now there was a woman who got straight to the point without dillydallying. She must have been a force to reckon with in her prime; indeed, she likely would still be someone whom one would prefer as an advocate, rather than as an adversary. Lord Brandon was an absolute charmer. There was no doubt where Tommy got his charisma.

It had been a relief when both sets of parents found common ground for conversation despite their different backgrounds and interests. Marcy had always been aware of her parents' abilities and accomplishments. In fact, as a growing child, she had mused more than once that she would never be able to live up to their record. It took her awhile to recognize that such thoughts were self-defeating, and that only she entertained such comparisons. Neither Jeremy nor Elizabeth ever pre or post judged her, but had instead encouraged her to try (and try again) as she sought to find her special place in the world. As a result, she had developed the confidence and freedom to reach for the gold ring of her dreams. Now, with her professional life well seated, it was time to direct her attention to her personal life. Marcy hated the thought of drama. Everything in her life was as she liked it. Why did outside issues have to complicate matters?

"As I was saying, dear heart, I cannot fathom what is ailing Demiluna. She took the trip just fine. Actually, she's done it several times, as you know. But when I worked her, she seemed a bit heavy and loathe to take even the smaller jumps that she can do in her sleep. I should appreciate your looking at her as soon as you can. We've only a few weeks before she must be ready to take on the competition. Marcy? Are you with me?"

He took her shoulders, turning her to him. As he looked down into her eyes, his usually smiling face turned serious. "Marcy, look here, I know we've been great friends for years, and we've spent a helluva lot of time together, particularly most recently. Actually, it's even better now that you're '*the*' established vet here. I get to see you more frequently. And there's no one I'd prefer to see more than you. Damn, I'm botching this horribly."

As he kissed her, Marcy felt herself stiffen with surprise, and then relax into his embrace. 'Wait a minute,' she thought. This was most definitely *not* the casual hello and goodbye kiss that they previously shared. This was a real, honest-to-goodness-full-blown KISS. Worse, she was enjoying it. Worse yet, she felt no guilt at all. What about Tre? Was it right to kiss Tommy like this? She cared deeply for Tre, and had kissed him like this, but it felt different somehow. Did it really, or was she just swept up in the moment and the fact that she and Tommy just reached a different plateau in their relationship? 'Hold your horses, girl.

You're about to take a jump that may be too high for you to make,' she thought.

"Tommy, whoa, whoa, this is moving too fast. Can't we just keep things just as they are?"

"I'm afraid not, Marcy, darling. Surely, you could tell from all the parental tattling tonight that I'm mad over you. When I saw how impressed Lord and Lady Brandon were with you and your family, I could hardly wait to get you alone and tell you . . ."

"You what?" exclaimed Marcy. "You wanted to make sure that I and my *family* passed m*uster?* Of all the unmitigated, egotistical, pompous . . . just who do you think you are, Thomas Brandon? Here's a news flash: You may *think* you are God's gift to all the women on the planet, and you most certainly are in a class by yourself as far as I'm concerned, but that *class* doesn't start with an upper case letter, despite how upper crust you and your precious pedigreed family are"

"Marcy, no, I . . . my word, you're absolutely gorgeous when you're like this!" grinned Tommy, "It's just that I had to make sure that you and they would be all right with each other before I spoke to you of my feelings, That's not unreasonable, is it?"

Marcy gave him a withering look and turned on her heel for the house. "I'll take a look at that mare on Monday at *precisely* 10:00 AM. Make sure someone is there to hold for me who is capable of exercising her. I may have to do a nerve block, depending upon how she presents," she called over her shoulder. 'In a pig's eye,' she thought, 'I am *not* a chattel on the market block. Hell will freeze over before I ever . . .'

At that moment, Matthew's voice called to her. "Marcy, you've got a long distance call from Washington. I told him you were in the barn, but he said he'd wait. Hurry up!"

'Oh great,' she thought, 'another complication. Why is everything suddenly so turned upside down?'

She stomped up the path to be greeted by Luke's singsong, "Marcy's got a-nother boy-friend. Whatcha' gonna' tell this one, Marce? I'm thinkin' it's gonna be lots of fun around here pretty soon. Yup, things are really warming up." She punched him in the gut as she strode up the porch stairs. Luke bowled over with a yowl, calling after her, "It *is* temper, just like I said!"

"Hello? Oh, Tre, what a surprise. Is everything all right?" It was, as far as Tre was concerned. Instead of arriving solo late Sunday afternoon, plans had changed and his parents would accompany him. He had booked them a room at the Gables Inn for the week, and looked forward to her joining them for lunch or dinner on *Monday*. He also hoped that he could bring them for a visit to Windward Farm to meet her family, perhaps Tuesday or Wednesday.

'Great,' thought Marcy. 'Tommy's parents will be here until Wednesday, and I can't avoid seeing them again, particularly as they've already invited me for Monday lunch or dinner. How do I explain to them? And how do I still remain natural with them during their visit, even though I've just had a serious falling out with their son? Oh, damn, this is turning into a mess.'

"Tre, look, let's leave the arrangements for a bit until I can check my schedule. Yes, yes, of course I'd love to meet your folks. It's just that this is the interval just before the trials. I'm glad you understand, yes, I'll check and let you know. Why don't you phone me at the office on Monday morning, okay? And Tre, make it well before 10:00 AM, okay? I've got an appointment I promised to keep. Talk to you then . . . yes, looking forward to seeing you, too. Have a safe trip and give my best to your folks. Bye."

'Just my luck,' she thought, 'if only I'd taken up Doc Rawlings' offer of going to that veterinary conference, I wouldn't have to deal with any of this.' Taking a deep breath, she walked toward the sounds of their parents' animated conversation in the living room.

"Hello, my dear," said Lord Brandon. "Do come and join us. We're just enjoying your clever mother's elderberry liqueur. Now then, where have you left my son?

ChAPTER 4

Austrian Alps 2007

The ice storm had rendered the middle chair lift all but barely operable. Skiers were forced to carry their skis and leap off the chair onto the icy egress area dotted with gravel and scurry away before the oncoming chair knocked them down or caused them to topple off balance partway down mid-slope. Then they could don their skis to ride the last lift to the top of the mountain, braving the mid mountain icy slopes on the way down and safely ski to the bottom armed with stories of crashes or narrow escapes for the evening's gluvein before the fire.

Amid the combination of raucous laughter, shouts, and epithets (mostly in German), Andy gritted his teeth as the chair approached. He was not worried about mimicking the example himself—as he was an excellent, strong, and agile skier—but his chair companion looked frozen in body and mind. Given one could *not* remain on the chair and ride back to the bottom, she had no choice but to jump. Andy had little confidence that Aniela would be able to master the exercise without getting hurt. It was bad enough that in the best of situations, she was obstreperous, willful, and disdainful of Americans; she was also not physically well and wilting fast. Since he needed her to guide him *off piste* for his meeting with Anton, he could not afford for her to be taken out of the equation by the ice.

"Aniela, hold fast to my arm as we leap off, and I'll steady you," he yelled in almost flawless German. She looked at him with flashing eyes and muttered something indistinguishable. 'Okay,' he thought, 'you give me no choice. I'll deal with the consequences later.'

As they neared the top of the hill, Andy deftly placed his arm behind her, scooping her off the chair with the combined thrust of his legs and the impetus of the moving chair. He scurried forward, awkward in ski boots, balancing their combined weight on the slippery mound along with his skis. The unexpected movement caused her to lose grip on her skis, one of them clattering to the ground and skidding perilously close to the edge of the hill. Safely out of the way of the advancing chair, Andy put her to the ground as she ripped away her mask and goggles to give him a tongue-lashing.

"*Besserwisser!*[4] *Dummkopf!*"[5]

"*Stille, stille,*" said one of the other skiers, as he skied to them to pass the errant ski to Aniela. "He did right, don't be mad. It is hard enough for us in these conditions. Do you not see how many have fallen? Be glad. Now you are all right to go to the top and ski down *mit* no sprain. Come on. There is little time to catch *da* lift." He rejoined his friends after a clap to Andy's back.

"I do not need help," said Aniela levelly in English. "Make to tighten your boot to let the rest go. Then we take the chair to the top, and I bring you to Anton." She thrust her boots into her bindings and moved away, still a bit wobbly.

"Are you dizzy?" asked Andy as he glided to her. "Maybe we should take a rest here for a few minutes? I'm worried you won't be able to manage the terrain. If you get hurt, it could be hours before I could get help, to say nothing of our lost opportunity with Anton."

"*Nein, nein,*" she said, again lapsing into German. "You just worry about keeping up with me. There will be no time to waste, and the way is difficult. I cannot be looking back for you or I *will* get hurt. I hope you can ski as you told me. You Americans always exaggerate. If you fall behind, I will leave you. Do we understand each other?"

Andy nodded grimly. Since he had met up with her, she had not given him one friendly word. So much for European undercover counterparts. He would have a word with Liam Corruthers when he returned. The past three days had been a test of his patience.

They let six chairs pass and then boarded. By the time they reached the top, the flurries had magnified to true snowfall. The view was stunning. Having skied his share of America's peaks, Andy was an accomplished skier turned instructor for school holidays. At one point, he thought he might attempt one of the Olympic ski division streams, but chose to pursue time abroad to hone his language skills. These mountains were the real deal: endless peaks connecting Germany, Austria, Switzerland, France, and Italy, farther than the eye could see.

They had arranged to meet Anton somewhere on the Kitzbüheler Horn at an outpost cabin once used by rescue teams. Home to the legendary Hahnenkamm downhill, paradoxically Kitzbüheler Horn was only about 1965m, and the medieval walled village center of Kitzbühel with its cobbled streets lined with colorful frescoed buildings was one of the prettiest mountain villages he had ever seen.

Aniela smoothly debarked her chair with Andy close behind. Just as quickly, she disappeared into a cloud of white, veering hard to the right. Once on the run, the pair skied in perfect synergy, negotiating the difficult, steep slope with ease. Aniela's pole flew out to the right as she cut into the conifers. From there, the going got really tough, and their speed slowed significantly. She slalomed in and out among the trees.

A groomed slope is one thing; powder skiing *off piste* is quite another, and requires a different technique than Nordic or Alpine skiing. If one does not lean back on the haunches to raise the ski tips above the snow, they bog down and the skier stops dead. Andy's flexible knees and strong thighs were burning with the effort, because he knew that if his tips were buried causing him to stop, he would sink. He could not afford to catch an edge or fall. There were sections of unexpected rock face, deceiving powder that collapsed under their weight, the ever-obstructing pines, roots, and patches of ice.

Andy was just able to make out the lip of a crevasse ahead, jutting into the air like a ski jump. She wasn't serious! Just as he had that thought, Aniela lifted off the rock lip and disappeared airborne into the thickly falling snow. 'Next time, it's going to be a quiet little village on the Mediterranean for me,' he thought as his stomach fluttered on the approach.

When a skier is in free fall, concentration is key. Andy tried not to panic; this was totally different from the familiar ski jumps he had taken at various times in his skiing career. Between the wind, the falling snow that obscured the ground and distorted spatial perception, a bubbling sense of panic, and loose rubble scraped from his takeoff that followed him midair, Andy struggled to keep his tips high and aligned for the landing. The ground loomed before him in a flash, and his skis slapped the snow. He fought to keep his balance and avoid jagged rock faces to his right, but he caught an edge and his shoulder careened off the sides of the protruding rocky crag. He flinched with the pain, but his impulsion left him little time to consider any damage sustained. He was moving too fast, his poles virtually useless in the close quarters of the path. On he sped, determined to catch up to Aniela. Where the devil was she?

Just as he broke through the woods, he saw her. She stood leaning on her poles, chest heaving, and head down. When she heard the slide of his stop, she looked up into his eyes. "So, the American is tougher then he looks. You've torn your coat."

He had temporarily forgotten his narrow escape with the rocks, but now his throbbing shoulder and upper arm drew his attention. He glanced at it, surprised to see that his sleeve was bloodied.

"Come," barked Aniela, "we must arrive before dark or all will be lost." Again, Andrew followed the elusive and brusque Aniela, as she whooshed away from him down a broad expanse of snow that seemed to lead to nowhere.

Chapter 5

Alpine outpost, Austria

He nearly cried when he saw the tiny cabin. He and Aniela had had to push themselves because of the storm, stopping infrequently to catch their breath to allow Aniela to reorient herself. Both of them were exhausted, but Aniela was close to the point of collapse, given she had been unwell at the start of their journey. They stowed their skis against the side of the hut and rapped on the door.

"*Gott sei dank*![6] Come in, come in," greeted them in a husky but friendly voice. Anton rose as they entered, rushing toward Aniela as her legs gave way. She and Andy were encrusted with snow from head to foot. He muttered a few words of explanation about their difficulty, as he and Anton stripped off Aniela's outer clothing. She began to shake uncontrollably.

"Is good, will be all right," said Anton, concern lacing his gravelly voice, "she is strong. Help me." Together, they guided her to the bed against the wall, and Anton covered her in quilts and a fur throw. Andy staggered to the table, sitting heavily on a wooden chair.

"Get things off and sit by fire," Anton directed in heavily accented English. He busied himself at the wood stove and by the time Andy had peeled off his outer garments, had produced a steaming mug of black tea for Andy and a small cup for Aniela, holding her up to help her sip the warming liquid.

"You rest now, *bitte*," he said to Aniela. Turning to Andy, he extended a huge hand. "You like to ski, *ja*?" he said with a broad smile.

After several minutes of conversing in German with occasional lapses into English, Andrew learned that Anton was native to these mountains, and had worked for years in a variety of interconnected capacities in the study of early cultures with languages at the root. He was a retired professor having held various Chair positions, a prodigious author, and noted expert in his field. Added to his academic prowess, Anton was a self-proclaimed philosopher whose life had been devoted to opposing violence and helping people escape its clutches, despite their affiliations. The safe passage of information and people arose from his political and ethical beliefs borne of his understanding of humankind. A man of peace, he found solace in his considerable library and endless stacks of notes that would one day find themselves organized into another book (sixth of a series), and gratification in looking after "God's clowns" when they infrequently intruded into his otherwise distracted, esoteric life.

"So, you have come as my Jewish friends promised. It is good, and you must have some more of Anton's special tea, *ja?* We have little time and you must listen carefully. I will tell you why this is so important, *ja?*" Anton poured more of the dark, steaming brew into Andy's metal mug.

"'Qumran' is only a type of shorthand used by us scholars to refer to the scrolls. The word itself is Arabic and names the locale in which the scrolls were found. The caves where the scrolls were discovered in the late forties and early fifties are along the shores of the Dead Sea, as you know. There were several, and each has its own story. But the one you must learn is from Cave 4, discovered in 1954 after the partition of Palestine.

"It will help you to understand the content of each by learning the chronological order in which they were discovered. Cave 1=1Q; Cave 2=2Q; Cave 3=3Q, and so on. There are further designations for manuscripts and fragments such as 4QD=the Damascus Document from Cave 4, as opposed to CD, that refers to the recent inclusions of the same part discovered at the end of the last century. That part of the document was found in a repository now known as the *Fairo Genizah.* But this you will know in time.

"You see, part of the difficulty is that it took a very long time to access the materials from Cave 4. The Jordanian Government set up a team to try to control the process, but the team did not work as a team. It was not international as it should have been, and the process of translation and editing was endlessly delayed.

"The Israel Department of Antiquities, the '*Ecole Biblique*[7], the Jordanian Government, all of them and others did little but to frustrate scholars with their delaying tactics. From these important relics, the first of which were discovered around 1947 by two Bedouin boys, it was not until about 1990 that two teams set to work to catalog, organize, and publish the almost 1800 photographs from the various finds. Can you imagine it? Over forty years!"

"Is there more tea?" asked Andy. "Please don't think me rude, professor, but I see there's more cheese and bread. Could I have a bit more? I'm starving." Andy grinned sheepishly.

Anton shook his head, rubbing his face. "*Ach*, forgive me, my young friend. We old men get talking and forget about hospitality. My wife used to chastise me all the time for forgetting to eat. Of course, help yourself. But there is little time, so we must continue." He placed the board with cheese and bread before Andy.

"Remember, the original team put into place by the Jordanian Government had 'official' stamped all over it, and the public viewed the editions it produced as authoritative. Why? Because *they were* the *official* authority. The problem was that those works were rife with interpretations scraped together from this international team that was not international. Bah!" he snorted in derision.

"It was not scholarly, nor was it archaeological in approach, nor was the team populated by historians, nor were respected translators included in its ranks, and on and on. So when the public read these interpretations, despite the team's complexion, those interpretations also were viewed as authoritative. Don't you see, my friend? Control of the documents meant control of the field."

"Excuse me, professor, but are you saying you take issue with all their interpretations?"

"Of course! And so do my respected colleagues."

Andy offered meekly, "I hope I'm not embarrassing myself, but I'm still unsure as to why you doubt them."

"Because the documents and these interpretations were allowed access only by the *chosen*!" he sneered. "Other reputed scholars might have challenged the interpretations, had they been allowed to study them. There was no competing analysis, no large group of minds and abilities to ferret out hidden meaning or classifications or translations. And so, the published interpretations became accepted as 'official scholarship.' This was utterly improper, and the rest of the community scoffed at the closed access and prevented investigation. Scholarship, 'schmolarship'. Humph!

"'Why,' you might ask, 'is this of any importance' when most of the material was a piecemeal recording of prayers, traditions, the number of amphorae[8] left, and so on?' Simply, remember that control of the documents meant control of the field. All of the work must be considered as a whole, particularly by other experts, to sufficiently describe or interpret the totality of the work discovered at Qumran. So nothing of precision can be said with accuracy without the proper approach. They published only that which they wanted the world to know, and all of it colored by their ideologies.

"This is important for you to keep in mind, as well, as you begin your particular work. Always be mindful of using the *proper* approach. Be comprehensive in your thinking and in your work.

"Regrettably, it follows that those who were involved in these interpretations and their editions, controlled graduate studies in the field worldwide. If one wished to study a particular document, one had to go to them as the faculty member controlling that manuscript, at the appropriate institute. All new chairs and positions in the field, as well as reviews of work, etc. were dominated by them. If you opposed their view, they dubbed you as second-rate. If you supported it, they crowned you first-rate. That perpetuated the same opinion.

"In turn, that opinion influenced minds: minds of academics, scientists, students of all levels, politicians, and common people. That affected politics, which affected governments, which affected national and international policies. And through all of it, Time marched on: countries took politico-cultural stances, skirmishes evolved into minor wars, trade was affected, religious factions clashed, and people were imprisoned or put to death for a host of reasons. Can you begin to appreciate the scope, my friend?

"Understand, we are talking about the scrolls which are somewhat ambiguous, sensitive, ancient documents that speak to the history of mankind and civilization in the West, as well as the Middle East! Perhaps the most important thing is not the reconstruction of the culture or traditions, even though as an historian, it hurts me to say this. But the beliefs, the philosophy of the time, the political implications, the religions! My friend, hear me well. The 'lost scrolls,' we believe, contain an ancient message that will rock the foundations of the world. And the copies of the scrolls I have for you have been hidden for many years. There can be no justification for this type of indignity to mankind."

Anton pounded the wooden table so soundly that the cups, plates, and cutlery jumped.

Anton stood and began to pace the small room, gesticulating with his hands. "The academic world should be committed to the kind of free debate that welcomes all minds, as well as those with opposition theories, not a closed camp that promotes its own theories to the exclusion and condemnation of others."

Aniela murmured as she awoke.

"Come, sit, and drink with us, Aniela." Anton poured her a fresh cup of spiked tea. "Anton knows what is good, *ja*? I am telling our young friend about the scrolls. Now, Andrew, pay attention. The next part is important for you and your friends," Anton said as he scratched out a rough diagram on a rumpled piece of paper.

"Most of the texts are in ancient Aramaic. As you know, Hebrew is the main language of the Hebrew Bible, and Aramaic accounts for only about 250 verses out of a total of over 23,000. But Aramaic—the language of Jesus time—is closely related to Hebrew, as both of them are in the Northwest Semitic family.

"One of the Hebrew texts includes another cryptic writing that requires decoding. I know only a bit about ancient Sumerian, less about Akkadian, Assyrian, or Old, Middle, or Neo Babylonian. *And*, I am not so good with ancient Hebrew either. The one your talents must address has a mix of Aramaic with several other ancient languages. This is where you come in, because the rest of us are not up to the task. There are few in the world good at ancient translations, as well versed as you with the symbols and the writing systems. And I tell you as an historian and archaeologist, that few archaeologists are apt translators.

"You are also from a free nation, my friend. America is well known for laundering its dirty linen in public. The rest of us laugh at you for that. But it is part of your charm, also. And it is part of your strength . . . this openness, this freedom of speech, writing, and publication.

"So! Back to my lesson. As you know, even through the times of Jesus the Christ, Aramaic was preferred for testaments and incantations. Hebrew was considered the holy tongue of the Books of Moses and was used for the more sacred writings.

"About 580 separate manuscripts can be identified from Qumran, with roughly 380 sectarian, non-Biblical texts. These sectarian texts, although often ignored by theologians, have great importance to historians, myself included. Why? Because the beliefs, trends, and culture of Judaism that formed the backdrop to Christianity in the last century BC and first century AD are expressed as eyewitness accounts in these scripts. I look forward to working on them one day. Maybe you, too, will want to join me in this after you complete the work I give you.

"But for now, the most important thing is to work on The Message. It was never part of what was published because, well, you will see for yourself. My colleagues and I have been able to make out just enough to know what it seems to be. We need others to clarify what our old eyes have seen and suspect."

"Surely you could have gathered a group of scientists, Anton. Why have you gone to so much trouble to get *me* here?"

Aniela snickered. "You Americans can be such children sometimes. The copies of the scrolls he wants you to translate and take to America are *stolen*! They were smuggled out to Anton. He cannot *publicly* gather with others to undertake such a task without risking his reputation, all that he has worked for, even his life and that of the others. They would kill . . ."

"Now, now, calm yourself, little one." Anton frowned, placing a restraining hand on Aniela's arm, negatively shaking his head. "We will not speak of this part for now."

Then to Andy, he explained, "Andrew, from what we have been able to piece together of The Message, it reveals a completely different interpretation than the theology accepted as fundamental to most Christians, Jews, and Arabs today. This much we have been able to surmise."

Andy rocked back in his chair, looking from one to the other. "Are you serious?"

"Understand the magnitude of this, my young friend. I can see your confusion and doubt. What you will learn will be unfamiliar to you, in fact, a completely alien Christianity of the first century as we commonly refer to it and understand it.

"The way Christianity has developed *is not* the Christianity in Palestine reflected by the scrolls' first hand witness in the first century. What you will confirm by your translation of the material after you decode it, could have a monumental effect on Judaism and Islam as well.

"Think of it, Andrew. Christians, Jews, and Muslims account for some of the highest percentages of the religious on the planet. What you will have in your hands is the power to overturn thousands of years of their history. This information will shake their very roots."

Andy sat in the chair, staring vacantly toward Anton. His body began to shake. Aniela cast him a furtive glance and rose to place the fur wrap around his shoulders as Anton continued.

"But the real egg within the egg—like the Russian *matryoshka* dolls[9], you know them? Well, the secret of it all is that the texts change all religious interpretation promoted by humankind all these years, and actually link Christianity spiritually with Judaism and Islam. Further, it is proved by these Holy Treasures, that each has a specific mission. You see? It is much like the story of the brothers fighting each other for the Father's favor. But in this case, the fight will earn the father's disdain. What is more, the expectations for the sons are clearly laid out. With the brothers trying to thwart each other's mission, they cancel out eternity for themselves. Staggering, is it not? The thought of no eternity to millions who believe in it.

"At least, that is our conjoint opinion. I admit, we have filled in a lot of the blanks because of our insufficiencies, but where else could it lead? You can determine this accurately, and *only* an accurate, complete translation will have any hope of acceptance. And, as I have said, acceptance will have no chance of even being put to the test unless a power as great as America is behind it.

"The scrolls also speak to the Jews and the Holy Land, and what we think is suggested does not at all resemble what man has done today. It is mind-boggling. It is only since these long-lost scrolls have been retrieved and examined that this has come to the light, and only partially. This is why we need you, my young friend. You must see now that it is critical that this information finds its way to the appropriate leaders to stop the madness that has spread through today's world."

Andrew raised a finger, feeling much like a student begging a question of his tutor. Anton's explanation had been long and rife with fantastic theory. "Forgive me, Anton. Muslims believe that there is only one God, that Islam existed long before Muhammad, and that the religion has evolved with time. Correct?" Anton nodded.

"Even the Qur'an describes many Biblical prophets and messengers like Adam, Nuh[10], Musa[11], Isa[12], and the Apostles as Muslims. The Qur'an states that these men were Muslims because they submitted to God, preached his message, and upheld his values. We know historically, that Islam's development followed Christianity, and Judaism preceded both. Are you saying that the message in these long-lost scrolls speaks to both the development and tenets of Christianity and Islam?"

"Yes, my friend, but now I should say no more on the subject. There is just not enough time, though I would dearly love to talk the night away. Would that I could work with you on this. But, it is not possible.

"I have the material for you in two ways: first, is a document with reduced text and all the pertinent information that must be decoded. All the images, symbols, and letters are clear. The little we have been able to put together from the original manuscript is too piecemeal to be reliable, but it is included. Do not think too badly of us, my friend. We had few resources and little time. You are good at this and also the languages in which it is written, once you have broken the encryption that stymied us.

"Next, is a little disk, some kind of compressed computer record one of my people made of the manuscripts in whole, raw form. They tell me you can view this and enlarge the writing. Time is short, so you must rest and then leave with both. You must protect them with your lives." He looked from Andy to Aniela.

"Where are the originals going to be?" asked Andy. "It's not that I don't trust you or your colleagues, Anton, but there will be others who may assume you *doctored* the reproductions and the photographs you've given me."

"Now listen to me, both of you. You must know this and believe. It has been difficult for me to get these things to you and people have suffered who have helped me. There are others who would suppress these facts because they threaten to upset powerful politics. They have suppressed them for years. They have killed for less, and the loss of these treasures will begin a storm. It is because of an old friend in Ha-Mossad le-Modiin u-le-Tafkidim Myukhadim[13] that they were recovered. They arranged for several of us to meet securely and carry out some preliminary tests and examination before these copies were made. Then the copies were passed through our network at great cost to many, many of our people. My friend and several others placed themselves at risk to bring me to this moment.

"Those who would have prevented this meeting and the revelation that the documents will bring to the world have hounded me and all my friends for a long time. I know not for how long I can make my trail cold. That is why we had to meet in such circumstances. But the snow has been our friend. It will cover you as you leave, and it will protect me as I leave. No one should be able to put us together in this place. The original manuscript—the scrolls—were recovered from the Arabs and will remain with the Jews, specifically the Mossad. Where, I do not know, which is best for the safety of the scrolls. Above anyone, they are capable of protecting them.

"I am sad to give such a mission to ones so young. I entrust the possibility of world peace to you. Ach, such a great burden for only one man. For all our civilized ways, our technologies, our armies, our governments . . . such a great responsibility for the safety of a timeless treasure rests with a handful of humans. Such foolishness! But it is all that could be arranged. *Bitte*, eat a little more, then rest. Tomorrow you leave at first light."

Andrew's head was spinning. What in the world? This was incredible, if it was true. Even if it could be verified, would the opposition accept it? Would his government use it for peace between nations, or would they suppress or misuse it? According to Anton, this would 'shake the very foundations' of the world's religions and political basis. Even if it were suspect, undoubtedly there would be those antithetical to its claims that would wish to destroy it. He had no desire to tangle with them.

Recent memory of his attempts to smuggle a list of persons involved with Taliban brought shivers. He had run from that bunch of thugs for three weeks, barely escaping to Port Grimaud to pose as a tourist, getting lost among the bathers. He had buried his clothes, shoes, and "special material" in the sand and jumped into the surf to come up beside a naked beauty on a raft. Using his charm, they were happily conversing in seconds floating listlessly in the sea making him virtually invisible to his pursuers. Later, that liaison proved not only convenient, but enjoyable for almost a week. What was her name? Francine?

Andy glanced over at Aniela, who had returned to her pallet. She lay with eyes closed, chest barely rising. "Aniela? Are you awake?" whispered Andy. She did not move. He wondered if she had heard all of Anton's disclosure. 'I feel like I'd like to sleep for two days straight after that run, and I don't have the flu,' he thought. 'She must be bionic,' he thought ruefully.

The trip back to the slopes would be brutal, but necessary. His shoulder was sore as a result of a bad scrape and a few deep slices, courtesy the rock face. The sleeve of his ski jacket was shredded where he kissed the stone in his careening flight downhill. Anton had mended it as best he could, to help protect Andy's bandaged arm from the effects of the cold. He mused that heroes and characters in suspense movies or books never seemed to succumb to things like the flu or the common cold. They were always at the top of their game, ducking bullets, eluding capture with uncommon feats of physical gymnastics, always strong, never exhausted, never afraid. 'What the hell am I doing in the middle of this mess,' he thought as he lay down on the hard bed. 'How nice it would be to smell the sheets at Windward Farm,' were the last thoughts as sleep overtook him.

Anton looked at his guests for a long time. He shook his head, smiling sadly.

"So, it has come to this," he said, as he sipped the last of the wine, thinking *'Alea iacta est. Fiat Voluntas Dei.'*[14]

Chapter 6

White Birches Farm, Maine,
Monday 10:00 AM

Demiluna, a usually alert and proud Hanoverian, stood head down in her stall. When Marcy finished her peremptory examination with no certain result, she directed the groom to ready her for exercise. Tommy rounded the corner just as Marcy was labeling the blood vials.

"So, doctor, what do you think? Not herself at all, is she?" Marcy did not look up from her work, and continued to make notes on her exam sheet. "Come on, Marcy, don't let's take Saturday into today, shall we? We can have a chat over some wine later, yeah?"

"Why is it you Brits mess up the English language?" she said with a wry half-smile. "I agree she's off kilter, but I don't know why just yet. And you're right, perhaps I overreacted a bit, but what you said hit me all wrong. Anyway, it doesn't really matter. But I think we *do* need to talk some things over, so if you're free when I'm done here, I'll meet you for drinks at the Club, okay?"

"How many more have you got to do? Perhaps I can tempt you with lunch?" said Tommy. "Then, when we are sated, I could take you for a drive along the coast. Nothing like fresh sea air to clear the mind. We could talk, we could walk, and we could, umm, likely find some other interesting things to fill the hours. What say you?"

"Whoa, there boy. You're starting today in the same mode as Saturday. Slow down and stop making assumptions. I think you're way too used to getting your way with other women. Another news flash: *I am not other women.* I make my own decisions; I determine what I will and will not do, and from now on, I will set the pace, *comprende amigo?* By the way, the operative word is *amigo.*" Marcy collected her clipboard and tray and walked toward the arena with Tommy in tow.

"Yes, my Lady. Whatever Her Ladyship wishes, is my command . . . for now," he said with a twinkle in his eyes. "Just now, I shall concentrate solely on Demiluna."

"Good," quipped Marcy, "because after I do a block and some other things, I want you to ride her through her normal paces. No jumping, just walk, trot, and canter, unless I direct you otherwise. Deal?"

"Of course, whatever you wish . . . excuse me . . . direct. But don't blame me if my attention span fails because you're such a delicious distraction." Just as Marcy was about to chastise him for getting personal again, he ran into the arena where Demiluna was down on her knees.

"My God! What's happened here?" demanded Tommy of the groom.

"I don't know, sir. She just sort of went down all of a sudden. I didn't do nuthin' but stand here, and . . ." explained the groom as Marcy rushed to the horse's side to check her color.

"Okay, girl," she said, patting the horse's neck, who was groaning loudly. "We've got to get her up. Tommy, help me." Between them, they encouraged Demiluna to her feet. She kept shifting her weight and groaning more loudly. Marcy donned a sleeve and prepared the mare for a rectal examination, instructing the groom to set up her portable table and plug in her Ultrasound machine. The mare was shaking so badly that Marcy did not dare return her to her stall. She had a sense of urgency and began barking orders to Tommy and the groom. Another came to attend, and she gave him terse instructions.

Marcy frowned as she withdrew her arm. She changed to a new sleeve, lubricated it, and inserted the Ultrasound probe. "What in the name of heaven?" she said, quickly scanning the screen. She moved with deliberate care, concern etching itself on her pale face. "Tommy, something's really wrong here. Dismiss the grooms and fetch me one of those dark plastic bags from my box." He complied and rushed to her side with the bag as she withdrew several small plastic packets from the inside of the mare. The last one was split, the white powder covering Marcy's sleeved fingers.

"Tommy, if this is what I think it is, we've got to flush this mare at once. It looks like only a little leached out, but even a small amount could be very serious. Do exactly what I tell you, keep your mouth shut, and we may be able to salvage this situation. Now listen closely," Marcy ordered.

Later, as they sat together listening to the call of the seagulls at a seaside restaurant, Marcy sighed contentedly. They had decided to catch a late lunch to plan their next steps. She needed to ground herself after this morning's developments, and the lilting flight of the gulls, the sea breeze, and the sunshine cleared her mind and soothed her spirit. Absorbing the peace of a seaside afternoon, Marcy sipped her tea thoughtfully. For once, Tommy was quiet, perhaps sensing her need, perhaps reacting to his own contemplations.

Demiluna should be fine, barring no unforeseen extreme reactions to the exposure she had sustained that Marcy suspected was a drug. She was fairly sure that the amount that had escaped from the plastic pouch was small, based upon her weight comparison of secure packets versus the compromised one. She had given the mare all the support veterinary science and good judgment offered. She and Tommy had gone immediately to Dr. Rawlings' office, but he had already left for the veterinary conference, not expected to return until Wednesday (coincidentally, the day Tommy's parents departed for California).

"Clearly, someone implanted that mare with those packets, and I'll lay odds they're illegal drugs. What a despicable thing to do, but then those types aren't exactly motivated by ethical considerations, are they?" said Marcy, her mind going over the day's discovery.

Tommy shook his head, still stunned by the revelation. "Blow me down, Marcy, I've never encountered or even *heard* of such a thing. My God! It's absolutely criminal. And to think, in *my mare.* Good Lord, that brings everyone into question, from the grooms both sides of the Pond, to the trainers, to the cleaners, to the shippers, even to my friends." Marcy nodded agreement. "You know, we can't discount vets, either. That means that you, Dr. Rawlings, old Larraby, and any of his compadres in the U.K. All are on the list. Blast . . . we've got a hornet's nest here."

"I think the most sensible next step is for me to keep trying to connect with Dr. Rawlings. He'll have to collect his messages some time, and I've left urgent appeals with the hotel staff and the conference people. He doesn't have a cell phone—too "modern" for him he says—so we'll just have to wait until he phones us. Meantime, we should make a list of everyone we can, everyone who has had any contact with Demiluna here. And you'll have to list all the U.K. contacts. Do you have the details on the shippers handy?"

"No, not on me, but of course there's the arrival paperwork. I can do my best with the British side of things, but frankly, I've never paid that much attention to things here except for the few staff I interact with directly. Good Lord, you don't think this suggests a network, do you? I mean people over there conspiring with people over here? Can you tell when she was infected?"

"Not infected, Tommy, *implanted.* And no, I'm not sure I can tell the when of all this. I suppose one could speculate based upon her blood work and the amount of time required for transfer to affect her blood levels, assuming we get definitive results from the tests I ordered from the lab. Then again, how do we know when the packet ruptured, much less when it was put in place? We can deduce how much powder leached out, but I'm certain there would be no reference data on affectation times in horses in such a condition.

"But more important, we have to get in touch with one of the law enforcement agencies. Frankly, I think this is too big for our locals, although maybe it's proper that we contact them first. That's why I want to speak with Dr. Rawlings. He'd know the right procedure. One wonders whether the state vet board needs to be apprised as well. Whew! This gets more complicated by the minute," said Marcy, putting her head in her hands.

Tommy reached across the table to cradle her elbow. "While this is terrible stuff, and I'm worried as hell about Demiluna, can we shove this aside for just a moment? You look all in, and unless I'm as thick as two short planks, you could use a glass of wine to relax." He signaled the waiter and ordered. "Now, you and I have something else to settle, my lass."

Marcy stiffened. "Tommy, it just doesn't seem right to speak about personal things just now, particularly not with all *this* swirling around the two of us." She sat straight and placed her hands in her lap, removing her elbow from his touch.

"Nonsense, we've laid out what we must do as a next step, and we've yet to finish our wine. It's more efficient to use our time wisely while we can. I have a feeling things will be in a bit of a whirlwind in the next several days. And there's Lord and Lady Brandon to consider, as well. I put them off for today because of the circumstances, though I did not elaborate. Instead, if you agree, we're on for dinner tomorrow—1800 at the Inn, okay?"

"Tommy, I really like your parents. I want you to know that. They're lovely people, and I wouldn't hurt them for the world. But . . ."

"You wouldn't hurt anyone for the world, I know that Marcy," said Tommy cutting her short. "I've a sneaking suspicion that you're about to 'launch into the deep,' as the Biblical saying goes."

Marcy smiled, knowing that his reference was designed to impress her. Tommy was Church of England like his parents, but formally so and not given to serious conversations about belief in God or life values. At least, such topics had not yet been explored between them.

"What I was trying to say was that dinner would be fine, as they're here for only a short time. But it's dinner only, do you understand? Don't try to make it into something more than polite social occasion with parents of a dear friend." She looked at him pointedly, trying to enforce the mettle of her words with her expression.

Tommy looked down at his laced fingers for a time. A light breeze picked up, ruffling his curly, dark hair, the blazing sunshine accentuating its shiny highlights. He looked at her, his face serious and troubled.

"It's rather awkward, I know, in view of how badly the other night went between us. No, hear me out," he said to the shaking of her head.

"You obviously have other suitors, or at least other friends who are attracted to you. I'm not a total clod. But I have to make it crystal clear to you that I am *more* than *just interested*. I've been around the block a time or two, and sampled all the pastries. I know you think me brash or perhaps too unsettled and flippant. But I intend getting my foot into the stirrups for the race, if indeed there is one. Please, Marcy, don't discount me. I grant you, I'm not used to being dismissed. In this case, I will *not* accept it, unless you tell me there's absolutely no hope and you cannot stand me at all. Surely, I haven't misread everything in all the time we've spent together, have I?" He looked at her imploringly, prepared to give her time to digest what he had said.

'Oh brother,' she thought. 'Now, what are you going to say? How can you get yourself out of this entanglement without hurting him? And do you really want to? What about Tre? Damn! Mother, you were oh so right, and your timing was spot on, as usual. Damn it all!'

"Tommy, listen to me. You and I have had a long friendship, and I treasure our times together. We've had great fun, lots of thrills, and gratifying moments connected with the horses. I love your parents.

They're wonderful people. It's just that too much is going on in my life right now to think of . . ."

"Blast, Marcy," he interrupted. "There's *never* a right time or a wrong time. There shall always be interference of one kind or another. What the devil is so difficult about it? You're a vet; you have a great job that satisfies you and earns the respect of those around you; you've got a fine family; you're healthy, beautiful, independent, and smart; the world is your oyster.

"This other thing will ultimately be handled by officials, and your only involvement will likely be in terms of recap and explanation, perhaps with a bit of guidance from a veterinary perspective. There's zero reason you cannot focus on the 'you and me' part, unless there's something you've concealed from me. Is that it? Do I repulse you? Or is there someone else serious hiding in the wings?"

She looked straight at him and took a deep breath. "Tommy, occasionally only because of distance, but for a long time now, I've been dating a very nice guy. He's a Navy Commander based in Washington, and we've known each other for a few years. A 'friend of a friend' type of thing for starters, but well, we hit it off and when there's time, we see each other. In between, we write and phone.

"Sort of like you and me. You go off into the blue to this show or that, this side of the Atlantic or in Europe, and when you're here, we pick up where we left off. The only technical difference is that you don't write at all, and phone very little. Hold your horses," she said to signs of his imminent interruption, "that's not a criticism, merely a comment. I listened to you; now it's your turn to listen to me . . . fully. Okay?" Having his assent, she continued, glad for the moment's pause. 'Make it good, girl,' she thought.

"I don't know exactly how to put this, Tommy. Tre is a great guy, and so are you. I never intended that there should be two men in my life; it just happened, and you both have turned up the gain all at once. It leaves me, well, a bit confused. I mean, we were all just dating . . . well, not even really dating. You and I, I mean.

"We'd catch a lunch or a dinner or maybe drinks, but it was all so casual, particularly since all the other girls are always fawning over you. I really never thought about a *you and me* type of thing. Not the way you mean it. You never seemed to be settled or serious for more than two seconds with people. It's only with the horses that you demonstrate true dedication and with them, you're incredibly focused. And don't get me wrong, that's fine, I mean, fine with me. And not strictly because of Tre, either. I admire that side of you. And I share that same dedication and focus.

"Like I said, Tre and I have dated for a few years, and I'm very fond of him too. He's a great guy, very solid, and we have friends, family, and sailing in common, among other things. I guess I just didn't think beyond what was. It was all so safe and easy, you know?

"I had my job, my horses, my family, and my friends. Everything was neat, tidy, and comfortable. I'd see you when you were in town or the spirit moved you; I'd see Tre when he was in town or I was in his locale for whatever reason, and that was that. I just didn't think beyond those relationships to, uh, getting more serious. Heck, I don't even know if I *want* to get serious about anybody right now." She hurriedly continued, afraid that she would lose her nerve if she allowed him to interject.

"Then, when your parents came to dinner and you opened up that can of worms by the barn, it just hit me all wrong. No warning, you know? All of a sudden, I was under a microscope to ensure that I was an appropriate candidate for the son of Lord and Lady Brandon. It all seemed so medieval to me . . . and insulting.

"You know my parents, Tommy. You know how I was raised. It certainly wasn't like your upbringing, I understand that. But, *when* I settle down . . . if I choose to spend my life with someone and get married . . . I want the kind of relationship they have together. I want feelings to develop freely, without clinical analysis and private agendas. That's why I reacted so badly. It wasn't only the surprise, which left me feeling totally off balance, but also the idea that I was being scrutinized for suitability by all of you. Mostly by you, Tommy. I never thought you'd be like that since you've always made light of your background. I guess, rightly or wrongly, your behavior actually hurt my feelings."

"Bloody Hell!" Tommy frowned and looked thoroughly miserable. "I've made a cock-up of this entire affair, haven't I? Can you ever forgive me, Marcy?" She smiled demurely, and nodded a silent 'of course.'

"Look here, I know you've a right to have other interests. I'm no fool. Equally, I know I've handled things poorly with little regard to your feelings or reactions. Sorry about that. I confess that I don't usually encounter resistance. Oh God, I know how awfully pompous that sounds; I didn't mean it that way.

"In short, we got along so fabulously that it just seemed natural that we should proceed to the next round, you know? Stupidly, it never occurred to me how it might seem to you, or that you might have other plans. I am truly sorry, and—though I absolutely hate to admit it—I'm very embarrassed. Seems you're the only female besides Lady Brandon who has the ability to knock me down a peg or two, what?" His infectious grin made Marcy laugh.

"There, that's better. The whole world lights up when you smile . . . at least for me," he said, his eyes misting. "The long and short of it is, Marcy, that I'm falling in love with you. There, it's out in the open. So the ball is in your court, as it were, and I can do nothing but wait on you. However, I want to be absolutely clear on this: I intend to pursue with vigor! This Tre fellow shall have a challenge on his hands. He's not going to win the fair damsel without a fight!"

"Oh, Tommy," chuckled Marcy, "you are such, oh, I don't even know how to fully describe you. Listen, I'm at fault, too, so let's let it go at that, okay? I guess after all is said and done, we can't really go back to the way things were, can we?

Marcy sighed, shaking her head. "And it's going to get even more complicated in that we've got your parents in the mix for dinner. I don't want them to have a false impression, so I'll leave you to sort that out. And then there's Tre. He doesn't know anything about you, I mean, this part. I've mentioned you to him, of course, but just in conversation in terms of the horse connection. He knows we're friends and associates, but that's all.

"I'll have to be honest with him, which brings up another problem. He's already in town with parents in tow. I'm to have dinner with them tonight. He wants to bring his folks to the farm Tuesday or Wednesday. I'm being totally up front with you so you'll understand the overall dilemma in terms of your folks and their suggestions. Add to that, this current mess, and I'm feeling a bit under the gun."

"Hmm, yes, I see. Well, the obvious thing is for you to have dinner with Tre and his parents this evening. Then let me know whether or not you set up Tuesday or Wednesday with them, though Wednesday would be more sensible, clearly. We'll take whatever is left, and I'll see to Lord and Lady Brandon's schedule.

"Meantime, we'll both work on our lists and contacts, and liaise sometime tomorrow when you get to the barn. I shall be there all day, what with Obsidian and workouts, as well as spending time with Demiluna. I have a few touch-up lessons I promised to some of the others, and a meeting before the trials start in the next weeks. You know the sort of thing: receptions, committees, awards, etc. Did you know we're getting the braiders in by end week? I think I forgot to tell you that, so all the first stage vetting needs to be completed by Thursday at the latest."

"Great, one more thing to have to work around. Well, we'd better get going, don't you think? And, Tommy, thank you for being so understanding." Marcy smiled genuinely at him.

"Look at me like that, my darling, and the world is yours," he said in all seriousness. They walked to his car to head back to the farm, both compatibly and comfortably silent.

Chapter 7

County Seat, Maine

The building had been steam cleaned recently and shone brilliant white in the morning sun. The friezes, columns, and statues lent both majesty and authority to the facade, reminding all those who entered that this was a hall of justice—a place where important decisions about life were taken. The words from *Superman* popped into Marcy's head, "Truth, Justice, and the American Way."

Detective Murphy had accompanied Marcy to the county seat to meet with the FBI, all arranged by their local Chief of Police. As Marcy had concluded, this matter was of potentially too large a scope for local law enforcement alone. Tommy, Marcy, and Detective Murphy proceeded to the second floor conference room with not a little trepidation. FBI agents Harry Lochmere and Sandra Dunne rose as they entered. Tommy hovered protectively near Marcy, his hand lightly at her waist.

"We have reviewed your account, Dr. Stanton. Very thorough, I might add," said Agent Dunne. "We have just a few more questions; please make yourselves comfortable."

Sandra Dunne was a petite, wiry woman dressed in the expected dark suit, the only acknowledgment to female gender, the pale pink blouse underneath. Her hair was almost black, shorn close to her skull in pixie fashion; her nails unpolished and short. She wore no makeup, save a sheen of pale lip gloss. The only "bling" visible was the metallic flash of her badge. Her partner, Harry Lochmere, was a bull of a man: blocky but fit, biceps straining at suit material, crew cut, and piercing gray eyes that stared from a square face with a large nose. These two did not resemble the Hollywood depiction of FBI agents even remotely. She could have been a gymnast; he, a professional wrestler.

"At the outset," Tommy said in an attempt to take charge of the situation or, in the least, level the playing field, "Dr. Stanton and I wish to offer you our full cooperation as, indeed, we did to the local constabulary. However, we do have limited time, so we would appreciate getting on with it, as there is little more we can add to the statements we have already provided." He flashed his most fetching smile at Agent Dunne whose expression was more one of amusement than compliment.

"And you're the Limey guy who rides horses, right?" said Agent Lochmere in a surprisingly high-pitched voice, nonetheless devoid of any friendliness. "What do *you* do for a living?"

Tommy was taken aback. "I, well that is, at the moment I'm competing in the remaining horse trials stateside. Depending upon the outcome, I shall proceed to the finals in Europe. I might say that there is a strong likelihood that I shall be in the finals *again* this year," replied Tommy with an edge of haughtiness and a disdainful look in his eyes.

"So you *don't work,* that right? Supported by Mommy and Daddy, uh, let me see . . . Lord William and Lady Madeline Brandon of Hampshire and London, England. Daddy is a Peer, and Mommy is a socialite. And you, their only son, are a globetrotter. That about size things up?" said Lochmere sarcastically.

"By the way, what town in Hampshire, and is it a Life Peerage or one of bloodlines?" glared Agent Lochmere, seemingly keen to keep Tommy under his thumb by his dismissive description, yet intent on letting everyone know that *he knew* that Hampshire was a county, not a city or town, and that there were differences in classes of peerages.

"Alresford." Tommy fairly seethed, now determined to change his tack and *withdraw* his previously cooperative attitude. 'Let's see just how well these two can *think* by asking the *appropriate* questions' he thought.

Lochmere scribbled on his pad and, without looking at her, asked Marcy, "Dr. Stanton, you're the local vet, right?" She nodded. "Dr. Stanton?" Agent Lochmere said, looking up with eyebrows raised.

Marcy realized that she was expected to speak. "Yes," she said, "I am First Veterinarian at Dr. James Rawlings Veterinary Clinic, currently assigned to oversee the needs of all the visiting participants and their horses for the trials. I've been proposed as senior vet at the finals, but we've not yet had approval of that." At Lochmere's bored stare, Marcy wondered if she had provided too much information.

This was confirmed by the agent's comment. "A simple yes or no will suffice, Ms. Stanton. Thank you." The question and answer period went on for nearly an hour. Detective Murphy was silent the entire time; indeed, his presence was barely acknowledged by the two FBI agents.

At the close, Agent Dunne directed herself to Detective Murphy, handing him a folder. "There are some forms in here that need to be completed and returned to me as soon as possible. We'll be in touch with your department chief. In the meantime, we'll be carrying out our own investigation, and will need an office provided for our local use. You'll see to that?"

Murphy replied in the affirmative, adding with notable emphasis, "My *Chief* and *all the detectives* will be fully cooperative, agents, in return for your full disclosure. This is not just an FBI matter, as you're aware. Because the facility in question is in our domain, we have a vested interest. These are *our* people, and we . . ."

With a withering glance, Agent Dunne said, "Spare me the TV drama, Detective Murphy. The FBI was brought in precisely because this is too big for you, and may or may not have broader implications *outside* your domain, as you put it. Insofar as full disclosure is concerned, let me make myself clear: Your department will receive whatever information we deem appropriate on a 'need-to-know' basis. We're here to do more than effect a Band-Aid fix, detective. Loose local lips rarely help matters. Do we understand each other?"

Detective Murphy bristled and mumbled that he would inform his Chief of the FBI position and needs. After that exchange, Tommy asked, "Are you quite finished? We have places to go, people to see, and *horses* to ride." Murphy ducked his head in a sheepish smile, Marcy colored, and Tommy brazenly stared at both agents with a mock expression of innocence.

"You're dismissed," said Agent Lochmere. "but keep us informed of your whereabouts," he said, handing each person a business card. "And Brandon, you are *not* free to leave the country until we say so, got it? That, of course, goes for the rest of you."

"I'm afraid that may be a problem," said Tommy looking at his fingernails. "You'll recall—I'm sure it's there in your notes, if you can't remember, Agent Lochmere, *or* on the tape in Agent Dunne's pocket—that I am scheduled to compete in the finals. For your information, even though you neglected to ask, the finals stateside are in two weeks. Thereafter, everyone congregates across the Pond, and the main event begins in the early spring. However, the horses need to be *in situ* well beforehand for reasons only a *horseman* of international participation would fully understand. In other words, the horses have to be in *England.* That includes the mare in question, about which you *also* did not inquire. Provided *Dr. Stanton* gives the all clear, I shall necessarily need to oversee matters here and *there*. Keep in touch won't you?" Having delivered those zingers, Tommy stood, taking Marcy's chair. Detective Murphy nodded a curt goodbye, and Marcy smiled nervously.

"Good God, those flatfoots were supercilious. And did you see that blockhead flex his muscles? Ah well, I suppose he has to rely on his physique, because clearly his brain is in dysfunction. Arrogance personified, that's what! I'll be blowed if they think they shall wreck my show record with their puny, fatuous demands. Humph! They've got no power over me, or the rest of us for that matter, by God."

"Calm down, Tommy. Let's just be grateful that it's over. I must admit, their questions covered little new ground beyond what we already told Detective Murphy and the Chief. Don't you agree, Murphy?" asked Marcy.

"Yeah, well, they can't bitch that we didn't follow protocol. But in my experience, they always try to take the upper hand right away. Something to do with that pep talk they all get when they join. When push comes to shove, they end up losing the attitude, particularly when they waste time and ground. They learn pretty quick and, if they don't, our boys will make sure they do. *We're* the ones who know this territory and its people. They'll recognize they have to play ball with us, sooner or later."

"Hmm," said Marcy remembering her mother's admonition, "I hope it's *sooner rather than later.*"

When she returned to Windward Farm, Jeremy was just walking up the path from the barn. "Hey, honey, you've got a date tonight, don't you? Running a bit late, huh?" Her father gave her a wide grin and a bear hug. "I've done the horses. Your Mom and I were just going to have a drink. You have time to join us for a bit?"

Marcy could not help but think how her father's arms had always made everything all right in her world, no matter the circumstance. They walked with arms around each other up the porch steps, as Marcy filled him in on the day's events.

"Well, quite a bit of excitement for our bucolic little town, huh? Do you think you'll have much more to do with it as time goes on?" Marcy shook her head.

"No, Dad, I think my contribution was merely in the discovery part, unless there are some other horses suspect. I imagine they will request a summary exam of all of them, just to be sure. That's not a big deal, just a time eater. But I hope no others were used as carriers. Likely, no one would have known had that one packet not split. If Demiluna hadn't gone punky, we'd have had no cause to examine her so thoroughly. I guess if you ignore how loathsome it was to use her that way, the idea *is* pretty clever of the drug runners—using a horse that routinely travels abroad and back. It makes me wonder just how and when they were going to retrieve their booty. What do you think?"

Elizabeth overheard the last of the conversation. Presenting the two of them with a glass, she said, "Marcy, has it ever occurred to you that even though you chose a relatively normal profession compared to your brother, you're involved in a potentially dangerous international situation? I'm not sure I like the fact that *someone* close to you might be involved in this. Anything to do with the illegal drug trade can be linked to violence or something nasty. Watch your step, okay honey?"

"I know, Mom, I've thought about that too. But I think I'm pretty well out of it. Whoever was going to be the pick-up person this side of the Atlantic will be walking softly with all the police involved, assuming that the retrieval was to be here. Maybe it was supposed to go the other way, who knows?.

"But, I admit, the whole thing gives me the shivers. I guess nowhere and no one is safe anymore." Marcy sipped her drink. "Hey, Mom, way to go. This is delicious!"

Elizabeth beamed. "You know, when Lord Brandon was here, he suggested that I might like to try Pim's in one of my concoctions. So I did, and I agree, it turned out pretty well, didn't it? Now, if I can just remember the recipe . . ."

They laughed together in recognition of the fact that Elizabeth was constantly creating this treat or that dessert or drink and rarely recorded her ingredients. Amazingly, she always managed the rank of "delicious" in whatever she prepared.

"You haven't got much time, honey. I think Tommy's message said he'd be by to pick you up at 5:30 PM, or something like that. If I remember correctly, you're due at 1800 at the Club—that's 6:00 PM, isn't it? Here, let me give you a top up. You can take it upstairs with you," said Elizabeth, grabbing the pitcher. "By the way, how is it going between the two? Tommy sounded rather down when he called, not his usual bubbly self. Have you had a chance to speak with Tre?"

"No. Tre and I need some private time together, and Monday was spent with his folks. Tommy and I did have a talk on Monday afternoon. It was difficult, to say the least, but he does know about Tre. Now I have to get the other side up to speed. Honestly, Mom, it's really awful. The part that gets me is that I don't seem to have any control of the matter. I mean, I'm being forced to deal with a situation that *they* created, and I don't like it one bit. I liked things just the way they were. But there's no going back now, unfortunately." Elizabeth smiled, nodding, and looked up at Jeremy.

Taking the cue, he said, "Honey, you *did help* to create this thing, you know. It's because you are what and who you are that both men are attracted. When one was here, the other wasn't, and vice versa. Now the ends are coming toward the middle magnet—you. I'm afraid there's no avoiding it: you've got two men in love with you. There *are* worse positions to be in, you know."

"Ha, ha, very funny. Well, I guess you're right, but I didn't do this deliberately. Honestly, I never even thought about the next step with either of them. Now that I've *had* to think about it," said Marcy walking around the kitchen trailing her finger along the woodblock island, "I'm not sure that I want to get more serious about either one of them, and I certainly don't want to get married just now. I mean, how can I choose between them? They're both great guys. And what if I make the wrong choice? Then the one I *should* have chosen will be out of bounds anyway, so I'm screwed no matter what I do. Then there's my job at the clinic, all my patients, my carefully planned future, and it wouldn't be fair to reneg on Doc. I just hate all of this," she said, making a face at her parents as they stood close together smiling at their beautiful daughter.

"Trust yourself, Marcy," said Jeremy.

"You'll do what's right for all of you," said Elizabeth. "All you need is time, courage, and honesty, and you already possess the last two, so give yourself enough of the first." her mother said wisely.

Marcy smiled at them: two beautiful people; two wonderful, wise, and loving parents; two people who together had carved out a life for themselves that kept them still in love.

"That's what I want for myself," said Marcy.

"What?" they said in unison.

"What you have," said Marcy smiling, "and I won't settle for less!"

Chapter 8

Kitzbühel, Austria

Having trudged up the slopes for half the morning through gently falling snow, Aniela and Andy stopped for a rest and a swig from their bottles. They had been making good progress considering that they had had to skirt the deadfall and propel themselves with poles and a skater's rhythmic gait on the flat. Four more hours' hard slog would put them within reach of one of the ski runs by mid to late afternoon. The plan was to join the run from a lateral position, ski the middle of the mountain, and reach the bottom and the welcoming warmth of the hotel for a meal, a hot bath, and the luxury of a bed with quilts and pillows.

Andy was puffing hard as his skis shushed next to Aniela. "Man, I've about had all I can take of skis for awhile. How do you people do it, day in and day out?" He stamped his legs and flapped his arms against his body. The burning in his muscles gave way to a throbbing ache.

"It is not so bad," said Aniela, "you get used to it. But I tell you true, I am tired," she admitted. "Not too much more now. Can you do it? We must get to the half point on the hill before the sun gets to there, you see?" she said, as she pointed to a position on the horizon. Andy nodded, swallowing the last of his water, and pushed off. Aniela came up beside him and flashed him an encouraging smile with a nod of her head. "Come on!" she said, racing away.

When they reached the hotel and stowed their gear, they joined the press of skiers moving through the doors into the lounge. "I'll just order us some food and drink to be sent to the room," said Andy. Aniela assented with a tired nod and went to the elevator. He joined her shortly, and they boarded in silence.

Their room was next to the Exit stairwell and opposite a bank of windows that overlooked an interior garden with a blazing fire pit surrounded by knots of people laughing and socializing following a good day on the slopes. "I haven't the energy for *gemütlichkeit* [15] tonight, how about you?" he asked her. "All I want is some food and sleep. I can't remember when I was so tired."

"*Nein*. I do not want to go down there. We must eat, *ja*, but then I go to the tub first. Then to the bed. You must go to the tub or you will not be in the bed with me. Okay?"

Andy laughed, pulling off his jacket and ski pants. "Are you saying that I smell? Well, you're probably right." Standing in long underwear, he removed his sweater and shirt, wincing. Aniela came to him to inspect his bandaged shoulder and upper arm.

"This is making blood again. We must change the dressing. There must be something here we can use." Aniela checked the bathroom and Andrew went to the bedroom. "Nothing in here except towels," she called out. The doorbell rang and Aniela went to answer it. "Room Service," she shouted to Andy. "You stay there; I will see to it."

She admitted the waiter who rolled in a cart, delicious aromas wafting from covered plates. He set the cart near the small dining table by the windows and, turning to ask Aniela if he could do anything else for her, his eyes flicked to the sofa and Andy's bloodied shirt. Aniela caught the glance. Speaking to him in German, she offered a handsome tip, and made a flourish of tossing the shirt into the wastebasket with a laughing denigration about her husband's clumsiness getting off the ski lift chair in icy conditions.

"These Americans, eh? They actually think they know how to ski their little hills, until they come to our real mountains and find out what skiing really is, *ja?*" The waiter smiled empathetically, bowed, and left.

Andy came through the bedroom door once the suite door closed. "Gee, thanks. Don't hold back what you think of me. And here I thought I was gaining your approval by keeping up with Aniela the Great." He plopped grumpily down on the couch, clutching his upper arm with a grimace.

"Oh, you fool. Do you not think it is suspicious to have a bloody shirt at a place like this? What do we know who is watching out for you? I had to make a cover with something. This is what I could think to do with no time when I see him looking so hard at your shirt." She went over to the cart and opened the doors beneath to remove some fresh linen napkins.

Andy felt thoroughly miserable. His arm hurt and he had just been a jerk by criticizing Aniela, who had acted quickly to provide a cover story. She was right: he was acting like a fool, despite all his training. She was right again: who knew if anyone was tailing him or her. It wasn't as if he had a low profile in certain circles, and if the information passed to him was as explosive as Anton intimated, there was a strong likelihood that "someone" out there wanted to get their hands on it. After all, hadn't Anton said that other of his contacts had met with danger at the worst and difficulty in the least?

Something bothered him and scratched at the back of his mind as a hanging detail that might be important to the success of his mission or, more important, his survival. There hadn't been sufficient time to ascertain exactly how Aniela *knew* Anton, or whether their association was merely as contacts through a network or a longstanding, personal association.

Aniela retrieved the bloody shirt from the wastebasket and began tearing it to shreds. She doused the clean linen napkins with some of the vodka Andy had thoughtfully ordered for her, and came to sit next to him on the couch. "Here, hold the bottle." She removed the makeshift bandage Anton had provided, dabbing at the deep cuts with one of the napkins.

"Hey, go easy there, nurse." Andy's face winced each time the vodka-soaked cloth touched his wounds, feeling like fire. 'So much for John Wayne or Clint Eastwood managing to ride a horse for miles with a bullet in them, losing blood, and bearing the pain,' he thought ruefully, as he involuntarily yelled, "Ow, ow, ow!"

Having cleaned the wounds on his upper arm, Aniela applied a fresh linen napkin, wrapping it snugly with the strips of his shirt. "It is not so bad as it looks. It will heal, but you must try not to use it so much as this morning. Your shoulder is a big swell with very bad bruise. We will rest to give us strength before we leave. We must plan our way to make for England." Having tended his wound without so much as a glance at him, Aniela crossed to the cart and table saying, "If you wish to eat, the food is still warm. Then I shall bathe and sleep. You would do well to do the same."

"Look, Aniela, I'm sorry," said Andrew as he rose and crossed the room to sit at the table. "It's just that I'm dog tired, everything hurts, this damned arm is a fly in the ointment and feels like it's been through a meat grinder. I'm short-tempered because I need sleep. Every bone and muscle in my body aches. Am I forgiven?" He smiled at her, looking sheepish. "After all, you took all that trouble to get me to Anton, which wasn't easy. *And* you got me all the way back here. I guess you could say you saved my life. If this stuff is as important as Anton says, maybe you've saved a whole lot of people's lives. By the way, the word is 'swollen'."

"I said it right before. You are a fool. Now sit down before you fall down or I push you down. Eat." At least she smiled up at him.

After both had had a hot bath—separately—Andy and Aniela relaxed for several minutes looking out over the panorama of the mountains from the balcony.

"Is beautiful here, yes?" Aniela turned to him and reached up to give him a kiss on the cheek. "We must sleep together, but we must not sleep together. Do you understand?"

Andy laughed and slung an arm over her shoulder as they walked toward the bedroom, each of them moving slowly because of body aches and tender feet and legs.

"Trust me, Aniela, all I'm capable of doing right now is passing out. This scotch has relaxed me, the food has relaxed me, and the thought of a soft pillow and clean sheets calls to every sore bone in my body. You've nothing to fear from me," he said with a yawn.

"I do not have fear of you, Andrew. I was talking about me. Good night."

'Damn that woman,' thought Andy as his head hit the pillow. 'She always has to throw me for a loop by getting in the last word. What did she mean by that, I wonder? Did she . . . 'But he could not finish the thought, as sleep came like an overpowering wave, and he surrendered immediately.

They both slept deeply.

Yacht Club

Chapter 9

Deep Harbor Country Club, Maine

"What do you mean by that, Tre?" Marcy was flustered, struggling to regain her composure. Tre had just dropped a bombshell by announcing that he wanted Marcy to accompany him and his parents to Washington for a week's visit, and would not take "no" for an answer. "I have a life, you know, and a job, and responsibilities, and . . ."

"I'm fully aware of all that, Marcy, but I have limited time. You know that. I told you the dates of my leave. Surely, you can arrange some time off for something as important as this. We can't go on with this *now and then* relationship forever. If we waited for the right time, that time would never happen. We're both busy people living in different parts of the country, and frankly, I'm fed up with this long distance relationship of ours.

"A week would give Mom and Dad the time they need to introduce you to our family and friends and do their social bit with dinners, the Club, and all that. During the day, we could investigate places to live, and you could poke around the other clinics to inquire about a transfer. It would work. Come on, Marcy, what's the problem?" He reached across the table to take her hands.

Marcy recalled her family's teasing about Tre's upcoming visit and their remarks that it might involve a proposal of marriage. Although she suspected they might be right, her focus on work and recent events had pushed it to the back of her mind. She now recognized that avoidance of the likelihood had left her unprepared. 'Great, Marce, shot yourself in the foot again, didn't you? Just because you don't want to deal with something, doesn't mean you *should not* or *will not* have to deal with it. Idiot!'

"Tre, it's just that, well, it's all a bit sudden, that's all. You could at least give me time to think about this. I mean, well, we've been dating for a while, I know, but we've never really spoken about the future. We haven't really talked about love."

Marcy was struggling to explain her needs without insulting or hurting Tre. Great, here they were in the midst of a romantic evening, Tre had dropped The Question, and all she could do was sputter. She felt like a tongue-tied teenager.

"I care deeply for you, Tre, you know that. But this has come on rather suddenly, and I'm in the middle of something at work, and . . ."

"It's that English guy, isn't it? I knew there was something fishy about the way he was sniffing around the farm all the time. Oh yeah, I've heard all about him from the twins. A real operator it seems, playing the big hero role with them, flattering your Mom, and yakking it up with your Dad about various sailing adventures. He's been after you, hasn't he? How much do you see each other?" Tre's eyes were blazing, and Marcy was shocked at his display of emotion.

"Hold on a minute, I don't like this at all. You don't own me, Tre. We've been seeing each other for a long while, true, but I've also known Tommy a long time, too.

"Neither of you is in any position to stake any claim on me. Neither of you has earned the right, nor have I given either of you any indication that I expected more than friendship. For Heaven's sake, neither relationship qualifies as committed, and both are only every now and then, so I'd suggest you get off your high horse. At least let's talk this through calmly, okay?" she cajoled, giving him her brightest smile.

Marcy had sensed Tre's rising angst, and tried to lighten up the conversation by her soothing tone, a smile, and reaching for his hand across the table.

Tre sat, shaking his head. "So he did try to 'stake a claim' as you phrase it. Well,"

"Marcy, darling, what a surprise!" Tommy wheeled around the table, planting a kiss on Marcy's cheek, extending a hand across the table toward Tre. "Delighted to see you again, old man. Believe we met a while ago on the courts. I was partnering that little Spanish fellow, what's his name? Ah, yes, I think it was Miguel. As I recall, we trounced you, what? Great match, that. Having the salmon? Good choice, it was delicious. Mind if I join you?"

Without waiting for a reply, Tommy pulled out a chair next to Marcy, placed his left elbow on the table, and draped his right arm over the back of her chair, grinning.

"Tommy! Well hello. I didn't think you'd still be here. Aren't your folks in California? I thought perhaps you went with them, or that you might be busy tying up loose ends," said Marcy reddening.

"No, no, my darling," interrupted Tommy. "I decided not to go with Lord and Lady Brandon to the West Coast, mostly because of that little matter you and I have been attending. And there's been a change of plan overall. They're actually going to come back this way before hopping the Pond to the U.K., extending their stay a bit, if you will.

"By the way, you look ravishing tonight. Yes, now, what was I going to say? Ah! I phoned your parents to let them know about my parents' invitation for Saturday week, and they accepted. So I'm taking this opportunity to corral you, as it were, on the happenstance that you and Tre were having dinner in the same place as me. Heaven knows, there are precious few places to get fine cuisine. Lucky coincidence, eh?"

Smiling broadly, unaffected by Tre's glare, he pressed, "So, can you join us? Oh, and I forgot to tell you, those dreary Suits want to see us again in the late morning. I reckon I can collect you by 11 AM at the clinic, all right with you, *mon ami*?"

Tommy looked at Marcy, awaiting her reply. Tre cleared his throat. "Sorry, Tre, didn't mean to ignore you, old chap, a bit of business, you know?" said Tommy to Tre's obvious annoyance at the interruption.

"Marcy will not be in town a week from Saturday, so I'm afraid she will have to decline your invitation." Tre's voice was leaden and his response clipped.

"Is that so?" said Tommy pointedly. "And since when does the lovely Marcy not speak for herself?" Tommy retorted with upturned eyebrows.

"Okay, you two, that's quite enough," said Marcy placating. "Actually, Tommy, I'll make my own way to the meeting, and see you there. As for your parents' invitation, I would be delighted. My parents and I will meet all of you here at the Club or The Gables, if that suits better. Just phone and leave a message as to the time and your choice of restaurant. I'll see you tomorrow," she said, rising to collect her purse.

Then, looking directly at Tre, she said, "I'll just be a few minutes in the Ladies Room. Perhaps we can continue that chat over dessert. Dory said the cheesecake is to die for, so I think I'll have that." Marcy stood; both men stood; she smiled at each, and made her way from the table.

"Right, well I'm off. Good night to you then, Trevois. Enjoy the rest of your evening." Before Tre could reply or initiate any other comment, Tommy was gone as quickly as he had arrived.

"Cocky Englishman!" he muttered to himself. The waiter appeared on cue, and he ordered their desserts. He was no longer fuming when Marcy returned. She smelled like a fresh ocean breeze, her eyes were like the depths of the earth, and her hair glinted bronze and gold in the candlelight. She was stunningly beautiful, and the sight of her made his heart skip a beat.

"I gather from your reply to him that you've decided not to come to Washington?" Tre asked dully. "I don't want to argue, Marcia, but I want you to know that I'm very disappointed that you'd accept him and turn me down. Should I read something into that?"

She smiled at him genuinely. "Not at all, Tre. As I told you, it's impossible for me to come to Washington just now. It is not impossible, however, for me to have dinner with Tommy's parents. They are coming here where I live and work. I've explained that I need time to think about what you've said. That's the best answer I can give you right now. I'm truly sorry that's not what you wanted to hear. I wouldn't hurt you for the world."

"Well, that's something at least." The cheesecake was superb, as Dory had promised. They both ate in silence, sharing only occasional, embarrassed smiles when their eyes met.

The evening ended much the same way, both tentative, embarrassed, and sensible enough not to attempt a kiss goodnight. Tre's frustration had been palpable which served only to deepen Marcy's concern over her predicament that seemed to be spinning out of control. She was more than confused, and determined that she had to sort out her feelings for each man as quickly as possible in an attempt to be fair to all involved. 'How in the world can you put a time limit on something like this?' she thought dismally. 'This is not at all the way it's supposed to work!'

She was in a temper by the time she mounted the stairs to her room. She was furious with Tre; she was equally furious with Tommy; and she was beyond furious with herself. "Stupid, stupid, stupid!" she said as she stomped around her bedroom.

How could she have let this situation progress to this point? Two simple, alternating relationships had developed overnight into Mt. Vesuvius. All of it was clearly her fault. She was so confused about her feelings that she wanted to scream. How dare Tre answer for her! How dare he insist that she go to Washington and choose the when, where, and how of it? He had no right. And how dare Tommy interrupt what was obviously a date with a counter proposal for another date? He knew exactly what he was doing, and did it quite deliberately. Both of them were staking a claim, without so much as even asking her opinion. How dare they!

When her tantrum abated, she sat morosely on the bed. Even the tree frogs were no solace. She put her head in her hands and began to cry in frustration. Four years of college, three years of vet school, two years' internship, work, work, work. Now that things were just beginning to come to fruition for her professionally, she was being asked to throw it all down the toilet, pick up and move to an area far away from home, and settle down as Tre's wife.

'Crap,' she thought, getting more depressed by the minute. She didn't even know if she loved Tre in that way, because she had never let herself really think about it. She had been too busy laying the foundation for her life here. And the thought of leaving Windward Farm and the sea for some inland hothouse full of politicians and Navy folks was repugnant. Tre had been so downcast when she refused to go to Washington, that she had felt guilty. How could she have hurt him like that? He was a sweetheart, and like the Rock of Gibraltar. He was handsome, intelligent, the strong, silent type, and had a good heart. She was the envy of many of her friends; they told her more than once that she was lucky. She had felt good about that, hadn't she? But why couldn't she remember what it was like to kiss him? Maybe because they hadn't done much kissing. But she had always felt so comfortable with Tre, hadn't she? Was that enough? Was that "it"?

Then there was Tommy: Dashing, outrageous, funny, sweet Tommy. He had fairy dust under his feet, and reminded her of Peter Pan sometimes. But he had shown a different side with the FBI, hadn't he? He clearly had steel in his backbone. He was obviously well educated, of good stock, had shown sides of fun and lightheartedness that had banished Marcy's routine tiredness from hard work, but he had also soothed her spirit with sensitivity to her moods and needs. He had passion. Somehow, that passion touched her deeply in a way that had nothing to do with their shared passion for horses. But was Tommy too flighty compared to Tre's solidarity?

There was only one way to sort things out. She was going to go for a midnight ride. As she left the farmhouse, the breeze picked up and the leaves on the trees fluttered whispers of greeting. The grass was covered in dew and her dampened boots shone in the moonlight. Rex whinnied as she entered the barn. Faithful Rex was always the first to sense her presence. She quickly saddled and bridled him, leading him to the aisle. The other horses shuffled, and she spoke quietly to reassure them. She and Rex left the barn to the sound of munching hay and soft whinnies.

The broad estuary was peaceful this night, offering up a chorus of soft lapping sounds to the night symphony of shuffling birds and animals. Rex walked lazily along the shoreline down river, following the well-worn trail to the open, seaward pasture where he and Marcy often raced together uplifted by the power of the ocean.

Without so much as a signal, Rex picked up his pace. The trail opened to a 50-acre parcel that was the promontory end of the farm, cosseted on three sides by the ocean. The full moon and starlit sky glinted off a silver sea casting a glow over the field, dewdrops glinting like a myriad of diamonds in the grasses.

By mutual agreement, they launched into a run. The cleansing air rushed through Marcy's hair as it did her heart, and she and Rex rejoiced in the abandon of free gallop. After a time, he slowed and nickered softly to Marcy. She laid her head on his neck and hugged him, the sound of their joint panting a soft metronome against the swish and lap of the waves along the rocky shore. Rex nickered again softly.

"Good boy. It's fine now, we can go home," Marcy crooned as she gathered up the reins. They turned for the upriver path and, in a short time, the welcoming outline of Windward Farm rose from the bluff against the wakening sky.

Chapter 10

White Birches Farm, Maine

Marcy chatted with the show officials, signing off on the horses she had examined and filing the appropriate papers. Lars Borst was a dream to work with. So far, the trials had progressed like clockwork, and Marcy appreciated the efficiency, record keeping, and professional accommodation she received from Lars as General Manager. He had his finger on the pulse of the entire operation, and it was a huge job requiring great resources of energy, patience, and broad-scale ability. Everyone respected and liked him, despite that he ruled with an iron hand.

"Lars, barring the unforeseen, I think I'm about wrapped up here. You have my cell number if you need me, right?" Marcy gathered her papers into her folder making ready to go.

"Yes, thank you very much, Marcia. And of course, if an emergency or weekend call occurs, there's always the clinic answering service as backup. But there is one matter. Hmm, how do I say this without creating undue concern or insult?"

Lars was frowning uncharacteristically, and his body language tightened visibly. These signs gave Marcy pause. She had long ago learned to be observant of horse body language as a clue to underlying emotions, and her sensitivity in this area underwrote her success as a veterinarian and therapist. The same principles applied to humans, although many people are able to mask their responses, whereas most horses cannot. Lars, however, was an open individual in virtually every way: what you saw, you got.

"Just tell me straight out, Lars, like you always do. You know you don't have to walk on eggs around me," replied Marcy reassuringly. She placed a hand on his arm and looked up into his troubled, distant eyes.

"Yes, you're right. Okay, here goes. You're one of the best vets we have ever had, except for Rawlings when he was in his prime. These days, he's . . . well, let's just say he's not up to the rigors of this anymore. I think you know how much I think of you, and how many compliments you've received from other participants.

"No one could ever accuse you of being less than thorough, Marcia, but lately we've had some unusual things going on with the horses. Nothing I can really put my finger on, mind you, but shortly after you gave inoculations, several of the horses just were not acting right, and certainly were not performing to their usual standard. I've been closely monitoring the situation, obviously, and we've been judicious in our standards of care. However, I was wondering if you had changed serums or something. Maybe the marketplace is touting a new, live vaccine or a newer, stronger formula that may be harder on the horses' systems.

"I would never question this in view of your standards, only we're ending the trials shortly, and then the finals will be upon us in no time. If something is wrong, I'd like to get it fixed while there is time. Some of the clients are beginning to buzz about it, so I thought I should raise it with you."

Marcy was overcome with a feeling of dread. There was nothing in her treatment and care that should cause the nagging conditions he was describing. Between his record keeping and scheduling, and her own anal record keeping, she was sure she had made no errors.

Could there be any linkage to Lars' report and Demiluna's condition? None of the other horses indicated any similar symptoms in parallel with Demiluna's timing. What could she have forgotten? Summarily, she had completed an overview of her Health Watch sheets on all the registered horses, and there were no unusual remarks. Rather than examine each and every horse on the premises (which would have been overkill, excessively and perhaps unnecessarily expensive to the owners, and could have caused general panic), she had quietly observed workouts, walked through the barns and chatted with owners, and checked the daily records—all with no results that would warrant concern. During the times she was there, nothing had flagged.

"Lars, are any of the horses involved mares? Or put it this way, are the horses involved *only* mares?" Marcy held her breath as Lars thumbed through the file to check names against his hand scrawled list.

"Well, let's see. We've got over 250 horses at this trial, so it's hard for me to remember all the genders, but, yes, these seven horses are mares. These other two are geldings, but their complaints were sore stifles with the one, and a popped abscess with the other. Besides, you treated both of them, see? Here are your initials on the Health Watch sheet with your treatment log stapled to the back.

"Now, let's just pull these others. Here we are. The mares all seem to be acting the same: not willing to jump and therefore showing strong resistance, diminished spirit, lethargy, lying down and rolling a lot in their stalls, a bit off their feed. They have no temperature and don't appear lame or colicky, but they are hangdog, if you know what I mean. Nothing seemed definitive enough to mark on the HW sheet, and it was on and off, not specific in presentation, and not consistent symptomatically in any way. I found out in the usual way," he said with a sly smile, indicating his habit of chatting up the grooms, handlers, and stall cleaners.

"I know exactly what you mean, Lars. Don't worry; I think I may know what's wrong. No, that's not accurate. I have a suspicion as to what may be wrong. Perhaps I should have done this before, but now you and I have to sit down and talk. I was asked not to have conversation with others on this matter, but the current situation makes that request inappropriate. Is there someplace we can have total privacy?"

Marcy's blood was up, and she walked purposefully behind Lars to his private offices. 'Okay, they want to play rough? Let's see how they like playing rough with me!' She would get these monsters if it were the last thing she did. Next stop after Lars and examining the horses would be Dunne and Lochmere's office. This time, it would be Marcia who would not take "no" for an answer.

She was careful how much she revealed to Lars, even though she was certain that he was not a security risk. Technically however, she was breaking her word to the FBI, even though it was with the best of intentions and potentially critical to the horses' health that she gain clearance to examine them. It qualified as taking matters into her hands without the knowledge or permission of the two FBI agents in charge of the case. But how could she let this news pass and still call herself a good vet, to say nothing of potential liability if she did nothing and waited for the slow wheels of the investigation to turn? Although concerns about her license and reputation were legitimate, Marcy's main thoughts were for the horses' welfare.

"So, Lars, it seems that the horses that have come from abroad may have been used as live vehicles for smuggling. I don't know whether the intent is from there to here, or here to there, if you understand me. That accounts for a significant number, in any case.

"I really can't say more, because I've already placed myself in a difficult position by telling you this much. There are authorities overseeing the matter, and I'd prefer that they divulge the remainder. Can you come with me to a meeting?"

Marcy filled him on the time and place of the meeting with the "Suits", as Tommy called them. They had only two hours left before they were to be at the FBI office at the Police Department in town.

"Meantime, let's look at the workout schedule to determine which of these I can examine right away. It'll take only a few minutes per horse to determine if they're part of this scheme. If they're clear, the exam will of course take a bit longer, and I'll also pull blood and do a rush CBC on them, just to be sure. What do you say?" Lars nodded his assent, and Marcy said firmly, "Then let's get cracking!"

Marcy and Lars compared the work chart to his list. It occurred to her as they jotted down times and barn locations that Lars might qualify as a suspect. No! That was simply impossible, or was it? No, Lars couldn't be involved, he was too comprehensive in his management style, had been running this event for years, was held in deep regard by almost everyone, and it was totally out of character for the man. Nonetheless, it would be up to Agents Dunne and Lochmere, and it was a good idea for him to come to the meeting. She would justify it as a "need-to-know" basis, particularly given his comments about the other horses she was going to examine. Besides, the Suits had made zero progress. This was where all the action was and where potential clues could be discovered. She felt like Nancy Drew or Miss Marpole.

"Okay then, that about does it. Ready?"

They walked from Lars' office toward the barn aisles. Lars was silent, somewhere between confusion and worry, she deduced. Marcy was determined, quelling a rising sense of foreboding. Two mares examined; two mares clean to all intents and purposes. One had shipped from Denmark, the other from Germany. Five mares to go. The next mare was a Hanoverian bay of size and beauty. She pinned her ears and made to kick as Marcy cleaned her for examination.

"Easy girl," said Marcy, as the groom snapped the chain lead shank on her halter and steadied her head. The Ultrasound machine showed a mass that should not be there.

"Oh dear," said Marcy to Lars, who was standing beside her outside the stall door opening. "Look at this." She pointed to the image. Lars was conversant with horse physiology and had seen enough Ultrasound images to know that this was abnormal.

"What is it, Marcia? I confess it doesn't look right to me, not something I've seen before." Lars looked at her quizzically.

Marcy withdrew the Ultrasound probe and proceeded to the next step of the exam with rising apprehension. Saying nothing to answer Lars' question, she gently eased her fingers toward the mass, which she suspected to be the same type of packet she had removed from Demiluna. Bingo! With extreme caution lest movement or pressure compromise the packet, she slowly withdrew the object. Exactly the same. Additionally, the material enclosing the powdery substance had again breached, although this one did not show a slit, as with Demiluna. It was slightly punctured, just sufficiently to allow both seepage of the powder into the mare, and absorption of the mare's fluids into the packet. As a result, it had expanded to its maximum stretch. Had it not been removed, likely it would have fractured internally with dreadful repercussions to the mare. It was, after all, several days after Marcy's examination of Demiluna. She surmised that both mares had been implanted within the same or a similar time frame.

"Obviously, whoever placed these packets didn't take into account the integrity of the material versus the environment—the inside of the mare, you with me? It looks as if this one was pushed into place, perhaps with a finger, and the fingernail may have punctured the packet. See the shape of the puncture? It 's somewhat crescent-shaped, and lies pretty much dead center." Marcy made some notes and cradled the packet gently in cotton before wrapping it loosely with 4x4's and placing it into a plastic case.

"We're going to have to flush this mare, Lars. There are a few other things I can do preventively, but she'll have to be watched for the next several hours and be on stall rest with monitoring." Marcy quickly outlined the regimen used with Demiluna.

"Choose an attendant who's conscientious and have him report to no one but you, discussing nothing of this matter with anyone. Just tell him that the vet said the mare had a cyst that was close to bursting which was causing the funkiness, and has been given a shot to shrink it. He should buy that."

Having finished the procedure, Marcy frowned as Lars informed her that the mare had traveled from Ireland in relatively the same period as Demiluna's journey from England. He promised to check the manifest to determine if any of the same people from shippers to handlers were linked between the mares. Marcy made more notations. Their meeting with the FBI should be interesting, and they had still had four more mares to check. Depending upon the results, it was likely that they would be late for the meeting. Lars deduced the same as Marcy was thinking it.

"Do we have enough time to get all this done before the meeting?" Lars whispered. "I have the impression that FBI agents are not the most understanding of law enforcement officers, but that's just from TV, of course." Lars was clearly tom between the need for immediate examination of the mares and risking the ire of agents he had not yet met, at a meeting he was going to attend without their knowledge or invitation. He gave Marcy a chagrinned smile.

"Let's just get on with it, Lars. I'll handle Dunne and Lochmere. When I finish with them and reveal what we've found, I doubt they'll be of a mind to chastise either of us for being late," said Marcy in hushed tones. Shaking her head and eyeing the groom, she said more loudly, "There, that's done. Now, where's the next mare? Let's get moving. I've got limited time."

Marcy hurriedly followed Lars down the barn aisle, making notes on the way. The groom followed like a pack mule, loaded down with Ultrasound equipment, Marcy's case, buckets, folding table, and totes. 'This is one hell of a no-nonsense lady vet,' the young man thought to himself, 'no one ever orders Lars around like she's doing.'

Chapter 11

Romantische Straße
(Romantic Road), Bavaria

The drive through Bezirk Kitzbühel toward Munich was uneventful, except for navigating the snow laden back roads they had chosen to take between the two points. Aniela had called ahead to arrange overnight room accommodation in Munich for them before arranging flights for Paris and London. It seemed more sensible to take a circuitous route to England, just in case they were being tailed.

Kitzbühel bordered Bavaria (Germany) in the north, the Kufstein and Schwaz districts in the west, and the Pinzgau region (Salzburg) in the east and south. They could have left Austria via the Swiss Alps, swinging to Geneva to spend some travel days and nights at Lake Geneva and the remainder of the "Seeland" (the land of lakes) at the westernmost of Switzerland. They could then have moved on to Bern and Lake Neuchatel, then Biel, before heading toward Paris. But Aniela decided that they would take the "*Romantische Straße*" (Romantic Road), Germany's most famous tourist route that runs through Bavaria from the baroque city of Würzburg towards Füssen near to the Alps.

On the 353 km journey, they would pass more than two dozen towns like medieval Rothenburg and Augsburg, or spectacular Neuschwanstein castle. This was Aniela's territory with which she was very familiar. Her decision was rooted in her determination to successfully complete their mission and keep the sometimes-impetuous American safe, in spite of himself and the fact that she was growing more and more fond of him.

"Andrew, we should stop soon and refuel. In a few kilometers, there will be a town. We can get food and petrol there." Aniela kneaded her neck and rubbed her eyes.

"Headache still with you?" Andy asked as he glanced over at her. She had been stalwart throughout the last few days, despite having had the flu. How she had managed to ski that rough terrain in freezing weather, he would never know. This woman had guts and incredible drive. As her health improved, so did her attitude. She had actually laughed a few times, and they shared infrequent bursts of conversation. Even though much of it related to their trip or their circumstances, Andy had managed to wangle a few bits of personal information from her.

She was single; she was a university graduate with joint honours degrees in natural science biology and physical anthropology, followed by a graduate degree in paleontology, and a doctorate in paleoanthropology. She had bolstered those credentials with significant study in archaeology and spending parts of various years either on site digs or related research of findings. It was through her work that she and Anton met. They shared a deep affection one for the other, although their paths did not cross frequently. His fatherliness and scholarly nature filled the hole from the loss of her parents, tragically killed in an airplane crash years before. They shared similar political views despite the disparity in their lifestyles and ages.

Aniela had volunteered to house some of Anton's "unusual" visitors from time to time. In the beginning, she had no idea how valuable and in demand her guests were. In a short time, her suspicions that there were hazards attached to her hospitality were confirmed by some disturbingly dangerous encounters. Anton had claimed that, by keeping her in the dark, he was protecting her. Were she to be questioned about the people, their backgrounds, or their ultimate destinations, she would legitimately know nothing. She had merely been asked by "Uncle Anton" to host some of his friends. Her cozy house was a far cry from the musty digs of a professor's apartment. With her relentless challenges, he finally told her the truth of associations.

Thereafter, Aniela adopted a more assertive role as and when it became necessary, as she had done in Andy's case. Occasional guests became charges to be connected with or delivered to persons who would pass sensitive information or establish them with a new identity in another region or country.

Through it all, Aniela had remained pragmatic, somewhat insular, and necessarily detached. According to her code, she was serving quietly to right the world's balance both in her professional life and through her "secret" life. She was a scientist, first and foremost. Science pursued the truth of things; politics, people's greed, the press, and governments perverted that paradigm. The archetype of placing the truth above all considerations was, in her view, the epitome of man's accomplishment, and his responsibility to himself and his world.

Her secret contributions might be small, but they supported her principles. Her choice had never been a choice, but an essential duty, intrinsic to her character. Her life included little that was unnecessary, including frivolity, flattery, empty conversation, waste, laziness, romantic entanglements, etc. She was stoic, straightforward, very bright, capable, and very real. And although she tried to repress it, she was also a sensual woman. As such, she exuded raw sexuality made all the more tantalizing because she denied it, and the attentions of those who responded to her magnetism.

As they pulled into the baroque old town of Würzburg, Andy became excited. "Aniela, look. There's a bread cart." He parked the Citroën, leaving the motor running, dashing over to the cart just as the man was preparing to leave.

"Can I still purchase a few loaves?" he asked. "*Danke*." He clapped the man on the shoulder with a broad smile, nodding to Aniela in the waiting car. The man smiled back at Andy, sure that his delay had helped the young man redeem himself with the fraulein. Ah well, they would have a good night, and all because of Klaus' bread. Beaming, Andy returned to the car with several baguettes. "Now, if we can buy some wine, cheese, and tomatoes, we'll have a feast."

Aniela grinned at Andy, not in the least because she, too, was famished, but mostly because of his boyish enthusiasm. He continually surprised her, shattering all her illusions about soft, spoiled Americans. He had distinguished himself physically on the slopes in their grueling journey to meet with Anton in the obscure mountain cabin. There had been no time to reschedule when the weather turned nasty, and the conditions on the mountain had turned from bad to worse. She was also surprised at how knowledgeable he was when he and Anton were talking about Qumran.

Further, he had matched her time for time in matters of drive, lack of creature comforts, and focus with cooperation and grit. He had moments of being a grumpy, little boy, but did not they all? He had spoken lovingly of his family and early life, and had displayed moments of sensitivity and care for her—a virtual stranger. He was good to look at in every way, even in the late nights of exhaustion or the early mornings of sleepiness. She shook her head to regain her steely reserve. This was no time to allow distraction because of attraction. It simply would not do for the likes of Aniela.

They found a green grocer and purchased some tomatoes and apples, then bought wine and cheese, and located rooms at a charming *gasthaus*. Aniela knew that these pension guesthouses were spread all over the country. They were very popular because they offered well-priced accommodation and had good standards. Guesthouses were cheaper than hotels and their furnishings were more basic, although the rooms were comfortable, with shower/bath/WC, but no kitchen. They were usually in private houses, which offered single apartments and/or vacation apartments. Sometimes they hosted a café or restaurant, but mostly guests were served a good, rich breakfast buffet in German style. This choice was far more acceptable in every way than a hotel, particularly if they were to maintain the facade of their spontaneous holiday.

Aniela charmed Frau Becker from the outset, and she led them proudly toward their rooms. The sitting room had a small fireplace flickering with welcoming flames, the ambient warmth promising to soothe their bodies and spirits. Once Frau Becker left, Andy set the small table with their purchases, while Aniela unpacked their meager toiletries.

"Fraulein, dinner is served!" he said, with a mock flourish, a towel over his arm. Aniela joined him before the fire. He poured the wine, and they clinked glasses.

"I could get used to this," he said with a smile. "I could get even more used to being with you." Aniela sipped her wine looking straight at him, and smiled.

CHAPTER 12

Windward Farm, Maine, Late Autumn 2007

Andy was temporarily *incommunicado* with Washington, (having made contact only with his European counterpart) and their incoming reports were less than encouraging since the last verified sighting was in one of the frescoed cafés with Aniela in Kitzbühel before their ski run. They were reported to have been on the chair lift to the midpoint of the mountain, just before it was closed due to the storm. No one had seen them since, and reports from European contacts were coming in slow and empty.

The assumption made was that he and Aniela may have been dispatched by any of sundry unsavory individuals tracking them under cover of the storm in the mountains. The head of the European contingent had had no word from Anton, nor had he reappeared at the university or his flat. Washington had no way of knowing that the two had even made contact, particularly as the Austrian agent who was to make contact with them had not reported in since the revelation that they and he would have to elude not only the Arabs, but "The Romanian" as well, who was working for the Russians. This latest development bode poorly for the young U.S. agent, as The Romanian was one of only a few at the top of the CIA's list of most dangerous international agents.

Because Andy and Aniela had returned to the hotel only to sleep and leave early the next morning, the hotel "plant" could pass no information to his contact about their reappearance. The pair expected that they might be tailed, which reinforced their plan to continue a carefree romp under the guise of a tryst. By their deduction, they were among several "individuals of interest" whose prior activities and/or associations made them suspect to the more watchful and organized security, undercover, and other agent forces worldwide. That they had successfully functioned on previous missions without leaving a sufficiently evidentiary trail, was to their individual and joint credit. Nonetheless, Andy's and Aniela's circumvention had made them elusive and unreachable for the last two weeks of Andy's nearly three months' tour abroad.

The prepared letters had long since been used, and it had been weeks since any of the Stantons had heard from Andy. Although they knew to be prepared for intervals like this, worry overtook logic. It had always been a sore subject that Andy would not elaborate on his job, even to the extent of defining the type of work he did for the government, other than that they employed his linguistic skills.

Because his parents were cosmopolitan (even though they chose to live a provincial existence), they were well aware that the CIA's Director had directed the rebuilding of the CIA's overseas presence and the overhauling of the agency's clandestine training facility—the "Farm"—at Camp Perry near Williamsburg, VA, also allowing the Defense Humint Service (the Pentagon's human intelligence agency) to send its students there for training. Additionally, as part of the overall intelligence/security reorganization, a covert joint intelligence organization was formed that married the clandestine skills of the CIA with the technical capabilities of the NSA.

The CIA's status as an intelligence collection and covert action agency had long since hit rock bottom as the year 2000 turned on everyone's calendar. Thus, the role of DCI (Director of Central Intelligence) as chief of the entire intelligence community atrophied, as the DCI controlled only a small portion of the overall assets of the intelligence community (which had many entities). No one authority could practically manage all the agencies, much less marshal the required funding, and almost 90% of the agencies were operated and funded by the DOD (Department of Defense). The reality of the network guaranteed stalls, leaks, and bickering over priorities. Moreover, the NSA's supercomputer research, surveillance, and technology, as well as its crypto logic and linguistic capability was a natural bedfellow for the CIA. Their growing closeness created the SCS.

It was, in fact, to one of the alphabetically denoted "groups" born of this reorganization merger to which Andy belonged. What was once the CIA's "Group D", was now the SCS (Special Collection Service). In "difficult" countries, clandestine SCS agents often appeared in disguises: businesspersons, academics, scientists, journalists. Andy was such an agent. Technically, he was CIA, but he worked very closely with the NSA, and ultimately reported to both.

Elizabeth's motherly intuition became as intense as a gale force wind. She *knew* her son was in trouble. When his parents inquired of his status with one of his US counterparts (Andy had, at least, provided them with a contact to cover an event such as this), they were dissatisfied with his answers to their questions, despite his reassuring, kind, and solicitous manner when he gently confirmed their worst fears: MOA—Missing On Assignment. Elizabeth knew that she was powerless to do anything but wait for definitive word . . . and pray.

The twins were lodged safely at college, undoubtedly leaving their unique mark. They weren't due home again until Thanksgiving, and were not at all as good about phoning as Andy and Marcy had been.

Marcy was heavily involved in her practice and the overhanging mystery concerning the competition horses, to say nothing of the distraction caused by Tre and Tommy.

Jeremy had immersed himself in farm matters, the refinishing of the wooden sailboat he had built, and late night meetings of the newly formed regional Environmental Committee.

All the fruit and vegetable harvest had been either canned or frozen weeks ago; the Garden Club was in hiatus; the cold weather had descended, causing everything to slow down from summer's bustle to autumn's quiet ebb.

With little to provide distraction, her thoughts enveloped her eldest son. Wandering aimlessly in the comfort of their home brimming with memories, Elizabeth sat down at the piano. 'In you, O Lord, do I put my trust,' she whispered in thought. The haunting strains of Chopin's Prelude No. 10 reached Jeremy in his workshop over the intercom. He paused rubbing the satiny wood on the stern for a moment and listened. A tiny droplet fell from his cheek to the waxen teak and shimmered. It did not splatter; it did not run; it stayed whole, refracting the last rays of sunlight that poured through the window. Jeremy smiled, whispering softly, "He's going to be all right, Liz, honey. Our boy is going to be all right."

CHAPTER 13

Winter, Germany 2007

Andy had worked out a relative timeline list of translations of the Qur'an in an attempt to parallel the working list he had compiled of the early development of Judaism and Christianity and their related writings. Although there were many, each on his list had earned note because of reported accuracy in both translation and transliteration without losing the essence of the overall message and its intent, and was accepted to be a moreorless reliable representation:

A.	600s	Salman the Persian translated Fatiha from Arabic to Persian
B.	1000s	Latin Lex Mahumet pseudoprophete by Robert of Ketton
C.	1500s	Latin reprint of Lex Mahumet pseudoprophete (1143) edited by Theodor Bibliander
D.1.	1600s	French, L' Alcoran de Mahonet by Andre du Ryer
D.2.		English, L' Alcoran de Mahonet by Alexander Ross
D.3.		Dutch, Mahomets Alkoran translated from the French by Hendrik Jan Glasemaker
D.4.		Latin, new rendering made by Father Maracci
E.1.	1700s	English, Koran, commonly called The Alcoran of Mohammed, translated from the original Arabic by George Sale (one of the copies owned by American Founding Father Thomas Jefferson, on which Keith Ellison, the first Muslim elected to Congress, was sworn).

E.2.		German, text of the Koran edited by Gustav Fluegel
E.3.		Polish, Koran (al Koran) by Jan Murza Tarak Buczacki
E.4.		English, The Koran by John Medows Rodwel
E.5.		English, The Qur'ân by Edward HenryPalmer
E.6.	1900s	English, The Holy Qur'an, by Maulana Muhammad Ali (Ahmadiyya sect)
E.7.		English, The Meaning of the Glorious Koran, by Marmaduke Pickthall (Sufi sect)
E.8.		English, The Holy Qur'an: Text, Translation and Commentary, by Abdullah Yusuf Ali (Sufi sect)
E.9.		Bosnian, Kur' an, by Hafiz Muhamed Pandža and Džemaludin Čaušević
E.10.		English, Noble Qur'an, by Muhammad Muhsin Khan (Sunni sect)
E.11.		Polish, Koran, by Józef Bielawski
E.12.		English, The Qur'an, by M H. Shakir (Shi'a sect)
E.13.		Swedish, Koranensbudskap, by Mohammed Knut Bernström (Sunni sect)
E.14.		Hebrew, Al Qur'an, by Josef Rivlin
F.1.	2000s	English, "The Message" God's Revelation to Humanity, by Progressive Muslims Org, 2003
F.2.		Hebrew, Ha Qur'an, 2005 by Uri Rubin
F.3.		English, "Quran: a Reformist Translation", 2006, by Edip Yuksel, Layth al-Shaiban, Martha and Aisha Bewley

Although his list did not claim to cover all translations, it verified that sufficient copies were available to the major land blocks and cultures, and were valid translations, as distinct to those printed with exclusively private agendas religious or political. Part of Andy's initial research would focus primarily on providing a comparative background between Islam, Christianity, and Judaism with a view to the analysis of timelines, development, similarities, and differences. The legitimacy of each would provide their connection as a backdrop for the translated message of the scrolls passed to him by Anton.

Those in his field and associated scientific disciplines accepted that *translation* communicates the meaning of a source-language text by route of an equivalent target-language text. *Transliteration* was essentially the exchange of text from one writing system into another, word by word, or (ideally) letter by letter. Further, *transcription* mapped the sounds of one language to the closest matching script of another language, and could therefore be opposed in some cases to transliteration.

Translators *en masse* always risked the inappropriate use of idiom in the source language finding its way into the target-language translation. The Ancient Greek term for translation—μετάφρασις—*metaphrasis* (or a "speaking across") provides a literal, word-for-word translation, as distinct to *paraphrasis* (paraphrase or "saying in other words"). Metaphrase relates to "formal equivalence," whereas paraphrase is considered "dynamic equivalence." Formal equivalence ("literal" word-for-word) renders text "literally," sometimes at the expense of elements natural to the target language. Dynamic equivalence ("functional") puts across the thought expressed in text, sometimes at the expense of literality, word order, linguistic sememes, etc.

All apt translators know that the metaphrase concept is imperfect, because words in any given language often hold more than one meaning, and similar meanings might often be signified by more than one word. Despite this and recent developments employing automated machine translation to mechanically aid translators, the actual practice of translation has not changed since antiquity.

Translators were an uncommon breed, showing carefulness and dedication to seek literal equivalents where possible, and paraphastic equivalents only when necessary. They tried to safeguard the context by replicating the original order of sememes [a linguistic sound] and word order, only reinterpreting the actual grammatical structures when necessary because of differences between fixed-word-order languages and free-word-order languages. Faithfulness and transparency to these ideals helped to conform grammar, syntax, and idiom.

Because he was a pre-eminent linguist, Andy knew that part of the complexity of translating the antiquities involved the application of the concepts of translation and transliteration as applied to an ancient language. The evolution of ancient languages revealed capabilities of distinguishing differing numbers of consonants and vowels, with conflicting conformation, *e.g.*, Cv or vC (C = consonant; v = vowel).

Further, Andy knew that the origins of the target language in the scrolls had to be considered and mapped. Semiotics (the study of signs and symbols) would necessarily come into play as well, since ancient symbols had been integrated into the scrolls' text as a kind of cryptography to protect the message, and had defeated initial analysis by Anton and his learned associates.

Sumerian cuneiform script had approximately 1,000 signs and variants, which number was reduced to about 600 by the time Akkadian records began. Akkadian is the designation for a group of closely related East Semitic dialects from the early third millennium until the Christian era in the Middle East. Akkadian is written with signs originally devised for and evolved from Sumerian, which resulted in a mixed method of writing: logograms mixed with syllables of vC, Cv, or CvC. This language system gave way to Old Assyrian, Old Babylonian, Middle Babylonian, and Neo-Babylonian—from which sprang the Semitic language of Aramaic.

Aramaic was a common language of the Eastern Mediterranean during and after the Neo-Assyrian, Neo-Babylonian, and Achaemenid Empires through to the 1st century AD. Along with some Hebrew and Greek, Aramaic remained the common language of Israel (eventually to become dominant among Jews both in Israel and elsewhere in the Middle East around 200 AD).

It was generally agreed by scholars that the towns of Nazareth and Capernaum, where Jesus lived, were primarily Aramaic-speaking communities, although Greek was widely spoken in the major cities of the Mediterranean Basin. Jesus and his disciples would have spoken a Galilean dialect clearly distinguishable from that of Jerusalem. As an example of the concurrence of languages, in the same time period the Mishnah (the first major writing of the Jewish oral traditions (Oral Torah) and the first major work of Rabbinic Judaism) was recorded in Hebrew; Josephus (37 BC-100 AD/CE, a 1st century Romano-Jewish historian of high ancestry who recorded 1st century Jewish history) wrote in Aramaic; and Philo (a Hellenistic Jewish Biblical philosopher born in Alexandria) and Paul of Tarsus (a zealous Jew of the Tribe of Benjamin who persecuted early followers of Jesus Christ, but who became a Christian and evolved into Paul the Apostle) wrote in Greek.

Andy viewed his comparative analysis as a critical step toward validating both the legitimacy of the scrolls themselves and their content, and setting the stage to help convince the adherents of major religions to accept the message of the scrolls. He knew he was taking a bold leap of faith by accepting the deductions and initial finds of Anton's group. However, his government would not have assigned him to this mission had there been any hint that Israel's request for help had been frivolous or ill-conceived. That was not the way things worked. *Ergo*, there had to be something to all of this to warrant the level of interest from all quarters. As he completed preliminary background while making his way out of Europe, his government and others were supposedly working on putting together a team for final analysis and investigation.

So many had risked so much to secure these long-buried, then hidden and suppressed documents. It fell to Andy and Aniela to properly assemble the framework of all the resource information before submitting what they had been led to believe was a life-shattering message to . . . to whom?

They had wrestled with the question for many hours and days. Governments, agents, mercenaries, scientists, and common people: all had risked themselves in a millennial labyrinth of intrigue and power, with life, death, and survival as the stakes. Cultures, ways of life, economic and political effect (much less supremacy) were the face cards in this game, with plots within plots within plots. It left the mind spinning. The "what if" quotient was never-ending.

How could they assume such a vast and long-reaching responsibility in the face of all that had been and what was? Although Andy had been sent by his government to connect with those who had risked their lives to protect the fragile manuscripts and sequester them until their content could be properly verified and revealed, he found himself questioning even the government he believed in. It was, after all, the construct of men. Therefore, it was flawed and subject to internal pressures exerted by private agendas. Nonetheless, it was the lesser of evils as governments went. In the least, the overall system provided for the freest pursuance of life, and most prevalent and effective system of checks and balances in the world. As if their minds were in perfect synergy inwardly searching for answers to parallel queries, they looked up at each other.

"Andrew?" Aniela's voice quavered with intensity. He rose and moved around the square table strewn with books, notepads, rumpled sheets of notes (in his undecipherable shorthand), abstruse diagrams, maps, and the leftovers of snatched meals. Andy gathered Aniela into his arms, and they stood together looking through the windows at the seemingly mindless busyness of routine village life beyond their cloistered existence. "Is it ever going to be over? Not this trip, I mean this uncertainty about life, about tomorrow. All this that we do, will it have a good ending? Will it help to stop the madness?" Aniela shivered.

He spoke softly, his lips resting against the upper side of her head. She smelled so clean and fresh, her body soft and warm within his arms, her hands cool on his bare forearms. His heart was full: full of passion for her, and full of passion for his beliefs.

"I don't know, Aniela, I can only hope that what I do, what you do, and what so many others have done, will be worth the effort. That's all we can hope for. It's what keeps me going, you know? Someone has to work to maintain the balance. Today it's you and me. Tomorrow, who knows? But from where I stand, it's definitely worth it." As he held her, thoughts of home warmed and comforted him.

"There are some people in my life I'd like you to meet one day. Then you'll better understand why I do what I do. It's like that for all of us: we all have someone or something we want to protect, things we want to survive without being changed or threatened. We do it because we have to, because it's the right thing. Nothing more, nothing less."

She turned toward him without breaking the embrace, looking into his eyes for several moments before kissing him softly on the lips. He shivered with the ecstasy of the moment.

"Come on, enough of this for a while," he said pulling her toward the door, snatching their jackets. "We need some air, some exercise, and some food and wine. Let's let the magic of this place brush away the cobwebs."

She smiled at him, altogether ready to abandon their troublesome work with its shadows, threats, challenges, idiosyncrasies, and burdens.

"And then, liebling?" she asked playfully. Andy smiled and waggled his eyebrows in response. Laughing, the two rushed from their rooms, eager to embrace a few hours of fragile freedom.

The man watched them through his dark glasses, slowly turning the page of his unread newspaper. He casually sipped the last of his coffee, placing a few Deutsche marks on the table before departing the café. Removing his phone from the inner pocket of his tweed jacket, Martine pressed a button.

"The little birds have left the nest. Send the hawks as soon as possible. There is no way to tell when the migration will begin." He followed the two at a distance, crossing the square to pause at a kiosk, then proceed through the market a safe way behind.

"You know, we've taken care to be inconspicuous, but I have a bad feeling starting in my gut," said Andy. He was all too used to employing ruses, double-backs, and the well-used routines of covert operations. Experience bred constant caution and a developed "sixth sense" promoted survival. Survival meant success in this business. Although he was a relatively low-level agent, his function was valuable, more so because of his comparatively low profile, erudite professional associations, and innate abilities.

His occasional courier use was employed under cover of international conferences or unsuspicious meetings with colleagues abroad. Barring one or two previous, close calls involving dangerous liaisons, his primary worth to his government was intellectual. He possessed a natural gift with languages and mathematics, and the cultivated time spent abroad honed those skills enabling him to speak like a native throughout much of Europe. As a linguist with degrees that covered Middle Eastern history, languages, and culture, he also had more than a peripheral association with linguistic anthropology, and (to a much lesser extent) archaeology. These links made his presence in certain parts of the world in the company of related individuals very plausible.

He had become more than useful in meetings that were in reality investigative in scope. He had proved himself apt in ferreting out information and connections for his missions, as well as to transmit directives or arrangements to covert agents and/or contacts. However, his greatest value was with cryptanalysis and translations with accurate context, particularly in those scenarios when the quick analysis of documents, messages, or information in less-than-friendly circumstances was required. His scientific mind functioned mathematically with ease. His linguistic talents made his translations unerringly accurate. His expertise in ancient languages made him the ideal candidate for this assignment, particularly since he knew some of the contacts involved through past association. Thus, Andy was not only the natural choice for the retrieval and work to follow, but likely the only one whose abilities exactly matched the needs of the operation.

If anyone checked his identity or wished to verify his credentials, he would flag as a brilliant but harmless academic who, as a young American, was also reasonably athletic and somewhat of a lady's man, according to reports. That he should spend some extended time with the lovely Austrian girl was in keeping with his profile, scant though it was.

The double life he led, and the believability of the cover he presented, made him a valuable asset.

Because of his particular gifts and their widespread potential, his was a deep cover position insulated and sufficiently buried from prying eyes. His work spanned the usual barriers between the CIA and the NSA, although he reported directly to the SOO (Staff Operations Officer) in the still independent CIA's Clandestine Service. Normally based in Washington, he was logged in as a Language Officer for access security purposes. Moreover, he was dispatched for foreign travel only when his Special Services training and abilities fit the task or mission.

"You learn to trust these feelings, *ja*?" Aniela took his arm and pointed toward a café whose low roofline was brimming with baskets filled with cut greens, berries, and cones, forming a cascading screen that provided shade in the late afternoon. "So now we must play the game of lovers, Andrew. A man or a woman may be watching us, *ja*? We must give to them something to think about. This should not be too difficult for you, my Andrew."

Aniela smiled at him teasingly, then ran ahead to secure a table in a comer of the café's outdoor arbor. In line with her suggestion, he paused at a flower monger and chose a small handful of cut blossoms that the woman tied with a ribbon. He smiled at her, pressed money into her hand and winked, walking quickly to Aniela in the café. Making a flourish of presenting the nosegay, he kissed her hand. They huddled together over the menu, pretending to discuss the fare.

To all intents and purposes, they looked like young lovers. He, with curly blonde hair fashionably long, skirting a reddish blonde beard; a black tee shirt and worn jeans under a well-worn waxed coat and hand-knitted muffler; scuffed boots and dirty tan leather gloves that had seen better days. She, a lanky, muscular Nordic-type with white blonde hair braided on each side of her head, framing piercing gray eyes ringed by thick, dark blonde lashes; tight black pants tucked into hiking boots, revealing well-shaped long legs beneath a green Tyrolean boiled wool jacket and ski cap, the only hint at femininity the white ruffles of a shirt peaking out of her bulky black sweater.

The man had a watch, but no rings or noticeable personal effects except a cell phone. The woman wore no jewelry or makeup, and carried no handbag, opting for a small leather purse attached to her chunky hip belt. They had only the paper sacks containing their market square purchases. Thus, they melded into the tapestry of townspeople without the earmarks of foreign travelers: no fashion statements or bright colors, somewhat worn clothing familiar to the region, slightly scruffy, no telltale tightly clutched traveling gear, and not boisterous in their demeanor.

The man in the beret stroked his goatee thoughtfully. He had found his quarry, but they were not acting at all like two people desperate to get away from the region. Perhaps their contact was in Germany after all. These two seemed to be thoroughly enjoying themselves, enrapt in each other's company with no suppressed urgency or watchfulness in their behavior. Could Intel have made a mistake? Was it possible that the American was merely enjoying an affair with the beautiful Austrian girl?

But no, she had a profile of association with other questionable people. These academic types, bah! They were always on the fringes politically, tampering with things they did not understand in pursuit of their unrealistic ideologies. Well, once the hawks arrived, he would know if these two had led him on a goose chase. They should just about be arriving. Once he made contact, he would report in for further instructions. Meantime, there was no reason to deny himself the luxury of another pastry and a warm drink while he watched. 'Lucky man for now, American,' he mused.

Andy and Aniela tucked into their meal with gusto. The sauerbraten was succulent, and the cheeses complemented the hard, dark, crusty schwarzbrot bread. Between mouthfuls, they traded observations.

"There, by the corner, in the beret. He was behind us from the corner of the piazza. I noticed him because he looked so foolish in that beret with no hair. He has such big ears! Here it would make more of sense to wear a whole hat, *ja*? No one from here would dress so. Even a Frenchman, which he is not, would forsake the beret for a warm hat in this cold. Even Frenchmen abandon fashion when their bald heads are cold," said Aniela with merriment in her eyes.

"Yes, I see him. I didn't notice him before. He may be a tag. Right now, everyone is suspect, even the lady at the flower stall. She keeps looking this way, so pay attention to those flowers will you? I know they're not roses, but . . ."

At that point, Aniela interrupted him with a soft, lingering kiss on the mouth. As she drew back looking into his eyes, Andy cleared his throat.

"Uh, was that part of the play acting, or was that for real?" Stroking her cheek, he thought, 'She is truly the most beautiful woman I have ever seen.'

"Whatever you think, that was from me to you, and it was real. So good, if it looks good to them, too. If they are watching us, then they see that fire is between us." Her eyes were moist as she traced the outline of his lips.

"Aniela, you can't . . ." Andy was interrupted again by the hungry press of her lips.

"So, the little birds make love in the café. They will be wanting their bed before long. Where are the hawks to be found?" Salid mouthed quietly into his cell phone to the watching Martine.

"I am expecting a call from them at any moment. Do you wish to maintain surveillance?" Martine removed his sunglasses, studiously cleaning them as he spoke into the concealed microphone attached to his cell phone. "Their rooms were tossed and revealed nothing out of the ordinary: a few books in his area of study, some notes, mostly scribbles, and travel maps. The search was fruitless. I do not recommend . . ."

"*You* recommend? Watch them closely and mark every move, every person. The days wear thin, but we have enough time to eliminate this wrinkle in the plan. The pair will not risk leaving the area with the weather front rolling in. It will soon be dark. Post a watch throughout the night, just in case, and call me with anything. Otherwise, I shall speak with you first thing in the morning. I assume your team was careful to leave no sign of their visit."

"There were no mistakes; my men are experienced. But if they have something on them, the only way we can get it," Martine stammered. He was interrupted by what were obviously terse instructions, as his facial expression became pinched.

"Of course, I will meet up with Fakar, and it shall be as you say," he said. As he placed the glasses in his breast pocket next to the Beretta, he pressed the button to end the cell call, unnoticeable to people nearby. After a suitable time, he withdrew his cell phone and hit the speed dial for Fakar.

Hundreds of miles to the south and east, Salid irritably snapped his phone shut, turning his attention to the young men practicing tumbling drills in the courtyard. "This new breed of faithful soldiers will make it unnecessary to rely on outside security and manpower. It will be better for my blood pressure," he thought with satisfaction.

Having finished their dinner, Andy licked the crumbs of the gingerbread-like lebkuchen from his fingers, saying with a forced smile, "Well, beautiful one, time to return to our rooms for some rest before we make our way out of this paradise. Let's just hope this little extended trip discouraged our tail while giving our friends enough time to get their act together. I was able to make contact via a secure line earlier, so they know where we are currently."

As they entered their rooms, Aniela sniffed and held Andy back with a light touch on his arm. "Someone has been in here, and it was not Frau Becker."

Slowly, they removed their scarves and jackets, feigning casualness while their eyes darted around the room. As Andy turned on the lamp, he checked it for a bug; Aniela did likewise across the room. The rooms were small; there were no pictures on the busy, shabby wallpaper; and the heavy drapes (which when closed were used to cover the windows for privacy, and provide some insulation) could not be used to disguise sensitive monitoring devices. The bed frame was iron with old-fashioned springs and a single mattress: it checked out clear. The square wooden table and two chairs were clear as well. The small chest of drawers and side bed tables, as well as the utilitarian lavatory and separate bathroom were as before: without frills or suspicion. Only the few books and pamphlets, some of Andy's notes, and their maps had clearly been moved, as if someone had rifled through them.

"How did you know?" Andy asked her, after receiving the "all clear" nod. He sat in one of the chairs to remove his boots. She came to him, kneeling to help.

"You Americans and your cowboy boots. How can you not wear sensible boots like mine?" she said, as she tugged them off, tumbling back onto the floor laughing. "I could smell whoever was here. There were two of them, I think. One was a smoker of cigars, the small ones that really stink. The other one had bad body odor with cheap perfume smell over top of it, like he was making it better, *ja*? Frau Becker smells of sauerkraut and onions or flour most of the time. So I knew it was not her, and no one else is here, but us. Just logic, my Andrew, and a trusty nose."

"Okay, Sherlock, I get it. Well, that also confirms our suspicions about being tailed. Let's have a look at that map and plan our next movements. I'll have to rely on your knowledge of the area, but I think we'd better mix it up a bit to look like we're casually sightseeing. If we can find the right place, we'll have to give him or them the slip. So much for taking that flight direct to Paris. That wouldn't be such a hot idea just now, would it?"

"We have enough time to make our way to our contact without attracting attention," said Aniela. "There is a wonderful place I want to show you on the way. I spent many times there with my parents, and it has happy memories. I have not been back since they were lost to me, so it is special that I take you there, Andrew." Aniela looked at him through her lashes, coloring slightly. He could see that her eyes had filled, and his heart welled with emotion, partially in sympathy that the distant loss of her parents still evoked such sadness, but mostly because she was opening herself to him, sharing a place of bittersweet memory, and revealing her vulnerability.

"Look. Here, this is the route I think is good we take." Aniela traced a finger on the map. "Everyone knows that Kitzbühel is home to the legendary Hahnenkamm downhill and has plenty of on and off piste skiing, so that little journey of ours was not suspicious, *ja* ? You had the first time handshake with one of those 1000 meter vertical descents through the steep bowl and gladed forest. How did you like it?" As she spoke, her eyes glinted mischievously, and Andy merely grumbled as he massaged his arm.

"Now, we will take the Tirol's Eagle Walk. It is well-known route for the vacationer to this region. See?" As her finger traced the proposed route, she explained to Andy. "It winds through Tirol's most beautiful places from St. Johann to St. Anton am Arlberg. Mostly, it follows hiking trails and mountain footpaths. There are difficult segments that require the high skill hiking, like here to here, and here and here, ending here."

Aniela's finger tapped the trail section from Steinberg am Rofan all the way to Trittscharte Notch and Ulmer. "Our friends will not have an easy time to follow and, if they dare to do so, we will be able to see them clearly and disappear. I know these places well from when I was a young girl."

Andy stared at the map for a long time. After their grueling ski through wild, frozen terrain, his injured arm (which was still sore, but healing), Aniela's illness, and the promise of more cold, snowy weather moving in, he was not certain that her plan was the best course.

Essentially, the most important thing to accomplish was to offload the reduced printed material to a contact, keeping the chip with them as backup, or vice versa, as the situation allowed or demanded. Aniela had skillfully sewn the chip into one of her hair ties, then woven each into one of her luscious braids. If things went wrong and they were searched, their clothing, pockets, backpacks, and boots would reveal nothing.

The second challenge was to make it to England to connect with his SIS contact (colloquially MI6—Secret Intelligence Service) and the safe-house in as casual a fashion as possible, either discouraging any potential watchers by their relaxed vacation meandering or giving them the slip by virtue of their circuitous route. Both options were sufficiently believable to remove high level suspicion.

"Don't call me chicken, but are you sure we're up to this? It looks pretty strenuous and it's over rough terrain that's pretty high up."

Aniela burst out laughing and walked to the chair to fetch Andy's cowboy boots. "American, you are having freezing toes, *ja*? Tomorrow, we go to get you better boots and some other things to make you feel better. My American is a chicken, not a rooster!" Peals of laughter tumbled from her.

"The expression is having 'cold feet', and 'chicken' has nothing to do with gender," Andy retorted petulantly. "It just seems crazy to go careening around the mountains when we could take a more direct, civilized route for the hand-off. We're not in the Olympic Games here, Aniela."

"Andrew, do not be so upset. It is a beautiful walk, and is just under 50 kilometers. Not so much for you, *ja*? Although, some of the climbs are steep, like the one to Aschau."

"Steep? How steep?" Andy asked suspiciously, keenly aware of the limits of Aniela's descriptive English.

"That one? Oh, only about 1150 meters vertical rise. But the walk to the top to Leutkircher Hut is 2261 meters up, and you will get to see the wide, open world of the alpine. Think of it, Andrew. In the high Karwendel Mountains, you can watch chamois climbing up nearly perfect vertical slopes. Andy's response was to shake his head and frown.

"Then . . ." she said, raising her eyebrows in challenge, "we spend the night at Bayreuther Hut."

Grumpily, Andy said, "Yeah, sounds just ducky."

"My Andrew, stop this. You will love it. It is so beautiful, you will see. This is the special place I told you about. Do not worry, there are hundreds of places along the way and alternate climbs and paths to lose anyone, if we need to do so. And we are being normal, like everyone who comes to this place. That is the beauty of it all, do you understand now?" Without waiting for his response, Aniela shook her head once affirmatively to denote that the subject was closed.

Andy sighed in resignation.

"Now, to sleep. We have big days ahead of us. But first, let us have the last of the wine, *ja*?"

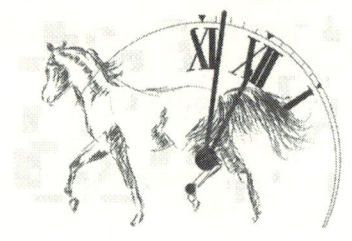

Chapter 14

Local Police Department, Maine

"So you see, agents," stated Marcy, having outlined her examination findings, "more than Demiluna was used as a carrier for their nefarious work. I've prepared a chart indicating treatment details, physiological data, including the results of the blood tests at the time of discovery—as well as following my treatment—through to final blood and other tests that register normal after removal. That window is somewhere between two and four days, depending upon the horse.

"Also listed are horses' names and owner contact information. Happily, they're more or less within the same clearance period with no known significant after effects, likely because of rapid discovery and removal of the pouches. All stall locations are on the second page of the chart marked on the site diagram, with photograph, registration certificates, health forms, and Coggins certificates. I'd remind you that these animals are worth many thousands of dollars, some in the high six figures."

Having finished this segment of her report, Marcy looked around the table for questions, her heart still pumping rapidly. She was certain that her complexion flushed, though her hands and eyes were steady. Anticipating acceptance of her work with perhaps a grudging compliment, Marcy was surprised at Harry Lochmere's explosive reaction.

"What?" exclaimed Lochmere. "Who would be stupid enough to pay that sort of money for an animal? You've got to be kidding, doc."

"It might surprise you to learn, Mr. Lochmere, excuse me, *Agent* Lochmere, that many people all over the globe are prepared to spend those amounts, particularly in the Thoroughbred breed, where purchase prices can be in the millions. And, for your edification, they are not considered just animals to their owners and those who care for them. Because of their value and function, they often receive care and accommodation that would be the envy of many people," Marcy said indignantly.

"Yeah, and in France I've heard they eat horses. Go figure," sneered Lochmere grimacing.

"I reckon I could find you a horse, *Lochmere*, that would make your work with the FBI superfluous in terms of cash. Much better investment, what? Anytime you want my recommendation, do call, won't you?" Tommy tossed his calling card on the desk.

Marcy flashed her eyes at Tommy's dig, removed a second report from her folder, and presented the sheets to the Agents. "Here is the tracking information on each horse replete with egress/ingress detail. In each case, we have put together a list of individuals who had known contact with the horses. I'm afraid it goes only so far, as we were unable to determine what officials may have had contact at the point of exit or entry. That part would be up to you, of course. Still, it's noteworthy that each of the affected horses either began their journey or had a stopover in England, be it from Ireland or The Netherlands."

"Good work," said Agent Dunne. "Your thoroughness is admirable, Dr. Stanton."

"I couldn't have done it without Tommy and Lars. In fact, Tommy gathered the majority of the contact data for you, and Lars was vital in listing some of the interactions presented in these reports, as well as details on the owners. Additionally, had he not mentioned the other mares, we might have overlooked the connection. Worst case, we could have had a tragedy of greater proportion. Whoever placed those packets, clearly did so in a hurry, I believe. Not one was without breach, and none were in exactly the same position within the individual horses.

"Speculatively, I guess one could say that the level of discomfort to the mare may have caused the mare to contract her muscles and change the positioning somewhat. But, I doubt that the differences can be attributed to normal exercise or internal muscular flexion.

"Also, note that the packet material doesn't withstand long-term exposure to bodily fluids without compromise. When an area is weakened, as in Photograph #3 of Packet #1, any undue movement could cause the rupture highlighted in Photograph #2. In the other cases, there were clear indentations that probably were made from a fingernail during the placement process. Given there was no lubrication added, at least none remaining on either the packet or surrounding tissue via several swab cultures, we can potentially rule out other chemical reactions beyond bodily fluids, except of course for possible assimilation of lubricants. Certain of the packets show thinning in the central areas, particularly the one that had at least twenty percent absorption of environmental moisture. The mucous membrane in that mare was seared at the point of exposure."

Tommy rose and signaled Marcy with a glance and an almost imperceptible nod. She was grateful for the pause. "Yes, if you will, agents, I suggest you focus on another nasty little aspect of this thoroughly disagreeable matter that Dr. Stanton's very meticulous report raises."

He looked at Marcy and smiled. With his hair slightly ruffled from their walk from the car, and his hand on his hip with his jacket thrown back, his stance and manner made her think of a feudal lord acknowledging and paying compliment to one of his chevaliers.

"Although we have no real benchmark to judge whether or not these mares will suffer any long-term effects from this criminal exposure, I imagine that the owners—once they know, and I assume you two will be notifying them *post haste*—may want to sue someone. What's your best guess, Lars?" Tommy may have delivered that comment disdainfully, but he was right, nonetheless.

"Therefore, it would behoove you two to include Lars Borst on every aspect of this issue, as the FBI may find itself involved right up to their white socks!" With this last quip, Tommy peered under the desk at Lochmere's ankles, with a wink to Marcy. Agent Lochmere caught the look and bristled.

"Certainly, it would not only be wise to include Lars, but necessary in terms of owner liaison, corporate and organizational considerations, and further details or information," declared Marcy. "Also, it is critical that this investigation be a tight one. These owners are deep-pocketed, and none will tolerate a less than satisfactory close to the matter. They all have the means to pursue this to the bitter end, civilly if not criminally." At this last comment, Lochmere raised his eyebrows to Dunne.

They discussed the matter for over two hours, each offering possible scenarios, exploring the most unlikely avenues, narrowing down connections and contacts. In the end, it was Agent Lochmere who offered their joint thanks. The man had been won over somewhat by their thoroughness and cooperation.

"I know this has been difficult and upsetting for all of you, particularly to you, Mr. Brandon, as owner of the first mare discovered. I confess we don't usually enjoy this kind of help. In this instance, it's more than welcome as this horse business stuff is, uh, unfamiliar to both of us. We may have gotten off on the wrong foot to begin with, but I want to thank you for your help. We'll be talking with you again in the next few days."

From Marcy's perspective, Agent Lochmere had apologized for his abruptness and initial insulting behavior. She squeezed Tommy's leg under the table in a signal of triumph.

"Why thank you, Agent Lochmere. Do let us know if we can be of further help to the FBI, or if you come up with any additional information beyond all we've provided you. Let's hope you nail the cunning blighters." Tommy, too, had taken a step forward, thought Marcy, though he had not been able to resist mentioning that they had all laid out the case detail work for the two agents.

Following the usual admonitions about physical movements, Lars, Marcy, Tommy, and Detective Murphy left the room. Murphy waved them a "thumbs up" sign as the three departed the Police Department and walked toward their cars, all feeling proud of their performance and work.

"Did you two have to give all that personal detail?" asked Lars. "There for a while it seemed as though they were treating me like a suspect, for Heaven's sake."

Marcy and Tommy reassured Lars, but Marcy retained a vague sense of uneasiness about the agents' reaction to Lars. Agent Dunne was particularly relentless in her questioning of him, and she had cast furtive glances to Lochmere several times during the interrogation.

By the time Marcy reached Windward Farm, she was overcome with a sense of exhaustion. Tommy had suggested they catch a quick dinner, but she had demurred on the basis that they would be together with Lars most of the following late afternoon through early evening, completing the last of the data preparation Agents Dunne and Lochmere had requested of them. The three planned a dinner afterward, and Tommy had suggested they drive up the coast to a sweet little place on the water famous for its seafood. She entered the house to the muffled sounds of crying.

"Hey, what's going on? Mom?" The house was dark and cool, illuminated only by the setting sun streaming through the glass. Her parents stood holding each other before the kitchen wall of west facing windows. The pastoral backdrop of Windward Farm's pastures rolling down to the sea framed their silhouettes.

Elizabeth turned to look at her daughter and whispered, "Andrew."

Her father merely stared out at the sea.

ChAPTER 15

Winter, Germany 2007

Würzberg, as the capital of Lower Franconia, became famous as the center of Franconian wine production and its atmosphere was beautifully embedded in the valley of the Main River, surrounded by wine-covered hills. The mighty fortress of Festung Marienberg was a famous landmark from which they had viewed the famous sights of the town. On a hill above Würzberg was the pilgrimage church Käppele, and it was in this idyllic spot that Andrew Vale Stanton acknowledged to himself that he had found his mate in the most impossible and unusual of circumstances.

"This is lovely, *ja*? I want to make for the Cathedral St. Kilian today, or maybe you want to see the late Gothic Church of St. Mary? Which, my Andrew? Either one will do. I wish to light candles for my parents."

Andy absently fingered Aniela's loose white gold tresses, cognizant that she had one braid running down the back of her luscious mane, which contained the hair tie with the chip. 'Always dependable,' he thought. He brought her fingers to his lips as he gazed over the town. They had left the market square and crossed the bridge over the Main River—Alte Mainbrücke—which was lined with an array of statues of saints which brought to mind the passage of historical time, the trail of his own life, and the family he had left behind.

The twenty-minute walk up the wine-covered hill took them to the Fortress Marienberg. They had shared a delightful, unfettered time in the beer garden sipping Pilsener, their conversation full of laughter and recollections. Aniela had unveiled her plan for their journey to proceed to Rothenburg ob der Tauber, a preserved medieval gem. The 70km trip would make it easily reachable in an hour, as was Nuremberg.

"My Andrew, you still have not told me: Rothenburg or Nuremberg? And is it to be St. Kilian or St. Mary?" said Aniela, as she roused him from his reverie. Just as he gathered himself to answer, the sun glinted off something below them and to the left.

Andy absently looked below as he said, "Oh, I think the cathedral is more fitting for you to light your parents' candles. In any case, I want you to know that this afternoon has been the most . . ." Andy's voice cut off and he brusquely shoved Aniela to the ground, lying over her, his lips pressed to her ear saying, "Lie still, darling."

"Andrew! What? This is no time to," she protested.

"Lie still and be quiet. There are two men who are no tourists coming up the hill to the far left, but not on the path. There are two others on the far right. One of them has a club or a metal stick or something that caught my eye when the sun hit it. It may be nothing, but my gut tells me it's not good. We should get out of here now." The intensity of his eyes burned into Aniela, dissipating the fairy tale they had been living, snapping her back to the reality of their situation.

Aniela and Andy scooted back, allowing the brow of the hill to provide them cover. As they gained their feet, they ran toward the far side of the Käppele. Breathlessly, they careened down the hillside to traverse the opposing side of the hill dominated by the church with a view to rejoining the path well below the men. As they carefully closed the circuit, the men were just reaching the crest of the hill, hand signing to each other.

They crouched into the hillside, grateful there were no other tourists present who might look in their direction and give them away. As the men disappeared over the brow, they tore down the path toward the fortress and the bridge beyond. In a little over fifteen minutes (halving the time they took on their walk), they were safely walking by the baroque Falkenhaus in the city center, albeit perspired and somewhat disheveled.

"It is good that you are fit, Andrew," said Aniela, who was still slightly out of breath. She squeezed his hand and smiled up at him.

"I'll take that as a compliment coming from you, however rare," he retorted with a crooked grin. "I'll never again complain about my farm upbringing and its hours of physical work, or the training I received from my government. All of it has come into play times over, but I'm particularly grateful for it just now." He steered her into a café, one of the many for which the region was famous, and they ordered double espressos and pastries.

"So it is now that we must be serious, my Andrew. I think we will be safe in our gasthaus for a while since our watchers are still on the hill, and there must be a hundred places like ours. We should go there and rest, *ja*?"

Andy sipped thoughtfully, wondering whether he should alert Aniela to his disagreement. He was, after all, the trained agent; she was merely a European contact. He was concerned not only about her overall safety, but also her mental ability to cope with what he assessed was the gravity of their situation.

Physically, he was certain she could meet most challenges; emotionally, she was a woman of enviable self-control; the mental pressure, however, was sure to escalate. Could she sustain her focus and composure over the long haul? Up to the current situation, her involvement in matters like this had been short-lived, of low profile, and significantly less dangerous.

"How did they know to go to the church, have you thought about that? Likely, they already know where we're staying, and tailed us from there. I wouldn't be surprised if our every move has been monitored since Kitzbühel. The thing we have to concentrate on is that they—whoever 'they' are—have stepped up the game. Those guys were not just tailing us. They meant business, and I can assure you, it would not have been friendly."

There. It was out on the table. Aniela looked levelly at Andrew, reaching across the table for his hand. It hurt his heart to tell such a beautiful creature, such a gifted scientist with elevated, unselfish ethics, his partner over the last weeks, a woman who had accepted him, helped him, joined herself together with him and his destiny, that her association with him had placed her in serious danger. "I know you didn't sign on for this, Aniela, and . . ." he whispered.

"Shush, liebchen," she cooed. "It is all right. I knew you were different from the moment we met. I am with you because you interest me. The rest, well," her hand made a sweeping gesture, "that just happened. You did not make it so. It is not your fault. We could do nothing but what we have done. The question is what now do we do? First, we must eat or we will look like, how do you say, a sore finger? The pastry is good, have some," she said, taking a healthy mouthful.

Andy smiled and reached across the table to whisk away sugar from the side of her mouth. "The expression is 'stick out like a sore thumb' and I agree, this little rest and food is called for. But then I think we should make our way to our rooms and scram. It would probably be a good idea to arrange a different car before returning to the gasthaus. Do you feel comfortable splitting up for awhile?"

"*Ja*, it is fine. You get the new car while I pack us up and settle our bill." She scribbled a name on the bottom of the paper menu, carefully tearing off the corner. "Get the car at this place. Is a good place with much business and they speak English. You know my code; here is my card. Get some more cash at the kiosk on the corner."

"No, no, I have plenty. You can't use your bankcard, Aniela. It's a dead giveaway as to where we are. Although on second thought, it might be useful to my people when they try to track us. If they know who you are, anything can pop up from credit card use. And if there are others besides those four guys from the church, we don't want to tip our hand, now do we? No, we'll forget about the credit cards for now. At least we've got some contacts, and my people also have satellite surveillance." Andy looked grave. "Crap, in this weather, satellites probably won't be much good, so we'll have to hope we can link up with a friendly."

"I know we must be careful, Andrew. Do not speak to me as to a child. But I also do not know where we draw a line to decide how much or how little we act like lovers on a European vacation. Now after all the acting, we will move in secret, looking for bad men around every corner? I wonder if this makes sense. Nein, I think we should be as normal. We must continue with our plans as if we have no cares. Even if in the mountains we have to lose the ones who follow, it is a thing that is explainable. It is not a thing that will look deliberate. Do you see?"

As she spoke these words, despite that they were delivered with a passionately whispered tone, Aniela looked like a woman who was merely having a casual conversation with her beau, while relishing the demolition of her pastry. She licked her fingers noisily.

"There, done. Now we go." She peremptorily nodded her head, indicating to Andy that her mind was made up, and the subject was closed.

He had been on the receiving end of that gesture many times previous. He had to admire her and the pragmatic way in which she seemed to deal with whatever came her way. Grudgingly, he also admitted to himself that her instincts made more sense than his initial reaction. Although she didn't realize it, the fact that she was not a trained agent, but a normal woman, made her a valuable asset he decided. Sometimes, but only rarely, experience could be a handicap.

"Not because you've totally convinced me," Andy said while placing money on the table, "but I'll go along with your point because it's more prudent to roll the dice, all things considered. But you'd better understand that there might come a time when you'll have to do as I say immediately and without question. Agreed?" He stretched his hand across the table with a rakish grin.

Aniela smiled, blew him a kiss, and stood. He noted that she failed to shake his hand in bargain.

"I shall wait for you at the gasthaus and pack all our things. I will be ready, and then we go to Rothenburg. Tschüss, goodbye." She winked at him, her long legs taking her out of the café in a few moments, male heads turning with appreciative glances as she went.

"Damn that woman." Andy muttered. Even as he said it, he had to smile.

CHAPTER 16

Rothenburg ob der Tauber, Germany 2007

"It seems like we're driving through a time warp," Andy said as they neared the beautiful little town with intact city walls that formed a ring around Rothenburg ob der Tauber. "I can just about picture knights coming through the gates on their steeds." Ahead, massive towers loomed above the stone walls like ages old sentries.

"We should leave the car outside the walls because traffic problems can be bad here. Look, over there. Go to that car park and choose a place near the exit, if it is possible." Aniela pointed to an area next to a tourist office kiosk that boasted guided walking tours in English.

"Humph, typical. They give 90-minutes of a tour that is supposed to cover hundreds of years of history and architecture. Never does the tourist spend more than an hour and a half to make their mind bigger. Maybe they can walk no longer than that. This is for the fat, unfit Americans, *ja*, Andrew?" quipped Aniela.

"Come on, Aniela. Americans aren't the only overweight humans on the planet. Some of us are very health conscious and in good shape. Besides, they say English on the sign. Last time I checked, the good ole USA wasn't the only country that speaks English." chided Andy.

Aniela retorted, "True, but all know that the English people are walkers and do not overeat because their food and cooking is so bad."

"Give it up, will you? Let's agree to disagree on this one." Andy pulled into the parking slot relieved to see that he could prepay for a long or short-term ticket. 'Uh oh,' he thought. 'Temper flaring a bit, slightly grouchy, getting more and more bossy: all signs of wear and tear borne of anxiety. I was afraid of this. Or maybe it's her time of the month? Nah, she's just crabby because of the pressure.'

Their departure from Würzburg had been tense, more resembling flight, although they pretended to be excited about their continued sightseeing as they deliberately lingered in their goodbyes with the landlady at the gasthaus. They had kept a fair watch for a tail on the short journey, and none seemed apparent. Still, given they were open about traveling the Romantic Road, it was not unlikely that someone or several would track them here. It was a dangerous game, but Andy had come to the conclusion that acting as naturally casual as possible might deflect the necessity for their pursuers to get nasty. He was all too familiar with how quickly a situation could degenerate, and he wanted to avoid it at all costs for Aniela's sake. Dealing with danger was his bread and butter. He was not only experienced and well trained in the art of covert operation and defense/offense, but had become sufficiently hardened through previous trials.

Aniela was a different story. It was one thing to lay traps or foil attacks if one had only oneself to consider. It could be fatal to have to ameliorate what should be instant response because of the burden and care of an ingénue. Besides, it was next to impossible to separate his love and protectiveness toward this woman from the harsh reality of their situation and the actions that might be required for their survival.

He did not like exposing her to any of it, fully understanding that she would likely suffer wounds of the heart and mind, as well as potential physical ones. She had had no preparation for any of it. All she had was Andy, and this additional role complicated things and threatened to compromise his judgment. All of that, coupled with the certainty of Aniela's spirited character leaning toward obstinacy, caused Andrew worry.

"Liebchen, I give to you the city of eternal Christmas," beamed Aniela as she spread her arms expansively. "It is not the time of the Christmas Market, but the shops stay open all year. You can get your family some lovely handcrafted gifts here."

At the end of the main shopping street—Schmiedgasse—they stopped at the Plönlein, a scenic fork in the road that is a famous landmark of the town.

"Andrew, go and buy a camera," pleaded Aniela. "I want to have a photo with you, and where better than here?" He complied, nipping into a shop and reappearing with a disposable camera at the ready.

"Over here. First take one of me and then I take one of you, *ja*?"

As they completed their snapshots, an older man approached and asked if they would like a photo of the two of them together. Aniela was delighted. The man took several photographs and handed Andy the camera. Curtly nodding his head, he walked away with a smile.

"How nice of that man," said Aniela. "Now, my Andrew, I shall always have a memory picture: Aniela and Andrew visiting the city of eternal Christmas, as part of the journey on the Romantic Road. I shall put the photo on my mirror for the time when . . ." her voice choked on the last words.

He almost did not respond because, as the man had handed him the camera, he felt something else in his palm: a small, folded piece of paper that he slipped into his pocket with the camera, planting a kiss on her cheek.

"None of that now, sweetheart. This is our time, remember? If we have to combine business with pleasure, I say we tip the scales toward the pleasure side. Come on now, show me those shops that will make me a knight in shining armor to the women in my family." They linked arms and headed toward Herrengasse 1 for the shopping Aniela had suggested.

Having spent time in the market place, they climbed the platform of the Town Hall, which was only a short walk from the Christmas Village. "Wow," said Andy, "impressive!" as his gaze fell over the town with its patchwork of winding, cobbled lanes lined with picturesque half-timbered houses. Beyond the city, the Tauber River languidly meandered. As Aniela walked to the opposite side of the platform, Andy withdrew the slip of paper from his pocket. On it was penned "Heilige Blut Altar 1800."

They wandered silently through dark dungeons and exhibitions in the historical vaults of the Town Hall. As they re-entered a brilliantly sunny winter afternoon after the obligatory tour, Andy. inhaled deeply, glad to put gloom and doom behind him; they had enough of that in front of them.

They returned to their apartment to rest from the afternoon's outing. After looking at some of his purchases again, Andy re-wrapped strings of ornamental lights with surgical care, placing them in his rucksack.

"I think my mother will love the lights we found in the shopping district. She always decorates the house beautifully at Christmas, and I can just see her stringing these around the living room. They'd also be great during summer on our porch. I can picture it now: The lintels strung with these lights with the wood and glass ornaments tinkling in the sea breeze, sitting with the family and sipping one of Mom's soothing summer punches, with Luke and Matt serenading us on the cello and guitar. You'd love it, Aniela. Oh yeah, Mom's going to love these all right. We don't have anything like this in the States. Wow, such intricate workmanship."

Aniela smiled at his images of family life on Windward Farm. He came from such a different world than she. Yet, they shared many interests and abilities like love of the outdoors, skiing and hiking, swimming—in general, both were very athletic and fit; he had a great love for his family and kept them close in his heart, just as she cosseted the warm memories she had of her parents; they both were people who cared about the larger world and its direction, disliking the turbulence caused by power mongers, dictators, thugs and terrorists.

He was comfortable with and appreciative of all things European. They often lapsed between languages unconsciously. His family life was obviously not provincial, which (she deduced) meant that his parents were sophisticated. She mentally opined that she might never get to meet any of them. Curling on the sofa, she continued to watch him in silence, smiling and nodding at his enthusiasm.

"Marcy will flip over this carved music box. She loves Rachmaninoff, and I never expected to find something that had the Variation on a Theme of Paganini. It's one of her favorite pieces. She has it playing in the barn all the time. That and various of Chopin's Preludes, with a bit of Mozart, and a smattering of Debussy and Mahler. It's not that common to find a box with two masterpieces. I figured that most of the music would be by German composers. Not that she doesn't like Bach or Mozart. Well, I mean she likes Austrian composers too, but she loves Chopin, and to have a Pole featured in a German music box after the war and all, well . . ."

He prattled on and on, all the while orchestrating the music that flowed from the music box. He chatted her through the review of his purchases for the boys and some smaller trinkets for other family members and close friends. It was not unlike watching a little boy under Tannenbaum.

"And this, my darling, I bought for you," Andy said, extending a small, black velvet pouch to Aniela.

"Oh, Andrew, you would think to buy me something." She felt very special having been included with his family shopping. She withdrew a delicately filigreed gold heart on an almost invisible chain. Immediately, she burst into tears. "It is so beautiful, my Andrew, but when did you?" she said, shaking her head as her voice failed. "*Danke*, thank you, liebchen."

"It seemed perfect, especially since we travel the 'Romantic Road' together," he said, hugging her close. "Turn around and let me fasten it. The chain is delicate, but the goldsmith assured me that it was strong. It's 18 karat gold. Fairly rare in these parts, just like you." He turned her around to admire the heart against the hollow of her neck and bent to kiss it.

"There, now I've sealed it with a kiss, so you'll always be able to feel me close."

She looked up at him tentatively, tears gently falling from her beautiful gray eyes onto her flushed cheeks. Her hair, loosed from its braids, rippled in cascades around her shoulders and down her back, its white blonde looking like liquid silver in the dim light accentuated by candles flickering on the coffee table.

He drew her to him once more in a close embrace, kissing each part of her face, whispering, "My darling Aniela, I love you. I love you, I love you. I will love you forever."

She buried her face against his neck, hugging him back. She said nothing.

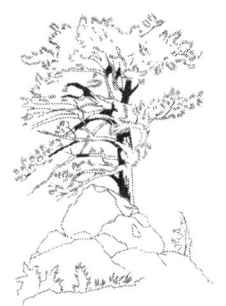

ChAPTER 17

Thanksgiving Holiday, Windward Farm, Maine 2007

The strains on Rachmaninoff's Variation on a Theme of Paganini wafted through the barn as Marcy swept the aisle. The horses were enjoying the run-in shed and rolling in the fluffy snow that was still falling. It had been months since the family had heard from Andy, and everyone had been cautiously avoiding the subject. Last night at dinner, Luke—always outspoken Luke—had called a halt. She remembered her father's pinched expression and her mother's involuntary flinch when he had said it was time for them to stop walking on eggs around the subject and face up to the fact that Andy was either in trouble or had had to "go to ground."

"It doesn't mean he's dead, for Pete's sake. It just means we don't know where he is or how he's doing. We all knew this could happen. So how about having a little faith in Andy? He's a strong, smart guy. He'll come through okay; I just know it. That's what I think we all have to believe."

He had stared at his parents, looking from one to the other. For once, Matthew had not punched him for his usual straightforwardness, which, had the comments come from Matthew's mouth, would have been more diplomatic. Matthew had nodded his quiet assent, indicating that the two had addressed this subject between themselves beforehand. Their mother had smiled at the twins after a few moments.

"You're absolutely right, Luke. From now on, this family is going to be a bastion of positive thinking. I didn't mean to shut you boys out, or you either, Marcy. I've just been so overcome with worry that I was afraid I'd lose my composure if we spoke about it. I didn't want to spoil your school break," she said to the boys, "or compound your stress levels," she said to Marcy. "We'll just keep the candle burning so brightly that Andy will come back to us, safe and sound. Agreed?" Jeremy reached for Elizabeth's hand and brought it to his lips.

"Good, that's settled. Now would someone please pass the mashed potatoes?" said Luke, and everyone burst into laughter. That was when Matthew did punch him in the arm.

The intercom in the barn chirped, and Marcy ran to get it. Jeremy informed her that Tommy had left a message requesting that she telephone him tonight, and they had just received a fax from Tre saying that he would be coming to Maine after settling some business regarding closure of naval bases in the Northeast. Tre hoped to spend part of the Christmas holiday with her and her family. Jeremy said that Marcy had to fax him back right away.

'Here we go again,' she thought. 'Can't those two ever manage not to complicate my life at the same time?' She hurried through the last of her chores and trekked up to the house, frowning while she formed the faxed response in her mind. She would call Tommy after faxing Tre.

Another difference between the two men popped unbidden into her mind. On more than two recent occasions (and many previous), Tre had either demanded things of her or set the stage for instant decision or action. Tommy, on the other hand, wafted in and out of her life like a comet. He asked things: a request to telephone; what did she think about having dinner at that darling coastal hideaway; he knew she needed time, but asked her to consider him in the running, etc. One demanded and expected; the other asked and waited. She had not previously focused on the difference. She decided that she preferred consultation to direction.

Windward Farm was gorgeous in the winter. It was gorgeous in the summer, too, but in winter it looked like a depiction from the most beautiful of Currier & Ives. Her father had made small wreaths for all of the windows on the ground floor, and her mother had placed candle lights in each window of both floors from all aspects.

When Marcy rode back from the promontory, she and Rex were guided by those beacons. When she walked up from the barn, the north face of the house looked like a sentry tower with its broad fireplace wall and chimney pots towering against the night sky, flanked by pinpoints of candlelight from top to bottom. The snow covered the shrubs that nestled into the house; the fruit garden and vegetable patches always had wildlife meandering through them in forage for deliberately left nibbles. The branches of tall pines, oaks, and hickories were laden with a mantle of fluffy snow. In the center, the farmhouse beckoned welcoming warmth from the glow of its windows and the smell of wood smoke spiraling from its chimneys.

Marcy knew that inside that house waited love, understanding, and care in all its forms. This was where she belonged. These were the people to whom she belonged. This was where she wanted to be. She realized it was not a revelation that struck her at that moment, but a confirmation of what she had known all along. It was what she had known deep inside for all of her life. And most important, it was what she would never deny or forsake. Windward Farm, and all it represented, was her center.

Chapter 18

Pre-Christmas, Maine 2007

All of the lab reports were back, confirming Marcy's suspicions. The substance was indeed a powdered form of an illegal drug. Early labs matched latent ones; there could be no doubt on the findings. Dr. Rawlings had returned her phone calls and had begun a subtle investigation among his associates at the conference regarding the hypothetical narcotic effect in equines. She had notified Dunne and Lochmere of developments and was not surprised at their hesitation to include another group, as Dr. Rawlings suggested when Marcy raised the matter with him. Although their initial reaction was to balk at the potential compromise of information (and therefore their case), Marcy relentlessly argued necessity and propriety issues. In the end, she was able to convince them to have a tentative assurance in the state veterinary board's ability to maintain confidentiality, as well as their sworn commitment to do so under the law's admonition and privilege. Grudgingly, they granted her permission.

She had updated Dr. Rawlings. Thereafter, he had forewarned the state board, instructing Marcy to forward copies of all her analyses and reports to them. Marcy sealed the Federal Express envelope in satisfaction. All the loose ends had been dealt with and she felt a sense of relief. Perhaps now, life could return to normal. 'Normal? What's normal about my life, or me, for that matter?' she mused.

She recalled something Andy had said a few days before he left. "Sweetie, nothing about you is average or normal. You're one of the most scintillating women I've ever known, even if you are my sister. And you fill the air with your own brand of electricity. I reckon that's why your hair is so fluffy. Come to think of it, that's probably why you're such a successful vet. The horses have an 'electrifying experience' every time you touch them."

"Ha, ha, very funny." she had said. "I'll give you 'electrifying . . .'" as she chased him.

She smiled at the memory. She had thrown her bed pillow at him, and they had launched into a pillow fight like they were kids again.

The subject had arisen when she had asked Andy if he thought she could settle into a normal, quiet, and predictable life, describing the likely scenario that the Virginia/ Maryland/ Washington connection would guarantee. She never did get a straight answer from him.

As she reviewed past months and recent weeks, she acknowledged that she was not much closer to a "fix" in her personal life than she had been at summer's end. It had been all too easy to concentrate on the enigma of the situation into which she had been thrust. She had enjoyed the mental and professional challenge, and although relieved that it would shortly end, she recognized a slight disappointment. One part of her wished she could play a vital role in bringing the vipers that had abused the horses to justice. But that was up to the "Suits," as Tommy always referred to them. Tommy . . . she was to see him before he left for the UK. Her heart began to beat faster, and she laughed aloud.

"This is crazy," she said, not aware anyone was in hearing range, "you're acting like a teenager."

"What did you say?" said Lars, as he came into the office smiling. "Don't tell me our good vet has taken to talking to herself? Has all this finally driven you to distraction?"

"Oh, no, Lars. Don't mind me. I was just thinking out loud about something silly. How's it going? Oh, here," she said, handing him her dailies on the horses. "I've rechecked those specials and finished all the others. Everyone's in good shape and everything's done." She held his gaze and gave him a meaningful look to avoid the secretary taking undue interest. "Have you heard anything more from our friends?"

"No, not recently. But I did get an interesting letter. I was going to call in on you at the clinic to discuss it." He gave her a worried look. "Do you have your diary with you? Why don't we schedule something now, if that's all right with you?"

"Uh, sure. Let's see . . . I can do Friday afternoon, if that's okay with you?" Marcy penciled him into her diary at his nod. "Good, see you then."

Looking quizzically at him as she passed, she stopped at the secretary's desk. "Margie, if you see Tommy, could you please tell him that I couldn't wait? I need to get this to Fed Ex right away. I've left exercise instructions for his horses posted on their doors. Thanks."

Walking toward her car, she was not surprised to see Lars hurrying after her. "What's up, Lars? You seem jumpy."

"Yeah, I am. I just don't like the way things seem to be developing. Thanks for being careful in there. We don't want any more problems than we've already had, and I want to keep a lid on this thing."

At her frown, he continued, "Marcia, I'll explain in detail on Friday. I'd rather not discuss it now and especially not here. But I will tell you, don't plan on being free of this mess for a while. You'd better start buttoning up outstanding things, and don't make any forward appointments." Then he turned on his heel and was gone, leaving Marcy standing in astonishment.

As she pulled into the driveway of Windward Farm, Marcy felt excited. Thanksgiving was a warm memory, and Christmas would soon be upon them with all its special preparation, surprises, comfort, and security. This was her favorite time of the year. As usual, Rex cantered to the fence at the sound of her car. "Hello, boy," she said, walking over to scratch the special place under his chin. She slipped him a peppermint and made her way through the snow to the house.

"Hello?" she called out to the silent house. Wonderful smells filled the kitchen. A note on the white ceramic message board on the counter informed her that her parents were snowshoeing before dinner and would return by 4:30 PM. "Just enough time for a hot bath," she said as she poured herself a glass of white wine and headed for the back stairs.

Tommy was due to stop by at 8:30 PM, or '2030 hours,' as he said, to say goodbye to all of them before heading down to Portland for the night. He had an early morning flight home and wanted to spend his last evening with all of them. The thought brought a smile to Marcy's lips. She had purchased him a Christmas gift and would present it tonight.

Her friend, Peter Fergus, was an excellent photographer. She had arranged for him to visit White Birches Farm on a day Tommy was exercising Obsidian. Tommy had not been aware of either of them as he and Obsidian focused on their patterns. Afterward, she and Peter had reviewed over thirty photos, finally reaching consensus on "the" one to have enlarged. She had found a beautiful sterling silver hand-tooled frame and Jeremy had mounted the photograph. She looked at it one last time before placing it in tissue and carefully wrapping the box. She smiled to herself.

Peter's eye and expertise had captured the essence of Tommy and Obsidian's partnership. The photograph depicted grace, strength, beauty, and the oneness shared between horse and rider. Obsidian's mane was fanned in the air as his powerful thrust launched them over the rails. His beautiful head and large, expressive eyes reached forward over perfectly tucked legs. Tommy's form was perfect: arched over Obsidian, rippled thighs grasping the horse's glistening ebony sides, heels down with elbows in and forward, his handsome face revealing the focus and exhilaration they both experienced in that moment. Horse and rider were painted in defining, golden sunlight, the jeweled autumnal surroundings slightly blurred against a darkened background. It was truly a "once in a lifetime" shot, as Peter proudly exclaimed when he gave her the enlargement. Marcy was excited to give it to Tommy, particularly since Obsidian had triumphed by returning from serious injury to performing better than ever.

Stamping noises and laughter from downstairs drew her attention. She skipped down the stairs, calling out to her parents. As she reached the bottom clad only in a towel, she was surprised to see Tommy sitting in front of the fire. Jeremy was pouring him a glass of wine and Tommy and her mother were laughing together.

As all three turned to stare at her, she said, "Oh! I thought it was just the two of you returning from your trek," said Marcy in embarrassment.

"Well, hel-lo!" said Tommy with a grin. "This is one image I shan't forget in the months ahead. Quite a send-off, what?"

"Honey, your Dad invited Tommy for dinner. We left a message for you, but I guess you didn't get it. Sorry." Elizabeth rose and walked to Marcy, whispering, "Don't just stand there, sweetie, go get something on." Tommy just sat there, smiling at her.

Marcy turned on her heel and bounded up the stairs. 'Wonderful,' she thought. 'This is not how tonight was supposed to go.' Nonetheless, she found herself smiling.

Dinner was delicious, as usual, and peppered with anecdotes about Marcy and family life, courtesy her parents. She had endured some good-natured ribbing, and reveled in the relaxed atmosphere. Tommy helped her clear the table; Jeremy poked at the fire; Elizabeth sat at the piano, her sensitive fingers rendering Debussy's "Clair de Lune" magical in the firelight. Jeremy stood by the fireplace looking at his beautiful wife with such tenderness and love, it wrenched Marcy's heart.

"Just look at them, will you?" she said to Tommy. "If ever there was a perfect match, there it is," she sighed.

"Yes, they're amazing. You're a lucky girl to have them as parents. I really like them, and I'm going to miss them and this place, the dinners, the horses, the boys . . . and you, Marcy, most of all." He continued to fold and refold the clean linen in a detached way. Finally, he looked over at her. "You, my sweet, I am going to miss very much."

Marcy smiled, and said, "Well, then, you'd better keep in touch so you don't forget me." She slipped her arm in his and they joined her parents.

After chatting for a while, Marcy excused herself, and ran to her room to fetch the box she had wrapped earlier. Tommy was sipping coffee when she returned, and immediately put down his cup and stood as she re-entered the room.

Taking a seat next to him on the couch, she said, "Since we all know you're going home tomorrow, I wanted to give you something to remember your time in the States, and all of us." She held the box out to him.

"For me?" he said with delight. "How marvelous! I certainly didn't expect any present. Your mum's dinner was a treat fit for a king, and spending my last night with all of you was sterling. But, thank you, Marcy."

"Oh for heaven's sake, stop talking and open it up," said Marcy excitedly. As he withdrew the frame, he stared at the photograph for a long while, his eyes misting.

"This is . . . I can't believe it . . . when did you? Oh Lord, it's incredible." He reached for her and hugged hard.

"Hey, go easy, you'll break my ribs," she laughed. "I gather you like it?"

"Like it? I love it!" he beamed. "Thank you so much. I shall keep it prominent always to remind me of this season, but most of all I shall think of you when I look at it. Without you, none of this would have been possible," he said, gesturing toward the photograph. "I shall always be in your debt. Ah, sorry, correction: we shall always be in your debt." Tommy smiled broadly, and passed the photograph to Marcy's parents. "Now, dear friends, I have something I want to say to all of you." Tommy stood and walked over to the fireplace, one hand in his blazer pocket.

Marcy laughed. "You look so serious, Tommy. And that pose makes you look like the Prince of Wales." She giggled and her mother gave her a frown.

"Marcia! He looks like nothing of the sort. He's far better looking. Pay her no attention, Tommy. And you look better in breeches than he does, too."

"Okay, ladies, that's enough from both of you. Let the man say his piece," said Jeremy with a nod to Tommy to continue.

"I want you all to know how very much I appreciate your past and present hospitality to me and my family, but especially to me." 'Another outrageously gorgeous smile,' thought Marcy. 'He really is a handsome man. I am going to miss him.'

"Sharing time with your family and enjoying all your support has meant a great deal to me personally. As you both know," Tommy said to her parents, "Marcy and I have spent a great deal of time together, brought to a head first by Obsidian's difficulty, and latterly by this unsavory matter at the barn with my Demiluna and some of the other horses, discovered by your brilliant daughter." As he finished the sentence, Tommy walked to the refrigerator and extracted a bottle of champagne.

"I brought this tonight to celebrate the deepening of our joint relationship and to thank you for all the love and good cheer you've extended to me," he said, giving the champagne magnum to Jeremy.

Jeremy produced glasses, popped the cork, and poured. 'How come the glasses were at the ready? They're usually in the dining room corner cupboard,' thought Marcy. As Jeremy gave Elizabeth and Marcy a flute, Tommy continued.

"With great thanks and abiding affection, I salute you . . . the Stantons!" he beamed. They all raised their glasses, exchanging pleasantries.

"Now, there's one more item on the agenda that I must raise before my heart bursts." Tommy looked at Marcy, no trace of a smile visible, his face concentrated and nervous.

"I know you to be an independent woman, Marcy. I know, too, that you dislike being placed in awkward positions. But I must beg your forgiveness for doing just that. I've no choice, given I'm leaving the country in the morning."

Marcy looked at her father briefly, and saw that he was smiling like the Cheshire Cat. When she looked at her mother, Elizabeth blew her a kiss, then focused great attention on sipping her champagne. Marcy understood at once that they were "in the know" and she wasn't. She felt a flush rise to her cheeks. Tommy had told them what he was going to say.

"I expect no answer from you, Marcia, let me make that perfectly clear at the outset. I ask only that you take to heart the fact that I love you and would like you to consider becoming my wife, my partner, and my soul mate. Yes, yes, I know there are other complications," he said as she opened her mouth to speak. "But as someone famous said, 'He who hesitates is lost.' Hmm, who that was escapes me just now, but never mind.

"I know you have a relationship with Trevois, and I intend no implied unfairness to him by my action, but there you are. I love you; I cannot imagine a life without you; I'm leaving and shall have no chance to champion my cause in the next months. You know me, Marcy, I simply had to speak my mind."

They all looked at her in expectation. Tommy said, "Um, well, I see I have left you momentarily speechless, but that's all right. What I'd like you to do is keep this for a time while you think over what I've said. If you come to a happy conclusion, I'd like the chance to put it on your finger myself at a later time, if that meets with your approval. But for now, please accept this token of my feelings and the promise of a life to come, if you'll have me."

Tommy removed a dark green velvet ring box from his pocket and held it out to her, deftly flicking open the lid. Inside shimmered an emerald surrounded by diamonds.

"Oh, Tommy, it's so beautiful. I don't quite know what to say." Marcy's eyes filled with tears. "Thank you for understanding that I, well, it wouldn't be right to accept your proposal when I don't even, I mean, I'm not sure, and I haven't . . ." Marcy shook her head as if to clear it.

"Sweetheart, I know it's all a bit of a shock, and not the way things are usually done. I don't expect you to do anything but consider, all right? And I'll try to graciously accept a refusal, if that's the way things end up, though I confess I'd find it hard to wish Tre good luck." Tommy grimaced. "Well, for now, all I ask is that you keep the ring as a reminder that I love you. I thought the emerald would go with your coppery hair." Clapping his hands together, he said, "Now, I must be off!"

She sat as though cast in stone, looking up at him. Despite her shock, she was touched that he would choose an emerald for the reason stated.

'He thought about my hair,' she pondered silently, unconsciously raking her waves from her face. Elizabeth rescued the moment by rising and hugging Tommy, expressing their fondness for him and wishing him a good journey with a winning ride in the championships. He and Jeremy shook hands, and Marcy rose to hug him goodbye.

He gently kissed her cheek and then her mouth, raising her hand to his lips. "Goodbye then, my beautiful, brilliant Marcy. Until next we meet, my darling, I shall carry you in my heart."

"Oh, Tommy, goodbye and safe journey. I'll be cheering for you both at the Show with all my heart," she whispered breathlessly. Raising the box, she said, "Thank you for this, and for understanding, and for being you." As she smiled up at him, tears glistened her eyes. Though her kiss was soft and brief, it carried a wealth of emotion and connection for them both.

He gave her a lingering look, as if memorizing every feature, briefly ran his fingers through some errant strands of her hair, then smiled, and turned to go. Jeremy and Elizabeth walked him to the door, their voices a murmur, as Marcy's concentration clouded with snippets of memories of the last several weeks flashing by in recollection.

She sat down before the fire in a daze. Their Irish setter trotted over from his pallet to sit at her feet, whining. "Oh, Samson, what am I going to do now?" she said stroking the beautiful dog's head. He smiled at her and pawed at her lap, knocking the ring box to the floor. The lid opened as it fell, and the beautiful ring's stones danced in the firelight.

Chapter 19

Rothenburg ob der Tauber, Germany 2007

The hands on the clock moved with excruciating slowness. The Heilige Blut Altar was said to contain a drop of Christ's blood. Andy was not a superstitious man, but in the circumstances, he hoped that if it were true that the 14th century building was a consecrated place, it would offer him a protection of sorts. He had no idea what to expect.

St. Jakobs Kirche was a long block's walk from Herrngasse, which was in the relative vicinity of the Marktplatz and the streets he and Aniela had traversed earlier. He felt somewhat familiar with the general area, but felt little consolation as the minutes ticked toward 1800 hours.

The totally uncommercial Jakobskirche was sober and Gothic, St. Jakobs Kirche itself covering two blocks with dual spires rising above the surrounding buildings like sentinels. He entered quietly, enveloped by the slightly musty, cool, damp atmosphere. He breathed deeply letting the scents of ages past sharpen his senses. The carved altar was superb, and stood alone in its glory. The man was not yet in evidence. Andy sat by a stone pillar near an exit door, praying that—should he need it—the door would not be locked. Candles flickered, their waxy scent adding to the pungent air. He thought, 'I can almost hear the stillness.' Even the faint sound of his breathing seemed inordinately loud in the surroundings. As his eyes strained to focus in the darkened interior, it seemed as if the air itself quivered.

"*Gott mit un*,"[16] said a voice to his rear. Miraculously, Andy did not jump, though it concerned him that he did not hear the man's approach.

"*Grüß Gott*,"[17] Andy replied with relief. The code phrases eased the tension, and he turned to behold the man who had passed him the note after taking his and Aniela's photograph.

"I am glad you were able to come," said the older man, "you may call me Erich." The man extended his hand over the back of the pew, smiling with a nod of his head.

"I'm Andrew. You have something to tell me?" Andy was still a bit cautious.

"The one who was to meet with you could not, as he is giving a bit of trouble to those who follow you and the fraulein. I have come instead. I have a car for you, but I cannot get it until late tomorrow. Does this cause you problems?"

"We have a car, but it would be good to have a change. That's fine. Anything else?"

"Mr. Liam Corruthers says to tell you not to get to like *lederhosen*.[18] He said to tell you that Kaufman will give you beer and arrange to get you to the Celts. That is the end of his message." The man paused to ensure that Andy had understood. As Andy nodded, he continued.

"I have to tell you that we have some luck. Everyone is believing that all interest is focused on the Copper Scroll. I have a little gift for you. It is what has been translated so far of Columns I-XII of 3Q15. As soon as possible, you and the fraulein—or you alone, as you wish—must disappear until this contact is made.

"Go to Zum Franziskaner, Residenztraße 9, Perusastraße 5. Order the *wießwurst* and Franziskaner beer[19]. It must be Franziskaner and the white sausage, *ja*? Kaufman will say to you, 'There's a mistake in the bill.' You tell him '*Könnten Sie das bitte aufschreiben?*'. He will then write down your instructions. If you get into trouble, you can let this disk go to cover your real purposes. But, for it to be a successful trick, it must not be easy for the others to get the disk. Do you understand me?"

Erich dropped a brown envelope over the back of the pew that Andy slid into his breast pocket. As he accepted the guidebook Erich passed to him (in which, presumably, was hidden the disk containing the translation of the Copper Scroll), he said somberly, "*Ja, leider; Das verstehe ich. Das stimmt.*"

It had been the subject of controversy since its discovery, because it differed significantly from the other Dead Sea Scrolls found at Khirbet Qumran. The others were of leather or papyrus; this scroll was fashioned in metal: specifically, copper mixed with about 1% tin. The others were literary works; the Copper Scroll contained a list of locations at which various hoards of gold and silver purportedly had been buried or hidden, amassing to tons of treasure.

Also, the style of writing in the CS was unusual and different from the others, in that it was similar to Mishnaic Hebrew. Many had searched for the treasures alluded to in the Copper Scroll for years, including its reference to a duplicate document containing additional details that was thought to be the Silver Scroll, as yet undiscovered. Scholars held that the Copper Scroll text had been copied from another original document by an illiterate scribe because of errors and mistakes in the text. They considered this unlikely from one who spoke the language in which the scroll was written.

The treasure described in the scroll was presumed to be that of the Second Jewish Temple (rebuilt following the return from Babylon, as listed in the books of Ezra and Nehemiah). Alternatively, there were those who believed the treasure to be that of the First Temple destroyed by Nebuchadnezzar, King of Babylon in 586 BC. For the First Temple theory to hold water, the scroll would have to have been left in a cave during the Babylonian Exile, perhaps with caretakers who were forerunners of the Dead Sea Scrolls community.

It was largely held that since the treasures had not yet been found, there remained un-deciphered secrets in the text. To date, no one had "cracked" the supposed mystery. The Copper Scroll was in a guarded display at the Archaeological Museum in Amman, Jordan. Thus, close access was rare and available to only a privileged few, and those few would certainly be only Arabs. In the current political climate with virtually impossible conditions of access, that Andy was the bearer of a smuggled copy of the text was a clever diversion in his view.

"*Alles in Ordnung.* It may not go easy for you. But for it to be believable, that is best. I am sorry."

"*Danke, Erich. Auf Wiedersehen.*" Andy extended his hand, and Erich held it longer than normal. They had spoken exclusively in the German language after their initial exchanges, when it became readily apparent that Andy was more fluent in German than Erich was in English.

"*Gute Nacht*, Andrew, my American friend." Erich left quickly and quietly. Andy did likewise, cognizant of how leaden his pace had become.

The frail, old groundskeeper nodded to Andy as he passed, tunelessly humming and scratching his gray beard as he neatened the earth around the sparse shrubbery, removing leaf and other natural end-of-season debris. Fleetingly, Andy reflected, 'That's odd; Mom always lets the leaves serve as mulch for winter.' His mind, preoccupied by more important speculations, he did not give it a further thought.

The groundskeeper rose from his task with ease staring after the tall, young American. Leaving his piles, he rapidly walked around the building to a waiting sedan. Once safely inside, he removed his cap and his beard, saying to the driver, "*Allez!* I'm cold. Get us to the hotel." Peeling off a stage mask and wig, Sofia rubbed her dirty knuckles against her scalp. "Oh, *mon Dieu!*" she said in disgust and relief.

The recent activities of the Arabs and the presence of the Romanian had been flagged to Sofia and Claude, and they had been dispatched to monitor the situation. She had received a veiled warning from one of their embedded agents from Saudi Arabia, Madame Colette Franqua.

Sofia and Colette had trained together and become fast friends. Where Sofia was small, quick, and athletic with pixie looks, Colette radiated sexuality, was soft and curvy, had bedroom eyes, and the kind of mouth that made men forget themselves. Opposites in looks and manner, both were equally as deadly.

Colette had fallen in love with Yuri Vasiliev, a cellist who had played at a soirée she was attending. His music had touched her soul, and his looks had stirred her hormones. Shortly thereafter, they became lovers. When Colette's work for the D.C.R.G[20] required her to become an intimate friend of a well-heeled and powerful Arab, Yuri had been killed summarily when the Arab learned of her divided attentions. With no care for her own life, she had thereafter accepted a posting laced with danger as courtesan to the high echelon of those known to fund and control terrorist activities. Yuri's death heralded Colette's manic commitment to the downfall of those responsible, often recklessly endangering herself.

Sofia had received one white, one yellow, and one red rose a week ago. That was their private signal to each other to check a postal box maintained in an alias. They had long ago worked out language to be used in desperate situations, and because they had such a long history, "double talk" even if discovered, would have meaning to no one but them. Colette's note made Sofia aware that her benefactor had launched a special team to Germany in search of an American accompanied by a beautiful Austrian girl, to secure whatever material or information they possessed.

The Romanian was also alert to the scent, and had contacted Colette, as she had several times functioned as a double agent with him as well. She had given Barbu just enough information for plausibility, albeit sufficiently old, to keep him just behind the Arab team. Then, she had contacted Sofia.

The D.C.R.G was sufficiently curious or, more likely, concerned at the increased activity of two of the most lethal groups under their scrutiny. The recent entry of the reviled and feared assassin brother/ sister pair into Germany, called Sofia and Claude into immediate action as two of the best French agents. Their mission was cloaked to everyone but D.C.R.G, until one of the other agencies broke the silence.

That the American had contacted a German agent at the church, raised Sofia's hopes that several of her European counterparts would join with them to face off this latest threat, because it was far too big a nut for just the two of them to crack.

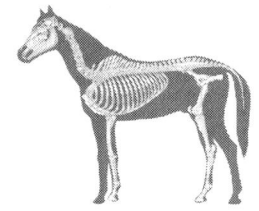

Chapter 20

Seaboard Equine Clinic, Maine 2007

Marcy had just finished cleaning her instruments and reloading her exam bag when Lars came through the door to the front office. Ben buzzed her in the clinic lab on the intercom, and she asked him to show Lars to her office with the requisite cup of black coffee. 'Well, I guess I'll find out what's been bothering him,' she thought as she rinsed off at the sink. Shedding her work scrubs, she frowned at her reflection in the mirror, and headed for her office.

"Lars, glad you could make it." She gave him a hug and they sat on opposite sides of the sofa, the center cushion occupied by a snoring Samson, enjoying his afternoon siesta.

"Yes, well, perhaps you won't be so glad to see me when I tell you the news," Lars said grimly. "The approval came in. You're not only the vet for the finals, but you're to be the head U.S. vet, Marcia. It was a unanimous vote. I took the liberty of informing Dr. Rawlings, who backs you 100%. It's fine with him if you accept, by the way."

Marcy shook her head, saying, "Wow, that's great, Lars, but I don't understand. I'd hoped you'd be pleased. Apparently, you're not. How come?"

"Oh, no," Lars said earnestly, "forgive me, Marcia. I didn't mean to imply that I was unhappy with that news. I couldn't be more supportive. It's the other bit that concerns me," he said morosely.

"The other bit?" Marcy's stomach tightened. Lars wasn't given to dramatics, so when he showed signs of something festering, there usually was a legitimate problem.

"Yes, my dear. I have your letter here, though why they sent it in care of me, I have no idea."

He handed her an envelope bearing the FBI insignia. As she quickly skimmed the contents, Lars continued.

"Those two agents are expecting further cooperation from us, it seems. Not that I object to helping, Marcia, but I'll have my hands full at the finals. I'm not looking forward to the distractions that those people will undoubtedly provide. And we're supposed to be part of their cover. Can you believe it? Just how are we supposed to bring them up to speed in the little time left? They know nothing. That ludicrous muscleman acts as though he'd jump on the nearest hay bale if a horse even came near him. How in the world is he supposed to pass as part of my labor team? After all, I have a reputation to consider." Lars' face was red, his eyes flashed, and he kept clenching and unclenching his hands.

"Oh, Lars, now I see why you were so upset the other day. I'm sorry I've been so busy lately. Poor you. You've had to carry this worry all by yourself with everything else on your plate," said Marcy in an attempt to soothe his mood.

"Not to worry, I'm in it with you now. All our heavy work is finished, even the late fall shots are all done, and I've prepared all the slides for the clinic Dr. Rawlings gives each winter. I haven't booked anything major, as you suggested, so after a chat with Doc, I should be able to clear out enough blocks of time to take the Suits under my wing for a crash course." Marcy gave him one of her brightest smiles.

"Thanks, Marcia," said Lars, visibly relaxing. "I confess all this hubbub has gotten to me. I don't like the unexpected marring my operation, and involvement with those two, well, it's very upsetting. I simply cannot . . . no, I will not jeopardize things because of their needs. They can't demand that of me, can they? And don't they normally deal with things only on U.S. soil? Since when do they travel abroad?" Lars rose to pace, sipping his coffee.

"I don't honestly know, Lars. I think they're U.S.-based, but my understanding from our previous conversations is that they also work with other agencies, both in the U.S. and in other countries. I don't know to what extent, and I didn't know they pursued their cases out of the country, as distinct to merely 'being in touch' with foreign law enforcement.

"But even if they do, don't worry. I can get them infused with enough of the basics so they won't look out of place. Then, if they have to do anything with the police in the UK, well, that's their problem to solve, isn't it? We'll have done all that we can to help them catch the 'cunning blighters,' as Tommy said. Right?"

Marcy poured him more of the imported Italian coffee she kept sequestered for special visitors. "I can actually think of a few chores for Lochmere that would suit all his muscles, can't you?" she said with a mischievous grin.

"Ah, my girl, you always know how to make me feel better. Yes, I agree. I think he'll just love pushing wheelbarrows, mucking, loading and unloading, come to think of it. Why, I can think of a host of heavy tasks to keep him out of our hair." Lars grinned from ear to ear.

"We'll show him how real men work . . . uh, and real women too. Hah! He'll be begging to get back to his pencil-pushing desk job when we're through with him, by God! I've had about all I can take of his deprecating remarks." Lars was practically rubbing his hands in glee, metaphorically speaking.

Marcy grinned back at him, pleased that she had been able to allay his concerns. She mused that he, like Tommy, had taken such umbrage at Lochmere's remarks about the horse industry. Usually, people who adopted that posture did so out of ignorance. Didn't they realize that? 'Is the male ego really that fragile?' she wondered. Both Lochmere on the one side, and Tommy, Lars, and Detective Murphy on the other side had sniped at each other consistently. It was only Marcy and Agent Dunne who had managed to keep the peace on their respective sides. 'Hmm,' she thought retrospectively, 'interesting.'

"So, Lars, it looks like we start Kindergarten on Monday. How about if I bring them to Windward Farm for starters? If it's okay with Mom, and if I can get hold of them this afternoon, maybe I can even start them out over the weekend. Lord knows, between my stallion, the mares, and the youngsters, there's plenty of tuition and lessons available at Windward. What do you think? That way, they won't be as clumsy when I bring them to you and the show barn," Marcy suggested.

"Perfect. I'll set things up with Margie at the barn. Just give me a ring when to expect you. I owe you big for this one, Marcy. I insist you let me spoil you once we hit British soil. Perhaps a lavish night in town or time off for a shopping spree, with a bonus for good measure? Of course, it would have to be a small bonus, you understand." Lars was back to his charming, in-control self.

"Deal. Oh, Lars, have you updated Tommy yet? I think we should do that, don't you?" Marcy queried tentatively, surprised at the butterflies fluttering in her stomach at the mere mention of his name.

"No, actually, I haven't. Could you take care of that, Marcia? I've got to visit my mother in the nursing home before leaving the country, and with all the other details, it would be just my luck to overlook it or run out of time. I'd hate to leave it to the last minute; that would be an unnecessary insult to someone of his caliber. You know, it's funny, I got so used to his being around, I actually miss the guy a lot. He's so full of life, isn't he?"

"Yes, I know what you mean," said Marcy, smiling inwardly. "Sure, I'll be happy to take care of it. So, I'll ring you in the early part of next week, depending on my progress, okay Lars?"

She walked him to the door as they chatted about more congenial subjects and, waving him goodbye, she turned back for her office. Ben handed her a pink message slip.

"I didn't want to disturb you, Dr. Stanton, but this call came in during your conference. I promised the gentleman that I'd give it to you personally before day's end. Do you need me for anything else before I take off?"

"No, thanks Ben, goodnight," said Marcy absently, as she brooded over the message:

To: *Dr. Stanton*   From: *Trevois Hattingley Swift*

Re: *Christmas arrangements—he wants you to call back no later than tonight by 9 PM with confirmation times and dates. Said you had his number and refused to leave one. Sorry—Ben*

"Charming, just charming," sniped Marcy. She called to Samson, and left for home.

Chapter 21

Washington D.C., Winter 2007

"Well, do you think it's Double Abdullah[21] or the MEK[22] that's after them?" said Lassiter, striding down the hallway with such alacrity that Jordan had to occasionally skip to catch up to him. "I'm due in Corruthers' office with the whole skinny, and I'm not getting hung out to dry on this one, kid, understand me?"

Lassiter was in a fury, and Lassiter's fury was like a Midwest tornado. He cut a swath through their offices nearly as wide, and people seemed to vanish at his approach. Jordan wished he had stayed at home like he had been tempted to do.

Instead, he sniffed loudly, saying through a stuffy nose, "Well, sir, the Intel coming in is sketchy, to say the least. We know The Romanian is interested; we have confirms that Double Abdullah's tentacles have been searching; and the Mujahedin-e's organization is all fired up about something over there to do with some kind of translation. That could or could not involve White Horse, but we've taken the position that it does, just to be safely watchful. Interestingly, foreign security agents are also . . ."

"What? Foreign government agents are involved? Who, exactly," Lassiter interrupted with a glare, "and why is this the first I've heard of it? Are you all idiots down there?!"

"Yes, sir, I mean uh, no sir . . . well, the Direction Centrale des Renseignements Généraux and the Bundesnachrichtendienst,[23] that we know of so far, sir." Jordan sniffed loudly.

"Blow your nose, you sniveling little twerp, and didn't anybody down there tell you that it doesn't impress anybody upstairs just because you can pronounce foreign agency names? You need to know more than how to pronounce names? You're supposed to know something about them and their activities. Idiots, I'm surrounded by idiots!" Lassiter trundled down a flight of stairs and made for the connecting hallway. Jordan skipped beside him breathing hard.

"Sir, we only just got word about the foreign security services. They're the ones who told us he finally turned up, because we couldn't find . . ." Realizing his admission of ineptitude, Jordan cringed.

Lassiter's eyes narrowed, and he hurriedly continued, "Uh, the professor, I mean. He's considered a dissident in some circles, but he's pretty harmless overall. Seems he was secluded doing research on another of his books, at least that's the story we get. He's written about six academic tomes, and . . ."

Lassiter's bulk seemed to increase exponentially. He whirled on Jordan at the same time as yanking him to a full stop. "Next, you'll be reporting on the color of his eyes and whether or not he changes his underwear! I don't give a rat's ass how many books he's written. What I need to know is whether or not he and White Horse connected, when, whether it was successful, and where everyone is now. Can you give me the answers to those simple questions, Jordan, or not?"

"Yes sir! We were able to confirm that he—White Horse—and the girl actually connected with the old professor. Unfortunately, our man lost them after they returned to the hotel." Jordan reported those last words dully, expecting an eruption. Why oh why hadn't he stayed home today?

Lassiter slapped his forehead with his hand. The acerbic phrasing of Lassiter's reply made Jordan involuntarily shiver.

"They had what I know must have been a grueling ski to meet up with the old prof, God knows where in those mountains. They make their way back to the trails and the town in a blinding snowstorm, and our guy loses track of them in the damned hotel?"

Jordan jumped at the loud and explosive utterance of Lassiter's last word, shrinking under his furious gaze. "Uh, yes sir. Seems there was a problem with timing. Apparently, they slipped into the hotel while everyone else was partying, you know, après ski, and all that."

Lassiter clamped his eyes shut at the après ski remark. Jordan winced, continuing intrepidly in a small voice.

"Then, they must have left in the wee small hours, because there was no sign of them at all the next morning, even at an early breakfast call. Sir!"

"Fancy that," said Lassiter sarcastically. "In other words, our guy—whose ass is in a sling at this moment—had a nice snooze and didn't post a night-watch, right? He just figured they'd waltz down for waffles in the morning? Do I have it straight, Jordan? Is that about right?" Lassiter's tone was dangerously measured and clipped.

"Uh, yes sir, that's about the size of it. They just slipped away from Watchdog and, well, Europe's a big place. There was no telling where they went until Hermann checked in with a confirmed sighting after White Horse was able to contact him. That bit, at least, went according to plan. Based on what he told us, if you don't mind my saying so, sir, it seems as if White Horse is just having a bit of time off with the Euro girl, sir. I mean, we don't know of any other verified activity, and all reports give indication that . . ."

"Jordan, do me a favor and shut your hole," Lassiter snapped, grabbing the folder from Jordan's hands with such force as to throw him off balance for a moment. "Our guys do not swan around Europe, idiot!"

Jordan sneezed a "Yes, sir!" shifting uneasily from foot to foot.

"Damn it! Stand still and pay attention. If he's moving around casually, it's because he's got a plan and there's a reason for it. Now get back to your department before you infect the entire unit, and dig me up something useful. I want a report on my desk pronto, and it had better be good. Move it!"

Jordan sneezed explosively again. Lassiter ducked to the side and sent him a shriveling look that sent him scurrying back down the hall, scrambling to grab his tissues from his pocket as he ran.

"God help us, if that's all the talent we can recruit," said Lassiter bitterly as he rounded the corner to Liam Corruthers' office. He took a deep breath and knocked smartly on the door. Julia Styles buzzed him in, smiling and motioning for him to proceed to the inner office. "What's the temperature?" Lassiter inquired with raised eyebrows.

"Hotter than the coffee I just made," she said, biting her lip. "Chin up."

"Wonderful, just wonderful. You don't suppose you could make me a coffee with some of that special reserve to brighten it up a bit, do you?

Just to bolster me up in view of his mood, you understand." Lassiter gave Julia his best smile.

She made a point of looking at her watch and raising her eyebrows.

"No, I didn't think so," he said miserably. His pace slowed as he neared the inner office door. Looking back at her, she nodded to him, and he entered.

Chapter 22

Windward Farm, Maine, Winter 2007

Agents Lochmere and Dunne had been blessedly quiet on the drive to Windward Farm. Occasionally, Marcy made small talk, pointing out a scenic cove or explaining the history of the region. As they drew into the drive, Rex cantered through the snow alongside the Jeep, calling to Marcy. The mares in the opposite pasture did likewise. The young stock galloped and bucked in the large paddock by the barn.

"Wow, do they always do that? That's quite a welcome home, isn't it?" said Agent Dunne, leaning out the rear window to watch the horses.

Marcy nodded and smiled. "They're part of the family. Oh, there's Sam. Be careful, he's usually pretty good about jumping, but sometimes he gets exuberant when we have company."

"Pretty place you have here," said Lochmere. "Thanks for having us."

"You're welcome, but it's really my parents who deserve the thanks. I'm only your teacher; they're your hosts. I think you'll find it comfortable here, for the most part." Secretly, Marcy smiled to herself thinking 'Except when you're with me in the barn . . . oh yeah.'

Elizabeth stood at the front door beaming a welcome, and Jeremy joined them from his workshop. "Hello there," he said, closing the outside door. They trudged through the snow in the parking area to the shoveled walkway, Agent Lochmere's leather shoes slipping badly. "Hope you brought some boots with you," Jeremy called out with a grin.

Lochmere reddened, saying "Yeah, that would have been a good idea, wouldn't it? Things are pretty well cleared up in town, and I . . ."

"Never mind," Jeremy said good-naturedly, "we've got plenty of spares here. I'm sure we can fix you up with something. Right, Liz honey?" He took Lochmere's arm to steady him and received a curt but nonetheless grateful nod in return.

"Welcome to Windward Farm," said Elizabeth, extending her hands to the agents. "I'm Elizabeth Stanton, Marcy's mother. And that's Jeremy, Marcy's Dad," she said inclining her head toward Jeremy, who had just rescued Lochmere from another potential fall. "Come in from the cold and we'll get you settled. How about some mulled wine to warm you up?"

After introductions, pleasantries, settling the agents into their respective rooms, and Elizabeth's wonderfully relaxing mulled wine, Marcy said to her charges, "Well, let's start out on the right foot, shall we? First off, I'm Marcy. Let's skip the formal side of things so we can get right down to business, okay?"

"Okay by me, doc. I'm Harry and she's Sandra," Lochmere said, pointing to Agent Dunne.

"Actually, Marcy, I'd prefer 'Sandy,' since we'll be working closely together." Sandra Dunne gave Marcy the first hint of warmth. "Harry and I really appreciate what you're doing for us. We know it's above and beyond the call, as they say," she said, smiling sheepishly.

"Well, whatever proves to be of help, I'll always do what I can. Now, let's get a couple of things straight before we begin. First, there will be daily tuition and exposure to build your familiarity, general knowledge, and physiques. Next, there will be down time conversation to fill in the gaps, so you can feel comfortable and appropriately conversant.

"When we get to the U.K., it's essential that you fit in, or the gig is up. You'll both be part of Lars' team. He normally brings a small work force with him. So your days will be busy, and your nights can be spent integrating with the other staff or doing whatever else you have to do.

"Lars and I will be busy most of the time, so we won't be on hand to bail you out. You'll be on your own. So these next several days are critical to bring you up-to-speed enough to pass muster. All we can hope to do is give you a surface buff so you can function without sticking out. We're going to have to compress years of experience and instinct into a few weeks, so I'm going to have to push you, okay?"

"We're in," said Harry. Sandy nodded her agreement. "Besides, it can't be that hard, can it? We'll only have to last a couple of weeks, and we should have plenty of backup over there, so I'm not worried, how about you, Sandy?" Harry languidly sipped the last of his wine with a smirk.

"Whatever you say, goes, Marcy. If things go as planned, we should be able to get a handle on this ring pretty swiftly. At least, that's what I'm hoping. Meantime, we'll try not to let you down on the horse side of things." Sandy said.

Harry rubbed his hands together. "No worries there. Like I said, how hard can it be? Piece of cake! How about we get started?"

Marcy smiled to herself as they left for the barn.

CHAPTER 23

Bavaria, Tirol, Germany 2007

The mountain peaks, with their breathtaking jagged rocks, served as the milieu to a myriad of mountain streams that had cut paths through the rocks to create picturesque ravines. The clear, unpolluted waters of the many lakes of Bavaria, created by a melting glacier, glistened like diamonds, as they caught the last of the sun's rays.

In the Alpine spring and summer, meadows would become rich with a plentiful variety of wildflowers, including the Alpine pasque flower and the Alpine thrift, with its round heads of pink and purple. On the lower slopes, mixed deciduous woodland outlined the meadows to give way to coniferous Alpine forests. Here the chamois roamed the foothills.

Above the tree line, dwarf mountain pine grew, and still upper stretches of high-altitude meadows were home to wild goat, the Alpine ibex, with its long, backward-curving horns, and wild mouflon sheep. Dots of color created by Alpine rock jasmine still graced the mountain slopes, peeking through where windswept snow revealed patches of southern exposure. From their vantage point, Andy and Aniela could see endless majesty fashioned by the Master Artist.

"*Splendor sine occasu* . . . magnificence without ruin," whispered Andy hoarsely, "*Opus Dei!*

Aniela reached for his hand, responding, "*Ad maiorem Dei gloriam*, to the greater glory of God." They looked at each other wide-eyed, as Andy lifted a finger to catch a tear from her cheek. The cracking sound broke the spell.

They stood on the crest, turning their heads to seek the origin of the noise, as another and another round grazed off nearby rock. Shards skittered against Andy's boots. It all happened in a matter of seconds. "Down!" he yelled, pushing Aniela off balance.

"Schnell, here!" called Aniela. They crabbed over to a group of small boulders on the opposite side of the hilltop's crest. "They shoot at us, *ja*?" she asked, her eyes wide—this time with fear. "We must go down. Here we are seen. Is no good!"

"We're not going anywhere until I can figure out where the shooter is," hissed Andy. "Wait here and don't move. If I get hit, go and go fast, as best you can. Understand?"

"Liebchen?" Aniela said, her lip trembling, "I could not leave you. No, we do this together or not at all, *ja*?" For once she asked, as distinct to making a pronouncement with that famous nod.

"Sweetheart, you promised me you would do as I said when the time came. It's here now, and I want you to keep your promise." The steel in Andy's stare pierced her heart, but she nodded her assent.

He sidled toward the edge of the eastern face of the crown, peering over, conscious that his silhouette would be made clear by the sun. Below, he spotted slight movement off to the left, followed by the noise of sliding stones. The man was having difficulty climbing the steep slope, which Andy understood all too well. He also remembered that there was a spot without any overhang and few handholds. He and Aniela had eased themselves slowly and laboriously over that lower terrain with each other's help in a lark to get to the summit for the view.

"Aniela," he called in a sharp whisper, "anything over there?" She shook her head. "Gather some of the larger stones and push them over to me. Stay low." She complied, crawling over to Andy with the last two, which she dragged in her vest.

"I'm going to try to nail him when he hits that open part, remember? You get over to the far side and keep your eyes open for anything coming at us from there. I'll be with you in a flash," he said with a poor attempt at a smile.

As the man below spread his arms and legs to belly over the smooth open area with only irregular edges for toeholds and precarious finger holds, Andy let loose with a stone missile that he hoped was his most accurate pitch. It hit the man hard in the shoulder, causing him to grimace, lose his grip with that arm, and look upward, all at the same time. Their eyes met for only a brief moment. Then Andy hurled another large rock at his target with deadly aim. There was a sickly thud and a grunt. The man's head snapped back throwing him off balance, and his body fell away from the rock face to lurch toward the bottom, bumping and scraping as he fell several hundred feet.

'Where there is one, there is always another or maybe more,' Andy thought grimly. As luck would have it, the climbers were linked together by rope, likely because one or more of them was inexperienced. As the first man fell, the second man screamed pitifully. The third, well below, had cut the tether and merely watched as one unconscious comrade toppled, dragging the second terrified man with him to his death.

"Okay, sweetheart, now we go. There's one more bad guy, and it's up to you to help us to lose him like you said you could. Let's go!" He kissed her quickly, and she nodded her head in determination. It was cold and it was slippery. The combination of frozen scree and some newly fallen snow made for rough going, but both were strong and driven by adrenaline. Together, they descended the western side of the rock face, doubling back below the third man, slipping into a crevasse that led to a cavern.

"I know where this cave comes out on the other side of these peaks. To go over the top and down again and then up the other where we will come out, will take many hours. We go there the short way. Come, stay close."

Aniela seemed to have a perceptive knowledge of the cavern and Andy trusted her certain lead. There were so many turns that, were he on his own, he would surely have gotten lost . . . or worse. Occasionally, fissures allowed weakly filtered light to penetrate the gloom, adding to the meager beam cast by their small flashlight, providing just sufficient illumination for them to move through the grotto without seriously stumbling.

After an hour's draining, slow trek, they began to climb upward, and the air lost its dank odor and clammy feel. Finally, they burst into the crisp, open air of early evening.

"*Dum spiro spero!*[24]" said Aniela breathlessly.

Andy hugged her to him, saying "*Dum vita est, spes est!*[25] You got us through!"

As they made their way back to the trail, they laughed together. It felt good; it felt better than good. The exhilaration at being safe and alive re-energized them."

"Aniela, I didn't know you knew Latin," exclaimed Andy. "You continually surprise me."

"Ach, my Andrew, what kind of a scientist would I be with no ancient language? But I tell you, I too, am surprised at you. Very few can speak Latin anymore, particularly barbaric Americans. And to think, the man can climb and he can ski!" Aniela gave him a magnificent smile as she nodded her head curtly only once, true to her inimitable style.

"*Nunc scio quid sit amor*,[26]" he said, holding her close. "You're perfect for me."

"*Nunc scio quid sit amor*," she repeated. "Now, let us make our way out of here."

Chapter 24

Downeast Maine 2007

It was on a snow-laden, brilliantly sunny day in December just before Christmas, that Trevois Hattingley Swift touched down in a Navy jet at NAS Brunswick (Naval Air Station), just north of Maine's largest city, Portland, on the Casco Bay.

"Tre, Tre, over here!" Marcy waved her arms beyond the barrier. 'Mm, mm, mm,' thought Marcy as she looked at his handsome, muscular body accentuated by his uniform. As he strode toward her, he broke into a happy grin.

"Hello, beautiful! Thanks for coming to meet me," he said gathering her into his arms for a bear hug. "I certainly prefer driving north with you than alone in a rental car. By the way, were you able to arrange one for me in town?" Tre fumbled with his hand luggage, extracting a paper with phone numbers. "Sweetheart, I just have to make a call, and then we can be off, okay?" Without waiting for her reply, he walked away, dialing his cell phone.

"Why, yes, of course Tre, that would be fine, and yes, I arranged your rental car. Not that you waited to even hear my reply. Ooh!" Marcy said to his retreating form, stamping her foot in exasperation. 'Calm down, girl, don't make judgments where none are called for,' she thought. 'This better not be a forecast of the way things are going to go this week.' Waving at her from the other side of the aisle, Tre held up his forefinger. Marcy began to pace, breathing deeply to calm herself.

"Sorry about that. A bit of business. Now, where were we, oh yes," said Tre, dropping his bag to the floor, pulling her to him by the shoulders.

He looked into her eyes and kissed her for a long time. "The rest of the time is for us, agreed?"

Breathless, Marcy said, "Yes, but I thought you had to go away for three days or so . . ." He stopped her with another kiss.

"Yes, I do. But for now and until then, no business, agreed?" Picking up his bag and grabbing her hand, he grinned, saying, "Now, it's to Old Portland and a romantic lobster dinner for you, my girl." They walked from the terminal to find Marcy's jeep, Tre chattering excitedly about recent events to fill Marcy in on changes to his career.

To Marcy's relief, dinner was delightful from the food to the wine to the conversation. Tre had received a promotion and, although still based in Washington, would be required to travel frequently in connection with the reassessment of naval bases and assets, particularly in the Northeast. That schedule left him considerable leeway, which would enable recurrent visits to Maine to see Marcy, or time to take trips elsewhere together. Marcy did not address the latter part of his remark, but congratulated him on his new promotion. She brought him up to date on the horse matter, and had him laughing until he cried with her stories of Harry and Sandy at Windward.

"If you could only have seen him, Tre, it was as if Rex knew just what to do as my conspirator. He turned his butt, raised his tail, and just let loose! Harry just stood there for a minute in complete shock, then jumped back shaking his leg and foot, using every curse word in the book until the retching took over. It was absolutely hysterical! Poor Harry," Marcy said through fits of laughter, tears streaming down her face at the recollection. "Even Sandy was giggling, but she had to be careful not to be too obvious. He is her partner, after all."

"When are they due back?" Tre asked.

"They're not, actually. They've achieved as much as anyone could teach them in such a short time, even though we gave them the intensified, accelerated version. The next I'll see them is when we leave for England," Marcy offered lowering her eyes, waiting for the expected exclamation to erupt.

"England? What do you mean, England?" Tre sat straight in his chair, pinning her with blazing eyes.

"The England as in final competition. I'm the assigned U.S. Vet for the team, remember?" Marcy knew that Tre hadn't focused on this aspect during his last visit, nor had her appointment been made at that time. She knew that it was not the assignment that elicited such a heated reaction, but the proximity of Tommy that would inevitably occur with them both involved in the horse show.

"Why do you think I spent so much time with Harry and Sandy? They're going to go, too, but as staff. But Tre, you absolutely cannot say anything about them to anyone, promise? It would blow their cover. Damn! I wasn't supposed to say anything; it just slipped out. But I guess it won't hurt, because you're trustworthy and you're not involved with any of the players, so there's minimal risk of a leak." Marcy reached across the table to grasp his fingers.

"No worries, I won't spill the beans about them. I assume it's to do with their continuing investigation?" Marcy nodded. "Well, I wish them luck. Usually, the FBI doesn't go abroad, except in special cases. Given both the horses and people travel back and forth, I guess it's a special type of case. When are you supposed to go? And just how involved in this thing are you?" The flush of upset had abated, and Tre's expression showed genuine concern.

"Oh, my part is pretty much done. The only possible involvement is if any more mares are implanted. Then, I guess, I just tip them off and they take it from there. We've helped them all we can with background info and current data. The rest is up to them.

"I'll function merely like a vet at any show or event, except that I've also been appointed to head up the international veterinary staff. Isn't that great?" Marcy beamed, waiting expectantly for Tre's congratulations.

When she didn't get a reply, Marcy adopted a *laissez faire* attitude to stifle further discussion, and scanned the menu for dessert. "Yum, Molten Chocolate Volcano Cake for me."

After a time, Tre said, "You didn't answer the first question: when do you go?" He folded his hands beneath his chin, looking directly at her without emotion. "And how long will you be gone?"

"Well, I'm not exactly sure. We haven't gotten all the details yet, but I'll let you know. It'll likely be sometime in late February or early March that we leave. The horses will be cleared by March, since they left ages ago to satisfy quarantine regulations. But they'll have to be tweaked and readied for the ring, so including time for the actual Show, I guess it'll be just about a month or maybe a bit over, that I'll be away. I just don't know the exact dates right now, and our flights haven't even been booked. Is there any more wine?" Marcy smiled at him, extending her glass.

With the same even tone, Tre asked, "Where will you be staying?"

"For Heaven's sake, Tre, haven't you been listening to me at all? I said I don't know the details yet, so how would I know where we'll be staying?" Marcy was feeling both guilty and exasperated.

Guilty, because she knew Tommy had taken their relationship to a new level just before he left, and Tre was unaware of it; exasperated, because she disliked the dynamic created by the two suitors causing her to have to justify her actions. They had both made it clear that they were vying for her favor, and it was apparent that she was going to have to choose between them, and soon.

"This is sounding unpleasantly like a third degree," she said, gulping down wine. "I think it's time we got going. It's getting late." She nodded to the waiter, saying to Tre, "I'll just be a minute." He stood, taking the bill from the waiter, placed a tip on the table, his eyes following her form to the Rest Rooms.

'Yes, Marcy, I heard everything you said,' he thought, 'and I didn't like it one bit. I wonder just how close Tommy lives to where you'll be staying. Damn it!' He walked to the door, gallantly offering his arm to her as she approached. "Shall we, beautiful one?"

"Thank you, kind sir," she said smiling, but thought 'I have to be totally fair to him, fair to Tommy, and fair to myself. Now, just how am I going to manage that?'

The ride home proved to be a blessing: she and Tre lapsed into their old comfort zones, sharing stories, and events from the time they were apart. Conversation was easy and enjoyable, and Marcy realized that she was completely relaxed in Tre's company, mentally reminding herself of many of the reasons she was so attracted to him. It was not so much a rediscovery, but more a focused recognition. As the evening wore on and the tires rhythmically clicked on pavement seams, she closed her eyes, contentedly enjoying the relaxing silence. Her mind began to reflect.

Mentally, Tre was sharp-witted, a quick study, and very intelligent. He had excelled in college, graduate school, and the Navy. His career reminded her of the slow, steady, and sure rises of NASA's amazing and thrilling space launches, made so only by sage decision, hard work, and consistent dedication. Tre's professional life was solid and moving steadily forward.

Emotionally, he had extended the same patience and understanding the demands of his career required of him to hers. Although he did not share Marcy's passion for horses and other animals (except dogs), he had always seemed to be understanding of her zeal in the veterinary care of her patients. Until recently, he had not expressed any definitive plans for them as a couple, nor put her under any stress insofar as emotional commitment was concerned. Theirs had been a relatively trouble-free and thoroughly enjoyable relationship until lately, when Marcy bucked his ordained plans.

Socially, he was flawlessly mannered and considerate, putting everyone at ease, conversing with young and old alike effortlessly. He lit up a room with his strong, amenable presence when he entered; everyone liked him, and was attracted to him. His family occupied a place of importance in his life, and he had established himself as a comfortable fixture at Windward within her own family ranks.

Physically, he was "a dish," as her friends had dubbed him. He was athletic and a fine hand at golf, sailing, baseball, tennis, and skiing. Undeniably, Tre was not at all hard to take and, by any standard, was the gorgeous, manly, muscular, northeast sailor type.

Perhaps they both had erred by avoiding serious conversation regarding the future. Clearly, Tre had assumed that their ongoing relationship would naturally evolve into marriage. Even her family had teased about the probability of an upcoming proposal, much to Marcy's distress. She wondered why that possibility had dismayed her, as she played back the conversation in her memory. Had there been some niggling doubt in her mind all along, despite all of Tre's obvious qualities and her genuine affection for him?

Then came the advent of Tommy. Previously, he had been little more than a delightful diversion, a charming acquaintance, and a fellow equestrian of exciting caliber. While they had known each other casually for years, it was not until Obsidian's injury that they had been thrust together on a daily basis, single-mindedly working together to save the horse's health and career.

Then the Demiluna saga reared its head, concentrating their contact in an effort to solve the horrible mystery. Tommy had been as outraged as she, on behalf of the horses. He had been fearless with the FBI, and had brilliantly manipulated them into including her, Lars, and himself in the ongoing investigation.

Mentally, Tommy was on a par with Tre, and was a graduate of both Oxford and Cambridge with honors. As a barrister in the U.K., he was a member of one of the Inns of Court, the Honorable Society of Gray's Inn in London, which is linked to the University of Cambridge. He had chosen to take a sabbatical to pursue his dream of winning the

"Big Horse Show," as he put it. He played polo with the Royals, was respected and well liked among Peers and Lords alike, and had a good position and business reputation with a notable firm in London.

Emotionally, Tommy and she shared the same depth of passion about almost everything. She recalled his face as he looked at the churning ocean the day they had sought the peace of the shoreline following Demiluna's unexpected collapse. He had remarked on the overwhelming beauty of the sea, wondering whether people spent enough time honoring and appreciating the abundant natural beauty of the world. It had touched her heart that so high-powered, dashing, and busy a man as he could have such thoughts, much less be moved to spend dedicated time quietly sitting on a stony coast in contemplation, showing no embarrassment as tears rolled down his cheeks.

Tommy had seemed to understand her inner nature: her love and passion for all things in the natural world; her dislike of being cornered or forced into immediate decision; her need to analyze and consider, as distinct to being rash, impetuous, or even particularly spontaneous; her sense of responsibility; her selfless commitment in the pursuit of excellence at whatever task lay before her; her need to ground herself in nature and animals; her vulnerable sides; her silly sides. He always seemed to give her the space to just "be" and to express herself when she was ready to do so. He was the one person (besides her brothers) with whom she could be frivolous, girlish, and silly, if only occasionally.

Socially, he was the epitome of charm and perfection with a dash of alluring mischief. He had been an immediate hit with her family; they shared many of the same friends who liked him tremendously. His family was of the utmost importance to him, and he acknowledged Marcy's connection with and veneration of hers.

Physically, Tommy was Tre's opposite. Yet, he too, was "delicious." His dark, handsome looks combined with his rakish behavior stirred something within her. His athleticism matched Tre's, with the added bonus of excellent horsemanship, whether riding or handling in any situation. Because of her own prowess in that area, Marcy knew with certainty that such innate ability indicated a deep spirituality of sorts at the most, and being able to put oneself aside, in the least.

Neither Tre nor Tommy had raised spiritual beliefs with her, despite their long associations. She had not delved into their belief systems except peripherally, asking hypothetical questions or requesting clarification on their reactions to a person, thing, or event. They had all had benefit of

the usual Christian upbringing to varying degrees. Marcy deduced that
hers had been more in-depth and integrated into everyday life than theirs
had been. She chastised herself for not having addressed this important
aspect of their relationships. It was central to her existence; how could
she have been so lax?

Interrupting the peaceful silence, Marcy said, "So, Tre, do you
believe in God?"

Chapter 25

December, Germany 2007

They reached the inn just as twilight slid into dusk. Andy was humming the Roy Orbison song, "When the Blue Hour Comes." They had been walking hand in hand, each still stunned by their recent escapade, enfolded in the comprehension that they were still alive and well.

"Did you know that the Scots call this time of evening the 'gloaming'?" he asked. Stroking her hair he said, "It's reputed to be especially flattering for people with blonde hair, and the French call it 'l'heure bleue'." He raised Aniela's hand to his lips as they entered their lodging. After closing the door, he drew her to him and looked seriously into her eyes. "I hate the fact that you're involved in all this. Maybe we should split up, and you ought to head on home."

Aniela vehemently shook her head. "*Nein*! You do not tell me what I must do now, Andrew. I am here with you, and with you I stay until we finish what we do. When all is safe, then I go home. But for now, I am going to Munich. I still shake when I think of the bullets, but only a little. Could I have some cognac, *bitte*?" She shivered once more.

As he poured them a few drams, he said, "Calculating the distance, accuracy, and the power of the shots that skittered off the rocks, I'd say we're up against someone toting an automatic pistol like a Beretta, Glock, or SIG/Sauer. They can hold from 7-17 rounds depending on the model, compared to 6 for the average revolver," he said analyzing the situation. "Those guys were shooting from a disadvantaged position with strong, rapid firepower and accuracy. And they didn't have the time or ability to reload, hanging on to a rope like that. We both know how tough that incline was. If they hadn't had the sun in their eyes, and we hadn't been on the summit, we wouldn't be having this conversation."

He looked at Aniela as he passed her the glass. She looked cozy under an eiderdown, demurely sipping, then yawning. Yet again, she had shown steely reserve and a fierce loyalty to him and his mission, making it her own. He hoped her faith in him was well placed.

Andy turned away to look over his notes on the scrolls, flipping the spiral-bound pages, glad to change the subject. "You know, from Anton's perspective as an historian, we're clearly dealing with ancient history, or more specifically classical antiquity. Let's see," he said thinking aloud as he rubbed his eyes, "we know that Sumerian cuneiform is the oldest form of writing discovered so far and was spoken in Southern Mesopotamia since at least the 4th millennium BC, gradually replaced by Akkadian as a spoken language in the beginning of the 2d millennium BC, if I remember correctly, right?" Aniela nodded confirmation.

As he scribbled some notes, Aniela said, "And? Where do you go with this, my Andrew? Semitic languages were among the earliest to be in written form, *ja*? But Akkadian writing began in the middle of the third millennium BC. Phoenician, Aramaic, Syriac, Arabic, and some of the others are historically significant scripts too, *ja*? I am a paleoanthropologist; I know physical anthropology, and a little of cultural anthropology, Andrew. You are the linguistics expert. Now you would make me to talk linguistic anthropology. This is a big jump, *ja*?" Aniela scratched her head thoughtfully, setting aside the upset of their escape, once again matching Andy's pace.

"Yeah, I know. But we don't exactly have all the scientific minds we need at our disposal right now, do we? We're it, and I want to think through a few things with your input, okay?" Their conversation again lapsed comfortably between German and English.

"Once we get to England, we'll have more resources, but for now, we already know with certainty that the Pleistocene extinction has been radiocarbon dated to 11,000 years ago. The saber toothed tiger, the mammoths, and the giant beaver disappeared at that time, which incidentally, coincides with Noah's flood from the Holy Bible." Andy waggled his eyebrows. "Impressed, yet?"

"*Nein*," said Aniela, lifting her eyebrows in response in an attempt to look disdainful. "Every child learns these facts in school." She held out her glass for a refill.

"Okay, it's generally accepted. I grant you, it's not my field, Aniela, but I try to keep myself up to speed in general, just in case I need to pull a rabbit out of the hat, like now. My point is, overall, we can preliminarily conclude that we can depend on radiocarbon dating for the Dead Sea Scrolls as well, with only a relatively small margin for error in dating. Most of the scientists involved in their examination agree on this too."

It was clear to Aniela that Andy was building a step-by-step defined progression in his mind in preparation for the composition of his presentation, once he decoded and fully translated the material they had been given. She reflexively touched her hair tie. 'So many secrets you have held for so long,' she thought.

"If only Anton were with us. He is an avid student of eastern and western history, and would be a reliable lens to view the present and predict the future. We need his historian-archaeologist's mind. Two of us are not enough." Aniela sighed.

Andy carried on, oblivious to her plaintive mood. "Now, what we have is part of what was found in caves in the sheer desert cliffs at the northwest end of the Dead Sea. Let's see, it was 12 km south of Jericho, and 32 km north of the En Gedi oasis—that's in the West Bank, just next to the Israeli Kibbutz of Kalia. When that young Ta'amireh shepherd, Muhammad ed-Dhib chased that goat up onto the rocks and found the cave, little did he know what a can of worms he'd opened. One can only wonder where the scrolls went from there." Andy traced an area on his map in pencil.

"The brownish-red of the soil and rock of Khirbet Qumran was originally a thick layer of marl that came from deposits at the bottom of the Dead Sea. When the seabed rose to form the terrace of that low range of mountains, it created the threshold of the Judaean Desert. Over time, rainy seasons created brooks that flowed from the western slopes, cutting through that marl. Ultimately, it made what we know today as the terrain of the rugged Wadi Qumran.

"The caves and their clay jugs and tatters of leather and linens were found high above the Wadi Qumran, on the last ledge of the old marl terrace just before it becomes a steep rock precipice that plunges down to the Dead Sea. So, in essence, they were in the best place for preservation before their discovery, since the dry air near the Dead Sea preserved the scrolls for two thousand years.

"Radiocarbon dating of the scroll linen covers results in a period 167 BC to 233 AD. The only other Hebrew documents of comparable antiquity are the Nash Papyrus from Egypt that contains a fragment of the Ten Commandments from about 150-100 BC, and Cairo Geniza found in the 1890's, but dating from the 5th century AD.

"Yes, yes. These things are known, my Andrew. Since the finding of the scrolls and all the subsequent tests, no one is going to challenge these scrolls, since they were part of the original group. Why do you spend so much time on the background? I thought you were to translate them."

"Yes, sweetheart, I am. But you have to consider the general audience. If what's in the scrolls Anton passed to us is as shattering as Anton believes, then I've got to ensure that they're linked to absolutely authentic origins. Remember, what the scientific community knows and accepts, is a far cry from what the general public of any country even knows about. And I've got to convince my government, so they can convince other governments—a lot of them adversaries. Believe me, most government people do not share our mindset of truth only. They're politicians, and politicians pursue what's most expedient for their view of what's necessary."

"*Ja*, of course you are right." Aniela chuckled. "Were it not so, I would not have become involved with Anton's little network. Then I would not have known you, my Andrew," she cooed, rising from the couch to wrap her arms around his neck as he sat at the table.

The warmth of her body, the softness of her breasts against his back, and the scent of her stirred his loins. He leaned his head back and sought her lips, determined to pursue the distraction. After a long and tender kiss, Aniela disengaged, reaching for the fruit dish. Popping a grape into his mouth and then one into her own, she smiled impishly saying, "Enough play for now."

Watching her languidly rearrange herself on the couch, Andy cleared his throat. "Right. What we have here is completely different and stunning. The Dead Sea Scrolls represent a whole library, like opening French doors into a new garden, to a way of thinking and experiencing that characterized a Jewish sect from around the time of Jesus."

Having difficulty in concentrating, he begged, "Are you sure you want me to go on?"

Chapter 26

Christmas Season at Windward Farm, Maine 2007

"Who do you think you're feeding, Mom, an army?" Marcy stood in the middle of the kitchen turning slowly in a circle. Every flat surface was covered with prepared foods.

"Sweetheart, you know that Christmas is a time for showing love. Well, one of the ways I show my love is through sharing special foods with others . . . things that they wouldn't otherwise have or fix for themselves in a normal day-to-day life. Lots of this is going to go to the nursing home in town, and bunches of the rest to shut-ins. But there will be plenty left for all of us and our company." Elizabeth stood with her floury hands on her hips, surveying her work with satisfaction.

"Do you have time to help me box these things? I promised Reverend Sorensen that I'd have my contribution to the church by three. Come to think of it, you're home a bit early, aren't you?" Elizabeth hugged her daughter, handing her a large decorated Christmas tree cookie.

"Yeah, there's not much to do these days compared to the other seasons," said Marcy listlessly. "I guess I shouldn't complain, should I? I've reorganized the inventory, prepared three lectures with slides for Doc Rawlings, and caught up on all the work sheets and other stuff. Ben has enough billing, filing, and other chores to last him the rest of the winter, so Doc said we should take advantage of the quiet time by going home early. I actually have the rest of the month off, except for regular and emergency calls, so I guess I'm yours. Just give me a chance to get cleaned up, and we'll get all this stuff boxed and delivered, okay? It's the least I can do, since you've done all the work."

"Wonderful!" exclaimed Elizabeth, giving Marcy one of her gorgeous smiles. "You know, Marcy, I can't help but remember you joining me for so many years in the past. The folks at the nursing home just loved your stories about the horses and the boys' mischief." She hugged Marcy, her eyes watering. "It's been awhile since you've had time for the normal things in life, sweetie. Take the time to enjoy it, will you?"

"Yeah, yeah, Mom, I know. You're always telling me, 'life is fleeting.' But I've always been the type to get things done, you know that. Then there was this opportunity or that, and sure, it meant lots of work, but it got me to where I wanted to be. Then when Doc offered me his practice, well, it was like a dream come true. I know now that this is exactly where I want to be, and that this is what I want to do, period, end of story." Marcy's last few words were punctuated by the firm set of her lips.

"Hmm," said Elizabeth sipping her tea and extending Marcy a cup, "it seems you've defined a lot of things for yourself recently. Where does that leave your relationship with Tommy? And where does Tre fit in? Have you thought about those parts of your life too?" Marcy had, indeed, thought about both men . . . a lot.

"I can tell you this much, Mom. I really care about both of them. Who wouldn't? But they're both very different and appeal to different parts of me. They also present the possibility of changes to my life in ways I'm not sure I could accept.

"Tre more or less assumed that I would simply pick up and move to Washington because that's where his career is based. That really ticked me off.

"And Tommy's life is in England for the most part. That parting bombshell announcement leaves a lot to be discussed, and England as a base looms heavily in the background.

"Honestly, Mom, given the two scenarios, I'm not sure I'm happy with either, even though I adore both men. So where does that leave me?" Marcy's brow furrowed, and she looked pleadingly toward the mother who had always supplied wisdom.

Stroking her daughter's hair, Elizabeth said, "Darling, it doesn't take a wizard to know that the situation is complicated. But look at it this way: at least you know for certain that your professional life is on the right track. You also know that you've found your niche and your place here. Clearly, both those things are good for your soul. They give you peace and they give you purpose. In and of itself, that's a great deal, wouldn't you say? Not everyone is so blessed. Perhaps Time will make the rest clear. Remember the line from that hymn, 'Are you weak and heavy laden, take it to the Lord in prayer'? That's just what you ought to do, and have faith that the answer will be made clear."

"Yeah," said Marcy thoughtfully, "maybe you're right. I've been so busy spinning my wheels between this and that, trying to take hold of everything and figure it out, I never considered just letting things be. The guys turned up the heat, and I thought I had to respond one way or another right away. I just kept getting more and more up-tight about it because I couldn't come up with any sure answer, nothing that felt right or good, you know? Your way is a relief valve. It doesn't exactly get me off the hook, nor do I expect that, but it at least buys me some time to see how things will develop. Thanks, Mom. As usual, you're right on."

Elizabeth laughed, refilling her cup. "You didn't always think so, Marcy, any more than your brothers. Kids have a habit of growing up and realizing that their parents might know a little something after all." The two women laughed together.

"I know what you mean. The other day I found myself thinking, 'Oh for heaven's sake, I've become my mother.' It was when I was doing the inventory and found some perfectly usable leftovers, you know, unopened but broken boxes, all dusty, partially used. Doc said, 'Just toss them, missy. We have plenty new replacements unopened.' Instead, I bagged them up with instructions, thinking about the Moreland's and their large herd.

"The drugs were perfectly good, still had a long shelf life, and the Moreland's are somewhat hard up. There were some tubes of this and that, bandages, bits of this and that. Waste not, want not, and all that. So I took a big box of stuff over to them, and they were really grateful. I think I smiled all the way home, not because I did a good thing, but because I learned how to do good things from you, and I liked the thought that I was a bit like you." Marcy grinned at her mother.

That's when Elizabeth's eyes overflowed. "That's one of the nicest things you've ever said to me, Marcy." As she dabbed at her eyes, the telephone rang. "Could you get that, honey?"

"Windward," said Marcy. "Oh, Tre, hello. We were just talking about you," said Marcy, winking at her mother.

Tre was due to arrive at Windward at the end of the week with a view to spending 10 days in the Northeast, based at the farm. He would be away for three of the days attending to business regarding the closure of bases, but could manage to have time at Windward either side of his business trip. Inevitably, Marcy knew that this visit would address the status of their relationship. She and Tre had never finalized their discussion last time, helped along by Tommy's untimely interruption. This time, Tre would have all guns loaded. Funnily enough, that thought didn't fill Marcy with dread, as it would have done prior to her chat with her mother, even though her family's teasing about a proposal from Tre had made her feel off balance and stressed. But now, she was actually looking forward to spending time with Tre without any other distractions.

Tommy was in England; the agents had gone home for Christmas holiday; all her routine busyness was at low ebb; Lars was busy with preparations for the upcoming trip; and the joy of the Christmas Season was upon them. Yes, this visit should bring clarity. Marcy thought all these things as she swept the barn aisle. The comforting sounds of munching horses and Chopin provided the background for her contentment.

"Lord? If you have a moment, we need to talk," she said, sitting on a hay bale looking through the upper part of the barn's Dutch door. Fine snowflakes began to fall, lilting downward as if dancing to the strains of Chopin's melody. "It's me, Marcy, and I need your help."

Chapter 27

Germany 2007

Aniela busied herself with shopping in the marketplace for their food, jogging around the town, window-shopping to purchase small clothing replacements, keeping their clothes laundered, and their rooms tidy. Andy researched and worked, breaking only to join her for supper at one of the town's many cafés or restaurants. When she returned from one such jaunt on the second day, she found Andy in a grumpy mood, noisily slamming books closed, and shuffling his notes together.

"Liebchen? Was I gone for too long?" she asked softly.

"No, no, that's not it," he snapped, turning toward her. "It's just that I'm frustrated. This is going to take so much time with me on my own, and it's neither a safe way to proceed nor fair to you."

"Ah," she acknowledged. "Well, about the first, we should talk. About the second, put your worry aside. I have quite enjoyed the role. It is as being the wife, *ja*?"

"Oh really?" quipped Andy. "Well, in that case, my dear wife, how about satisfying your obligation to conjugal rights?"

"*Nein*. Did you not listen? I said it is as being the wife, not your wife am I, my Andrew."

"Not yet," he mumbled out of her hearing. "Okay, okay, you win. So let's go out and get something to eat."

When they returned to their rooms, Aniela cuddled next to him on the couch, encouraging him to go over his notes with her.

"Hmm, where did I leave off with you the other day? Oh yes, the dating of the Qumran scrolls. They're from the 3rd century BC to the 1st century AD. Their significance—other than that they include one complete Old Testament book, Isaiah, and thousands of fragments that represent almost every other OT book—is that since their discovery, we can confirm the accuracy of other manuscripts discovered much later. The period from 200 BC to the time of the destruction of the Second Temple in 70 AD, was the era from which both Rabbinic Judaism and early Christianity sprang.

"In fact, many of the world's great religions trace their history through this region, if not from it, but that's fodder for another paper." He looked up at her and grinned, saying, "So, babe, maybe I ought to give up all this cloak and dagger routine, and become just an academic. Do you think we could make a living writing about this stuff once I have it decoded and translated?"

Aniela scowled at him. "Do not be impudent, Andrew. Finish your thinking out loud, *danke*, and pour me another tot?" Andy jumped to comply, refilled her glass, and began walking around the room waving the bottle to emphasize his statements. When Aniela scooped the bottle of ginger wine from his hands, he didn't even notice.

"What's important is that the scrolls are from a unique formative period before the Rabbinical, Christian, and Moslem revisionists made their donations to the literature that comprises religious thought and tenet. They preceded all the editions that were tweaked to suit politics, power, control, and all the rest of it.

"Anton said that about 80-85% was written in one of three dialects of Hebrew. The fragments we're interested in represent the beliefs that depart from the mainstream structure and theology of the religious sects operative at the time." He plopped into a chair, scrutinizing some of his pages of notes.

Aniela paced in frustration, clearly thinking through what he had said. "Yes, my Andrew, I remember some of that from the time we were with Anton. But what is the point of it all? Everyone in the religious and scientific communities knows about the Dead Sea Scrolls. So they justify the Masoretic texts for the Jews . . . what has that to do with the rest of the world? It seems to me that just proving one group has legitimate ancient documents does not . . ."

"No, no, sweetheart. It's much more than that. Until about the 1990's, it was presumed that the scrolls were written by the Essenes, or maybe another sectarian group, residing at Khirbet Qumran. The presumption was taken that they hid the scrolls in the caves during the Jewish Revolt in 66 AD, before being massacred by Roman troops. There's a lot of significant evidence to support that theory, but it's not important to go into it now. It'll play a part, though, in our final presentation . . . that is, if we ever get to give it." Andy smiled ruefully, as he jotted down a few thoughts in his notebook.

"*Nein*, my Andrew. Do not speak so." She looked at him solemnly, gently nodding her head repeatedly. "We will get to England and you shall have your chance to make things clear. This is a promise I make to you. Ask Anton: I do not make promises often, because I always keep them, and to keep them is much work. Now continue with your thoughts."

He could not help but to smile at her soothing tone, which at that moment reminded him of his mother, Elizabeth, on the many occasions she had encouraged him to follow his dreams.

"Well, although there are a lot of theories about who actually wrote the scrolls and where, many of these scrolls may have been made after the Qumran period of occupation, and it's thought that the site was constructed sometime between 134 and 104 BC. There are other bits too, like Pliny[27], who describes the Essenes of the Dead Sea area as celibate, yet remains of women were found in the cemetery at Qumran. Only small portions of the graves were excavated, because under Jewish law excavating cemeteries is forbidden.

"If the scrolls are examples of major Jewish intellectual culture known only in Jerusalem during the intertestamentary period, then the scrolls are more important than they were previously thought to be, because of the light they cast on Jewish thought in Jerusalem at that time. And their documented thought reveals much about Jewish action and history, as well as speaks to early Christianity."

"Andrew, yes, I understand all you are saying, but it gets confusing. I do not see what is the point. I work with physical evidence. This evidence is physical yes, in that it exists, but it is in what it says that it becomes so important, *ja*? This is more intellectual it seems. And it is like we are running around in a circle. Where is the meaning? What is the value? Why do we risk so much just to prove that ancient Jewish documents are legitimate?" Aniela shook her head over and over, rubbing her arms in exasperation. Andrew knew he had to sort through this mental jumble for both their sakes.

"Look, Aniela. There's no easy way to get from point A to point P, except one tiny, verified and analyzed step to another. You know that as a scientist. All of this is important, from the terrain that preserved the scrolls to the societal development of the people of the time, to the religious fervor, to the political influences, and so on. All of them and many more are pieces to a big puzzle. Our job is to put the picture together so it's real, makes sense, and has enough legitimacy that it can be accepted by everyone, because from what Anton says, the message will be world shattering at most, and significant in the least.

"There's another important point to throw into the soup pot. One needs to consider that many scholars continue to believe that a small group of disenfranchised priests described in a portion of the scrolls, could have been Essenes like the ones described by Pliny. It's thought that this group established a sectarian community in the seclusion of Qumran. According to the scrolls, its members studied scripture and other sacred texts, meticulously following Jewish law. They were a kind of ascetic monastic community that retreated to the wilderness.

"Now for the whammy: In those scrolls, the person who led the community was referred to as the Teacher of Righteousness, and always carried that title. And better yet, there was only one Teacher of Righteousness recorded, to all intents and purposes. The timing is spot on. Make you think of the missing years of Jesus Christ? Didn't you ever wonder where he went after his appearance as a boy in the temple?

"According to common interpretation of the four canonical gospels we do have, Jesus was born between 8 BC and 6 AD. There are accounts of his activities in the temple at about eight or twelve years of age, I think. Then nothing. About 30 years after his birth, he was baptized by John the Baptist at the start of his ministry. His ministry lasted one year according to the Synoptic gospels—or three years according to the Book of John. He was then executed between 26 and 37 AD under Pontius Pilate during the period of Roman rule and occupation.

"Anton and his friends translated and analyzed other documents of like time and age. They believe the message in the documents he gave us is compatible with the words of Jesus. It could be that our scrolls and message might be the earliest extant New Testament documents in existence. It could be an undiscovered, unpublished part of what could have become an independent gospel containing Jesus' words. At least, that's the current line of thinking. I mean, if it has no real importance, why was it kept under wraps for so long? Why is it so precious that people have died to protect it, or perhaps more accurately, died to get it away from those who would bury it?

"Maybe it's only part of the earliest Gospel of Mark, dating somewhere between 30 AD and 60 AD, or a completely new gospel that the Essene scribes recorded . . . the actual words of their 'Teacher of Righteousness'. We won't know until I figure out the encryption, and then translate the ancient languages. But either way, it's groundbreaking.

"Now, do you understand the value? From what I've been able to determine so far, some of the words speak to the way peoples should live. Anton said that deeper into the document, the words refer to the Jews and the Arabs. It's thought that precisely because the message is so precious is why the scribes who recorded it, also made it cryptic. Whatever the words, once translated, the message would be incredibly powerful, Aniela. And anything binding itself with power in this region is incredibly dangerous. Now do you fully understand?

"Heck, even some of the scrolls now currently safe in museums were sold to the highest bidder in the years following their discovery. These scrolls, that Anton and his colleagues say are so controversial, had been separated from all the others, taken, and hidden for years. I guess it's not surprising when you consider the potential impact of their content, particularly the message. Even then the Jews rejected Christ's teaching and were warring with the Arabs, and the Arabs were warring with everyone. The more things change, the more things stay the same." Andy rubbed his face with his hands, showing exhaustion.

Aniela had remained quietly attentive. "I have some questions, Andrew. I can speak to you now?" Andy, looking a bit sheepish after his soliloquy, nodded his assent.

"We know this area was a critical trade route for the whole region. No ruler of Judaea would let them sit on such an important trade route without permission, *ja*? So the Essenes there needed the approval of authorities in Jerusalem at least, *ja*? They had to know about them. So the Essenes maybe were not outcasts, but those who chose to live in wilderness and who were allowed to live there by those in power in Jerusalem.

"And so also, these ruins at Khirbet Qumran were almost always occupied by someone during the entire time when the scrolls were stored, if not hidden, in the caves within plain site of Qumran's walls. The Hebrew revolutionary troops were there until the Roman soldiers took it around 69 or 70 AD, *ja*? Then the Roman soldiers were there until 100 AD. So who hid them under everybody's nose?"

Now, she rose to stand behind him, rubbing his shoulders. "The other thing, my Andrew, that does not make itself clear to me is who took these scrolls and hid them for so long? Anton did not say, and he also did not say how he came to have it in his hands. To me, this is important. It will tell us who hunts us now, *ja*?"

"Yeah, you're on target, as usual. Remember, Aniela, Muslims are also children of Abraham. The roots of humanity are deep in the Middle East." Andrew stood, pacing as he thought, reciting his speculations for Aniela's consideration.

"That was a time when there was a significant increase in cultural fascination and obsession with ritual purity. It was a time of religious, cultural, and political upheaval as well. It wasn't only the Jews who were obsessed with this, the Arabs were as well, and into each culture, traditions were woven to reflect just that. These scrolls represent a form of religious library that escaped centuries of suppression, censorship, and revision. They weren't subject to what happened with the canons of other religions. Two thousand years they lay undiscovered. Then for almost another 50 years, they were sequestered and suppressed from public viewing. When I think of it all, it never ceases to amaze me.

"Anyway, the founder of Islam was Muhammad, as we all know. He was born to an underprivileged family about 570 AD among the Semitic people on the Arabian Peninsula in the city of Mecca, almost 600 years after Jesus of Nazareth.

"A reflective man, the story goes that he often retreated to a cave[28] above Mecca as he grew older in the pursuit of discerning the true faith. Tthe Arabia of his day was generally lawless, although there were Jewish and Christian factions to which he was exposed. But even they fought between themselves and with the Arabs in the region.

"According to Islamic history, he was visited by the angel Gabriel at age 42. Gabriel—a well-established figure from Jewish and Christian lore as well—told him that he was to be the prophet of Allah, the true God, and that he would be the one to bring the true and complete will of the Creator to the world. This will was revealed over time in the form of 114 surahs, or chapters that eventually comprised the Qur'an."

"I know it is important that we understand the Arabs and their religion, my Andrew. They have become very powerful, *ja*? Maybe the most powerful and the most dangerous. They make more and more Muslims everywhere today in all countries. They are smart and they are patient. Most of all, they are committed to their cause, *ja*?

She continued, "I do not think these are a people we should ignore, but the rest of the world seems to be asleep. We may awaken to find ourselves in a blind, like the ones we herd the sheep into, you know?" Aniela sat in the dim light, steadily brushing her hair. Its silken, wavy tresses glittered like strands of silver spun by faeries. Andy looked at her and found it difficult to concentrate.

'Focus, focus, focus,' he thought. "Mmm, yes. So, within those writings was the mention of Christianity and Judaism and their major books, traditions, and prophets—Jesus, Moses, the Gospels, and the Torah—as those who had come before to help prepare the world for the revelation of the Qur'an. While the Jewish Torah and the Christian Gospels were accepted by Islam as being divinely inspired, Islam differed sharply on fundamental matters of doctrine.

"Without getting into tedious doctrinal analysis, ultimately the differences threw Islam into opposition primarily with Judaism and Christianity, and pitted them against each other with resentments growing like weeds in a fertile garden. All claimed to be the one true faith, and the growth of each undermined the others' claim to universal truth. That got translated into political hostilities that grew into armed conflicts that waged war for centuries. So that's the backdrop.

"The situation with Israel comes from its Arab-Islamic neighbors and Islam's dedication to Muhammad's command that forbade the existence of non-Islamic states in Islamic lands. That legacy prevailed over 14 centuries, becoming a bloody and constant challenge to those living on the borders of the religion's domination.

"Muslim armies visited violence on peoples across North Africa, the Middle East, Europe, and into Asia as far as the Indian subcontinent, in the cause of the spread of their religion. As I recall from my studies, Muhammad is to have said, 'I have been ordered to fight the people 'til they say: 'None has the right to be worshipped but Allah.'" Pretty much a blueprint for the world situation today, isn't it? So if this long-hidden scroll criticizes what Jews, Arabs, and Christians have done for hundreds of years on the basis of their beliefs over time, it's a very, very hot potato."

"Oh, Andrew. It was scary then, and it is scary now." Aniela shivered. "I did not know you were such a good storyteller. I hear you tell me the story of these peoples with passion. But I worry that others will not read or listen. You know well, my Andrew, that people become bored with serious matters or things that make them concentrate on uneasy things.

They want to hear only about what they will have to make their lives easier, or what is free, or what is fun. Am I wrong? They do not talk together as we do. The everyday people, I mean. And it's they who must realize these things."

She looked at him imploringly, her eyes welling. All of a sudden, her mood changed and she giggled, wiping her eyes. "Andrew! Tell me now, who is going to catch this 'hot potato', and who will hold it long enough for it to cool?"

"Very funny, ha-ha. But I guess you've got a point there. Anton's people tossed it around between them; then Anton tossed it to us. I guess it's up to us to hold it, figure it out, and then turn it over to . . . well, that part I'm not sure of yet."

Andy scratched his head and picked absentmindedly at his cuticles. "You know, all these years of cultivated complacency might just end us all up in another holocaust, God forbid. So it's not surprising that several factions might not want this information available for study, much less for public consumption. I figure we've got agents of the two tinderbox countries fueled by a powerful religion on our tails. It may be more than that, I don't know. And that makes for one heck of a headache."

"*Nein, liebchen.* We stay one step ahead, and we have God on our side, remember?"

"And you don't think that they think the same thing? They'll be just as driven as we are, maybe more, because to them human life is expendable for the overall cause." Andrew sighed, saying, "I'll give you two hours to stop what you're doing."

Aniela continued kneading his shoulders and neck. "Who do you think it is, *liebling*, that chases us? I know they want the scrolls Anton gave us, but I am unsure why they want them. Is it to hide them away again?" Each sentence was punctuated by a pause, and Aniela's voice was troubled.

Andy carefully framed his answer. "Well, *schatzi*,[29] remember the Arabs' agenda is for world domination, singularly under the mantle of Islam. That would of course give a huge amount of power to radical imams, if past and current trends are considered.

"Then there are the Russians. Their economy is in a mess. Despite the cessation of the Cold War and their ameliorated global stance, they're still a threat in many ways to democracies worldwide.

"My best guess is that both are tailing us. The Russians would like nothing better than to ransom the scrolls for billions to a rich Arab country or broker. They'd immediately accomplish two things: create a much-needed cash injection for their failing economy; and further stir it up between Islam, Christianity and Judaism, putting the US and Israel into an even more desperate fight for survival against the main Arabic countries who sponsor terrorism and support jihad, or rather, the Jihad they are waging.

"The only ones who could tip the balance in that equation are the Chinese, and we all know they're a sleeping dragon. I really don't know who is dogging us. But one thing I'm sure of: whoever it is won't make it easy for us to elude or defeat them."

Aniela smiled, kneading her strong fingers into his muscles. Her glance followed the contours of his upper body, as he lay with his head on his arms. The table creaked slightly with the movement caused by her manipulations. His shaggy hair fell over his brow, his lips parted slightly to release heavy breathing. On and on, lighter and lighter, she stroked. "Sleep, my Andrew. Soon, you must become the angel Gabriel. Perhaps you already are . . ."

Chapter 28

Washington D.C. Post Christmas 2007

Lassiter was distinctly uncomfortable. Less, he admitted to himself, because of the straight-backed chair in which he sat waiting for Corruthers to finish his telephone call, but more because he knew he was not as prepared for this meeting as he should be (an unusual and unacceptable position for him). 'Damn those sniveling, little office twerps!' he thought.

"So, Bull, what do you have for me?" Liam Corruthers slammed the phone in its cradle noisily, indicating to Lassiter that he was short of patience . . . this from a man who rarely demonstrated any emotion. He was as cool a cucumber as Bull had ever met, even when facing down those whiners on the Congressional committees. The CIA had all-source capability covering the entire world: inside and outside US borders. The covert action with which Corruthers was immediately concerned—White Horse—fell under the umbrella of an activity conducted by the US Government to influence political, economic, or military conditions abroad, wherein the US role would not be apparent, much less publicly acknowledged.

Thus, the "black-out" tag on White Horse meant that probes had to be surreptitious and handled with extreme care, especially among foreign intelligence services. The CIA's Clandestine Service was the front-line source of clandestine information on critical international developments, and Corruthers sat at the top of that granite CIA/NCS mountain, navigating its crags and crevasses with unbelievable focus and attention to the smallest detail.

Not wanting to appear hesitant, despite feeling so, he said, "Well, Liam, I've got an update that we can confirm via the D.C.R.G. Seems they've got a pair on the scene monitoring, but no contact has been made. White Horse connected in the last of the villages, as reported by Hermann, so he's got the bogus goods, some cash, and new wheels. The girl is still with him, and seems to be an asset so far. Sofia and her big buddy, Claude—remember him? Well, they're still with them in Munich. If there's any luck to be had, the Munich contact will get them safely on a plane for the U.K. and MI6.

"Salid's cell is still sniffing around, but Sofia's friends have been causing them a bit of trouble. Great idea to use a dupe couple, especially one as good as Sofia. She's the best chameleon I've ever seen. For a change, D.C.R.G is playing ball, and the BND have been on the money with this one. They worry about Salid and his slime as much as we do. Difference is, by all accounts they've got more bad seeds than we do, so it suits their aims to play ball with us right now."

"Good. I sent a coded message I know he got, so he knows we're hawking. Is there anything more we can do from this end in the meantime?" Corruthers ran his hands over his exhausted face. He had not slept in 36 hours, and it was beginning to tell. He was getting too old for this kind of drain.

"Honestly, I don't know. We have precious little and that, only in dribs and drabs. I can tell you, I'll feel one helluva lot better once he's out of Europe and in a safe house with MI6. There's just too much that can go wrong from now 'til then . . . particularly with a civilian along. By the way, did you give him carte blanche for that? He's not the type who normally involves anyone. I admit I was surprised to learn how long they've been connected. Unless he's uh . . . well, she's quite a dish it seems," smoothed Lassiter, as groundwork for protecting or excusing one of his operatives should it become necessary.

"Yes and no. He had full authority to use his judgment based upon how unusual this assignment was. You should read your memos, Bull. Obviously, it was necessary. The thing that worries me is how everyone else found out so soon. It must have been someone associated with the old professor . . . a leak . . . or a mole. Better run that down, Bull, and right away. See what you can get on the old boy, and make another contact. You can always use Hermann. Let me know as soon as you have something."

Corruthers shook his head, flipping through some of the papers on his desk. "On second thought, Bull, let's leave Hermann out of this for the time being. How about pulling in Ileana Muscovici from Vatican coverage. She could get to Munich in a few hours, and she speaks Romanian. That's a plus with Niculaie Barbu on their tails. Do we know whether Barbu has his sidekick with him? What's his name?"

"Humph, that fiend Covaciu? He's a nasty piece of work. No, I don't know, but I'll find out before the night's done." Bull scribbled "Gheorghe Covaciu" on his notepad, doodling deep-penciled arrows around the name. "Liam, what do you think about dropping a tight black ops team in to tighten up this deal? I just don't like having one of my guys out on a limb unsupported like this, particularly given the surrounding circumstances. It's been too long a time, and the odds get worse every day."

"I know, Bull, but I've had to play this one by the book. It was meant to be a quiet and easy transfer, but somehow someone got wind of it, and now White Horse is in the thick of it.

"So far, our Euro friends have kept a reasonable perimeter around him. And he's been confounding adversarial Intel by moving leisurely through Europe with the girl. No one's made any serious moves on them, at least insofar as we know. Weather hasn't been helping either. It's all but knocked out our satellite surveillance and real-time contact.

"If you do send our people in, have some of them focus on the old professor and plug that leak, whatever or whoever it is, as soon as possible. Split your team, Bull, but make sure the shadows are capable of dealing with Barbu, especially if that viper Gheorghe is tagging along. Make sure the team is heavy enough to get the job done. They'll have two fronts to deal with. This is a nasty one, Bull. We can't afford any foul ups. *None*, hear me? Plug that leak, Bull, plug it for good. Whatever it takes. And get White Horse out of there in one piece."

"Right," said Lassiter, rising from the uncomfortable chair, running his hand over his silver crew cut. Bristling slightly, he said, "Am I dismissed, sir?"

"Oh, yes, Bull. And thanks," said Corruthers abstractedly. Then, catching himself, he looked up as Lassiter turned to go. "Bull, sorry. I'm under a bit of pressure with this on top of all the other sticks in the fire. If this thing is what we're led to believe, we'll have a hornet's nest here, as well as every other place in the world where there are Muslim reactionaries."

Then more philosophically, he said, "I'm not a religious man, but this is one time that I sincerely wish there was something to the Second Coming. This is a potential firestorm. And it's a firestorm of worldwide threat."

Back to himself, he said brusquely, "Now get out of here and get me as much as you can. The world is depending on us it seems, even if they're oblivious to it, on our young White Horse and us. My God, what an ironic name for this turn of events. See you at Digby's for a Scotch at 2200? Cancel that . . . a bottle of single malt, okay?"

Smiling and somewhat relieved, Bull said, "Yes, sir, 2200 it is, and I'll choose the Scotch since you're paying." He shut the door on his boss, noting that Corruthers was staring at nothing, his mind hundreds of miles away, likely in Munich, probably wishing that he could be White Horse's guardian angel.

Before his promotion to administration, Corruthers had been one of their very best agents. Bull noticed that he was absently fingering the scar that ran down the right side of his face. Today, it was unusually angry.

As Lassiter's long legs ate up the distance to his wing, he phoned his assistant, Wendy, explaining what needed to be arranged. "Get Noonan, D'Orza and Hennecke to Munich, and tell them to take Bianca Romm with them. I want Morales and Kaiser to link up with Ileana Muscovici coming from the Vatican. That way we'll have the language bases covered as well. They'll be going dark, so SOP prevails with the usual links on the continent for necessary gear. And Wendy, tell them it's Andy."

On the other side of the world, Salid sat surrounded by exotic lilies and orchids in his climate-controlled garden room. The marble floor glistened, flowing veins of azure blue streaks alluding to sea currents creating an ambience of weightless, flowing peace against the vaulted high glass walls and ceiling. The fronds of fern and palm wafted gently in the cool, circulated air on which drifted the delicate scent of the fragile, remarkable blossoms. Having delivered a tray of jasmine tea, his satin slippers moving silently, old Wakir stood before him dressed flawlessly in white from head to toe.

"Mahdi, do you wish anything else?"

Salid contemplated Wakir with satisfaction. He had been a servant of his household since Salid was a young boy. Consistently loyal, old Wakir was less like a fixture than an integral part of Salid's inner circle.

"Wakir, my old friend, I wish you to deliver a gift and a letter for me . . . personally. You must ensure that you place both in Madame Franqua's hands, do you understand?"

"Yes, Mahdi, it shall be done." Salid handed Wakir a vellum envelope with his waxen seal, the scrawl of his small, deliberate handwriting flowing across the face, and a small gold box. "Shall I wait for a reply?"

"No reply will be necessary, Wakir, but you are to present the box to Madame Franqua first. When she opens the box, tell her she must have one of the sweets inside before she reads my letter. Once you see her take a piece of the chocolate, retrieve the box as if you are waiting to serve, and then give her the envelope. Understood?

"When all is completed, return the box and the note to me. Leave nothing behind." Salid smiled, envisioning the shock Madame Franqua would feel at his message, picturing blood rising to her cheeks, the faint sheen of perspiration gracing her beautiful, pouty lips and the cleavage between her firm breasts after she sampled one of the chocolates inside the box.

He knew that she would be intrigued by his ploy, expecting a special proposal for one of their infrequent getaways, replete with instructions for the games they routinely played. Thus, he knew that she would follow Wakir's instructions, placing a chocolate—one of her weaknesses—into her rosebud mouth . . . the same mouth that had brought Salid such pleasure in past months . . . the same mouth that had betrayed him. He wondered just how much she had told Niculaie Barbu, and how much he had paid her.

He sighed with satisfaction, knowing she would have only enough time to read his note and realize that he was the director of her last game, before she fell to the floor, dying. Such a waste of a beautiful cohort. But then, there were innumerable others to take her place for his pleasurable distractions. His heart was held and filled by only one: the glorious *Jihad*!

"Ah, my beauties. Come, sit, have some tea." Three women demurely garbed in traditional Arabic fashion had quietly entered Salid's private garden. They had been summoned to appear precisely before the call for afternoon prayer. Salid was not a Muslim in his heart, though he led an outwardly pious Muslim life. His was a life dominated by power, titillated by intrigue, and satisfied only by winning, be it the obeisance of his immediate circle or the high stakes of influence on world politics.

As the resonant tones of the *muazzin* calling the *azan* floated over the landscape, the women prostrated themselves in a row before Salid. Their four *Ra'kahs*[30] would begin once Salid gave them permission.

Allahu Akbar, Allahu Akbar.	[God is greater, God is greater.
Allahu Akbar, Allahu Akbar.	God is greater, God is greater.]

"Iffat, my sweet virgin, you shall be saved as reward for after the great moment of my triumph," whispered Salid in the gentlest of whispers, all the while stroking Iffat's presented posterior. She shivered under his touch as his fingers lingered in the cleft of her buttocks. Heat poured from her body through her silken gown to his hands bringing a smile of satisfaction to Salid's lips as he sneered, "God is greater, my ripe Iffat." Iffat's *hijab*[31] splayed over the floor in rich tones, catching the sunlight. Her tears were captured by her *niqab*[32] as she silently wept.

Moving to Rana, he raised and folded the hem of her gown over her back. "Your name means delight, Rana, and so you delight me." His hands explored her body with familiarity, and Rana moved to his ministrations. "But we must control our passions, my flower, until the moment is right. Fan the flame I light, precious Rana."

Ashahadu an la ilaha ill Allah.	[I declare there is no god but God.
Ashahadu an la ilaha ill Allah.	I declare there is no god but God.]

"Qahira, you will bring me to the plateau of my great moment. Speak now my private names," rasped Salid as he took her harshly.

Ashahadu anna Muhammadar Rasullullah.	[I declare Muhammad is the Messenger of God.
Ashahadu anna Muhammadar Rasullullah.	I declare Muhammad is the Messenger of God.]

"*Muhammad Ahkam Ahmed Abreeq, Mahdi* (strong and durable, most praised glittering sword, Guided One)," choked out Qahira in repetition, each word matched to Salid's thrusts, over and over to a chorus of muted sobs and whimpers from the other two women and the last of the *muazzin's* intonations, until he was spent.

Salid withdrew, composed himself, and walked away from the women, clapping his hands twice. "Now you must pray to Allah and rededicate yourselves to the One and Only God and to me, his servant." Salid sat sipping his jasmine tea and watched the women perform their *Ra'kahs*. 'Timing is everything,' he mused.

> *Haya alas Salah. Haya alas Salah.*   [Rush to prayer. Rush to prayer.
> *Haya alal Falah. Haya alal Falah.*   Rush to success. Rush to success.
> *Allahu Akbar, Allahu Akbar.*   God is greater, God is greater.
> *La ilaha ill Allah.*   There is no god but God.]

The utter defilement of the *salat*[33] was typical of Salid's twisted view of life and abuse of his personal power. The purpose of the *salat* is to present oneself before God as a humble servant. The Muslim combines physical movements with memorized passages and supplications as a means to enfold the self into a state of meditative, humble obedience, totally removed from all distractions.

In olden days the world over, when in the presence of a king or noble, the common response was to show deference and pay honor to the person by bowing. It has been so throughout many cultures. If when one prayed, one remained upright or stiff and recited memorized lines, one's emotions might become involved to a degree, but one's body would not demonstrate reverence. Accordingly, the Muslim bows before Allah to demonstrate respect. The obedient recitation of praise in the prayerful words are a structured way to honor Allah, committing the heart, not unlike the Christian recitation of prayers given by God to His people. Thus, the servant combines the three elements of mind, heart and body by reciting the prayers with a dedicated heart, concentrating on their meaning and committing daily to their message with the mind, and prostrating the body showing humility, demonstrating faith and righteousness before supplication.

Within Salid's personal world, his version of the *salat* was permeated by the requirement that Allah be honored, and that he also be honored as Servant of the Restorer, one of the leaders of the holy *Jihad*.

Truly devoted Muslims would be aghast at his perversions, not only of *salat*, but also of his alteration of the true meaning of *jihad*. Salid was well aware of this, but in his twisted and brilliant mind, he felt justified and would carry through with well-set plans. That his rituals embodied distortions worried him not in the least. They invigorated him, providing impetus for completion of his role and reassurance of his ever-growing power.

He had been apprised of the Romanian's dispatch and monitoring of the American. To Salid, this was only a minor complication. Martine and his hawks should be able to deal with the American and retrieve whatever the old German professor passed to him. Martine had remained one step ahead of Barbu thus far and, with not a little threat from Salid, would come through. If he had another misstep, Aatiq Ali had instructions to deal with him summarily, and Fakar as well, if need be.

Salid reveled in the thought of the purification of his network of operatives. Shortly, all would be Muslims with the likes of Martine and other European turncoat mercenaries pruned out. He had people embedded in towns and cities all over the western European nations and America, as well . . . faithful Muslims all loyal to him: men, women, and children. He looked upon this network as an extended family army of sorts: trained, put in place, guided, and maintained by the Servant of the Restorer.

If asked to do so, every one of them would go willingly to their death at his command in praise of Allah and for the holy jihad. They adored him; they were totally loyal to him; they feared him. So it was and so it should be! He was, after all, the Glittering Sword, was he not?

CHAPTER 29

Munich, Germany, End December 2007

Munich, the capital of Bavaria, is Germany's third largest city. It sits on the River Isar, and can be reached by seven autobahns and the regular ICE, EC and IC rail services. Flight time to London is only two hours, so Aniela wisely chose it as their departure city.

"The airport is around 28 or 30 kilometers northeast of the city center, but we can take the S-Bahn rail link to get there. There is a train every 10 minutes from very early in the morning until just after midnight. The train station is just west of the city center, so it will be easy for us and although a little longer in time, will allow us to leave the car. To take a taxi is expensive, and has too much risk. It is a long ride during which much can happen."

Aniela drove carefully, negotiating the roundabouts and traffic with ease. She had booked them into a small hotel because of the value and its location near the Viktualienmarkt with its open-air market, trees, and tables. Additionally, it was close to a train station. "It will not be unusual with all there is to see in this area for us to go to Zum Franziskaner. Erich advised this, *ja*?"

"You've chosen well, Aniela. I don't know what I'd have done without you." At her raised eyebrows, he said, "No, I mean it. You know so much about these areas we've traveled. Under the circumstances, I'd have been in trouble on my own for sure. I don't know how to repay you."

"It is simple, *ja*? Stay alive; finish the job; then is time for us and loving, *liebling*." She looked at him briefly, amusement flickering in her eyes.

"Simple? Baloney . . . nothing's simple about any of this." jibed Andy in retort. "Right now, I'd just like to be done with it. I'm beginning to doubt whether all this effort will come to any good after all is said and done. I mean, does it seem logical to you that one ancient document—fragile and sequestered though it be, and tied up in all sorts of ages old disputes—is really going to be accepted and have any broad scale effect on world politics? Does that seem even remotely feasible to you?" He shook his head doubtfully, his brow furrowed.

Determined, Aniela merely said, "Come." Andy followed deep in thought.

They had paid a bit more money for a private bathroom, but the accommodation was still very cheap by hotel standards. Unpacking their few belongings, they decided to rest before tackling the city. Checking the tourist map they had picked up, Andy was surprised at the efficient placement of public transport system routes, and how compact the center of the city really was. Against all the teeming vibrancy of urban life, the Alps served as a stunning backdrop.

The hub of Munich, the Marienplatz, was a few short blocks from their hotel. North of it was the former royal palace (Residenz), the famous student section of Schwabing, and the parklands of the Englischer Garten, one of the largest city parks in Europe through which the Isar River flowed. Andy speculated that he would be able to make contact easily from their location, and mentally planned contingency routes to the airport should such become necessary.

"Oktoberfest is long gone, and we have snow every day now. It is cold, my Andrew. We must get some more clothes. It is not good to wear these things for so many days. I have washed what we have, and we were fortunate to have a fireplace for drying, but we need other things. Tomorrow, we shop. Do we have enough Euros?" Aniela had been exceedingly thrifty and an "easy keeper" as women go. Her cautious query caught Andy off guard.

"You're right, sweetheart. I've been thoughtless. Uh, do you need girlie stuff? No, never mind . . . don't answer that. We do need some fill-ins, perhaps another sweater and shirt, and another change of underwear and socks. I sure wouldn't mind a hat. This headband is good, but the top of my head gets cold. And yes, we have plenty of money still, but I should break down some of the larger bills. We can do that when we go shopping, okay?"

The meeting in the church that provided him with the Copper Scroll disk, also supplied them with a glut of cash, which he discovered only after he'd left Erich. He regretted that he never had the opportunity to thank him for his kindness and help. He would eventually remedy that once they got to England. The European network impressed him so far. He hoped that they continued to maintain high standards because their lives depended on it.

"Andrew, can you come here?" Aniela motioned him to the window. Outside, two figures were standing together conversing in the cold, their breath fogging around their heads. One was clearly a slightly built female; the other, a burly male. "They have been so for over half an hour. Not a place to stand with so many cafés and bars around, do you think?"

The window had a semi-sheer curtain woven with a flower pattern. Aniela had sensibly left the curtain closed, peering out from the side edge of the window where the curtain was held away from the wall a few inches by the rod.

"Hmm, new friends, do you think?" Andy peeked over her head, noticing that the woman glanced toward the hotel before entering a taxi. The man stayed on the street looking around, it seemed, for a more hospitable post. Finally, he walked to the corner and entered a bar that advertised all-night music. "Well spotted, sweetheart. Looks like we've got company yet again. I'll bet they'll have lookouts at the airport, too. Damn, I'd hoped we gave them the slip."

"Not to worry, my Andrew. Our trail led to Munich as a natural next place. They have logic, and they know that this city offers much. No one would come to this region without visiting Munich. It makes sense. But this is the first we have seen a woman. And the man is not the man with the beret. Remember the one with the big ears? These two are different. I watched their lips, Andrew, and I am certain I saw the woman say 'oui,' which might mean they are French. I cannot think of another word that is made with the lips so, certainly not in German." She silently demonstrated with her lips pursed.

"You've become a regular little Mata Hari, Aniela. Well done. Whatever it is, it is. But for now, what do you say we spend some quality time together? Then we can go get something to eat, okay?" He spun her around, picking her up in his arms, the two of them collapsing on the bed in laughter.

ChAPTER 30

Christmas Season,
Windward Farm, Maine 2007

How many Christmases had the family spent at Windward decorating the house from top to bottom? It was the only home Marcy knew, and it was a large part of her foundation world. The house glittered from the outside, white fairy lights shining through the boughs of trees and shrubs and outlining the wreaths in all the windows. This year, her mother had decided to make deep blue bows for the wreaths, as a sign of unity, confidence, strength and steadfastness. Elizabeth had researched the symbolism of color in various cultures and decided that, in addition to blue being a significant color in many religious beliefs, its assigned attributes were appropriate for this Christmas without Andy, and the family's commitment to their faith and belief in his return.

As she threw the nighttime hay flakes, Marcy gazed through the barn door at the house, wisps of smoke lazily pluming from its chimneys, and the meadows and pastures beyond. The water was a dark gray and moving swiftly under an equally gray sky releasing velvety snowflakes. What a beautiful picture. She heard the storm door to her father's workshop slam shut, and watched him as he hopped over snow mounds to the sidewalk. 'Now there's a gorgeous man,' she thought. Jeremy Jon Stanton was, she realized, the benchmark against which she had always judged other males, from high school sweethearts to her current day suitors, Tre and Tommy. Even though well into maturity, he cut a strong and handsome figure. He was her personal Rock of Gibraltar. Marcy laughed, turning back to the horses. 'Those boys have a long, long way to go, methinks.' she thought to herself.

"Sweetheart, the table looks absolutely gorgeous. It's not even Christmas dinner yet and you're pulling out all the stops." Jeremy hugged his wife from behind, kissing her on the neck. Elizabeth smiled up at him.

"Hey now, you be careful or you'll make me muss the icing on this cake." she scolded, trying her best to frown despite that her eyes and lips were smiling. "Oh how I love the Christmas season," she whispered. "Did you notice how the boys have been preening themselves? I think it's lovely that they've invited Rebekah and Charlotte for the weekend.

"Tre should be arriving shortly, Jeremy, so I thought you could serve my punch with the appetizers in the garden room just before dinner, okay? We'll have the Pino Grigio with the first course; it's in the fridge, but not uncorked. Oh, and you'd best let the red breathe awhile. It's over there on the counter by the windows. There!" The four tier cake was perfect, its crown of toasted coconut tempting Jeremy, as he pinched a nibble. Elizabeth slapped his hand.

"Now, if you'll just light the candles since the boys aren't down yet, we'll be all ready." Elizabeth moved to the back door to call out to the barn for Marcy.

Jeremy could not help but smile at Elizabeth's unconscious direction. She always liked to have all details addressed well in advance. They had had many a dinner party in this home over the past many years, and had always followed the same routines.

All his family participated in decorating the house, particularly the tree. Yearly store-bought ornaments had underpinned their collection of well-worn child-crafted ornaments, but the angel they placed on the tree every Christmas had survived the hands of all the toddlers who were now adults.

Fragrant evergreen boughs adorned the sills and mantel; candle lights flickered in every window; Elizabeth's secret mixture of potpourri lay in attractive pots and dishes throughout the house, gently scenting the atmosphere. Everywhere the house bade welcome with loving touches. 'I am greatly blessed,' he thought, rubbing his sore arthritic shoulder. 'It's a good thing that boat is almost done, 'cause I don't know how much more this old shoulder can take,' he thought wryly, and chuckled to himself. 'I'll have it done by the time Andy comes home.' He nodded to himself, fetching the matches.

The aroma of dinner and baking bread permeated the house. Everyone always looked forward to Elizabeth's concoctions: her punches were always delicious, and each year would match the array of appetizers that seemed to flow for however long pre-dinner conversation flourished. She would present an amazing meal with a splendidly wicked dessert to follow.

Jeremy would always serve the appropriate wine with the courses, followed by Andy's offering either an after dinner Port or liqueur in the living room before the fire. Marcy would pass around fine European chocolates, and the boys would kibitz with each other as to who would clear the table and who would wash up. Year after year, they followed the same routine; it was both comforting and refreshing. Their family had rituals in which they confidently participated despite the passage of time. It was part of the glue that held them close to each other.

Again this year, his family would participate in the traditions that culminated another year of living and loving each other . . . except that one cherished member would be absent. As his mind focused on that empty place within his heart, a sob escaped his lips.

"Dad, hey Dad, oh come on. It's going to be okay. You know it will. Dad?" Jeremy was unaware that Matthew had walked into the kitchen. He looked up into the face of his grown son, so like Andrew at the same age, and dissolved into quiet tears.

"Dad, I know. We're all feeling it. But remember the blue bows we put on the wreaths and what Mom told us about the symbolism? You have to hold on to that, okay?" Matthew had put an arm around his father's shoulders briefly squeezing, knowing that it would be just enough comfort without spawning his father's embarrassment.

"Right, son, right. Sorry, it just sneaked up on me with no warning. I'm okay. Thanks." Jeremy turned, wiping his eyes, as Elizabeth came back into the kitchen. A sensitive wife and mother, she knew immediately that something was amiss. She glanced from Matthew to Jeremy and turned toward the stove. A wise wife and mother, she knew when to leave things be.

"So, Mom, did Charlotte call? I didn't hear the phone." Matthew walked over to the windows, peering out. "You don't think she'll have trouble with the snow, do you?" Charlotte had insisted that she make her own way to Windward, refusing Matthew's insistence that he drive her, as after the weekend she planned to visit her grandmother further north before Christmas.

"No, honey, I think she'll be just fine. It's not slippery out, just our usual snow laden wintertime roads, and she's used to them. What did you tell me she was studying?" Elizabeth glanced at Jeremy who was opening the wine. He felt her gaze and turned to look at her, nod, and smile. She blew him a kiss and he caught it, holding his fist to his chest, looking at her through misting eyes.

"I'm looking forward to meeting her," said Marcy as she sauntered into the kitchen, grabbing a handful of spiced pecans. "By the way, Matt, does she have red hair like Mom's and mine? I know how you and Luke love red hair." Elizabeth and Marcy erupted into giggles just as Matthew was about to answer back. But at that moment, Luke bounded into the kitchen.

"What's up? Am I missing something?" Helping himself to one of the cheese rolls from the basket destined for dinner, he grinned as his mother slapped his hand. "So, Mom, has Rebekah phoned? I didn't hear any ring, and I was wondering if anyone has heard from her?" He walked over to the windows looking out. "Is it bad out there, Marce? Do you think she'll be okay getting up here?" When everyone burst into laughter, Luke said, "What? What's so funny?"

In the midst of the jovial explanation, the doorbell sounded, and a very tall, handsome Naval officer came through the side door, escorting two lovely, young, blonde women, one on each arm.

"Commander Swift reporting, sir. Found these two on my way in. They belong to anyone here?" said Tre with a broad grin. The boys rushed to greet Charlotte and Rebekah and shake Tre's hand. Coats were hung, bags were carried to the stairs, and everyone chattered introductions and welcome. Marcy gave Tre a kiss and a hug, taking his arm to lead him to the couch by the fire. The telephone rang, and Jeremy answered on the first ring.

"Marcy, honey, it's for you . . . long distance." Jeremy put the phone on the counter and walked to Elizabeth, whispering in her ear.

Her heart raced as she stole a quick glance at Tre, who was staring into the fire. "Hello? This is Marcy," she said shakily. "Oh, hi, how are you? Yes, the same to you . . . Well, we're just about to have dinner . . . the boys have some friends over and," Marcy turned her back to the room, listening to the caller. She whispered into the phone, "Can I call you later? It's not a good time right now. Please forgive me."

Returning to the couch after ending the call, she placed her hand on Tre's. "To answer your unspoken question, yes, it was Tommy. I said I'd speak with him later." She looked at him questioningly. She was unsure whether her heart was beating so rapidly because of the telephone call or because of her concern at what Tre's reaction might be.

Tre held her hand to his lips for an inordinately long time, and then turned to look at her, smiling. "It's all right, Marcy, I understand. And please don't think I'm going to be overbearing about your return call. I imagine he'll guess that I'm here, unless you specifically told him, and that won't be welcome news to him anymore than his phone call was to me. But it's okay, sweetheart. I know he's in your life, but he's not here right now, I am. That's enough for right now. Let's not let it spoil our evening."

"I didn't say you were here, Tre, but I agree he probably guessed because I was so brief and unwilling to talk longer. I just didn't know how you would, I mean, I didn't want you to be," Marcy stammered, annoyed at herself for being so flustered.

"Sssh," Tre said, encircling her with an arm, pulling her head to his shoulder. "It's all right. I do understand, Marcy. Now let it go, okay?"

Dinner was, as usual, a raging success. The girls were relaxed and fit into the family dynamic as if they had been friends for years. After dinner, Charlotte asked if she might play the piano. Elizabeth was delighted and shot Matthew an approving look that made him beam.

As Charlotte played a soft Chopin Etude, Matthew took his cello from its stand to accompany her. Their music was glorious, and the two fit together wonderfully, revealed by the looks they shared. Their hearts flowed into the music, each instrument caressing the other by intonation and response.

"I never realized music could be so sexy," said Rebekah looking at the two of them. "Luke, you play too, don't you? Why don't you join them in something?" Rebekah's dimples framed a beautiful smile that lit Luke's face.

Matthew and Charlotte finished, and Luke suggested that the threesome play a piece he chose. "It's one of Andy's favorites," Luke explained to the girls, joining Matthew and Charlotte with his guitar, "and he can't be with us, so we'll do this one for him."

The strains of "The Little Drummer Boy" filled the room. Rebekah rose to stand next to Luke, raising a sweet voice to make a quartet. It was a special moment. Jeremy held Elizabeth's hand; Tre held Marcy's hand. As if they read each other's minds, the four adults rose and gathered around the piano with the young adults, joining in.

For one brief moment in time, the sounds of heartfelt holiday music floated from the house to the skies above . . . all the way to Munich.

CHAPTER 31

Munich Airport, Germany 2007

Saleh bin Tariq bin Khalid Al-Fulan and Fatimah bint Tariq bin Khalid Al-Fulan walked from the immigration entry desk to the supervisor's office. "Saleh Tariq Khalid Al-Fulan and Fatimah Tariq Khalid Al-Fulan, tell me, what is the purpose of your visit and how long do you intend to stay?" said the supervisor, eyeing them suspiciously.

"My sister and I have business in Munich, sir," said Saleh. "I am hoping that we shall be able to conclude such matters within two weeks or so." His German was flawless, albeit smoother and less guttural than native speech. "Is there a problem, sir?"

The supervisor looked through their passports and papers, snapping them shut. In English, he said to them, "It surprises me that you travel in western clothing. No *bhurka, fraulein*?" It was clearly a pointed remark designed to agitate. Fatimah stood stiffly, returning the supervisor's gaze without blinking. Her dark eyes glinted like polished steel, even as she offered him a coquettish smile.

"And so, inspector," she said in the Queen's English, "you think that all of us should dress in that drab, loose clothing? We do not. I prefer this style. It suits me, don't you think?" She moved her hands over her hips to her belly, sliding down to the tops of her thighs, amused as the supervisor's eyes followed her every move, his stare lingering below her navel in clear admiration of how tightly her pants clung to her body.

"Yes, well," he continued clearing his throat, "you understand, I must ask these questions." Returning their passports, he looked from brother to sister. "You look remarkably alike, are you twins?"

"No, sir," smiled Saleh, "Fatimah is my younger sister, but we are very close, perhaps as close as twins might be in more than looks. Thank you sir, is that all?"

The supervisor nodded brusquely, waving them out of his office as he busily shuffled the papers on his desk. 'Humph, funny way to describe themselves,' he thought, 'strange ones, these Arabs.'

Saleh and Fatimah worked their way through the airport moving through the exit doors to look for the car they were promised would await them outside. Both were unusually tall; both wore their hair cut close to the skull; both were dressed in tight, black leather pants, jackets, and boots; both wore silver earrings with a peridot/olivine gemstone[34] embedded at the center of the small disks. They made an imposing couple, moving with synchronized catlike grace through the crowd of travelers. Their presence turned more than a few heads.

Saleh nodded to Fatimah, and together they approached a Citroën parked about 10 meters away. The driver recognized the pair and leaped out of the car to assist with their bags.

"Take us to the *funduq* (hotel) immediately. Did you get the trunks from cargo?" Fatimah eased into the rear of the car, removing her sunglasses while surveying the other cars around them.

"Yes, all is as you ordered. Abdul Rahman awaits you." The driver quickly loaded the car, jumped into the driver's seat, and engaged the motor. Saleh snapped his phone shut, joined Fatimah in the rear of the car, and slammed his door. The car sped from the airport carrying two of the most adept and feared assassins whose reputations drew a shudder in international circles when their names were mentioned. Their moniker, "Al-Mumît" (Giver of Death, The Slayer) was rarely spoken, and then only in whispers.

Their accommodations were lavish: Covering the veined beige marble floor was an exquisite hand-loomed silk rug from whose colors the tapestries and décor were drawn. Cream-colored silk covered the sofas with soft chairs in plush sage velvet with bronze and sage striped cushions that matched the floor-to-ceiling draperies. In counterpoint, the wood paneling was a dark, rich mahogany. Even the vases of fresh flowers reflected the color scheme with delicate ivory roses, coppery chrysanthemums, and bronze asters. Fatimah bent gracefully to drink in their scent, and then snapped off a rose to place in her lapel.

Their contact, Abdul Rahman Yasin (another well-known purveyor of fear whose name showed on most international terrorist lists), greeted them. He reiterated the highlights of the briefing they had already received, providing them with snapshots of Andy and Aniela, as well as Martine and Barbu. "He is a hireling working directly for Salid," he said, as he distributed Martine's photo. "So we are not at cross purposes here, you work directly for me. Our aims are the same, but our alliances . . . or shall we say, our employers . . . differ.

"The Romanian may have another with him or coming soon. They usually work together on the more difficult assignments, although I would not classify this one as difficult so much as sensitive . . . yes, that is a better term. We want things expedited, which is why I contacted you.

"But," he emphasized, raising his forefinger, "we want things done cleanly without notice. You must ensure nothing is left behind, not one trace. If you require immediate extraction because of complications, you have my safe number and it will be arranged, but leave nothing to be cleaned up."

"Mmm, this American is very attractive. It would be a pity to waste such a one." Fatimah stroked Andy's photo with her long index finger, the short, white polished nail moving along the curve of his mouth. Saleh snorted in amusement, shaking his head at her with a lascivious grin.

"Your appetites are well-known, Fatimah bint Tariq, and you will not compromise this mission by satisfying them. Merely secure the information and get out. We do not wish to draw any more attention than is absolutely necessary. Praise Allah, this should be easy for you and over soon. Then you can return to your island." Abdul Rahman Yasin stared at the brother and sister as if dissecting them.

"So shall it be," intoned Saleh, inclining his head.

"So shall it be," crooned Fatimah in synchrony, likewise inclining her head.

Abdul continued. "Since the American met with the old Austrian professor, the pair carry on their holiday in a relaxed fashion which is clearly a ruse. The Austrian girl linked them up. We are not sure what her connection is with the old man, perhaps quite innocent. But the professor and his people got the package from the Mossad, so it is likely that he passed it to the American, since they love the Jews. We think he is using the girl as cover until he can make secure contact and divest himself of the information. I want it before he leaves Germany."

"And what about the man and the woman? Do you want them too?" Fatimah asked.

"We care nothing for either of them. He is of no value to us, a low-level courier from all accounts, an academic that the Americans use unwittingly. The girl is just a plaything, a nothing. But that said, you will not harm either of them, if it can be helped. But if there is an unexpected problem, they are to disappear without a trace and particularly with no connection to you. I leave that to your . . . judgment and experience. You must act quickly.

"I do not want Barbu or Martine to succeed. Insofar as they are concerned, or any of their henchmen, use whatever degree of your special expertise is required. Their loss would be our gain, and of course it would be amusing to make it look as if the Americans or the Germans were responsible."

His smile was easy and gentle, not unlike the smiles conferred from grandfathers to their grandchildren, except for the deadly, snake-like expression in his eyes.

As he moved to take his leave of the pair, he paused at the door, turning toward them. "It is written: Muhammad said, 'Allah has recorded both good and bad deeds. Whoever intended to do a good deed and did not do it, Allah writes it down with Himself as a full good deed. But if he intended to do it and did it, Allah writes it down with Himself as worth from ten to seven hundred good deeds, or many times over. But if he intended to do a bad deed and did not do it, Allah writes it down with Himself as a full good deed, but if he intended it and did it, Allah writes it down as one bad deed.' So, children of Allah, may your deeds be worth from ten to seven hundred good deeds, many times over.

"But remember, it is written in the Qur'an that 'every soul draws the results of its actions on none but itself: no bearer of burdens can bear the burden of another.'[35] I leave it to you. Make contact with me only if you succeed. Otherwise, I do not know you." As he spoke, he fingered his *masbahas*[36], raising his fingers to his brow in farewell.

"It shall be as you say, Hafiz.[37]" Saleh bin Tariq bin Khalid Al-Fulan said as he bowed at the waist. His sister, matching the timing of his bow exactly, smiled to herself in anticipation.

Righting herself once Abdul Rahman had departed, Fatimah put her arms around her brother's neck saying, "It is also written according to Muhammad, among the first words of revelation given to man were the instructions, 'If you feel no shame then do as you wish.'" She winked at him.

Chapter 32

End December, Windward Farm, Maine 2007

Just before he left for his three-day business trip, Tre walked out to Jeremy's workshop. "Mind if I come in and talk for a bit?" he asked. Jeremy was polishing the stern of the sailboat, sitting at the transom. "I know this is your private place, but I could really use some advice."

Jeremy looked up, saying, "Sure, son, come on in. But shut that door, you're letting all the warm air out. There's fresh coffee over there on the counter; no milk or sugar, though, but that shouldn't bother a Navy man. In fact, I'll take a break and join you."

"I suppose you know it's about Marcy." Tre rolled the steaming mug in his hands.

"Ayeh, I figured." Jeremy squinted at the steam as he sipped the hot brew. "What's on your mind, Tre? Just spit it out. No use worrying about how it's going to come out; it's just you and me in here. Besides, I heard the women talking over breakfast dishes that they were planning on going into town. There's a holiday soup sale on at the church, and Liz likes to support everything they do."

"Yeah, well, I guess it's best that things go on as normal for the time being, but I have to tell you, Jeremy . . . uh, excuse me, Mr. Stanton . . ."

"Oh horse puck, come on, son, I told you to call me Jeremy. No sense standing on ceremony. At least not with me. Now get to it, this coffee won't last forever."

"Well," sighed Tre, "it's kind of complicated. The whole family's been great to me all the while I've been seeing Marcy. I thought everything was fine. Then this Tommy thing developed almost overnight. Clearly, Marcy's in a muddle, which makes a muddle for me. I . . . I . . . just don't know where I stand, and I'm kind of afraid to push the subject with her. She can be temperamental, you know." Tre ran his fingers through his hair.

Jeremy laughed so hard it made him cough. Wheezing, he said, "No kidding, Sherlock. She takes after her Mom, that's for sure. The twins say it's their red hair." He grinned at Tre's discomfort. "Look, Tre, you're never going to know what she feels unless you ask her. I don't know myself. But if you're the kind of man I think you are, 'do not go gentle into that good night.'"

Tre smiled and said, "Dylan Thomas wasn't it? I love his poetry. Didn't he also write something about the 'meaning of life has been lost in the wind'? That's kind of how I feel these days."

"Ayeh, I love his poetry too, but that second line was from 'Let Me Die in My Footsteps', and I don't think you're about to die. Same poem, son, says 'Some people thinkin' that the end is close 'stead of learnin' to live, they are learning to die,' or something pretty close to that. The point is, Tre, are you learning to live or are you going to give up and die? Your relationship, I mean, of course. But then, if there's not enough in it worth fighting for . . ."

"Oh, no, I didn't mean that" Tre said in dismay. "It's just that I don't seem to be able to make any headway. I'm no match for the likes of Tommy with all his dash and international glamour. And half of it is that I think he's just turned Marcy's head. You know, he's got a wild reputation with the ladies, and I'd hate for her to get hurt."

"Noble of you." Jeremy stood and picked up his chamois.

"Naturally, I don't want to get hurt either. I mean, I want to marry Marcy. I think we could have a good life together. Hell, we've been seeing each other for years now. But every time I go to talk to her seriously, she sidesteps me. I'm about at my wit's end."

"So, what do you think you should do?" Jeremy said smoothly, stealing a look at Tre who was slumped on the bench looking thoroughly miserable.

"I'll make her talk to me, that's what. I won't take no for an answer. I'll tell her how I feel and that I want her to choose whichever of us she's in love with, even though both of us are in love with her. At least, I figure Tommy's in love with her. He's never stayed around any other girl long, so there must be something there, you know? Damn that guy, he always one-ups me, beats me to the punch. Sometimes I'd like to have it out, just him and me. I think I could whoop him. He's no pansy, but I think I could still take him."

Jeremy smiled. "Sounds like your blood's up a bit, son, with that cave man approach. How do you think Marcy would react to that?"

"I know," he drawled. "She'd hate it. She'd probably deck me or refuse to see me ever again. Hell, I wouldn't do it anyway. It's just that I'm so frustrated. She's everything I've always wanted, Jeremy, and I can't seem to make any progress."

"Tre, you're a sailor. What do you do when the wind changes?" Jeremy kept rubbing without looking up at the distressed young man.

Tre looked puzzled, thinking for a few moments, and then smiled in recognition. "Right! Thanks, Jeremy. Thanks for listening to me and giving me the answer. Yeah, I know what to do now, and by God, I'm going to do it today."

"Ayeh, sounds like a plan," said the father of the temperamental redhead who reminded him so much of the woman he loved with all his heart. He watched Tre leave with a smile and a knowing nod, thinking, 'I remember when . . .'

Chapter 33

Washington, D.C., End December 2007

The "CCC" (Command and Co-ordination Centre) provides a round-the-clock operation for any of 186 member countries of Interpol. It determines the priority level of each message received by Interpol's General Secretariat or any National Central Bureau in member countries, and replies to urgent requests in real-time. It also coordinates the exchange of all intelligence and related information for operations involving a few to several countries, and can offer specialized assistance, when required. It was to the CCC that Lassiter placed an innocuous inquiry.

"Oskar? That you? How are you, old buddy?" Lassiter laughed, but made his small talk brief. "Yeah, I need a favor, Oskar, and I need it to be black. You okay with that?" A smile spread over his face, erasing some of the tension. "Great, now here's the deal. And Oskar? I need it right away, like yesterday."

Lassiter's assistant and "right arm," Wendy Collins, had been a fixture in the inner sanctum domain of Washington D.C.'s upper echelon security for many years. She had seen directors and their top teams come and go with changes in government administration. She was a figure whose knowledge, flawless demeanor, comprehensive organizational ability, utter reliability, and personal strength commanded unequivocal respect . . . from everyone, including presidents.

Wendy monitored the blinking light on the secure line while stuffing the brown envelopes for the team sitting in her waiting room. She eyed them surreptitiously as she worked—bright, keen, and piercing violet eyes peering over her eyeglasses beneath elegantly coiffed steel gray hair.

James Noonan looked like a man just off a tractor from a wheat farm in Iowa: his face was craggy, likely from the sun or wind, with a square jaw, preoccupied hazel eyes, and a shock of unruly sandy brown hair. He had large hands and a powerful torso. Despite his bulk, he moved languorously as he bent to flit through the magazines, the bulges beneath his crisp uniform displaying very fit muscles always in control. Noonan was an expert in armaments, including small missiles, arms of all types, general weaponry, and associated equipment. He was also an expert marksman and sniper.

Angel D'Orza, the smallest of the group, fidgeted with nervous energy. He was the wiry type with dark eyes that flitted everywhere at once. He kept cracking his knuckles. His dark olive skin and nondescript features made him a shoe-in for various nationalities, as did his enviable language skills. D'Orza was also an explosives expert. Wendy supposed that one needed to have an "on-the-edge" personality to deal with volatile situations that demanded use of the unstable material D'Orza routinely handled in missions. His teammates aptly nicknamed him "Monkey" because of his propensity to achieve seemingly impossible physical feats of agility.

Conrad Hennecke was an average looking man, although he, too, was obviously physically fit. There was something contemplative about the slightly distant expression in his eyes, as if his mind was always working on something in tandem with his current monitoring of a situation. Hennecke, like D'Orza, spoke several languages and was proficient in dialects of some of the more unusual ones like Kurdish, Uzbek, and Farsi. He was an electronics and computer specialist who had grown up primarily in Germany, but had chunks of his childhood in the Middle East, Russia, and Europe in line with his father's work assignments.

Bianca Romm was the daughter of a brilliant German archaeologist and his Italian wife. She had spent her childhood carousing digs with her parents on assignment, and had achieved prominence in the field herself. She was also a martial arts expert and taught occasional courses (when available) for the government.

Rico Morales and Helmut Kaiser sat conversing with Ileana Muscovici, recently in from her Vatican assignment. A handsome Latino, Morales was flirting outrageously with Ileana, whose middle European looks captivated him. A petite woman, Ileana had pale skin, green eyes, and lush dark hair that trailed down her back. An adept translator, she had been on undercover assignment to the Vatican under the auspices of Cardinal Monteverdi, who was in charge of the Vatican's endless and enviable library. With her background qualifications as a published academic whose knowledge of the development of world religions made her a favorite in religious circles worldwide, her translation work for the Cardinal was not suspect. In reality, she was there to help ascertain the "who and how" several irreplaceable documents had been stolen from the vaults. Ethnically Romanian, Ileana was a valuable asset who had worked on most of Lassiter's special ops teams for the last several years. She possessed a flawless cover *persona*, was physically alluring, immensely bright, and ruthlessly capable with a knife.

The son of German immigrants, Helmut Kaiser was 100% Teutonic in looks and bearing. An accomplished seaman and diver, Helmut backed up Noonan in the brawn department. He was a clear thinker who never hesitated to act or lead. His crisp judgments had more than once saved his team and their mission. Almost assuredly, Helmut would be assigned leadership of this operation as well. His emotionless organizational skills, brute physical strength, and indomitable character had earned him the respect of all who had worked with him. His profession as a marine biologist usually found him aboard research vessels lending his undersea abilities and scientific mind to the project at hand.

Morales was the bright copper penny of the group. Nothing ever got him down, not the worst developments, bad weather, poor equipment, or being outnumbered. Lassiter had once remarked to Wendy that he believed Morales had been vaccinated with some type of "gung ho" serum, since it was abnormal for anyone to be so happy and positive all of the time despite the circumstances. He was the confidence booster of the team, as well as an inveterate ladies man. His well-built, medium frame with curly, dark hair framing a handsome face could easily be the envy of most male models. In civilian life, Morales was a Dapper Dan, dressing in silks and tight sharkskin as owner of one of a string of prestigious clubs. He was also a fearless fighter and one of the most reliable members of the team, often achieving the impossible against poor odds.

The light went out on Lassiter's phone. Wendy waited a few minutes, expecting a buzz or the light to reappear, indicating her boss had another pressing phone call. When neither occurred, she rose gracefully and walked toward his door. Everyone's head immediately turned in her direction, all conversation and movement brought to a dead halt. She looked at the expectant faces kindly.

"I'll let you know," she said, then proceeded through the door, closing it behind her.

"So, Ileana, maybe you'd like me to teach you the samba or the mambo? You look like you'd be able to master those dances with little effort," Rico said, moving his shoulders to unheard music.

"Just ignore him, Ileana, or he'll give you a demo right here and now. That's the last thing we need Lassiter to see." Then to Rico he said with a smile, "Cool it, chum. Time to drag your brains from below your belt back up to your head. We'll be going inside in a minute." Kaiser grinned at his friend, who smiled back, shrugged his shoulders, and winked at Ileana.

After a short time, Wendy appeared at the door. "Okay, kids, time to see the Headmaster."

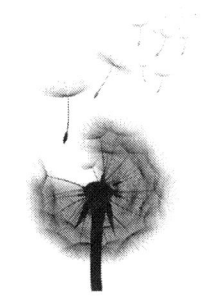

Chapter 34

Spring 2008, Maine

"Well, darling, I think that about does it. Are you sure you've packed enough warm things? It gets cold in England, you know. Their spring tends to be cooler than ours, and damp." Elizabeth fussed over Marcy's suitcases just as she had done when she left for college.

"Mom, it's okay, they do have washing machines there, you know." Marcy grinned at her mother, who sniffed and mumbled to herself. "Oh now, I'm not going to be gone for all that long a time. Come here." Extending her arms, Marcy held her Mother for a long time. "I know, it's me going away and Andy still being away, the boys away too . . . but we'll all be coming back, don't let go of that."

"I know you think I'm being silly, Marcia, but it's just," her sentence filled with quiet sobs. "I love you all so much, and I worry when you're gone, that's the long and short of it. I want you to go, honey. I'm so proud of you, and this opportunity is, well, an unexpected feather in your cap. I just don't like you being in such close proximity to all that nastiness with those drug people, you know?"

"Sure, Mom, I know. I don't like it much either, but we won't exactly be playing cops and robbers. My role is well removed, and our whole staff will have tons of protection from the Brits, as well as from Harry and Sandy, who will be right there with us the whole time. Oh, by the way, can I borrow your gold locket? I'd rather like to have family photos close to my heart while I'm away. I promise I'll take good care of it. I know how much it means to you. It's just that . . . ."

"Stop right there. Of course, you may borrow it." The locket had been a gift from Marcy's father a few Christmases ago. One side held a photo of her parents; the other a photo of the two sets of twins. The face of the locket was intricately engraved on the outer edges, with a shiny inner heart inscribed with the initials EVS. The reverse held the letters: Forever—JJS. It was her mother's favorite piece of jewelry.

"I'll just run and get it. Remember, it's 18 karat, so I'll take your word that you'll be careful, okay? It would be lovely with your emerald green dress and the ring Tommy gave you. Would you like to borrow my gold earrings too? They'd complete the outfit. I'll bring them, just in case." Her mother scurried from the bedroom, calling downstairs to Jeremy to take the roast from the oven.

'Just like Mom,' Marcy thought tenderly. 'God forbid she didn't have a wonderful going away dinner for me, even with everything else that's going on.'

Marcy was due to leave with the rest of the team the following morning. Tonight, she and her parents had planned a relaxing evening together. She was excited about the trip, even though two months away from Windward Farm and her practice was difficult to contemplate. The lengthy trip represented a complete change in her orderly, secure life. The prospect was at once exhilarating and unsettling. Although she had no reservations about her ability to perform well as the assigned head vet, she harbored a bit of trepidation about the veiled circumstances surrounding the show. Regardless, she would never let on to her mother.

Elizabeth had carried on life as normal, but Marcy could detect a subtle wearing down, an emotional cracking taking place. She did her best to hide her concerns, but Marcy could see through the façade. Her mother was suffering deeply from the distress of Andy's unknown status. The family had made a covenant over Thanksgiving not to give up their belief that Andy would come through whole and well, but the succeeding months of silence were wearing Elizabeth down with repressed worry.

Jeremy seemed to take it all in stride, remaining positively resolute, although Marcy recognized deeper lines in his face as well. Matthew had written his inner feelings to her, as had Luke. Both fervently believed with the guilelessness and innocence of youth that their brother was undefeatable. Marcy's heart refused to entertain that Andy was lost to them, but her mind became more troubled with the passing of each day.

Christmastime had been enjoyable, but each family member had deeply felt Andy's absence. Each had tried to hide it for the sake of the others, but everyone knew everyone else's tricks. It had almost been a blessing that Marcy had had to deal with Tre's proposal. It gave her something else to think about besides Andy's absence at their favorite time of the year.

It had happened at the most unexpected of times and places. She had been feeding the horses before dinner, thinking Tre was occupied with the twins and their girlfriends. He was due to leave Windward some time after the weekend for a few days, returning briefly before leaving for D.C. They would each spend Christmas with their respective families, and Tre had told her that he would visit again before her upcoming trip to England. She had mistakenly thought that his schedule would buy her some time to sort things out in her head and heart.

The horses had announced his presence in the barn. When she had turned to see who it was, she saw him standing in the doorway, his image dark but framed against the falling snow outside. Her heart had seemed to stop as she held her breath. Tre's silhouette so closely resembled Andy's and her father's that she had one, fleeting moment of unrealistic hope.

"Sorry if I startled you," he had said evenly. "I thought maybe you'd like some help. Dinner should be ready soon, and the kids have a surprise for all of us. They sent me to hurry you along."

"Oh, Tre, no, it's okay. It's just that for a moment . . . never mind. Come on in. I'm about done, just need to top off the water buckets and sweep," she had responded amicably.

"Let me help you," he had said, moving for the hose. Marcy had smiled genuinely at him, surprised that he was joining her in the barn since he had little affinity for horses and rarely entered her domain. As she rhythmically swept the aisle, Tre began his well-planned speech.

When he had finished, he had silently continued to fill the buckets, then drained and rewound the hose, all without looking at her. She recalled that she stood rooted in one spot, watching him in amazement, too stunned to speak.

He had covered the Tommy thing; he had declared his intentions toward her; he had expressed how fearful he was that they were growing apart because of Marcy's attraction to Tommy or that their relationship was deteriorating for reasons unknown to him. He had spoken evenly and sensitively, issuing no hotheaded demands or requiring an answer.

He had actually asked her to look deeply into her heart and mind and consider his proposal, the answer to which he would not hope for until he returned just before she left for the U.K.

As he left the barn for the house, he had paused next to her, gently touching her cheek. "I'll see you in the house. Try not to be too long. The kids . . ."

"Yes, okay, I'll be right there," was all that she could whisper.

The rest of the evening and weekend had passed uneventfully, if a bit strained between them. Tre looked like a hound from the shelter, wounded and eager for any scrap of attention or affection. Marcy had tried to be herself, but felt as if she were just going through the motions. She had immersed herself in domestic chores, assisting her mother until she was gently chastised for being underfoot. It was serendipitous that the twins had their girlfriends for the weekend, as they all provided much needed distraction. When it came time for Tre to leave, Marcy did her level best to be lighthearted, sending him off with a kiss, a hug, and a promise that she'd seriously think about what he had said.

Over the rest of the holiday, Marcy did just that. To her surprise, her father had left her a letter on her bureau just after Christmas day. It was a sweet reminder that he loved her, was proud of all that she'd worked so hard to become, particularly pleased that she exhibited so many of her mother's qualities, and perhaps a few of his own characteristics. It was also a message of support and wisdom as concerned her responsibility to herself and two wonderful young men, both of whom loved her.

The last part of his note read, "I know it's not easy, baby, but lingering at a decision will only bring pain to the pair of them and, more importantly, to you. All you need to do is think with that wonderful brain of yours, and listen to your heart. Maybe these will help . . . I love you. Dad" The envelope held two printed sheets: on one was a typed poem/song by a current, prolific, Christian songwriter and singer with many platinum records and albums; the second was a copy of William Shakespeare's Sonnet CXVI.

Marcy felt the tears release even as she kissed the pages, her heart full of love and gratitude. It was just the sort of thing her father would do; it was just the sort of thing her beloved Andy would do.

I WILL BE HERE

If in the morning when you wake,
If the sun does not appear,
I will be here.
If in the dark we lose sight of love,
Hold my hand and have no fear,
I will be here.

I will be here,
When you feel like being quiet,
When you need to speak your mind I will listen.
Through the winning, losing, and trying we'll be together,
And I will be here.

If in the morning when you wake,
If the future is unclear,
I will be here.
As sure as seasons were made for change,
Our lifetimes were made for years,
I will be here.

I will be here,
And you can cry on my shoulder,
When the mirror tells us we're older.
I will hold you, to watch you grow in beauty,
And tell you all the things you are to me.
We'll be together and I will be here.
I will be true to the promises I've made,
To you and to the one who gave you to me.
I will be here.

Steven Curtis Chapman

Callie McFarlane

Sonnet CXVI

By William Shakespeare

Let me not to the marriage of true minds
Admit impediments. Love is not love
Which alters when it alteration finds,
Or bends with the remover to remove.
Oh, no! It is an ever-fixed mark
That looks on tempests . . . and is never shaken.
It is the star to every wandering bark
Whose worth's unknown, although his height be taken.
Love is not Time's fool, though rosy lips and cheeks
Within his bending sickle's compass come.
Love alters not with his brief hours and weeks,
But bears it out . . . even to the edge of doom.
If this be error and upon me proved,
I never writ, nor no man ever loved.

ChAPTER 35

Munich, Germany 2008

Andy and Aniela had enjoyed a wonderful day. It wasn't surprising that the town had earned the moniker of "Athens on Isar", as its development along Neo-Classical lines made it a magical place to explore. They strolled along Ludwigstrasse and Königsplatz, admiring the impressive architecture. The interior of the baroque Asamkirche, built between 1733 and 1746, astounded Andy. He could have stayed much longer, but gave in to Aniela's pleading.

"Come, my Andrew, I am so hungry We are near to Viktualienmarkt. We must eat. Then we can bring our packages to our rooms, *ja*? Let us go, *bitte*?" She pulled on his arm.

"*Wie spät ist es*?" he asked, his head held back as he gazed at the intricate ceiling with its ribboned columns, statuary, and painted dome. Despite the dimly lit interior, he was overcome by the degree of embellishment on every surface, especially the dynamically shaped single nave. Andy's eyes were irresistibly drawn to the altar, which featured a magnificently sculpted group of the Holy Trinity.

"It's one o'clock!" exclaimed the frustrated Aniela. "*Entschuldigung*, sorry, excuse me, *entschuldigung*," she said to a group of passersby into whom Andy bumped as she pulled him from the church, his eyes drinking in the magnificence of the small, but unique, church. The origins of Munich had come from a handful of monks who had built an abbey there, giving the city its name (from the word for 'monks'), and it had become a bastion of Catholicism during the Reformation.

They had lunched "on the hoof," walking back to their hotel, Aniela laughing at Andy's American expression. "I must meet this family at

Windward, *ja*? And I must meet the horses! We will go riding together. Do you know how to jump? I used to ride with my Papa." Andy turned to her, surprised. In all their conversations, Aniela had not revealed any particular attraction to animals, especially horses. Now, as she prattled on about her youth, he realized they had more in common than he had realized.

'This is getting better and better,' he thought, listening to her and nodding at the appropriate times, laughing between mouthfuls. 'It all started out of mutual respect, then progressed to mutual attraction, and now there's a similarity in background, at least in likes and dislikes. There's way more to this woman than meets the eye,' he thought, 'and what meets the eye is more than most men hope for.'

Back at the hotel, Aniela dozed while Andy worked on speculative scribbles in the ancient and extinct Semitic language of Akkadian. Some of the images from the copy of the scroll Anton provided had confounded him initially, as the text was mixed with ancient Hebrew, Arabic, and Greek. While cuneiform was one of humankind's earliest forms of writing, it began as a series of pictographs created by the Sumerians in about 3000 BC. Its symbols were formed by drawing on a clay tablet with a blunt reed, creating impressions that were wedge-shaped (*i.e.,* "cuneiform"). It underwent alteration for over two millennia and was ultimately adapted for languages of ancient tribes (Akkadian, Hittite, Elamite, etc.). Thus, an original pictogram drawn around 3000 BC, became an abstracted glyph written by Assyrian scribes in the first millennium, until it eventually became extinct.

Akkadian cuneiform included phonetic symbols from Sumerian, as well as picture-based characters representing entire words or phrases, known as logograms. The system was not unlike classical Japanese, wherein some of the images are logographic in meaning, and others are phonetic characters. This method of writing continued until the end of the Babylonian and Assyrian empires, when laboriously spelling out words took preference to using signs.

Then in the sixth century, the Assyrian language was heavily influenced and virtually replaced by the Semitic language of Aramaic. Aramaic was the language of established empires, and also the primary language of religious worship of all kinds then prevailing. It was also the original language of the majority of the books of Daniel and Ezra (biblical books), the main language of the Talmud, and the native language of Jesus Christ.

Andy knew that there were different conventions for the transliteration of Akkadian and/or Sumerian cuneiform because scholarly studies had occurred for only the last century. Thus, names written from an older period brought uncertainty as to whether they were Sumerian or Semitic. So one always had to consider the Semitic influence in parallel.

Cuneiform script was capable of distinguishing 14 consonants (transliterated as b, d, g, h, k, l, m, n, p, r, s, š, t, and z), and four vowels (a, e, i, and u). Both as a fusion language, and as a Semitic language, its grammar was very similar to classical Arabic. Its form had gender, verb conjugations, noun, adjective cases, numbers, and unique verb conjugations, much like Latin. Thus, its words and images were "declined" by gender, number, and case. As an avid student of Latin (as was Aniela), Andy had an innate understanding of this structure.

One interesting difference that also provided a complication, was Akkadian sentence order: subject, object, and verb (SOV). This set it apart from most other ancient Semitic languages like Arabic and biblical Hebrew. These had a verb-subject-object order (VSO). To complicate matters, in the latter part of the first millennium BC to the first millennium AD, word order seemed to have shifted SVO/VSO, likely because of the influence of Aramaic.

Thus, it was both plausible and likely that the mixture of symbols between Hebrew, Arabic, and Greek—plus the Akkadian cuneiforms that contained phonetic symbols as well as logograms—would have been combined together in these scrolls as a means of early encryption by their scribes to safeguard the manuscript. Andy recognized that he would have to consider SOV, VSO, and SVO in his cryptanalysis.

Aniela awoke, stretching and yawning, "My Andrew, do you still work?"

"Yes, sweetheart," he smiled in satisfaction, "and I've made some significant progress, if only in my mind. Every small step brings me closer. Are you up for dinner out? I'm ravenous."

"*Wunderbar*. But you must wait a few moments so I make myself beautiful for you," she said, searching through their purchases in the side chair.

"You're beautiful at every time of the day, in whatever you wear, sweetheart. But you're especially beautiful when you're in the tub." Andy responded with a smug look.

"Ooh, you! And when have you spied on me in the bath? This is not what a gentleman does, my Andrew, I am shocked at you. I shall be making to tell your *bemuttern*, so you must now behave. Your mama will not be happy to know her son is so naughty. Do I have your promise?" Aniela stood waiting, hands on her hips.

With his hand over his heart (but with fingers crossed behind his back), he said, "I promise," trying for all the world to look contrite.

"What a beautiful evening," he said as they strolled back to the hotel. "I couldn't eat another morsel. I absolutely love German cuisine. And I love being with you. And I love you, love you, love you!"

"I love you too, *liebchen*. At this moment, I am the happiest woman on the planet," said Aniela, nimbly placing a kiss on his cheek. At that moment, all seemed right with the world.

They came at them without warning, grabbing Aniela from behind, striking only a glancing blow at Andy's back as his "sixth sense" caused him to turn when his attacker was in mid swing. To the right behind them, Andy heard the instantly recognizable click of an automatic revolver being pulled back and released. Then Aniela screamed. One of them had her left arm twisted up behind her shoulder with his other arm around her throat.

"Silence, bitch!" he sneered, as he dragged her struggling, kicking body back into the shadows of the alley.

Andy dove for the ground rolling, deflecting his fall by his still healing shoulder. At the same time, he kicked out with his left foot, which found its mark in the man's groin. His attacker was off balance, having followed the thrust of his misplaced blow. The forward impetus augmented the effect of Andy's well-placed kick. As the man bent over, stumbling forward and wheezing in pain, Andy rolled to his feet and punched him in the chest. He hoped he had hit the "soft spot" where the diaphragm is most vulnerable. He felt the feedback of the punch all the way to his shoulder, but it had been a good, solid hit that threw the man over backward, his head hitting hard on the pavement. With any luck, he might be dazed or out cold for several minutes . . . minutes that could mean life or death for both of them.

"Stand still," a voice called out, "or your little friend's neck will be broken like a bird's."

Andy stood panting in a bent position, hands on his knees, as the phantom materialized into a small man dressed in a dark, expensive cashmere topcoat. He came forward, the gun aimed directly at Andy's chest. He had gleaming, ferret-like eyes, the eyes of a predator.

"So," he said, "you are the famous American," walking around Andy, who was breathing hard. "Not so much of a man, it seems," he sneered, signaling to his associate to push Aniela forward. Her attacker had released his hold on her throat, but had her by the hair, grasping tightly and pushing her roughly. "You can let her go now, Nawaf. She will not leave, will you, pretty one?"

Aniela looked forlorn and confused as she shook her head in agreement. Rubbing her skull as if to soothe it, she sent Andy a look that acknowledged that the chip was still safely embedded in her braid.

As Andy rose to face his captor, the man swung to pistol whip him in the head. Andy's reaction was swift. He moved just enough so that the pistol swiped and bloodied only his cheek, rather than knocking him unconscious. Andy felt his face split with the blow, and blood streamed down his cheek and neck. Aniela crumpled to the pavement sobbing.

The man on the ground had regained consciousness, gathered himself, and moved toward Nawaf Fakar and the leader. "I will beat you to death while your woman watches you bleed!" he spat at Andy.

"Tazim, you bring us no honor," the small man said, wiping his revolver on Tazim's shirt to clean the bloodied barrel. Ali Atiq pulled the revolver back slightly, and aimed the silenced muzzle to Tazim's chest and fired once, dropping the man.

"Nawaf, place this garbage into the alley quickly, before he spills his blood all over this nice, neat German stone walk."

As Nawaf Fakar moved in front of Aniela to take hold of the fallen Tazim, she sprang to life, slicing his throat from ear to ear with the small, concealed knife she had removed from her boot when she slumped to the ground. She thrust his body into Ali Atiq with all her strength, whose second fired round hit the man's dead body. Agile, he sidestepped, throwing the body out of the way, raising his revolver to take aim at Aniela. He was not quick enough.

Andy leapt toward the man only a split second after Aniela shoved the knifed Nawaf toward Ali Atiq. He was taking aim at Aniela as the two collided. Andy's body bulk threw the man completely off balance. His chop to Ali Atiq's wrist released the man's grip on the revolver, which clattered to the ground, skittering out of immediate reach. In a frenzied defense, Andy kneeled on Ali Atiq's chest, grabbing his hair. He pounded his head into the stone until blood oozed from his smashed skull. It all happened in a few short minutes. Three dead men lay around them.

At that moment, a Citroën roared up to the curb. A woman leaped out, calling to them in French, "Hurry, here!" Aniela moved over to Andy, her knees bent with the bloodied knife in attack position. A large, homely man exited the car and opened the rear door, holding his hands up to forestall any action from the two victims.

"*Mon nom est Claude*. This is my partner, Sofia. I am a friend. *Bien fait*, pardon," gesturing toward the scene. "*S'il vous plait?*" The man swept his arm, signifying an invitation to get into the car. The petite woman ran from the side of the car and pulled Andy to his feet, all the while watching Aniela closely, gesticulating for Aniela to remain calm.

"Come! We can waste no time. I am a friend of Bull Lassiter. You must trust me," she said in accented English. Looking sharply at Aniela, she nodded, "You may keep the knife as a sign of good faith, but you shall not need it with us, mademoiselle."

As the car sped away, Sofia turned to the two in the rear. "Are you both all right? Here, drink this." She offered them a thermos filled with coffee. "Claude is never without his coffee; he is addicted to it," she said, trying to relax them with a piece of normality. Aniela sniffed it, murmured something unintelligible, and took a sip. Andy declined in French, asking her a question. "I will explain all to you in a bit. But first, my friend, I am sorry we were too late. Still, you both did well from the looks of things. Did you kill them all?" she said, switching to her native French in acknowledgment of his fluency.

Aniela burst into tears, burying her face against Andy's shoulder. He flinched and grimaced. "Easy, babe, that's the ski shoulder, and the one I fell on, and the same one that threw the punches. I think I've done some serious damage to it." It was only then that Aniela noticed that Andy's hand was dripping blood.

"Claude," said Sofia, "turn left at the next corner, *c'est urgent*. We need to get him to a *médecin*." Turning to Andy and Aniela, she said, "Do not worry, we have a trusted colleague," as Andy's head slumped forward, and darkness swathed him like a shroud.

After being examined, dosed with painkillers, his cheek stitched, and his shoulder and arm wrapped, Andy felt as if he were in the land of the living again. Sofia and Claude had brought them to a confederate, awakening the woman who proved to be a German and French speaking English doctor who had lived on in Munich following her husband's death. She served them all chicory-tasting strong coffee with cheese and biscuits, once her professional duties were completed.

"I'm afraid you've damaged the lateral head of the Triceps Brachii muscle, the Teres Major and Minor muscles, and the Deltoid muscle, with some minor damage to the tendon of the TB muscle. The fascia is torn, separated, and in contraction. That's where most of your pain is focused. I don't think the epimysium or perimysium is compromised on any of them, although the fascicles are sending nerve pain messages by the trillions, it seems!" She grinned, pleased with her diagnosis.

"In English please, doctor," groaned Andy.

"Right, too technical, what? Yes, well essentially you've reopened, torn and separated the keloid . . . umm, the overgrown scar tissue. Had a previous or recent problem, did you?" At Andy's nod and Aniela's embarrassed look, she continued.

"There you have it, then! Your little scuffle tore up the scar tissue, separating the sheets of tissue that hold the muscle fibers together, and tore the tendon that holds the muscle to the bone, as well as the erythema nodosum. Oh, umm, the fatty tissue under the skin, that is. But, the good news is that this type of injury heals itself well with proper rest, nutrition, and remedial exercise therapy. You must keep yourself wrapped, Mr. Stanton. Your body will heal, but it must be given time to do so. There you are, then. Understood? Good, how about some more coffee?"

They stayed long enough to partake in the doctor's hospitality, which gave Andy and Aniela much needed time to settle down and collect themselves after the evening's events. After the second cup of coffee, they bade the doctor goodnight with effusive thanks. Claude paid her handsomely and, as she and Sofia kissed goodbye, she cautioned Sofia to be careful.

"I got a note from Colette last week. She didn't sound herself at all. She told me there are some nasty things afoot, which of course means the two of you will be in the thick of it. Watch yourself, my dear. You're not invincible, you know." Sofia smiled, nodded, and hugged her one last time.

Safely lodged back in the French couple's rooms, Andy and Aniela recounted their frightening episode. Claude had gone to fetch some of their belongings from the hotel. Sofia expanded her initial explanations of their connection with Lassiter, which went back several years.

Although Lassiter had not contacted her directly, she had had a message from one of his operatives, Ileana Muscovici, who had been working at the Vatican and was a "special friend" of several years. Sofia shared with them the facts, as she knew them. Ileana had thoughtfully provided Sofia with the code word message to validate Sofia to Andy, which she had hastily blurted out before they entered the car at the scene of the attack.

"You must understand, my friends, that the nastiest of the nasty are sniffing for you. My superiors have had Claude and me on watch, and we have tried to keep a safe perimeter around you. But now, since our last instructions, it appears that we are mobilized in your defense and safekeeping until your people arrive.

"Ileana should be here tomorrow with some others. We will then decide how and when to safely get you out. But for now, you need rest." Rising, she walked to the sideboard and poured brandy into two snifters. "This will help you to sleep. I shall remain here with you to await Claude. You must not worry. You have done well."

Aniela helped Andy to his feet and together they followed Sofia to the bedroom suite, Andy's good arm leaning heavily on Aniela's shoulders. As she closed the door softly behind them, she thought, '*Mon dieu*! They have been through hell, she is not even an operative, and still she does not crumble, but helps him. There is more there than it would seem.'

She lit a Gitanes Brunes, her favorite brand of French cigarette. "Ah," she exhaled, slumping on the couch. Her thoughts drifted to Colette Franqua.

Chapter 36

Munich Airport, Spring 2008

Ileana had installed herself in the airport coffee shop while the men saw to the baggage and transportation. Francesca Virante should be arriving soon. It had been a long shot, but Lassiter was prepared to call in all his chits once it was learned that not only the Romanian (working for the Russians at the moment) and the Arabs, but the dreaded Al-Fulan siblings were all concentrating on Andy. In a very short time, White Horse had become a sensitive issue within the intelligence community.

Lassiter had decided that the quietest, and therefore safest, way to arm their team was for Ileana to work through Francesca, who was a Lieutenant Commander in the famous Italian Carabinieri. Although its official name was Arma dei Carabinieri, the Carabinier Corps was the national gendarmerie policing both military and civilian Italy.

They had met in Rome during Ileana's undercover assignment regarding the disappearance of some of the Vatican's most ancient works, including painted scrolls, carved tablets, and early papyri. She had been working under the auspices of Cardinal Monteverdi, a man who recognized no conflict in his loyalty to God v. his loyalty to those whom he called "God's soldiers."

Francesca normally worked with the Specialist Unit Division (Rome), but had been assigned to the TCP (Comando Carabinieri Tutela de Patrimonio Culturale-protects Italy's cultural heritage) in its work with the NTPA (Nucleo Tutela Patrimonio Artistico-specializes in protection of artwork and recovery of stolen paintings), both of whom had been called in to the Vatican to assist Cardinal Monteverdi by special request of the Pope.

She and Francesca had hit it off immediately. They had dubbed themselves the "Dynamic Duo" from Batman and Robin following an episode resulting in the capture of a well-armed, upscale gang of art thieves with deep-pocketed international collector-clients. They had used wiles, brains, fortitude, and their "special abilities" to solve one of the greatest, but unpublicized, heists in history. That little jaunt had resulted in Francesca's promotion to the rank of Lieutenant Commander.

It had taken only a phone call with limited explanation to get Francesca on a plane to Munich. Her network routinely supplied both ordinary and special weaponry to its staff members because of their diverse needs. When Ileana suggested it as a safe way to provide their team with necessary equipment on-site, Lassiter had jumped at the chance. Short of flying the team and required supplies in a special aircraft (which would raise too many questions and complications with governmental intrusions), their access to equipment and weaponry through Francesca was far more workable and time economic. Given the intelligence community is relatively small, despite one's affinity or connection to a particular group, it is common to extend and receive help amongst one's contacts.

Francesca and Ileana had arranged to meet in the coffee shop to then hook up with the men and meet at their hotel suite to plan the mission. 'This could be very interesting,' she thought, 'but in the least, it will be fun to see the dynamics,' she mused, thinking specifically of the handsome, sexy Morales.

Ileana's green eyes smiled as Francesca walked toward her. Previously a model, Francesca was almost six feet tall, had the longest legs Ileana had ever seen, and although slim, was very shapely in all the right places. "*Ciào, ciào!*" called the lovely Francesca, opening her arms to give Ileana a hug. "Look at you! Ah, I miss you, my best friend," she said, kissing both cheeks and laughing. Batman and Robin aka The Dynamic Duo aka Francesca and Ileana walked arm in arm toward the car rental desk, chatting incessantly.

"Hey, *cuate*, take a gander at what's coming our way." Noonan elbowed Morales. "Some Italian beauty, don't you think? I didn't know they made cops like that over here. She's just my size. Too bad for you, Morales, you'll need to put lifts in your shoes."

"Holy Molé, she's a looker. But don't they make a funny pair? Tall and short, light and dark, but . . . beautiful and beautiful!" grinned Morales, standing to attention as the women approached.

Ileana said, "Hail, hail, the gang's all here, guys. Let's go."

The remainder of the team rose from benches and chairs looking not unlike a business delegation. After hasty introductions and the inevitable teasing remarks, they proceeded to the rental car area. Hennecke had arranged two vehicles for their use: a large horsepower Mercedes sedan for Ileana, Hennecke, Bianca Romm and Kaiser, and a large SUV for Noonan, Francesca, Morales, and D'Orza.

"Wagons, ho!" jibed Morales, waving his arm from the back window of the SUV. The cars left together for the hotel, all occupants smiling and conversing, except D'Orza who kept cracking his knuckles. Francesca noted his unease and reached back to touch his nervous hands.

"Didn't your mama ever tell you that doing so would give you arthritis one day?" Her smile could light up the darkest corner. The small D'Orza felt electricity in her light touch, and stars bloomed in his eyes from her smile. He smiled at her the way one smiles when one sees an angel.

"You're cute," she said, turning back to the front to concentrate on their drive. D'Orza's heart skipped a beat, and he smiled like a happy puppy.

"Hey, what about me?" teased Morales, winking at her and leaning forward to hook his head around her seat.

Francesca blew him a kiss and patted his head.

Chapter 37

Birmingham, England, Spring 2008

The combined flight had been long, but Marcy and the others (seated in a block in the economy section) had made the time pass quickly. Once they were on the transatlantic leg, it was rather like a cocktail party—everyone moving about the cabin to stop and chat with friends; laughter, teasing, and bawdy jokes proliferating. Following a typical airline "cardboard" meal, everyone settled down to sleep, read, or don headphones. Before she realized that the almost 12-hour ordeal had passed, they were landing at Birmingham International Airport, then standing in the endless line for Immigration, and finally battling the crowds at the baggage conveyors to secure their luggage.

Her arrangements had been made by Lars' secretary, who had negotiated volume rates and determined hotel and car assignments for staff. The initial part of Marcy's stay was to be at the Crowne Plaza Hotel in the grounds of the Birmingham National Exhibition Centre, overlooking Pendigo Lake. It was only a 20-minute drive to the city center and about the same from the airport to the hotel. Unfortunately, Margie had been unable to secure a room for Marcy through the end of the event, and she would have to switch to the Copthorne Hotel at Effingham Park. Marcy did not relish having to pack up and move, but recognized that the event was attended by people from Europe as well as other parts of the world, not just the United States and Great Britain. Thus, rooms were at a premium. She was grateful that her hotels were so close to the show arena, as driving on the opposite side of the road would undoubtedly prove to be a challenge.

"Marcy? Over here!" called Lars. She waved and pushed the trolley in his direction. "Well, you look wonderful after so long a trip. Come on, I've got a car waiting." They moved out of the airport and, to Marcy's surprise, the driver of a large Land Rover signaled to them.

"Lars, is he waving at us?" Marcy indicated to the man.

"Yes, my dear, those are our wheels, and that is our driver. Name's Jamieson, if I recall correctly."

"Wonderful," said Marcy, "I've been worrying about driving over here for the entire flight. Remind me to send Margie some flowers."

Just as she moved to take one of her suitcases from the trolley, strong arms grabbed her from behind, sweeping her off her feet. "What the . . ."

"Hello, my darling," said Tommy, standing her upright after having swung her around in circles. "I couldn't wait to see you!" He kissed her square on the mouth in front of God, Lars, and everyone.

"Cheers, Lars. Welcome to merry ole England." Tommy grinned and embraced Lars, turning back to Marcy. "Well, my sweet, are you ready for the adventure?" Marcy was taken aback, not in the least by the sheer force of Tommy's personality, but also by her surprise in seeing him at the airport.

"Well, hello yourself. Wow, what an impressive sense of timing. A few more moments, and we'd have missed you."

"Lars, you have an incredibly efficient and romantic assistant in Margie," Tommy grinned. "She helped me plan this from front to back. Fabulous, what?" he said grinning like a chimpanzee.

"Plan? Plan what? I get the feeling there's more to this than your surprise of meeting us when we got in, am I right?" Marcy looked at Tommy suspiciously, noting that he could not stand still. He reminded her of Luke and Matthew as little boys.

"Ah, let me see . . . do I tell her now, Lars, or do I wait until dinner?" Both Lars and Tommy were enjoying teasing Marcy. She loved seeing Lars lighthearted; few smiles had graced his face in the last weeks.

"Blast! I simply cannot wait any longer. Marcy, I've rented a townhouse on Wellington Road in Edgbaston, just a bit outside of the town. Mummy thought it would keep me out of the various dens of iniquity so prevalent in Birmingham, or at least that's what she said. You'll love it. It's a period Georgian townhouse with a corner position. It's rather new, dating only from the 1840's, but with much of its original period features intact, so it's got some character, at least. It's got four bedrooms and four reception rooms, so when Lord and Lady Brandon come to visit, no one will be crowded. What say you? Are you surprised?"

"Good for you, Tommy. It's still close enough to the arena, isn't it? It wouldn't make much sense to have to do a long drive after an exhausting day." Marcy raised her eyebrows, but was secretly excited to see his house, knowing that it would be infinitely more comfortable than a hotel room during hours off.

"Yes, mum, it shan't take me much longer than the rest of the crew. Oh, maybe a few minutes more, but by God, it will be well worth it. Come on, I'll take you there. Lars, can you drop her things at the hotel for me?" Lars nodded, shooing the two of them away.

"You know, I hope you'll feel comfortable staying at "Wellington" some of the time. There's plenty of privacy, and you might find you need a break from everyone." Tommy's eyes remained on the road, but the muscle spasms in his jaw indicated his tenseness. Marcy lifted a finger to trace his jaw line.

"We'll see, Tommy, we'll see. Let's just take first things first, okay? I've got a lot to do initially, and then we should connect with Harry and Sandy. But if my days aren't hellish, then there's a good chance I can come and visit you. That good enough for now?"

"Of course, my pet, whatever you want. I just wanted you to know that my door is perpetually open to you at any time of the day or night, for however long." The Alpha negotiated the roundabouts with ease, zooming down the A38 until they turned onto Wellington Road in the Calthorpe Estate.

"Wow," said Marcy as they drew up to the white two-story detached period townhouse. "This isn't exactly like the townhouses back home," she said with eyes wide. "I like the royal blue door to the stable."

After his tour of "Wellington House," Tommy took Marcy to her hotel, accompanying her to her room. Her bags had been delivered, as per Lars' promise. On the side table was a glorious display of flowers, a tray of fruit, cheese, and biscuits, and a bottle of chilling Veuve Cliquot, her favorite champagne.

To her surprise, the note simply said, "Love, Tre." She was embarrassed, as she had been certain that Tommy had arranged the surprise. She turned to Tommy, saying, "Would you care for a glass of champagne before dinner?"

"Lovely," he said. "Here, let me get that for you. An admirer?" he teased, removing the card that had been taped to the bottle. Noting the name, the flare in his eyes was unmistakable, but quickly controlled as he removed the cork with a flourish. "To a successful show, and an even more successful visit," he said, smiling.

She showered and changed, leaving Tommy in the sitting area. They were to meet the rest of the staff in one of the Crowne Plaza's conference rooms later, as everyone was seeing to their own arrangements for dinner.

Dinner was peppered by various people stopping at their table, as both staff and competitors wandered in dribs and drabs into the avant-garde blue and gold room. The hotel was modern, decorated in bright colors, and devoid of any furnishings or artwork that might portend to British history and tradition.

Once the meeting was concluded, people filed out of the conference room clutching their exhibition packets, chattering excitedly, and making plans to visit the exhibition grounds or sample some of Birmingham's nightlife.

"Lord knows, this town is not an 'English gem,'" said Tommy frowning. "I know a lot of folks think it gets a bad rep simply because it's so industrial hereabouts, and I don't think it's because the town has become such a mix of ethnic groups. It's just that its ugly, uh well, unattractive to my eye, even with the recent upgrades." He corrected himself when he saw Marcy's expression.

"Oh, Tommy, that's an awful thing to say," said Marcy. "I'm sure there are lovely parts. Why only yesterday I heard someone talking about visiting Althorp House. That's where Diana, the Princess of Wales, is buried, isn't it? On an island in a lake on the grounds? I hear there are paintings by Van Dyck, Gainsborough, and Reynolds in the collection there. I just adore Gainsborough."

"Yes, my sweet, that's true, and good for you for knowing about Diana. But the point is, that's in Northamptonshire, not Birmingham, here in the South Midlands. Oh, it's still do-able, and there are other places one can visit on a day trip, but Birmingham itself, well, its only claim to fame in my book is that it has more canals than Venice!"

"Nonsense." said Marcy, flicking through one of the hotel brochures. "I'd like to go to the gay quarter south of New Street Station tonight. This says it's a sharp and trendy place that stays open until the early hours. I'm off tomorrow afternoon, so if you're available, I think the museum and art gallery on Chamberlain Square would be good, and then maybe the Think-tank on Curzon Street? It says here that the city's industrial heritage is . . ." Marcy interrupted her sentence when she saw Lars running toward them with a worried look on his face. Tommy followed the direction of her gaze.

"Oh, am I glad I caught the two of you before you left! You'd better get your bag and come quick. I'll meet you at the grounds in the veterinary building." Lars dashed off again calling after another of his staff members, leaving Marcy and Tommy looking at each other in bewilderment.

"Do you think it's starting up all over again?" she said to Tommy, whose face had already hardened. "I suppose I should change quickly; I've only brought a few dressy things with me, and it would be stupid to ruin this dress." He grabbed her elbow and steered her toward the elevators. When they got to Marcy's room, the telephone was ringing. "Would you get that, Tommy, while I just zip out of this dress into some work clothes?" she said, dashing to the bathroom after grabbing some clothes.

"Dr. Stanton's room." Tommy said crisply. "Yes, Tre, Marcy's here. But I'm afraid she's dressing, old man, and . . ." Tommy looked at the phone, shrugged, and placed it quietly in the cradle.

"Who was it?" she said, trotting in, clad in slacks and a shirt. She sat to put on socks and shoes. "Tommy? Who was it?"

"It was Tre. I'm afraid he didn't react well to my being here. He hung up before I could explain or take a message. I'm sorry, dear heart." Marcy's shoulders slumped. "But we've got no time for this now, come on. We've got to get to the grounds," he said, taking her hand and pulling her to her feet.

Chapter 38

Munich, Germany, 2008

"Okay, that about wraps it up," said Helmut. They had had a productive meeting and each of them had thoroughly discussed all elements of his/her assignments with the group entire.

Helmut Kaiser, Conrad Hennecke, and Angel "Monkey" D'Orza were to try to make contact with Andy and Aniela at their hotel after scoping out the locality, as they had a position courtesy the D.C.R.G. for them. They French had finally admitted to Washington that their team had been shepherding the pair, albeit at a distance. Their "take" on the situation based on the reports of their embedded agents had caused Washington to take some additional covert actions of its own.

Francesca Virante would take James Noonan to a safe Carabinieri-owned warehouse to choose arms, supplies, and other equipment the teams might need. She had already arranged for an unmarked panel van to be delivered to the hotel for their use.

Rico Morales and Ileana Muscovici would try to set up a meeting with Sofia Bertrand and Claude Fournier, either at their hotel or wherever the pair chose, if they were successful at establishing contact through Ileana's "insider" knowledge of Sofia's safe post boxes. Sofia and Claude had separated themselves from Andy and Aniela, after stowing them in a secure flat.

The women (Ileana, Sofia, and Colette) all maintained post boxes in several of Europe's main cities, with prearrangements for mail forwarding (failing pickup) depending upon their physical location while on assignment. Previously, Ileana had sent Sofia a note to three of her best guesses. Albeit somewhat delayed, Ileana was betting that

Sofia had been alerted that she and some others were on their way to help Andy.

Fairly certain that the French agent would be in Munich by now (since Washington had been in contact with the D.C.R.G.), Ileana and Rico headed for the post office. The D.C.R.G. would have no one but Sofia and Claude assigned to this gig, Ileana was sure.

It was not so much that Sofia and Claude would be unwilling to meet, but they might not have the same degree of flexibility to engage, as did their American counterparts. Although the D.C.R.G. was currently cooperating with Washington, it was a matter of protocol. Nonetheless, Ileana believed that the situation was developing such as to make Sofia lapse into her characteristic "renegade" instinctive behavior to safeguard her mission in favor of "towing the party line." She had risked reprimand by her superiors many times previous. Because of her shrewd judgment and almost prophetic read of situations, Sofia had earned much-deserved respect in cloak-and-dagger circles. Ileana also knew that Lassiter regarded her highly.

Bianca Romm was to remain at the hotel suite as liaison, transmitting information from one team to the other, and receiving any directives from Washington.

Everyone would keep in touch with Bianca at the appointed times, with a view to returning to their temporary HQ at the hotel suite by late afternoon or early evening. Looking at his team with satisfaction, Kaiser said, "Let's mount up."

Later, once everyone was in position, Kaiser posted himself on a stone bench under a tree opposite Andy and Aniela's hotel. He had a sketchpad and pencil, and his rendering of the architecturally detailed building was both accurate and could help him pass muster as an artist, should anyone look too hard at him.

D'Orza was fiddling with the engine of their vehicle parked slightly to the right of the hotel, a dirty rag hanging from his jeans pocket, and his hands suitably covered with smudges, as he repacked tools and examined a bogus fan belt.

Hennecke, the quintessential German professor, entered the building, with a knapsack and worn brief bag. His task was to make contact if they were in residence; to break into their room, if they were not.

Kaiser saw the pair stroll by the hotel shortly after Hennecke had entered. The man slowed, looking hard at D'Orza who didn't turn a hair, although Helmut knew that Monkey's antennae would have pricked.

He just kept mumbling and fiddling, occasionally uttering an expletive. Satisfied that he was legitimate, the man caught up with the tall woman with whom he had been walking. He whispered something to her; she looked back at D'Orza, and laughed. They paused at the corner one building past the hotel, crossed the street, and entered a small café.

'Come on, Conrad, come on, buddy.' thought Kaiser. Hennecke reappeared at the front of the hotel, looked at his watch, and placed a newspaper under his arm. He paused, seemingly intrigued by D'Orza, feigning a normal person's momentary curiosity, and then walked down the street passing Kaiser. The signal given, D'Orza slammed the hood of the car, started the motor, and drove around the corner to the pickup point.

Kaiser waited an appropriate time, rose from the bench, and walked into the café. The man and woman had chosen a table in the corner by the window, providing a diagonal view of the hotel entrance. Kaiser chose a small table near them, ordering coffee and a snack. He could just make out their quiet conversation, but unfortunately it was in Arabic, in which he was not fluent. 'Damn, Hennecke should be here.' he opined to himself.

Removing his phone, he placed a call, whispering a few terse words. As he left the café, he was pleased that the pair did not even glance at him. He passed Conrad at the door without even looking at him. Fortunately, Helmut knew that the two Arabs had not seen Conrad exit the hotel. 'For once, timing is on our side,' thought Kaiser, as he walked around the corner to D'Orza in the waiting vehicle.

As Hennecke sat devouring the grilled curryworst, he ordered more Federweisser wine, asking the waiter to bring a small portion of *zwiebelkuchen* onion tart with *spargelzeit* (thick, white stalks of asparagus, extremely popular in Germany), as he sopped up the sauce with a bread roll. Acting the part of a native was second nature to him. As he ate, he read a paperback book in German while unobtrusively monitoring the Arabic man and woman, his "hearing aid" amplifying their conversation. The early afternoon sun was shining strongly through the café windows, and Conrad noted that the woman was fidgeting and only picking at her food. She had removed her black leather jacket. Hennecke noted that she wore a provocatively low top, and was generously endowed for such a muscular, slender woman. He smiled to himself, thinking of Rico's reaction to the description he would later supply.

"I hate this country," Fatimah said to Saleh. "Just look at the food these people shovel into their mouths. There is not even any fresh fruit on the menu." She dipped her pita bread in the hummus. "What I would not give for some *taboula*[38] or *warak domali*[39], but no, only *würste*, potatoes, *spaetzle* and beer, and everything with sauce or gravy." She fidgeted. "It is hot in here; how long must we stay?"

"Calm yourself, Fatimah. We shall leave soon, but I want to see if our prey is about and look closely at these surroundings so we can make a good plan. Order yourself some wine, since you don't like the coffee. But be still, I do not want you to draw attention to us."

Conrad finished his meal, closed his book, and signaled to the waiter. As he rose, he glanced at the man and woman briefly, smiling at the woman as she looked up at him. He inclined his head and turned for the cash desk.

"At least the men know a beautiful woman when they see one," said Saleh, attempting to mollify his sister.

"Yes, perhaps this country is not all bad. They do make good-looking men. When our work is completed, you must promise me some time for fun. Maybe I will try a young German this time," Fatimah said, seductively licking the dripping hummus from her piece of pita, her eyes following Hennecke out the door.

The pen with which he had been underlining passages in the book had taken close-up photos of Saleh and Fatimah. Now back at the hotel, Hennecke was downloading the images onto the small computer that Ileana had purchased when she and Rico went to post a note to Sofia.

The note, if retrieved, would trigger Sofia's reaction. Ileana hoped they would soon be in touch, as she and Rico had no idea where the French team was staying while in Munich. They might have gone to ground; they might be in a hotel; they might be in safe house; they might be in a gasthaus. With the hundreds of places to stay in such a popular city, they simply did not have the time to do a search. Until they received some confirmation from Washington, all Ileana could hope was that other agencies were aware that the American and Austrian were the subject of concentrated focus by the Arabs and others, and that Sofia would frequently check her safe post box for incoming messages. Its use for direct contact had been used only a handful if times before by Ileana over many years; it was not a privilege one abused.

Conrad used an embedded safe access created long ago for occasions just such as this. The disk he had created and inserted into the small computer was protected by a complex network of feedback viruses, firewalls, trap doors, and Trojan horse worms in his security system, all of which prevented lurkers, hackers, and cypherpunks from intruding, including those working for the network of outside agencies. Additionally, his digital pseudonym changed every several seconds, and even that sequence was a mathematical codex known only to a few. As he suspected, the photos were identified as the dreaded brother/sister pair of assassins known as Al-Mumît aka Saleh and Fatimah [Tariq Khalid Al-Fulan].

The two were fearless, methodical, high-priced mercenaries, brutally successful in completion of their missions. They had consistently eluded capture and takedown, the most notable of which was when Corruthers was still in the field. The scar that ran from the corner of Corruthers' right eye to the point of his jaw had been a parting gift from Fatimah. Conrad knew that Corruthers was monitoring the same link, and could picture that scar reddening with long-promised vengeance and anger.

"USE CLYDESDALE / BARDOT DIAMOND / STOP HARLEYS / COSSACKS RIDE" read the enigmatic message that flickered on the screen for only fifteen seconds. Hennecke smiled, and the screen went black, as the link disappeared.

Bianca said, "Did you get that, Conrad? What does it mean?"

"It means we use maximum force; that Sofia Bertrand is a hard and brilliant asset for us to use, or rather, work with; and that we are to stop the black leather twins. Corruthers views them as his nemesis, did you know that? No? Well, I'll tell you about it later. The last part is obvious, right?" Hennecke's mind was already miles away.

"You mean that bit about the 'Cossacks'? No, I don't get it." Bianca prompted.

"Oh, that's an instruction to link up with our friendly Russkys, who are on the move. I think Aleksandr was with MI6 in England last I heard, so he should be here in a matter of hours, if he's not here already. He and Lev are a good team. I've worked with them before. You'll like them: they're all business when you need it, but they play hard too.

"The last time I saw Aleksandr, Lev and I had to carry him out of a tavern. But he won a pile of cash by out-drinking everyone and still dancing that crazy Cossack thing. You know, the one where they squat and kick out their legs? What a night that was!"

Noting Bianca's disdainful look, and the impatient tapping of her foot, he said, "Why don't you round up the others? I think we should let them know what we've got." Bianca nodded and patted Conrad's shoulder.

Ileana was just finishing a shower; Rico was setting out a tray of cheese and fruit; Angel was deep into Tai Chi forms near the curtained balcony windows; and Helmut was finishing his drawing. Jim Noonan and Francesca had not yet returned. The telephone rang and Helmut leapt to answer. It was Francesca.

"I've rented the most perfect house just outside the town. So, before I come to dinner, my friend and I are going to drop off our purchases there. I just wanted to call to let you know we shall be a wee bit late. We should see you by 7:30 or 8:00 PM, is that agreeable?" Kaiser knew that meant that Noonan and Virante had had a successful day.

"Do you need any help?" he asked, already knowing the answer. Noonan could unload two vans all by himself in jig time. The man was like a mammoth.

"How kind, but, no. We have it well in hand. See you soon. *Ciao!*" Francesca rang off.

Bianca touched D'Orza lightly on the shoulder, motioning for him to join her. They walked to the loveseat, the others all filling the remaining chairs and couches. Hennecke stood leaning against the doorframe of the adjoining suite door.

"Well, kiddies, Papa Bear has given us a bunch of green lights!" he said, grinning broadly. Smiles began to creep onto the faces of the team as Conrad Hennecke passed along Corruthers' message, received by exclamations of "Yes!" and "Finally!" accompanied by raised fists and D'Orza's back flip.

"I love it when a plan comes together," Conrad said grinning. "Now, if we could rein in our White Horse," he mused, "maybe we could be home for the start of baseball season."

Chapter 39

National Exhibition Center, Birmingham, England

By the time Tommy and Marcy reached the grounds and the veterinary clinic, several of their group had already gathered, everyone asking questions at once. One mare was standing inside the clinic waiting examination. The other had been returned to her stall after collapsing on the groom who had been bathing her after a workout. Apparently, Harry Lochmere had gotten the scrambling horse up on her feet, so others could drag the stricken groom to safety. The man had been more frightened than injured, had only some cuts and bruises, but had been sent to hospital to be checked out. Lars had checked the mare, and she suffered only a scrape and agitation. She would be second on Marcy's list. The mare in the vet clinic stall, however, was groaning and shaking, with quick respirations and a ragged pulse.

"Okay, Tommy, I'm going to need you to use your charm and clear these people out of here." Marcy held her hands up to forestall the questions that flew at her as she entered the clinic. Sandra Dunne was already there trying to calm the mare while the horse's owner paced.

"Marcy, thank God! Can you believe the luck? She makes it here just fine, and two days before the show begins she gets sick. If I didn't have bad luck, I wouldn't have any." Celia Browning stamped her foot in a display of frustration.

"Let's not assume the worst, Celia," said Marcy in a calm tone, despite that she felt anything but calm. She traded a glance with Sandy.

"Can you tell me exactly what happened?" she asked, as she prepared the mare for examination.

Celia recounted how she and her husband had come to the barns to have a walk-through, only to find her mare, Sissy, lying down in the stall, kicking and groaning. Fortunately, Lars was on the premises, and they had summoned one of the grooms to find him. He then ordered the mare to the vet clinic, and told her that he would drive to the hotel to collect Marcy for the emergency. Just after he left, the second mare fell on Hosea, the groom, when he had been bathing her. She had been only lightly exercised by her owner, who had returned to the hotel unaware of the episode or the mare's condition.

"Just you wait until Bernadette hears about this. If you want to see upset, just you wait!" Celia warned. "So don't tell me to stay calm. I'm calm. But Bernadette will be anything but calm, I can tell you. What the hell is going on here? I could understand one, but two at the same time?"

"Look, Celia, I totally understand how you must feel. But there's nothing you can do here, so why don't you go back to the hotel and try to relax? I promise I'll give you a buzz once I know what the situation is. Rest assured, I'll take good care of her and do everything possible." Marcy did her best to give Celia an encouraging smile. Apparently, she succeeded, because the woman nodded, happy to hand the situation over to someone else and be excused.

"Okay, thanks. I could really use a drink anyway. I'll talk to you later. Do your best for her, will you? I'd hate to come all this way with all the expense and not be able to show." Celia gave Marcy a brief smile, nodded to Sandy, and left the clinic without even patting or speaking to her horse.

"Charming," said Sandy. "Are they all so self-centered?"

"No, some are, but most aren't. Celia is just, well, 'everything's always about Celia,' if you get my drift. And Bernadette! Oh boy, I pity Lars. She's got some mouth. She's just plain spoiled." Marcy filled Sandy in on what she would be doing and what would be expected of her as Marcy's assistant. Just as she finished the preliminary exam and was placing her stethoscope around her neck, Lars came into the Exam Room.

"Anything yet, Marcia?" He looked as if he'd seen a ghost.

"Lars, let's all just take a step back, okay? We don't know for sure what this is . . . yet." As she palpated the mare, her face fell. "On second thought, maybe we do. Hand me my Ultrasound probe, Sandy."

It was 1:30 AM when Marcy had finished with the horses. "I feel confident we can leave them now," she said to Lars and Tommy. The same after-care regimen for these mares would follow the ones Marcy treated in the States. "It's the same M.O., I'm afraid," she said morosely.

Harry Lochmere and Sandy Dunne turned the corner, approaching the three of them. For appearance sake, they reported in to Lars. He gave them a look and said louder than necessary, "Dr. Stanton, perhaps you should interview these two members of staff privately, just to make sure you have all the facts for your report. I wouldn't want anything to be amiss when we speak to their owners. If you'll all come this way?" Lars led them to the veterinary office and closed the door.

"What is it now? Haven't we all had enough excitement for one night? I hardly need you breathing down our necks. Isn't that a bit dumb? You could blow your cover!" Lars unleashed his frustration on the two FBI agents, and despite that he was whispering, his tone was agitated.

Harry was about to retort, but was held back by Sandy's hand on his arm. She said, "Now, now, Mr. Borst, take it easy. We're following protocol by reporting in to you, right? That was quick thinking of you, getting us all in here together for an interview before our kind, lady vet has to speak with the owners." Mollified temporarily, Lars sat in a chair, scowling. Sandy turned to Marcy, asking for a copy of her examination results.

"Of course, we'll have to wait for lab confirmation to be sure, but I'm certain I'm right. I assume that's okay with you? I was going to send this stuff out, but come to think of it, we're in England and you might want your colleagues to analyze the results rather than the local lab."

"Yes, Marcy, I would. That'll keep a lid on it, for now. The mares were exactly the same?" Sandy asked, flicking through Marcy's comments on her report. At Marcy's nod and sigh, Sandy said, "Well, folks, that's good news and bad news. The good news is that we have confirmation that we've done the right thing by coming to merry ole England, because the bad news is that the bad guys are still workin' it, and we've got to find out who it is, and put a stop to it. Now, here's what we're going to do."

Tommy drove Marcy back to the hotel, neither of them speaking. When he parked the car, he said, "Shall I come up and tuck you in, my love?"

She smiled and leaned over to kiss his cheek. "No, if you don't mind, I'd rather just collapse. I've only just gotten here, and I'm exhausted after the long trip, a big day, and then this." She leaned her head back, looking up at the stars. "I think I'll just take a shower and go straight to bed. Oh, nuts!" she said. "Is it too late to call home? With all that's gone on, I totally forgot."

"There's about a six-hour difference, love, so that's up to you. I imagine you should call Tre," he said, his voice dropping off to a whisper.

"I was talking about phoning Windward, Tommy, but you're right. I should call Tre, too. Well, I guess we'd better call it a night. Hope you get some rest, Tommy. We've got nothing on tomorrow, so I intend to sleep in a bit. You should, too. I'll see you then. Thanks for all your help," she said smiling at him.

He reached over to open her door. As he righted himself, he touched her face. "I love you, Marcia. I love you by daylight, and I love you by moonlight." He kissed her gently on the lips, and she was surprised . . . not at the kiss, but at the feel of a tear.

Chapter 40

Munich, Germany 2008

Jim Noonan knocked at the door of the suite. As the door opened, he swept Francesca into his arms and strode through the entry hall into the sitting room where the rest of the team was gathered.

"What is this, James? I confess, not many men can pick me up, I am too tall. I like it just the same," she said smiling, "but why are you . . ."

"Ladies and gentlemen, if you please, our heroine!" he said, whirling her in a circle as she laughed convivially. Placing her down, he bowed low in courtly fashion. Returning to his full, impressive height, he related the result of their day to the team.

"Not only did we have the pick of the litter," he said, gesturing to Francesca, "but we had our pick of some mighty fine hardware. I packed that van to the gunnels, and it's all stowed safely at the house Francesca got for us. I can't wait for you to see all of it."

"My, my, how easily pleased you Americans are," she said coyly. "It was nothing but service to good international relations, *sì*?" Francesca accepted the glass of wine offered by Rico with a grateful smile. "Mmm, good, I am parched."

"So? What did you get? Do we have enough stuff for all of us?" Rico was impatient for details.

"*Sì! Abbiamo segnato!*" Francesca raised her glass in a toast. Everyone complied, grinning, but pestered James for the details.

"Well, we've got several Beretta 92's. They're the standard service arm for the Carabinieri, and we've got plenty of 9mm x 19 rounds. I also took some 8000 Cougars since they're smaller, lighter, and easier to conceal than the 92's, but use the same cartridges. Francesca says they use them for the officers, so I thought they'd be a good choice for the women.

"I could have had an FN Minimi, and a couple of Mod.Pm 12 S2 submachine guns as backup, but I opted for the Heckler & Koch MP 5 Submachine guns, because they're the most accurate and controllable. That way, we'll have only one type of box magazine to eliminate any chance of confusing ammo in a clinch. Plus, we don't know what we'll have to deal with. I'd rather be prepared for the worst case. That way, we're ready for anything.

"I figured Helmut could use the Accuracy International AWP for sharpshooting needs with one of the Heckler & Koch MP5's for quick lay down." With a wide grin aimed at Helmut, he teased, "You're gonna' just love that submachine, Helmut. That baby spits 800 rounds a minute, and the AWP has a detachable 10-round box with a replacement time of only 2 or 3 seconds. Not that you would need a second shot," he said with a wicked smirk, "but I figured in case you had to neutralize enemy targets quickly at distances, the long range capability of the AWP would be a huge advantage. I'll have an Accuracy International AWP like Helmut's for sniping or sharpshooting."

"We've also got a couple of Franchi SPAS-15 shotguns with lots of bore and ammo, but the effective range is only about 45 yards, so I figured Monkey and Conrad for those. There's plenty of smoke, tear, and stun grenades, lots of C-4 that I knew would make Monkey smile, and some of the other explosives and bang ware we're used to."

"I'm in love," said D'Orza to Francesca, who ruffled his hair with a smile.

"The icing on the cake, my friends, is that she managed to commandeer two BMW motorcycles—an R85-T and an F650GS. Man, they are sweet! How she did it, I don't know, but we've also got an Agusta-Bell AB 412 helicopter at our disposal. I can't imagine we'll need it, but it's nice to know we can call it up for use. We're solid in the wheel department. In case we need to change vehicles in a hurry, Francesca has arranged a small fleet of mixed cars to be delivered to the house over the next day and a half. They'll be stowed in the garage and other outbuildings."

"What kind of cars?" asked Hennecke and Morales together. They both laughed.

"Oh, a Toyota Carina 2, a couple Alpha Romeos: a 156 and 159, and two Land Rovers: a Freelander, and a Defender-90 hard top. Although

Morales could have a Fiat Punto 60 or ELX2 series, the Stilo 1.9 JTD, or the Ducato, if he prefers." Francesca said with a smug, self-satisfied raise of her eyebrows, looking straight at Rico.

"What did you say, Angel? You're in love? Well, so am I! *Bella, sono inamorato di lei*," said Morales, bending to one knee. D'Orza glared at him.

"*Sciocco uomo*, silly man. Everyone loves me right now. Is it not so?" retorted Francesca, going to sit next to D'Orza, asking for a refill of her wine glass.

D'Orza looked at her adoringly, refilled her glass, and whispered, "*Sí, usted es amado. Usted también es respetado. Todos estamos agradecidos.*"

"Oh, Angel, I am so sorry. I do not speak Spanish," said Francesca looking bewildered.

Angel blushed. "Uh, I said that yes, you are loved, that you were also respected, and that we're grateful. It's true, Francesca, you are, and we are."

"Okay you two, stop with the hormones already. Francesca, Angel's right. We would have had a helluva time getting the supplies we need over here. Things have gotten tight, and we're still black. By the way, that means that you're in for the full enchilada. I can't afford any screw-ups, even unintentional ones, okay?" Kaiser said, looking a little chagrined, hoping he hadn't insulted her by the reference to screw-ups.

"*Certamente*! I assumed it would be so when Ileana called me at the beginning. Besides, I can hold my own, and Ileana is like a baby *sorella*. I must watch her back, *si* baby sister?"

With that remark, Ileana bounded from her perch on the arm of the sofa squealing, and leapt into Francesca's lap, spilling her wine. The clowning eased the tension, everyone laughed, and Noonan suggested they all go to the local Ratskeller for a few hours, since they needed to eat, catch some rest, and be ready for the second phase of their plan to take effect beginning at 2:00 AM.

Across town in their hotel, Sofia and Claude spoke quietly at a card table in the corner while Andy sat scribbling in his notebook. Aniela cuddled close to him. "Have you had any word?" Sofia said, her eyes on the cards she placed on the table.

"No, nothing yet. But it is early. The Americans should be installed somewhere here, but Paris is quiet for the time being." He sipped his coffee looking over the rim at their guests.

"I don't like this at all. We should have heard something by now." Sofia looked over at their charges only to meet Aniela's stare. "Do you need anything, Aniela?" she asked.

Aniela shook her head. "You make plans about us, *ja*? We should know what plans you make, Sofia. Maybe we have plans of our own."

Andy looked up from his notations, looking from one woman to the other. "Let's just sit tight for the moment, okay? We'll be hearing something from my team when they're ready. I know them, and we can trust their judgment. For now, we seem to be safe here. Let's just spin it out for now. Agreed?"

Aniela looked insulted that Andy had not defended her statement, but swallowed her pride and snuggled against him more deeply, glaring at Sofia.

"Claude, I need some air. I will check my post box and bring some pastries back for us. Do you need more coffee?" Claude's face lit up, and he nodded his head emphatically.

Aniela finally smiled.

CHAPTER 41

Wellington House, Birmingham, England

More at ease in his house but uninspired about going anywhere but to the arena, Tommy inserted a disk into the sound system. He orchestrated the opening strains of Aida. Giuseppe Verdi was to Italian opera what Ludvig van Beethoven was to symphony, in Tommy's view. He had copies of serious works like Oberto, Nabucco, Macbeth, and I Lombardi from Verdi's earlier years. Although critics had dubbed his last three operas as his finest, Tommy also loved the height of drama and depth of musical expression in his masterpiece Rigoletto, the unexpected twists and turns of Il Trovatore, and the passion of La traviata. Today, however, the tragic love story of Aida suited his mood. He could not get Marcy's involvement with Tre out of his mind.

Earlier, he had had difficulty concentrating on riding, and Obsidian and Demiluna responded in like kind to his mood. They had thoroughly lackluster workouts. He ended up more discouraged than ever, particularly when he overheard other riders' denigrating comments. Marcy had been busy with Lars, some of the other owners, and horses. He had begged off lunch with friends and returned to his nest. As he listened to Act I, when the commander of the Egyptian army, Radames, dreams of gaining victory over the advancing Ethiopian army, and of the woman he believes to be an Ethiopian slave whom he loves (who is really the captured daughter of the Ethiopian King, Amonasro), Tommy sang loudly, *"Se quell guerrier īo fossi! Celeste Marcia!"*

"I'm flattered!" Tommy spun around at the sound of her voice, surprised and embarrassed. "I'm sure you know it's Celeste Aida. I've never been called 'heavenly' before." She gave him a dazzling smile. "Sorry to startle you, Tommy, but you didn't answer the door, I heard the stereo blaring, and well, I just thought to come to the side French doors. I hope that's okay."

"Of course, of course," he chuckled. "You've just caught me with my pants down, as it were. I love singing to my recordings, but I'm so dreadful that I always do it in private."

"Not at all, you have a . . . an . . . interesting voice," said Marcy diplomatically. In actual fact, Tommy's voice was better than average, but he had never learned volume control: it was all or nothing, a bit like his personality.

"Well, let's leave that subject alone, shall we?" Tommy grinned affably. "I'm delighted you've come, only I had no idea you would. You were very busy when last I saw you. Can I get you a sherry?"

"Yes, thanks, I'd love one." She sat on the sofa, tucking her long legs under her. "It's a bit chilly today, isn't it? I'm glad for the fire."

"Here you are, my darling," said a happy Tommy, perching on the arm of the couch next to her. "Will you let me spoil you a bit? You've been working far too hard, and the event hasn't even begun yet. Pamper me, and say you'll stay."

Marcy looked up at him smiling, and nodded her head toward the French doors. Her overnight bag sat like a ambassador of truce, its gold letters "MAS" gleaming in the afternoon sun.

"Marcy, I can't believe . . . are you sure? How wonderful!" Tommy jumped up to retrieve her bag. "Come on, let's get you settled upstairs."

"You did say there were four bedrooms, didn't you?" Marcy said emphatically. "Just so we understand each other." She hurried up the stairs after him, grinning.

The love between Aida and Radames developed, as the recording of the opera played on.

Springtime in England could be anything from chilly to cold or, conversely, mild and sunny. Later that evening, they sat again before the fire. Although dressed in slacks and a sweater, Marcy had wrapped herself in a chenille throw. They sipped a mellow port.

The British Open Show Jumping Championships were launched in 2003. Since then, they had been held indoors in April. For the first of its four years, the show was held at the Sheffield Arena, but was moved to the NEC Arena in Birmingham in 2007.

"So dear heart, you see that if I do well here, I shall then move on to the All England Jumping Course at Hickstead. That's West Sussex, by the way. There are two major international horse shows there each year: The Derby Meeting in June and the Royal International Horse Show in July. The Derby lasts four days and has substantial prize money. They've got an 1195 meter course with some very tricky jumps. It's probably the greatest challenge any of us have. Jumping the Devil's Dyke, I mean," he said in answer to her quizzical expression.

"The FEI World Final is at the end of April on the continent and, since I can't be in two places at once, if I do well here I'll opt instead for the FEI European Show Jumping Championships next year. They're held only every two years. We'll see how things go."

"Mmm," she said contemplatively, "so I guess I won't be seeing much of you after this little stint in Birmingham, will I?"

"Not unless you agree to marry me," he said softly, as he poked at the fire. "But, I promised I wouldn't raise that, so I'm not. It was just a silent thought that fell from my lips by accident. Forgive me?" He turned back to her smiling, holding his hand over his heart.

"Who could resist forgiving you? You look like a little kid sometimes, a wicked, wicked little boy!" They laughed easily together. "Oh, this is heavenly," Marcy said.

After a companionable silence, "You know, Tommy, I've been unfair to you. Not that I meant to be deliberately unfair, but in retrospect, I have been unfair."

Frowning, Tommy inquired, "How so?"

"Well," Marcy began, "I've benefitted from your passion and commitment concerning the horses. That was made clear to me by the reactions of some of the other owners over the last two days. I just assumed you'd join with me in this thing, with all its ups and downs, extra work, and inconvenience. I never even asked you. You've got a life of your own, things to do, plans to make, obligations. I feel as if I've taken advantage of your good nature. I owe you an apology, and I hope you'll accept it."

"Don't be a silly goose. Of course, I was willing to help by working with you. It was my mare, after all. Besides, don't you know by now that I'd do anything you asked of me, if it was in my power to do so?"

He pulled her close, lifting her chin. They looked at each other for what seemed like a long time, but was in reality only several seconds, before they reached for each other hungrily.

The passion of Rachmaninoff's Piano Concerto No. 2 filled the room. The fire crackled and blazed higher.

Chapter 42

Munich, Germany, Spring 2008

"*Salut, buna dimineata*," said Barbu, as he passed Ileana on the street. It took all her instinct and training to maintain her pace, but her heart was pounding. She knew his identity, and wondered if he knew hers. It could have been an innocent courtesy uttered in his own language, but no, Barbu spoke German, as well as French. Had it been innocent, he would have said 'good morning' in German. He knew who she was; damn! What were the chances that she'd pass him on the way to the post office? She felt a piercing sting at the back of her neck, and her legs went immediately weak. Her last recollection as she fell was of strong arms lifting her.

Sofia Bertrand was just exiting the post office. The message from Ileana she had retrieved yesterday afternoon engendered this meeting. She checked her watch. She was late, and that was not like Ileana. As a black sedan passed slowly by, the rear window wound down. Barbu's face painted with a leering grin looked directly at her. He tossed something from the car window. For a moment, Sofia froze, watching the car motor away. When she regained her composure, she quickly retrieved the item. It was a small, linen square embroidered with the initials, "IEM". Ileana Ecaterina Muscovici!

"*Sacre bleu*! He has Ileana. He knows." She walked hurriedly away, trying to think of a way to contact Ileana's team, even though she had no clue where they were.

Rico Morales had been following Ileana a block behind. He had witnessed the entire takedown, too far away to even attempt interference. It had happened very quickly. Her collapse was likely caused by either a well-delivered nerve block, or a small, quick needle jab filled with one of any number of fast-acting drugs one could use to get that effect. Morales had not gotten a good look at the man, as he was dressed in a jacket with the collar flipped up, and a fedora pulled low over his eyes.

As the woman approached, Morales started whistling the French national anthem, La Marseillaise. She looked at him sharply as he smiled, saying, "Mademoiselle Bertrand? Am I glad to see you. I'm a friend of Ileana's. Come on, I'll take you to the others."

Sofia drew her knife surreptitiously, backing away slowly. "Stay where you are!" she hissed.

"Hey, hey, go easy. Look, I'm Rico Morales. I'm not going to hurt you, okay? Let's just take it nice and easy and not cause any fuss. I'm going to walk alongside you to that bench over there. I'm going to put my passport on the bench for you to look at, okay? I'll keep my hands in plain sight all the time, once I get my passport from my pocket. Come on, you saw what just happened to Ileana. Let's cut each other a break. If I'm not who I say I am, you can just fade away, but don't stick me. My people wouldn't take kindly to that, and neither would I."

It all went slow and easy, just as Morales had promised. She confirmed his identity as an American; the rest would have to wait, but she tentatively accepted his explanation. "That *bâtard* abducted my friend," she said to Rico.

"She's my friend, too," said Rico moodily. "Do you know who he was? They were too far away for me to see or do anything, damn it. Ileana was on her way to meet up with you, and I was tailing. I was going to bring both of you to meet up with the rest of us, once she had explained things to you. She thought a mundane trip to the post office would be safe. It wasn't."

"Oh, *merde*! It is all my fault. Shit, shit! I suggested she meet me here," said Sofia stonily.

"Turns out we were all wrong," he said grimly. "Don't beat yourself up. Come on, let's get out of here and figure this thing out with the others." He took her arm and hurried her down the street toward the idling car driven by D'Orza. Holding the rear door open for Sofia, he said, "Step on it, Monkey, we've got trouble!"

Sofia paced while she explained the recent debacle, going back to Ileana's initial contact before she left the Vatican. "I cannot understand how he knew, unless there is a plant at either the Vatican or the post office. It matters not. What matters is that she must be rescued, but I have no idea where he is. I am certain he has Gheorghe with him. They always work together. He was probably driving the car."

"You're sure it was Niculaie?" asked Noonan. "No mistake?"

"Unfortunately for Ileana, no mistake," said Sofia in a flat, depressed tone. She swiped at a tear, showing an uncharacteristic display of temporary vulnerability. "He is a very clever man, a very efficient agent, but brutal. And Covaciu is an animal!" she spewed.

"*Cabron!*" D'Orza pounded his fist into the wall. Francesca went to him, stroking his back. Everyone on the team was shaken by this unexpected turn of events.

"Well, the one good thing is that you have Andy and the girl," Helmut said to Sofia. "If he knew where you had them stashed, he wouldn't have taken Ileana. Her kidnapping serves two purposes for him: One: he sends a loud and clear message that he knows we're here; and two: he's flexing his muscle to let us know he has the edge, that we don't have the upper hand, and that we'll have to deal with him."

Hennecke said calmly, "He'll contact us to bargain getting her back."

"How can he do that?" said Bianca sarcastically. "He doesn't know where *we* are, either."

"Are you so sure? If we can count on anything, it's that we can't be sure of anything where Barbu is concerned, except that he's dangerous." Hennecke sat quietly composed, inspecting his fingernails.

"Look guys, everyone's right here. We know he has her; we know he's dangerous; he took her for a purpose; he'll toy with us for a while, but eventually he'll let us know what that purpose is. The one thing I know about Ileana is that she won't be broken easily, and that'll piss him off. All we can hope is that we can get her out before he gets really serious about working her over." said Noonan, rising to load his sniper rifle.

Helmut said, "Yeah, Jim, you're right. It's my bet, he'll parade her. The only logical place is in the vicinity of the post office where he took her down. Conrad, can you get us images of that piece of crap, Covaciu? I know what Barbu looks like, but I'm not sure about him. Who else needs a refresher?" As Hennecke tapped keys on the laptop, some of the team raised their hands. Bianca looked at Francesca, whose hand was not raised.

"You know them?" she asked.

"Unfortunately, yes, I know them both. They are pigs, *i suini!*" Francesca stalked across the room to join Jim Noonan in loading the weapons they had brought from the house to the hotel earlier.

"Okay, everyone. Familiarize yourselves with the photos and the diagram. Then we're going to post a watch in several places with a little surprise of our own. You're in on this, too, Sofia. We're going to need your help to get Ileana back, and we're going to do a little dance together to get Andy and the girl away safely. Listen up." Helmut unveiled his plan.

Gheorghe Covaciu had driven the big Mercedes well out of town into the countryside. Ileana was slumped in the back seat next to Niculaie Barbu for the entire trip, slowly coming around. She did not open her eyes, even though she had regained consciousness. Using isometrics, she checked her body. Although she suffered a dull body ache and felt like she weighed 300 lbs, basically, she was all right. She knew that Barbu had drugged her to effect the kidnapping, and that her situation was precarious. She also reasoned that he would make use of her abduction in an attempt to either flush the team or coerce them into some sort of a compromise. She tentatively opened her eyes to look into Barbu's face.

"Ah, Gheorghe, the little *wed'ma* is awake." She spat at him. "Oh ho, not nice, witch!" To inspire fear and demonstrate a point, Barbu viciously backhanded her.

"*Svoloch'*! Bastard!" she screamed at him.

He smiled, hitting her again and again, this time with his fists. Gheorghe Covaciu began to laugh.

CHAPTER 43

Birmingham, England

Marcy and Tommy were enjoying a quiet dinner together before his parents' arrival. Lord and Lady Brandon were expected late that night and would stay at Wellington throughout the show in support of their son.

"Yes, Sean, could you bring us a bottle of the Dom Pérignon Cenothèque Vintage '93, please?" Tommy smiled across to Marcy. "It's not Veuve Cliquot, sweetheart, but I think it's time you broadened your palate. Oh, listen to me. That sounds horribly pompous, doesn't it? It's only,"

"Don't worry about it, silly. You're right. I drink champagne so rarely, that when I was lucky enough to find a really good one I loved, it became my favorite. But that was only because of inexperience, not because of discerning, experienced taste buds. But, you must admit, Cliquot is one of the better, luxury champagnes."

As Tommy feigned wiping his brow with his serviette, they laughed together. Marcy picked up the wine list and looked aghast at Tommy. "Are you kidding? That bottle is over $400 by my calculations! Cliquot is bad enough, but this . . ." she shook her head in disbelief.

He took the leather bound folder from her. "If you're going to nose around and complain about what I spend on you, I shall have to be more careful."

"Oh no, Tommy, I wasn't checking up on you. I just thought I would familiarize myself with other kinds of champagne. When I saw the one you ordered, well, naturally I looked, and . . ." Marcy was thoroughly embarrassed. "you don't have to spend a lot of money on me to impress me, Tommy."

"I know, I know, you're a country girl, and all that. Do you seriously believe I'd be that shallow? No, my love, you know I am not. I will admit, however, that this dinner replete with the champers is part of my scheme to sweep you off your feet. And I shall make no excuses for myself. I intend doing precisely that, as much as opportunity and time allows. Ah, here's Sean." Tommy nodded to the sommelier.

As they toasted each other, they were unaware that the braiders, Leonora and Philip, were skulking around the stalls at the show grounds.

"Phil, here, help me. I think she'll stand quiet; she's a pretty old campaigner." Philip released the mare's head with a pat, reached into the bag Leonora extended, and passed her a packet. She quickly inserted her slim arm. "What was that?" Leonora spun around just enough to place pressure on the mare's insides, eliciting a squeal. "Hush, girl. Phil, go check," she said, withdrawing her arm, yanking off the exam sleeve, and gathering up her bag.

"Hey, Hosea," Phil said in greeting to the approaching groom. "You look no worse for the wear. How are you, man?" Hosea stopped to chat to Phil, eagerly recounting the episode that had caused him to go to the hospital.

"They can't pay me enough to go through somethin' like that, again, man," he slurred. "No way, no how. And them bitches, never even gave me a tip for my trouble. Want some?" he said, holding out a half-empty bottle of bourbon to Philip.

"Nah, I can't take that stuff. Makes my ulcer act up. Where you headed?"

"Oh, nowhere, everywhere. Jus' kinda takin' a chill, ya' know? Whatcha' doin' here? Hey, Leonora," he said as she exited the stall with her bag. "Ain't it kinda early for you to braid? Tail'll be all rubbed out by show time." Leonora looked nervously from Hosea to Philip.

"Wait a minute, man, you ain't 'sposed to be here now. Lars said. Only us grooms 'cause we sleep here to keep watch, ya know? Whatcha' doin' here, huh?"

Philip worriedly looked at Leonora. He said to the drunken groom, "Ah, come on now, Hosea," slinging an arm around his shoulder. "No need to worry. It's us, man."

"Nah, nah, I gotta tell Lars, man. My butt's in a sling now, an' I don' wanna get in no more trouble, ya' know? Sorry, man, but . . ."

He never finished his sentence. Philip wrenched his arm around Hosea's neck and snapped it. The man slumped in his arms.

"Philip! Oh, God, Phil, what have you done?" Leonora asked aghast.

"Protected us, that's what. Don't stand there like a ninny, help me get him into a stall." Together, they half-carried, half-dragged the limp Hosea to an adjacent stall. Philip doused his body with the remainder of the bottle, tossing it in with the body.

"There, they'll think it was merely an accident. Perfectly plausible in his drunken stupor. Now, let's get the hell out of here."

Hosea was discovered the next morning when Bernadette came to check the order of go. She had brought some carrots for her mare, but decided on second thought not to give them to her in case the treat might upset her mare's digestion. She was hoping that she would be well enough to show early that evening, and didn't want to do anything that might compromise the horse. She decided, instead, to drop carrots into other horse stall feed tubs since she'd brought them to be eaten. One could never rely on the grooms to do as they were bidden.

"Charles, I won't be a minute. I just want to walk over to see Queen. Marcy said she'd be fine, but I want to see for myself. In the meantime, drop that note off for Lars. I certainly do not intend paying the vet for what is clearly their negligence. Queen's not a sickly mare, so they must have fallen down somewhere.

"I'll only be a minute. Then you can take me for brunch at the hotel. God knows, with all this stress, I will need to rest before tonight. You can arrange a massage for me. Yes, that would be good," she said peevishly as she stalked away. Just as her husband was nearing the show office to deliver the note for Lars, he heard screaming.

The grounds were in a hubbub with police vehicles, people milling about, excited horses, and general confusion. Lars greeted Marcy grimly, as she ran to the main aisle from the clinic office. "What in the world?" she said to him, her eyes questioning. "Not another mare," she said hopefully.

"No, it's worse, Marcy. Hosea is dead. Of all people, Bernadette found him a while ago. The mare next to hers was whinnying and putting up a fuss, kicking at the walls. She says she thought the mare might be suffering like her precious Queen, and when she looked into the stall, that's when she found him. What a mess! She's going around acting like the poor, put upon damsel-in-distress, saying all manner of rotten things about us, the show, the grounds, security, all of it. For Pete's sake, it's Hosea that's dead!"

"Where is he? Have the police taken him away yet? Do you know what happened?" Marcy had a hundred questions, not the least of which was her concern about the condition of the mare in whose stall he had been found.

"Yes, they've removed the body to wherever it goes for investigation and autopsy, I expect. They think he was drunk when he went into the stall. The theory goes that somehow he spooked the mare and she kicked him. He must have hit his head. If he was drunk, his reactions and judgment would have been impaired. But that just doesn't sound like Hosea, you know? He drinks, yes; they all do. But he'd never attend to a horse if he'd been drinking. He'd call someone else. This just doesn't make any sense, Marcia, I know the man. He's been with me for years. Can it get any worse than this?" he said, looking to Marcy for consolation.

"No, Lars, it can't. I'll go over and check the mare, and then have a talk with the constable to try to find out some more. Which one was it?" Lars hurriedly gave her the information, hugged her, and dashed off to do damage control with the gathering fray.

When Marcy finished examining the mare, she was immensely relieved. She found no evidence of tampering, nor was the mare compromised in any way other than slight nervousness due to all the commotion. She could not give her even a small sedative dose, because that was against drug practices for horses at show. Even small amounts of various restricted medicines would show up on the routine blood tests required. Instead, Marcy spent a few minutes with the mare, sharing one of the shortbread cookies she had taken a liking to since arriving in England. Tommy had teased her about always having a packet in her pocket. Now she was glad of her weakness for British shortbread. So was the mare.

As she stood in the stall stroking the mare, she lapsed into her unconscious habit of visually checking everything. There was something peeking out of the mare's left hind shoe. She raised the horse's leg to take a look. A plastic identity badge had gotten wedged just under the rim of the shoe. Fortunately, the open pin mechanism was facing the floor, and had not punctured the mare's sole. Marcy removed the plastic badge. It read "Philip Conover". 'What's that doing in here?' she wondered.

Clearly, with all the scuffle, it had become hidden under the straw, lying undiscovered when Hosea's body had been removed.

The constable told her that he had given orders to staff that nothing in the stall be touched. He had given her permission to examine the mare, of course, and had posted one of his men outside the stall. Marcy knew she had to declare this to the police at once. She would also alert Harry, Sandy, and Lars.

She scratched the mare, saying "Aren't you a good girl! You're going to be fine. In fact, you may end up the star of the show in more ways than one!"

CHAPTER 44

Munich, Germany

Kaiser, Noonan, and Romm followed Sofia to her hotel to meet up with Andy once the team meeting had concluded. Each took a different route at a different time in case they were being tailed, and each was in short wave contact for warning or emergency.

Andy was elated to see them, and filled in the background to their current circumstances. Likewise, Kaiser informed Andy and Aniela of the arrival details of Saleh and Fatimah, and a low-key description (for Aniela's benefit) of Ileana's snatch by Barbu. His update deflated Andy's mood instantly. Aniela remained aloof and silent during the introductions and conversations, the only reaction a curt nod and busy, analytical eyes.

When Helmut and Bianca joined Andy in one of the suite's bedrooms, he said, "Andrew, my boy, that's one spectacular traveling companion. How in the world do you manage it?"

"No thanks to me, Helmut. She was my assigned guide. But since then, she's proved herself times over to be my guardian angel and savior," Andy said quietly with a grim expression. "She's a civ, and yet she killed a man and helped me disable, well, kill, the other. It saved our lives. I took two more out in the mountains when they tried to shoot us, but I don't know who's who. I didn't stick around to find out."

Helmut whistled softly. "This has been a rough one, huh?" Bianca said consolingly, moving to Andy to give him a hug.

"No rougher than any of us have had before, I guess. But for her, having to be on the run, pretending all the time, getting shot at, climbing overland and through a dangerous cave to escape, threatened, roughed up. You know, nothing normal. Well, it's been a lot to ask of someone. She's done amazingly well, but she's starting to crack. I'm worried about her. She needs out of this."

"Are you saying she's no longer dependable?" Bianca asked. "It would be understandable, given what she's been through. How much do you know about her?"

"All I need to know. She's a scientist, she's brave and unselfish and strong. And I, uh, love her." Andy grinned sheepishly at that last phrase.

Shocked, Helmut and Bianca looked at each other, Bianca's eyebrows raising. "So much for keeping one's head and remaining uninvolved on a mission," she mumbled.

"Yeah, I know," Andy said. "I knew that would be your reaction, and I can't blame you. It's not what you think. I tried, but it just kept building and developing. The woman is full of surprises. Sweet, brave, unexpectedly strong surprises. Although it hasn't interfered up to now, I am concerned that either her good sense or my professional judgment might be compromised depending on how things develop. So as of now, I'm handing all decisions over to you and the team. That okay with you?"

"So, the feelings are reciprocal, I gather," Helmut said with a sigh. "Yeah, that's best for everyone concerned. That way, no matter what happens, no guilt, no official repercussions, no criticisms, right?" They all nodded their agreement.

"Bianca," Andy began as he showed her the reduced printed copy, "this will interest you. I've been able to . . ." Helmut left the two of them hunched over some papers and Andy's notebook, and returned to the sitting room. Aniela hadn't moved from the sofa. Claude was just serving coffee.

"Everything okay?" inquired Jim, looking from Helmut to Aniela to Sofia, and back to Helmut.

Having gotten the gist of Noonan's look, Helmut said, "Yeah, we're solid. But I think we should work out how we're going to get them out of here as soon as possible."

Turning to Aniela, he said, "That okay with you, miss?" Aniela smiled her beautiful smile, nodding her head enthusiastically. It melted Helmut's heart, and he thought 'Oh Andy, you never had a chance, did you?'

Together, they hashed out the pros and cons of two plans. The first would entail drawing out or waiting for contact from Barbu, and hopefully, retrieving Ileana. The second involved getting Andy and Aniela out of Munich to England. They had sufficient personnel, arms, contacts, and other resources. Barring the unforeseen—and there was always an unforeseen hitch in this business—Helmut felt reasonably confident their plans could work.

Claude and Sofia had committed themselves totally to the team's efforts. They had learned through one of their confederates embedded in Saudi Arabia of Colette's death at the hands of Salid. Since Andy and Aniela had decimated Salid's team before Sofia and Claude could intervene and help, they had expressed their feeling of an unpaid debt of gratitude, which translated into their cooperation.

"There is one last thing," said Sofia to Kaiser and Noonan. "Even though we know he will send others, there remains one of Salid's scum alive from the original group. His name is Martine. He is mine."

"You will know him by his big ears," piped in Aniela. Everyone turned to look at her.

"He has been with us since the days after we met with Anton. I think it was they who searched our rooms. They all smell." Helmut and Jim looked at each other and burst into laughter, joined by Claude and Sofia.

Two days had passed, and there had been no word from or sign of Niculaie Barbu or Gheorghe Covaciu.

Noonan and Kaiser had split shifts for prearranged sniper position from a low rooftop. Since they needed a woman with whom Sofia could make a fake "contact" to be observed by a watcher, Bianca Romm had enthusiastically volunteered to be the goat in an attempt to draw either Barbu's or Covaciu's attention.

She faithfully walked to and fro the post office daily with a little dog procured by Claude from a rescue shelter, waiting in-between on a bench under the trees, reading a book. Francesca Virante, who had firsthand knowledge of both the Romanians from previous encounters, was a well-armed post office plant covering all exits. Hennecke, D'Orza and Morales manned the vehicles that were parked unremarkably at opposite ends of the street. The two ex-patriot Russians had arrived and linked up with the team. Aleksandr Petrov and Lev Rossovskaya alternately strolled the streets, shops, and cafés, being careful to keep the mix uneven. Amid this background, Sofia Bertrand made her daily trip to the post office. The stage was set; they waited.

Saleh and Fatimah were aware of Barbu and Covaciu's presence in Munich. They were also aware that most of Salid's men had been eliminated by someone, likely the American. Scrutiny of the hotel in which Andy and Aniela had registered had proved fruitless. Saleh was convinced that the pair had holed up somewhere awaiting help from the American's home shores.

"You are likely correct," said his sister, who was lying nude on the chaise on their balcony, soaking up sunshine in the middle of winter. "But I think the easiest way for us to know for certain is to find Barbu. We can watch him, and he will lead us to them. Or, if you prefer, we can take him and I can make him talk. That could be fun." She turned to her stomach, the chill bite of cold air raising gooseflesh.

"Normally, I would not encourage you to sate your unusual tastes, my dear Fatimah, but on this occasion, I believe you are right." Before opening his satellite phone, he massaged some oil onto his sister's back and legs to her expressions of pleasure.

After a short time, he rose and said, "Come, my little viper, we have only a few hours. We must prepare ourselves."

Fatimah looked at him coyly. "You had better have a good reason for interrupting my sunbath, dear Saleh. I was just enjoying the most provocative daydream."

He smiled at her, admiring the tautness of her muscular body, discarding his robe." We shall pay them a visit tonight, perhaps."

As she looked up at him, as beautiful and alluring a man as she was a woman, Fatimah's eyes glinted with malevolent excitement. The prospect of the confrontation with Barbu made her body tingle. She accepted Saleh's hand, wetting her lips.

CHAPTER 45

Birmingham, England

The hotel concierge flagged Marcy as she returned from the show grounds. He passed her an airmail delivery: a letter from Tre. Marcy controlled her urge to rip open the envelope, as she headed toward the elevators. Later, as she relaxed in a hot tub with a glass of wine, she felt ready. Her hands shook only a little, as she withdrew the single page.

Dear Marcy:

Having had little success reaching you by phone, I decided to write. I hope England is all that you hoped it would be, and that your work at the show proceeds well. I miss you.

I would appreciate it if you could give me a heads up when you know the date of your return. If agreeable to you, I'll put in for special leave. We have some unfinished business, you and I, and after all this time, I feel we owe it to each other to settle things between us.

Tommy undoubtedly will be pleading his cause while you are there. There's nothing I can do about that under the circumstances. What I can do, is tell you that I love you, and ask you to keep that in mind during the time you are away.

Time marches inevitably on. I can only wonder if its trail will reveal your footsteps beside mine. You know what my preference would be.

Love, Tre

Marcy read and reread the letter, sipping her wine thoughtfully, the hot bath water making the room steamy. She called to mind Tre's face, his body, his laughter, the sound of his voice. She began to cry. Awhile later, she had regained self-control. A regrettable sadness lodged in the recesses of her heart.

Had she been at home, she would have spent time with Rex on the promontory. But she was not at home, and all her usual comforts were missing. She had to do it all alone.

"Marcia, my dear, so good to see you again," Madeline Brandon said, giving Marcy a warm hug. "Has my naughty son been behaving himself?" Madeline gave Marcy a questioning smile.

"Hello again. No worries; he's been sterling. That's the appropriate expression here, isn't it?" Marcy said, looking over Lord Brandon's shoulder as he hugged her as well. They walked together into the sitting room where Tommy was fussing over the corner table laden with a light lunch.

"Ah, my pet," said Madeline, clapping her hands, "you remembered. You are a darling boy!" Madeline was referring to the centerpiece of apricot-colored roses preferred by his mother.

"I couldn't very well forget to spoil my favorite girl, now could I? Particularly, after you've come all this way just to watch me ride." Tommy bowed obsequiously, then scooped his mother into his arms and swung her around and around.

"Thomas, oh, Thomas, put me down at once!" she giggled breathlessly, loving the attention.

Over lunch, Tommy filled his parents in on some of the latest news regarding the show, various individuals with whom they were familiar, his horses, and the forward schedule.

"I've taken the liberty of marking up a couple of programs for you," he said, presenting them to his parents together with their passes, box seat tickets, and badges. "You shall be able to go anywhere on the grounds at any time with these. Our box is well-situated; I hope you'll be pleased."

Afterward, Madeline and William retired to their room to unpack and take a rest. Marcy was cleaning up in the kitchen with Tommy and reviewing when he would show his horses.

"Tommy, I didn't want to mention it during lunch, but I think it would be a good idea for someone reliable to be around when Demiluna is braided. I know Harry and Sandy don't want to tip their hand, but from a veterinary standpoint, I'd rather not have her placed at risk. I know how important it is to catch the culprits red-handed, but if another mare is chosen because she's accessible, the alternate mare would survive it better, since it would be a first time exposure, and caught immediately. Do you know what I mean?"

"Oh my darling, you are simply the best. I'm overwhelmed that you should worry about Demiluna in the midst of all you're dealing with. And yes, you're absolutely right. I know it sounds callous of me, but I'd rather a mare other than Demiluna play bait. She's working wonderfully, Marce, but that's only because of your care and astuteness in discovering the problem in the first place.

"When this is all over, I'd like you to do a thorough pre-breeding exam on her. Whatever it takes, I want to ensure she has suffered no after effects from this, particularly nothing that might compromise a healthy gestation."

"Making plans, are we?" asked Marcy, looking askance at him. "Funny, I never pictured you as the sort who'd want to get involved in breeding," Marcy said softly.

"Really? Well, I suppose that's because I've always purchased, and I've bought many a youngster and raised them. It's just that she's so special a mare, I thought that breeding to the right stud might preserve a portion of her greatness, you know?" Marcy nodded, concurring with his line of thought. "And insofar as breeding is concerned, I think about it all the time. In fact, I lose sleep quite regularly," he said, grinning.

Marcy visibly reddened. "You are a rake, Thomas Brandon, a 'rake and a ramblin' boy.' Sometimes I wonder if the rest of that Baez song could ever come true. Do you know it?"

Marcy sang the first line, "Oh, I'm a rake and a ramblin' boy, there's many a city, lord, I did enjoy, but now I'm married, got a pretty little wife, and I love her dearer than I love my life."

Tommy laughed. "You've a good voice there, doctor. But, my answer would be . . . 'I'll go no more a'rovin' since rovin's been my ru-i-in, I'll go no more a rovin' for you fair maid," his happy, sonorous rendition of the sailor song rang through the kitchen. He grabbed Marcy in a do-si-do. Tommy's parents walked in during the second chorus.

"Now, here's a pretty sight," said Madeline to William. "Have you ever known him so happy?"

"No, my dear, I have not. I wager that this ginger-haired doctor has heart, well and truly, what say you, love?" said William, tapping his foot in time to the music.

Madeline just nodded her head. "The question is, William, does Tommy have her heart as securely as she has his?"

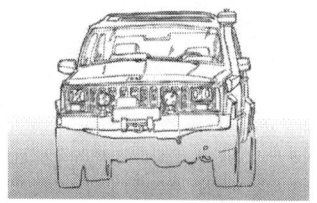

Chapter 46

Munich, Germany

Sofia walked slowly and deliberately toward the post office. Bianca was sitting on the bench reading her book with the little dog basking in the sunshine at her feet. Neither looked at the other.

As Sofia entered, she caught Francesca's eye and the almost imperceptible gesture signaling caution. Although she showed no outward indication, Sofia's heart began to race. She strode to her post box, opening it. The man next to her said, *"Pas un mot! Comprenez-vous?"* as he closed the adjacent postal box. She withdrew the junk mail and flicked through it, nodding to give indication that she would say nothing. She turned, dropping a tissue from her right pocket, as the man took her left elbow and they walked toward the exit.

With a flinch of understanding, Francesca knew that the dropped tissue signified Barbu's memento of Ileana's handkerchief. It was Barbu! From her position, she had been unable to see his face. Francesca tapped two long strokes on her button: the team was alerted. '*Prego Dio*, nothing goes wrong.' she thought.

Once outside, Sofia dropped her mail. Bending to retrieve it, she drew her knife, keeping it concealed. The dark sedan in which she had previously seen Barbu when he had snatched Ileana, was parked part way down the block, the engine idling. Barbu and Sofia walked casually toward it.

Aleksandr Petrov closed the distance with his long stride until he was only a few paces behind. Noonan had Barbu in the sights of his sniper rifle. The trees in front of the post office had temporarily obscured the target, but after the cluster, there would be a clear view.

Francesca walked outside, nodding to Bianca. They walked separately in the opposite direction, Francesca crossing the street, to ensure that no additional lookouts or other of Barbu's men could interfere with what was about to happen. As Bianca placed her book into her leather tote slung diagonally across her body, her fingers closed around the Beretta. The little dog trotted happily beside her.

Francesca's 8000 Cougar was stowed in her long jacket pocket. She walked purposefully, hands in her pockets, the breeze blowing her jacket lapels open to draw attention to her jiggling bosom and long legs that slinked under her very short skirt. With her long blonde mane blowing freely and her angular face clad in stylish sunglasses, she walked the street as if on a model's runway to many appreciative glances.

Rico Morales was leaning against a lamp pole licking an ice cream cone. Hennecke was behind the wheel of the SUV parked on the opposite side of the street, with D'Orza in the back seat cracking his knuckles. A small packet of explosives wrapped in black tape lay on the seat beside him. Kaiser's motorcycle was perpendicular to the curb one parking slot ahead of the Mercedes. He appeared to be glancing at a map, but the dark visor of his helmet hid eyes that were glued to the Mercedes.

As Sofia and Barbu neared the Mercedes, Aleksandr sprinted forward, wrapping Barbu tightly around his rib cage with his powerful arms. Sofia ripped her elbow out of Barbu's grasp, running forward and away. Barbu struggled against Aleksandr's hold, kicking backward with his heel into Aleksandr's left knee. The snap was audible. Knees bend in only one direction, and Aleksandr went down moaning in searing pain. Free, Barbu tore after the petite Sofia.

At the same time, Morales dashed across the street, just as Gheorghe Covaciu was getting out of the car. He rammed the door closed on Gheorghe's arm and shoulder with all of his weight behind the thrust, simultaneously punching the man square in the face and then in the throat.

Hennecke revved the SUV's motor, monitoring traffic and movement on the street. D'Orza said, "Come on, man, let's go!" A cool Conrad ignored the nervous D'Orza, waiting a few nerve-wracking seconds more.

Kaiser gunned his motorcycle and drove onto the sidewalk just as Noonan's bullet smashed into the back of Barbu's head, dropping him to the pavement. "Sofia!" he called. She sprinted the remaining distance and leaped onto the back of the motorcycle, Kaiser's protective arm circling back around her waist, as he maneuvered them onto the street to speed away.

Once Kaiser had Sofia safely tucked on his cycle, Hennecke said, "Okay, Monkey, get ready. Now, we go!" He gunned the engine, turning the big SUV into the street. D'Orza leaped out as it jerked to a screeching stop. Running to Barbu's car D'Orza yelled, "Any sign of her?"

Morales was repositioning the unconscious Gheorghe in the front seat of the Mercedes." Nothing! Check the trunk!" Morales delivered a stun blow to the side of Covaciu's head for good measure. "That feels better, you piece of shit," he said, flexing his hand.

D'Orza popped the trunk. To his great relief, Ileana was inside, bound and gagged, but conscious. She was bloody and bruised, but she was alive. At D'Orza's shout, Morales ran to the rear of the car.

"Oh my God, Ileana, it's okay, baby, we've got you now," he crooned to her, removing her gag as D'Orza cut her bonds. "Get Barbu," Morales said roughly to a grimacing D'Orza.

Morales carried Ileana to the waiting SUV, as D'Orza grappled with the limp form of the tall and lanky Barbu. Monkey was strong, agile, and used to carrying exceedingly heavy packs of explosives and devices on his back, often having to scale hills or climb ropes. Barbu's form posed no difficulty. He slung the man over his powerful shoulders and ran the several paces to the car, putting him in the back seat. Casually, he tossed in a small, black parcel.

"*Aqui van, bastardos. Acabo de odio que los hombres tartan a las mujeres mal!*"[40] D'Orza trotted to the waiting SUV leaping into the passenger seat, as the motor roared to speed away in the direction of Bianca and Francesca.

Francesca spotted the two men lurking around a small, parked Fiat, nervously smoking, conversing, and gesticulating. Their features, clothes, and manner marked them for what they were. They were on her side of the street, looking alternately in her direction, then toward the post office. She put some extra bounce in her stride. Their eyes immediately focused solely on her advancing form, drawing leers and chuckles. She smiled inside. As she neared them, one of them made a remark she could not translate, but clearly understood. Every woman understands that universal language.

She stopped, one hand on her hip, saying, "*Ciao, ragazzi. Ti piace? Si? Beh, non mi piace ciò che vedo.*"[41] The toe of her pointed designer Italian boot lashed out and connected with one man's groin, bringing him to his knees. The other drew a pistol from his shoulder holster just as Francesca fired her silenced Cougar into his abdomen. He looked at her in utter surprise. She smiled and shot him between the eyes, precisely 2 seconds after the first shot. Casually but efficiently, she leveled her weapon at the second man's head. "*Ciao . . .*" she said, flicking her hair, brusquely walking away. The episode took little more time than it takes to sneeze three times.

Bianca and the little dog encountered nothing remarkable. When she heard the muffled pops, her eyes flew to the opposite side of the street and Francesca. They exchanged a brief glance, and Bianca continued on her way. 'Way to go, girl,' she thought. She approached the corner to head for the vehicle they had parked earlier. Francesca would meet her there; together, they would return to the hotel.

At that moment, an SUV roared by. The driver's window was down, revealing an extended arm with the thumb held upright. 'Perhaps we should stop and buy some wine on the way,' Bianca thought. 'I'll bet we'll all need some fortification after today.' She bent to pick up the little dog, who whined and licked her cheek.

An explosion rocked the street behind them, no more than fifteen meters from the post office. In the SUV at the end of the block, Hennecke said, "I just love it when a plan comes together." Angel "Monkey" D'Orza grinned at him. In the back seat, a battered Ileana smiled weakly as she leaned against Morales, still cradled in his arms, tears of relief and gratitude spilling down her cheeks.

Rico Morales said, "I think this calls for a celebration. Who's buying?" Smiling broadly, he kissed the top of Ileana's head.

From start to finish, less than five minutes had elapsed. The plan had been executed faultlessly with perfect synchronism.

Chapter 47

NEC Arena, Birmingham, England

The show was going wonderfully. The weather had cleared somewhat, and the arena temperature was sufficiently moderate to allow maximum muscle performance for the horses and minimum overheating. Tommy's performances had been commendable, despite that he had not pressed either of his horses. He was not in first position, but remained comfortably in the top group of competitors.

Bernadette's horse had also performed well, carrying her rider cleanly through the course. Bernadette, true to form, had been more concerned with the applause and audience recognition, than acknowledging her horse's excellence. To Lars' chagrin and Marcy's disgust, she had taken a half lap around the arena at her finish, waving to the crowd. Celia had been green with envy, as she and her mare had had one rail down on the challenging oxer. She stamped her feet in displeasure.

"You'd better make sure Sissy is up to par for the next round, Lars. She never pops a rail. I'm sure it's only because of that incident, and we all know that's your fault! I've paid a lot of money and spent a lot of time, and I expect a better result. You people better have your act together," she said, traipsing away in a temper.

Marcy looked at Lars sympathetically. "Well, now that this session's over for us, unless you have anything for me, I thought I'd join Tommy's parents in their box for a bit, okay? You know where to find me if you need me, and I'll let you know when I leave the grounds. Maybe we can relax over a drink later?"

"Sure, you go on ahead. At least we're through this far with no serious problems. That thing," he said gesturing toward the retreating

Celia, "I'll handle. It never gets easier, but I'm used to it," he said in a resigned tone.

As Marcy approached the Brandon's box, the sounds of merriment reached her. She tucked in her shirt as she turned the corner to join the group. Tommy was standing next to his father laughing happily.

With her arm wrapped tightly around Tommy's waist, leaning her head on his shoulder, was a gorgeous raven-haired woman dressed in what Marcy imagined Coco Chanel would have worn to a horse show of this caliber. The woman's hair and makeup was impeccable. Lady Brandon might not have spotted her if she hadn't hesitated, fascinated by the woman and Tommy's obvious familiarity with her.

"Marcy, do come and sit by me, my dear. William, fetch her a glass of wine, there's a love."

"Hello, Madeline. Hello, everyone," said Marcy as she meekly took a seat next to Lady Brandon. She accepted the wine gratefully with a whispered thank you to Lord Brandon, happy to wrap her slightly shaking hands around the glass.

"Vee, say hello to Dr. Stanton. Marcy, this is Veronica." Tommy gestured to and fro, from Veronica to Marcy with his wine glass, smiling and oblivious to everything but his good mood.

"Hello, Dr. Stanton. Are you finished with work, then?" The woman deigned to remove her head from Tommy's shoulder as she assessed Marcy. She spoke in perfect "BBC" English. There was no smile on her face nor any in her eyes, as she awaited Marcy's response.

"Yes, I'm done for the day. I just stopped by to say hello before heading back to the hotel to get cleaned up," she said, smiling at Madeline, "I get pretty grubby around the horses." She smiled sheepishly, absentmindedly brushing her pants.

"Well, of course, you do. One cannot be around the creatures without getting mussed, can one? Why, just look at Tommy—all wrinkled and wet. Thomas, why don't you give Marcy a lift to her hotel on your way back to Wellington? You shall need to shower and change before dinner." Madeline smiled at her son, but gave him a raised eyebrow look with her eyes.

"Yes, capital idea. Well, all, I shall see you later, I expect. We're on for 1800 at Le Petit Blanc on Brindley Place. I expect everyone can find it, what? I'm told it's one of the best French restaurants in town, and I feel like some continental food."

"How about you, dear heart?" he said, bending to kiss his mother's cheek. "You and His Lordship can make your way back to Wellington on your own when you're ready, can't you? Father knows where the car is parked. I've gotten you one of those private sponsor spots right near the main door." Madeline nodded and smiled at her son as he kissed her again. Clapping his father on the back, he smiled at Marcy, saying, "Shall we go, *médecin*?"

"Tommy," said Veronica petulantly, "you haven't kissed me goodbye. And you also haven't invited me to dinner. Should I be hurt?"

"Sorry, Vee," said Tommy delivering a peck to her cheek, "no slight intended. Of course, you're welcome to join us. Nick, old chap, take care of Vee, would you?" Veronica shot Marcy a look of triumph as Tommy bent to collect his gear bag.

On the ride to her hotel, she tentatively asked him about Veronica. Unaware of Marcy's discomfort or Veronica's implied challenge, he explained that he and Vee had "been an item" years ago, and that she was a longstanding friend from childhood through early professional years after university.

"She's a lovely looking woman, quite stunning, in fact," said Marcy quietly, looking at her short nails and tanned, freckled forearms, tucking a stray strand of her hair behind her ear. Her ponytail blew wildly in the wind, as Tommy negotiated the route from the grounds to her hotel.

"Hmm? Oh, Vee? Yes, I suppose she is. Daughter of one of Father's associates from Parliament. She's what you might call in America, a society debutante. But to me, she's just Vee. We've known each other forever. Ah, here we are, my pet."

Before debarking, Marcy turned to him to ask, "How dressy is it tonight? I realize Birmingham isn't London, and a lot of the places seem to be casual, but Le Petit Blanc sounded a bit up-market. Any suggestions? I wouldn't want to embarrass myself . . . or you."

"Sweetheart, you could never be an embarrassment, not anywhere at any time. But, I take your point. A smart dress would be my guess. I presume you brought something appropriate?" Although Tommy was teasing her and knew perfectly well that she'd packed a few "nice" things, the comment hit her wrong because she had felt like an dirty, ugly duckling next to Veronica's polished appearance. She realized she had also felt a twinge of jealousy over their rapport, and the way "Vee" had been hanging all over Tommy.

"Oh, I think I can manage something. I brought a denim skirt and a white blouse with fringes and sparkles, and I can wear my cowboy boots, but without spurs, since it's not formal. I'll leave my hat in the room." She smiled at him and blew a kiss. "See you later. No need to come up when you come back to get me. I'll probably be downstairs in the bar with Lars. Check for me there. 'Bye!"

'Was she having me on?' Tommy wondered, as he drove away picturing Marcy in a cowboy hat.

The little gem of a restaurant flaunted true Parisian style, decked out in silver, blue, and polished blonde wood. As they took their seats, Tommy said, "Now, dear hearts, I insist you allow me to order a few things for the table. You can all order your entrees, but I've got special information for starters."

To the sommelier, he said, "We shall begin with a Charles Heidsieck, Blanc des Millenaires '95, if you will. Also bring several bottles of Perrier sparkling water, please." Then to his guests, he said, "Given it's the champagne of the royal houses of Europe, I thought it would suit us!" Everyone laughed.

To the waiter, he said, "My party would like the deep fried goat cheese with olive tapenade and tomato chutney as an appetizer, along with equal orders of the Jerusalem artichoke soup and the pumpkin risotto. Thank you, and please see to it that the bread is frequently replenished."

"There, now that's done, we can enjoy each other's company. Mummy, you know I'm told that the pan-fried sea bream filet is marvelous. Apparently, they serve it only in the French tradition with ratatouille and raw tomato coulis. And, sweet thing, they've a chocolate fondant with pistachio ice cream. I know that's a favorite of yours," Tommy smiled adoringly at Lady Brandon. Madeline nodded and she and William continued to peruse the menu.

Looking toward Marcy, he asked, "Doing all right there, Marcy?"

She looked up at him, not wanting to think he meant that she might be out of her element. "Yes, I'll have the confit of guinea fowl with wild mushrooms, thank you."

"Oh dear! The thought of all that rich meat swimming in all those fatty juices, ugh. Are you sure you want that, Dr. Stanton? I must say, I'm surprised. Tommy darling, shall I have the char grilled scallops or the trout? I prefer to eat healthily. Those of us who ride, must keep ourselves taut and trim, you know," she said haughtily to Marcy. "So, my love, would you order what's best for me?" she said coquettishly to Tommy.

"*Confit de pintades avec les champignons sauvages* actually is a healthful food, Veronica. It's very low in fat, has no carbs, higher protein than red meat, and three times more iron than fish. Add to that, all the calcium, A, B, and C Vitamins, and all the minerals at less than 200 calories, and you can't beat it." Marcy smiled broadly, reminiscently thankful to her high school French teacher's insistence on flawless pronunciation.

"Oh, and Veronica? I ride as well. So I understand what you mean, but I've never really had to watch what I eat." She knew that despite how matter-of-factly her little speech had been delivered, it was inexcusable. She had deliberately made Veronica look fatuous, and made herself look childish in the process.

"Well, there you are! I must say, Marcia, I had no idea. I shall have to take you with me for nutritional advice when I dine out in the future. I'm certain my physician would approve, because as we can all see by my figure, I love my food!" said Madeline laughing, trying to make light of an awkward moment. Everyone politely chuckled.

Nicholas Day, one of Tommy's and Veronica's friends of many years, broke the spell by recounting an episode from their youth during fox hunting season before it had been banned in England.

"I tell you, Marcy, it was a hoot. There he was at the very front of the pack, taking the last hedge, and his girth went. He went sailing through the air to land unceremoniously on the other side in a heap. He had to scramble and crouch against the hedge, as the rest of the horses jumped it. He's lucky he didn't get his head kicked in. All he had were some bumps and scratches, the lucky bloke!"

"Nicky, you lout, you're only trying to make me look bad in front of the woman I love. Now, cut it out!" Tommy said good-naturedly. It was at that moment that Veronica choked on her Jerusalem artichoke soup. She coughed continuously. The two young men leapt to her side.

"You all right, Vee, old thing?" said Tommy.

"Here, have some water," said Nicky. "Do you need a spot of air?"

"Nonsense, you two hooligans. Sit down. Veronica shall be just fine in a moment, won't you my dear? It was simply all that raucous laughter from your boyish tales. Now, behave like gentlemen, the pair of you. This is not a brasserie, or is it?" she asked Lord Brandon.

Looking appraisingly at Veronica, the astute woman knew that Tommy's declaration of love for Marcy was what had caused the coughing fit.

"Why, I've no idea," he said. "No matter, we all had a good laugh to clinch a fabulous day. Thank God, you've learned to ride a bit better, my boy. Wouldn't do at all for you to come undone at this show. No, wouldn't do at all." Lord Brandon raised his glass, "To Thomas, may he wear blue!"

"May he wear blue!" everyone cheered.

Tommy raised Marcy's hand to his lips, saying, "I see you've worn my ring, my darling. Should I read anything in to that?"

"No," she whispered in response, "only that I'm trying a lot of things on for size."

He nodded. "Speaking of size, you look absolutely ravishing tonight. That green dress suits you. Where have you been hiding that luscious figure? You look like a goddess." Marcy reddened, jabbing his leg under the table. He kissed her hand again, then moved his attention to the others.

As she raised her wine glass, Marcy's eyes flicked to Veronica who was staring at her, clearly seething. Smiling, Marcy raised her glass, inclining her head to Vee.

Casually sipping her Perrier, Lady Brandon quietly monitored the interchange thinking, 'You've chosen wisely, my son.'

Chapter 48

Munich, Germany

"We've not seen or heard anything from Martine, so we have no way of knowing whether or not he's ordered up some more rag heads," said D'Orza.

"Angel!" reprimanded Bianca. "That comment is beneath even you," she said indignantly.

"Sorry, Bianca, you're right. I meant Arabs. But since when we do we have to be politically correct around each other, huh? The guys we're up against aren't good Arabs, they're stinking Arabs who care nothing about the Holy Qur'an or Islam or Allah or praying. That group lives only to kill and create mayhem on the rest of the world. They're all about power, and they're using the power of their religion and the rest of the Arab world to . . ."

"Enough." Helmut stood and withdrew the pencil from behind his ear—a clear sign that he was about to make further assignments. "It's not our job to indulge in political debate. All we have to be concerned with is keeping a low profile, keeping ourselves out of trouble, and getting these two to safety without any of us getting hurt or killed in the process, got it?"

"Low profile, did you say? Like blowing up a car in the middle of town?" Bianca bit into her apple peevishly. Bianca was a proponent of effective, quiet, hand-to-hand combat to accomplish one's aims. Her prowess in martial arts and her previous value to the team attested to the merit of her remark.

"Yeah, that was sweet, Angel. Timing was perfect." Hennecke smiled at D'Orza.

"Relax, Bianca. It was necessary, and everything went so well and so quickly, we weren't tied to any of it. Just to be sure, we'll check the local paper to see what's written up about it, okay? We'd have heard long ago from Papa Bear if there were problems. But in my book, it would have been worth blowing up the whole damned street if it meant getting Ileana back." Kaiser stroked Ileana's head tenderly, before he walked around the room to pass out notes to his team.

Jim was massaging Francesca's feet as he spoke. "We get it, Helmut, and we agree, so let's get to these two hermits, okay?" grinned Noonan nodding at Andy, who frowned. Aniela, silent throughout the group's exchange, sat stone-faced, revealing no emotion whatsoever.

"Right," continued Helmut. "Well, if she agrees, I think Francesca is a shoe-in for Aniela. Both are thin, tall, and blonde. We have the extra bonus that Francesca knows how to handle herself in a pinch, although I'm not totally comfortable with it, given she's not an official member of our team."

Then he turned to Francesca. "You've been terrific, don't get me wrong. We wouldn't have had the ability to rescue Ileana without all your help and equipment. It would have been a much more face-to-face confrontation, sloppier and more risky, and may have had a very different outcome. But I do worry for you, even though our government has arranged your temporary loan to us with your superiors. If you want out, we'd all understand, and there'd be no cast aspersions."

"*Grazie.*" Francesca rose, walking to the balcony doors, the team's waiting eyes watching her without comment. After a moment, she turned toward them, a serious expression hardening her beautiful features.

"Understand this, *miei amici*. What I do is not for governments, yours or mine. What I do, I do for Ileana, and the others in our sisterhood. Maybe you forget so soon that I killed two of the scum? *Capito?* I am with you until it is finished." She moved to stand behind Ileana, bending to kiss the top of her head.

Ileana's tears flowed as she reached her hand to Francesca whispering, "*Sorelle . . . il mio amico più vicino . . . tutti I giorni, in tutto.*"[42]

"Okay, good," said Helmut, his voice throaty. "Right, let's get back to business." He nodded and smiled at the tall and stunning Francesca, then looked at the bruised, waif-like form of Ileana. 'Light and dark, so different, but both with guts and courage of steel,' he thought admiringly.

"Jim, even though you're bulkier, you could pass well enough for Andy. You're both tall and look like all-Americans. Okay with the two of you?" Jim and Andy nodded. "Anybody have any other thoughts?" Helmut waited, and then proceeded.

"The Russians are out of it, for the time being. When I spoke to Lev at the hospital, he said his contacts indicate a slowdown. Things can take a long time to get approval over there, anyway. Oh, by the way, Aleksandr's going to be okay, but that knee's going to require a replacement joint." Helmut made a face, and the others uttered commiserations.

Noonan remarked in support of his Russian comrade, "You know, if Aleks hadn't tackled Barbu at just the right moment, well, he gave Sofia time to separate herself from him to go for you, Helmut. There's no way I'd have had such a clear shot at only him. I'd have taken my best, but I hate to think of the possibility that I might have hurt Sofia. No one's perfect, and she was being held against him. It wasn't a heads-on angle, and the distance was significant. We owe him big."

Francesca tugged at Noonan's unruly forelock, saying "Really? You're not perfect? *Mio Dio*, you're pretty close, Mr. All-American sharpshooter. I could do with you in the Carabinieri, James."

"No stealing my team," Kaiser teased Francesca. "Now let's get back to it, shall we? We know that Al-Mumît are skulking around somewhere, although D.C. and none of Sofia's people have a tag on them. They're our worst problem, I think. If at all possible, which I doubt, I'd like to get Andy and Aniela out of here without tangling with them."

"Out? What do you mean, out?" Aniela queried, jumping to her feet. "You are here now, *ja*? You will take the scrolls and Andrew to safety, *ja*? I am going nowhere until I know that Anton is all right. I must return to my work, my life, my . . ." Andy looked stunned.

Rico, having put a tray of tea and biscuits on the coffee table, extended a cup to her, clasping her arm in a gesture of friendship. "Come on, now, sweet thing, you have to understand the way these things work. We'll get you home once this thing is over."

"Let go!" she screamed, wrenching her arm away from Morales, spilling the tea. "Do not touch me! All of you, leave me alone! I want nothing more to do with you, I . . ."

Bianca rose with the intention of comforting Aniela, but never got to take a step. Aniela pointed at her saying, "You! You can help now.

You are archaeologist, *ja*? I heard you speak about the documents at the other hotel. You go to England and help him; I cannot. You are part of the team, *ja*? I am not!"

Andy reached for Aniela, but she backed away from him. "Sweetheart, what's this? What's wrong? What's come over you? Here, come with me into the other room and we can talk this over, okay?" She slapped away his hand, and crumpled to the floor, sobbing.

"She's suffering from PTS, Andy. Think of what she's been through." Ileana looked at him, her bruised face and split lip bringing the point home. "She's not trained for any of this. She needs medical help, I'd say. She'll be okay, but we can't put her through anything more. She'll lose it completely and place the plan and all of us at risk. I vote we ask Sofia and Claude to help." Ileana looked at Helmut for affirmation.

"Andy? It's your call." Helmut watched his friend gently cradle the woman he loved whose crying had stopped, but whose eyes were alarmingly vacant.

"Is this something that will pass? It's probably a repressed reaction from all the kill . . . from what happened before Sofia and Claude found us. I told you I was worried. Now all I feel is guilt," said Andy morosely.

"She'll be all right eventually," said Francesca. "I had a bout with it myself when my brother was tortured. I went on a binge and took out a lot of *terroristi*. It was not a good time. I hunted them like a cat. No feelings, just the hunt. And when I found them, I killed them for revenge with no regrets. No regrets, just bad, bad memories, and ghosts who haunt my sleep."

Ileana looked up at her friend. "I never knew, *mia sorella*." Ileana rose to hug Francesca, whispering so that the others could not hear, "*Come devi soffrire! Mi dispiace tanto chiedere il vostro aiuto. Esse deve portare tutto indietro. Vi chiedo scusa?*"[43]

Francesca nodded, "Do not worry yourself. I do not often speak of it. It is a sadness, but I am fine." Knowing how deeply wounds of that nature scarred the soul, Francesca had sympathy for Aniela.

Aniela, however, was not fine. She had retreated into herself. Andy could have kicked himself. He should have seen this coming, particularly with how passive she had been since the team's arrival. Had he been more sensitive, he would have realized that she had shown signs of posttraumatic stress from their first days with Sofia and Claude. She had strained herself to the limit for the sake of his wellbeing and the mission's success. She had clearly exceeded that limit when she had reacted protectively and killed Yawaf Fakar. She must have been living in her own private hell, reliving the horror of it, and he had never helped her.

He had become so accustomed to doing whatever had to be done, that he had not given sufficient thought to the effects of the life they had been leading on Aniela. For a sensitive woman with no training and no familiarity with dealing with the level of danger to which he and the rest of the team had become necessarily if only somewhat immune, was it any wonder that she was in this state? Andy angrily brushed away tears of frustration. He had done this to her. He had done this to the woman he loved. What kind of man was he anyway? He had no answer to his own question. He felt bereaved.

"Ileana, call Sofia. Explain, and have her make the proper arrangements. Conrad, contact D.C. and tell Lassiter that D.C.'s going to foot the bill—no questions asked, or I'm out. Got that? Helmut, once we get her safe, and we have D.C.'s feedback, I'm yours. Whatever you want to do. Let's just end this. The sooner the better. Rico? Could you get me a stiff drink?" His face grim, Andy slumped onto the sofa as Ileana, Bianca, and Francesca helped a compliant Aniela to the bedroom.

"Look, buddy," Jim said softly, the tapping keys of Hennecke's laptop the only background noise, "you can't beat yourself up over this. She stayed with you because she wanted to. Until that thing the other night, it wasn't all that bad, was it?"

"No? Maybe you think she liked being shot at! How about that I killed two of them in front of her? Maybe you think she didn't feel desperate, hoping against hope that she remembered her way through the caves. The last time she was there was when she was a kid with her father. You think she wasn't nervous being followed all the time, or having our rooms tossed, or having to escape in the car driving like a bat out of hell? For God's sake, we barely had a meal without looking over our shoulders. And she never complained . . . not once. She just did and did and did, until she did one thing too much. She didn't deserve any of this." Andy just sat, shaking his head.

"We'll fix it, Andy. She'll be okay, you'll see." Jim patted his shoulder and walked to the far side of the sitting room to join D'Orza, who was fiddling with some timing devices.

Ileana returned from one of the bedrooms. "It's all settled. Sofia and Claude will come tonight."

At Andy and Aniela's hotel, Saleh fitted listening devices while Fatimah riffled through drawers and some scattered papers. "They will return, Saleh. From wherever they are, they will return."

She gave her brother a smug look, holding aloft Andy's rucksack filled with the gifts he had purchased for his family. Fatimah removed the tissue from one of the packages, lifting the lid of a box. The strains of Chopin plaintively filled the room.

Chapter 49

Birmingham, England

The NEC was a beehive of activity with distractions everywhere. Not only was the British Show Jumping Championship underway (when top British riders competed against some of the best in the world to culminate in the prestigious British Open title), but there were a host of events to attend: high speed Scurry driving, the world's top eventers challenging for the British Indoor Cross Country title, Barrel Racing, high goal Arena Polo, and the ever exquisite Dressage to music, along with other entertainment programs and displays.

Because of its popularity and the whopping prize money (over £150,000), the jumping competition lasted for four days with a Championship class every day, including the traditional Saturday afternoon class that revealed the top twenty riders to contest the British Open Final on Sunday afternoon.

Up to thirty international riders, including the top ten British riders, had qualified to compete, so rivalry was top drawer. There were additional show jumping classes interwoven over the four days, including the International Accumulator and the breathtaking British Open Puissance. Because of its success and popularity, the acclaimed British Open Indoor Cross Country competition would stretch across Friday into Saturday. That made the weekend schedule both tight, busy, and constantly exciting.

Once the show had begun in earnest, Marcy was kept very busy not only overseeing the health, wellbeing, and last minute checks of the horses associated with Lars Borst and the American contingent, but liaising with the entire veterinary committee covering competitors from other countries. She was the one to ensure that full compliance was met in line with the competition's requirements.

Although Tommy was riding on behalf of the British, two of his horses (Obsidian and Demiluna) were under Marcy's care and Lars' umbrella. He also competed with two other of his horses lodged with a prominent British stable.

While she was busy, Marcy still managed to have surreptitious meetings with Harry and Sandy, who had maintained a low profile, blending into the tapestry of the army of workers. Lars had seen to their assignments to allow greater flexibility to watch over Leonora and Phil's braiding schedule. Lars had also increased security, and Marcy knew he furtively walked the barns at odd hours, as did she.

Before joining Tommy for a private celebration after one of his championship wins, Marcy decided to amble down the aisles, dispensing pieces of her coveted shortbread to her favorite horses. No one was about just before dinner, and the security people were making their rounds on the other side of the barn aisles assigned to Lars.

Like many vets, Marcy wore therapeutic clogs with a cushioned foot bed and a stout rubber sole. One's shoes had to be capable of withstanding the rigors of her profession, with its manure, iodine, and other stains, as well as providing much needed support and comfort for long hours on the feet. She had hosed her clogs and scrubbed up at the vet clinic, leaving her bag for retrieval after her stroll. Walking silently along, peering into stalls as she sauntered, animated whispers reached her ears causing her pace to slow, but her heart to beat faster.

"I tell you, they know! Haven't you noticed that suspicious air around Lars? And what about all the extra security?"

"Don't be a silly moo, Leonora. Everything's going to be all right, I'm sure of it. She said we have to do this only one more time. Look, it's Thursday tomorrow. These lovely girls shall be leaving I would think, as they're not in the final classes or the championships. We'll be shot of it and free to have a lavish lunch. I'll even take you shopping." Phil's whispered voice was filled with wheedling promises. "Now, get on with it!"

Marcy shook from both rage and anxiety. She quickly deduced there was no time to get help, but if she faced them off alone, it was likely that she would be in a precarious position. She doubted either of them would hesitate to cover up their reprehensible work by hurting her, or worse.

She thought of Hosea with a shudder. Just as she bolstered her courage to take a step, she spied Harry and Sandy at the far end of the aisle.

'Thank you, God,' she thought, motioning for them to remain quiet and approach with caution, pointing to the stall that held the scheming pair. Harry signaled that they understood. Marcy watched them draw their weapons and creep stealthily toward her and the stall. One of the mares whinnied, and Marcy flattened against the stall walls. Harry and Sandy halted immediately, waiting.

"What was that?" Leonora whispered, sounding frantic and nervous.

"Nothing, nothing, now hurry up. We're almost there, love, just keep your focus," Phil intoned.

Harry and Sandy reached the stall wall adjacent to the one in which Phil and Leonora worked. Sandy indicated that they wanted Marcy to make her presence known. 'What?!' she thought. 'The cavalry is here and I've got to be the one?' The mare in the stall with Phil and Leonora was nervously nickering, stamping her feet.

"Hold her, Phil! My God, I don't want my arm broken," Leonora ordered.

Marcy turned toward the stall, pretending she was just walking by. "What are you two doing?" she asked, stopping at the grating looking in at the two of them.

"Shit!" Phil mumbled under his breath. "Oh, we're uh just finishing up here," he said, walking to the front of the stall to block Marcy's view of Leonora's position, letting the mare loose. The horse walked away from Leonora, turning in a large circle moving toward the sound of Marcy's familiar voice. Her movement made Leonora's status plain to view, and also compromised her arm, as she struggled to withdraw it at the awkward, moving angle.

"I don't like the looks of this at all," said Marcy in a quavering voice, as Phil opened the stall door, reaching for her quickly.

"Now, doctor, why did you have to stick your nose into things that don't concern you," murmured Phil. As he grabbed Marcy around the neck, she struggled, amazed at his strength and how startlingly effective his grasp was at cutting off her air. She began to choke uncontrollably, as lightheadedness tried to claim her. It was then that Harry and Sandy descended.

"Okay, mister, that's all we needed. Up against the wall and spread 'em," Harry ordered, ruthlessly slamming Phil into the grating and expertly twisting his arm up, behind his back.

Sandy dashed past Marcy, who was gulping for air, and pulled a shaking Leonora from the stall, her arm still clad in a sleeve cradled against her body. "Marcy, are you okay?" At Marcy's nod, Sandy said, "Then check that the mare is okay, and bring out their bag, if you would."

"Did you put anything inside that mare?" Marcy asked the wilting Leonora, still breathing heavily from her encounter with Phil, and her voice raspy.

"N-n-no, I was just . . . I mean, I was . . ." she stammered.

"Shut up, you cow!" Phil interrupted, as Harry yanked his head back by the hair. "Ooooww!"

"Now you listen to me, you little creep, you are the one who is gonna shut up, understand me? You speak only when spoken to, got me?" With that, Harry delivered a kidney punch and Phil gasped.

"You can't do that, it's illegal! It's brutality!" Phil whined. Leonora only cried and held her arm.

"Oh really?" sneered Harry. "I got a news flash for you, Limey boy, I'm an American, see? I don't have to follow your polite Brit ways, now do I? I'm exempt! And guess what, Phil my man, guess what this is? Yeah, that's right, a pistol." Philip's eyes opened wide as Harry held the barrel close to his head, stroking it up and down his cheek.

"Your British cops don't carry them most of the time, do they? Well, we do. And they're a great little tool in the right hands," he said, jamming the butt of his pistol between Phil's buttocks. "How's that feel, you little prick?" Philip's bladder released.

Sandy had handcuffed Leonora, and while handcuffing Phil, gave Harry a withering glance. Turning toward Marcy, she said, "You sure you're all right, doc? Sorry we had to make you go through that, but we were right here. We needed an incident, if you know what I mean. So how's the horse?"

"I think they implanted her, Sandy. But, I'll have to check for sure. Their bag has all the stuff you'll need to charge them, and I found this in the straw." Marcy handed Sandy a packet identical to the ones already in evidence. "They must have dropped it when they were arguing."

"Good work, doc," beamed Harry, as he pushed a downcast Phil toward the office. Sandy took charge of the now wailing Leonora, and

Callie McFarlane

Marcy raised her hand in salute to the two of them, heading for the vet clinic to get her bag. 'This is one time I'll be relieved to find something inside a mare,' she thought.

Later, as she and Tommy sat sipping a mellow, rich Châteauneuf-du-Pape, Marcy felt the most relaxed she had been in weeks. The sound of his voice was especially pleasing.

"You know, my darling, the name of this wine translates as New Castle of the Pope, from when the Avignon was under papal rule. Did you know they permit thirteen varieties of grape to make it? I've always wondered about the French. I mean, I love the wines of Provence, but . . . Marcy, where are you? You haven't heard a word I've said, have you?"

"Hmm? Oh sorry, Tommy, go on," she said distractedly. Her head had been full of the events of the previous few hours, ticking off things she would necessarily have to do to make Harry and Sandy's case against Phil and Leonora airtight. She hadn't yet mentioned it to Tommy, because he was full of excitement over his winning class, and she hadn't wanted to distract the significance of the evening with her news. She had decided there would be plenty of time to tell him, but the focus of the evening should be a celebration of his achievement.

"Darling, now you have me worried. What's going on in that beautiful head of yours?" he said, reaching an arm across the table to stroke her hair. "Your hair looks like spun bronze in this light. You're quite lovely, you know," he said tenderly. "And, I reckon, I'm the luckiest man in all Britain."

They had decided to dine late at a little restaurant tucked into a former Georgian silversmith's workshop. The Bucklemaker managed to be traditional, contemporary, and welcoming all at once, and the atmosphere was definitely romantic.

"You know, I'm getting awfully spoiled, Tommy. My mom is a great cook, as you know, but I don't usually eat such exotic foods as I have here. I'm well known for grabbing a simple lump of cheese and bread for dinner after a busy day. And here I thought the English weren't known for their cuisine," she said, happily diving into the oysters with raspberry shallot vinegar Tommy had ordered for starters.

"Oh, we're not, my pet. But, we have the good sense to go to restaurants where the chefs are good, like this one. Do you like calves liver? They're supposed to have a fabulous liver dish here with sweet potato and red skin onion tartlet, piquant sauce and deep fried sage. Would that do you?" His mood was festive and expansive. "They've also got seventeen wine cellars, here, can you imagine? Birmingham has improved indeed!"

"Seventeen wine cellars? Unbelievable. The food here is so good, I can barely wait for what's next. I hope I have room for dessert," she said, comfortably passing mundane conversation, content in the knowledge that they could be "just plain people" together, with nothing out of the ordinary or exciting needing to happen all the time.

"Ah, Marcy, me love, I wish these times could go on forever," he sighed. "I wish . . ." he breathed thoughtfully, but then stopped. "Let me pour you some more wine, and when we're finished eating, we'll have a bit of a walk, all right with you?"

"Mmm, yes, fine," said Marcy with her mouth full. "Oh, I'm sorry," she said, patting her mouth with her napkin, "but this is delicious!" She was glad Tommy viewed sampling different cuisines as an adventure. One's attitude about the simple things in life could make the difference between a full and stimulating life versus a boring existence. Another "plus" to add to his side of the ledger.

Having finished dinner, they walked around St. Paul's Square. The breeze faintly rustled her hair and fluttered softly over her skin. They walked in silence holding hands, Tommy's fingers absently toying with the ring he had given her.

"Tommy, this has been a wonderful evening, but then all of my evenings with you have been wonderful," she said. "I'm so proud of you. You and Obsidian put the rest to shame. Congratulations."

"He was smashing, wasn't he? And though there's more to come . . . a long way to go, as it were, I think he's got plenty left. I'm really excited about Demiluna's class, too. Will you be able to see it, do you think?" Marcy nodded affirmatively, smiling. She wouldn't miss it for the world.

"Is Veronica here for the duration?" she inquired casually, to disguise her true feelings.

"Yes, I believe so. Nicky said she's been having a rough time of it lately, something about money or, should I say, lack of it. Seems her father's cut her off because of excesses. Not like Vee, you know? But Nick says she's been involved with some jetsetters, but the rogue-ish sort, as I understand it. Ah well, that's Vee, always living life a bit on the edge," he said. "She's made the most of herself and all her connections with our horsey set, so I reckon she'll be fine. She probably just needs a rest from the high life. So hanging around with all of us wholesome horsey types will be just the ticket, I reckon. What she needs is a good man to settle her down."

"Hmm, yes, I suppose you're right," said Marcy genuinely. "Tommy, I've got something to tell you. I think the time is right now, and I hope you'll be pleased."

He stopped dead and turned, looking expectantly toward her. "Darling, yes, of course, go ahead."

She realized her error at once. "No, no, Tommy, don't misunderstand me, please. It's not that." He sighed softly, and they continued walking. "It's about Demiluna and the others. We've cracked it, Tommy, it's over. At least, I think it is. There's some more to do, of course, especially with the authorities here. Harry and Sandy are still questioning and putting their report together. But in the main, we got them!"

"How, what?" Tommy's interest was sparked. "That's wonderful, darling, but . . ."

"Just listen. You won't believe how lucky we were," said Marcy as she began the tale.

When she had finished, Tommy rubbed his face with his hand, saying, "Do you realize you could have been killed, Marcy? Have you forgotten about Hosea?"

"Well, no, of course I didn't. But I was right there! I couldn't just let them do it again, could I? And it was pure serendipity that Harry and Sandy turned the aisle at just the right time. I think God was protecting me and His horses. Anyway, it all worked out for the best. The only thing we don't know is who the "she" is that Phil and Leonora were talking about, but I guess Harry and Sandy will get that out of them."

"Come on, let's get out of here. I think we should sample some of the reputedly wild nightlife here and celebrate. You're a heroine, my darling!" he said, swinging her off her feet. "I'm proud of you, but you never cease to amaze me. And I'm a champion, well, at least in that one class. So let's not lose the moment. Besides, celebrating with you is the best one could wish for," he said, kissing her hand.

They hailed a cab to make for the "quarter" and a night of merriment. Both of them were in well-deserved high spirits, though in the far recesses of her mind, Marcy acknowledged a flickering of guilt about Tre.

Chapter 50

Munich, Germany

In the arena of covert activities, the name of the game was to limit the options of one's opponent. Close . . . create fear . . . eliminate . . . that's the way the game is played. With this mission, however, the team had to accomplish their goals without revealing that the United States was involved whatsoever. That knowledge was limited to a very few, and those agencies and individuals were allied to the United States under a veil of extreme secrecy. It was a tall order, with which the team was altogether too familiar.

Thus, none of the team had any insignia or markings to indicate national or unit connection, no personal effects except wristwatches, and were clad in dark clothing that was both practical and relatively non-descript. All could effectively blend into the night, except for Francesca Virante and James Noonan, whose job it was to impersonate Andy and Aniela.

The pair cautiously entered the hotel, making certain that any watchers would notice their nervous demeanor. Once inside, Jim opened the door with the key Andy had given him. Francesca immediately began going over the room, signaling to Jim when she found the location of an electronic device, as he did with her. Pleased their expectations had been met and the room was bugged, they began their role-playing for benefit of the listeners. Earlier, they had agreed and memorized special "catch phrases" that would appear like innocent conversation, but were in fact flags to their listening team. As Helmut listened to Jim's relaxed Midwestern speech patterns, he nodded his head in satisfaction. He keyed "two shorts" on his button to put the team on stage 2 alert.

Fatimah, reclining on the bed in an adjacent room of the same hotel, snapped to attention when Saleh motioned to her, a finger to his earpiece, the other hand adjusting volume on a small receiver. She approached her brother who smiled up at her. "It is as you said, my sister, they have returned. You were correct to insist. *Shook-rahn*, thank you."

"*Tighyib*, now we wait until they are well settled and sleeping. Rest now, I will listen for a while. Then, when the time is right, we shall go and quickly end this. I cannot wait to get back to our island."

The luminous hands on the anti-reflective crystal dial of Helmut's Victorinox Swiss Army watch showed one minute to midnight. The entire team was outfitted with the Ground Force 60/60 Chrono model, and had synchronized them as they went over their plan for the last time at their hotel. Helmut checked the clarity of his night scope. The entrance was clear as a bell, and he could focus in on an item as small as the door handle latch from his position across the street.

Angel was posted on the roof and had already set hooks and ropes in readiness—one never knew how things might develop. Bianca and Conrad were inside the hotel at their stations. Rico was in one of the SUV's parked opposite the entrance. The team received one short click on their communicators, as Conrad spotted the two figures move stealthily down the hall toward Andy and Aniela's room.

Ileana had remained behind with Andy under the pretext of helping him with the translation, but more to prevent his involvement. He had seemed glad of her company, and the distraction of addressing the ongoing problem of the codex would be healthy for him, they had decided, as he continued to be preoccupied by his concern for Aniela. She was safely cosseted with Sofia and Claude, and they could be trusted to look after her and get her the proper treatment.

When push came to shove, Andy would do his job, nonetheless. The critical part of his job now that he was relatively safe with his team, was to concentrate on the reason he had been selected for this mission in the first place. The remainder of the team could and would deal with outside threats to the mission's completion.

The door burst open. Francesca and Jim, pretending to be asleep, were at the ready under the covers. Francesca was armed with her Cougar in her right hand, and a knife at her waist. Jim had one of the FN Minimi's, fitted with a silencer, nestled in his arm aimed at the door. When Saleh and Fatimah came through the door, both agents rolled from the bed to the floor, assuming a defensive position. The room was pitch black, as Fatimah had quickly closed the door behind them, preventing any illumination from the hall to leach into the room, and to help cover the sounds of any potential scuffle.

"Do not move, American," said Saleh, his voice calm and even. Fatimah moved slowly to the right, feeling for the light switch. Jim flicked on the high-intensity beam of the flashlight he held in his left hand, blinding the intruding pair before Fatimah could find the light switch.

"No, I think it's you who shouldn't move," said Jim firmly.

A silenced shot popped, and the flashlight went out. Fatimah leaped for the bed, only to find it empty. With her movement, Saleh slung the door open, moving to his left against the wall. Francesca leapt from the floor to the bed, landing on top of the wiry Fatimah. Saleh fired at the shape moving toward him, but it kept coming. Jim felt the slug enter his side, and searing fire erupted throughout his chest cavity. The earlier shot had hit his flashlight, only stunning his left hand, but now his entire left side was useless. He held the light gun steady and fired a few bursts, strafing along the wall, hoping to hit his assailant.

Fatimah and Francesca grunted and struggled, wrestling each other on the bed, each frantically seeking superior purchase. Fatimah effectively held the Cougar away from her head with her left hand, and punched a roundhouse blow to Francesca's left ear with her right fist, as Francesca leaned on her throat with the point of her elbow. Stunned, Francesca rolled to the floor, shaking her head, fighting vertigo. Fatimah leapt off the bed like a gymnast, somersaulting and landing on her feet a few feet from Noonan.

She kicked him in the side, eliciting a deep groan, as he went down. Fatimah kicked the gun from his hands. As she turned to check on Saleh, Francesca threw her knife with deadly accuracy despite the darkness and her awkward position. It struck Fatimah in the center of her left shoulder blade. The hit would have been square in the middle of her back, had not Fatimah turned toward Saleh. He lay against the wall, bullet wounds in his thigh and hip. He motioned Fatimah away. Fatimah turned on Francesca who, unarmed, squatted by the bed.

"Where is it, *akrootah*. Give it to me, whore, and I may let you live." Fatimah viciously backhanded Francesca. She tried to crawl away to reach for a bag on the side chair. Fatimah stepped on her hand, kicking her in the side with her other leg. Francesca rolled heavily with the blow. As Fatimah picked up the bag and removed the disk, placing it inside her jacket, she reeled at sounds from the hall.

Bianca burst into the room with Conrad on her heels. Bianca leapt for the floor in response to Jim's frail warning, as Conrad turned toward the waiting Saleh. "Drop your weapon," Saleh said, leaning heavily against the wall. "Get over there by your friend," he said. "So much for Americans," he said disdainfully. Conrad knelt by the bleeding Noonan, instantly assessing his damage and the overall situation.

Bianca and Fatimah traded blows. Because of her shoulder wound, Fatimah was not up to her usual par, and Bianca had the upper hand in the deadly earnest martial arts contest. Slowly, edging her position toward the door, Fatimah stood close to Saleh. Despite feeling faint from loss of blood and pain, he raised his gun toward the advancing Bianca. "Enough, *kelbeh*! Move back away, bitch. Now!"

Fatimah, bleeding from the knife wound from Francesca, and breathing heavily from several of Bianca's damaging blows, took Saleh's arm to help him upright, and then moved for the door. "*Khara!*" Saleh grimaced, putting weight on his leg. Fatimah said nothing, disappearing from the doorway. "Do not be foolish and follow. You will not be so lucky as your friend," said Saleh, leaving the room close on her heels.

As they left the hotel, moving as quickly as Saleh's leg allowed, Fatimah checked outside the door. Seeing nothing, she motioned to Saleh, who hobbled to their parked vehicle. She would have preferred to eliminate all of them, but the unexpected resistance from the American and the girl, had already caused too much disturbance and cost too much time. What should have been a quick in/out hit and retrieval, had been a fiasco. Fatimah did not like fiascos.

She would exact revenge for the failure they were not used to experiencing. They would not forget. They would have themselves satisfied by the last blood of those who caused their wounds. She vowed all this to herself, as she motored away from the scene. Saleh said nothing, his staring eyes fueled with rage and vengeance.

Bianca had signaled the team to let them escape. As Helmut looked through his scope, he ground his teeth. He would like nothing better than to put a bullet into each of them, but Bianca's signal indicated that they had the phony disk. He wondered how four of his team had fared. They'd clearly put up a good fight, since at least one of the fleeing pair was wounded. His ruse had worked, but at what price?

D'Orza quickly dismantled his gear and ran the interior flights to the room. Morales sprinted across the street to enter the hotel once the Arab pair drove away. When both men got to the room, they found Conrad attempting to staunch Jim's blood flow and Bianca supporting a shaky Francesca. In seconds, they vacated the room.

Bianca led the way taking point for the egress; D'Orza and Morales half-supported-half-carried Jim; Francesca was next, clutching Andy's rucksack to her chest, holding her side; and Conrad swept the room for weapons and other identifiable items, closing the door behind them.

They piled the still conscious, stoic Noonan into the SUV, D'Orza taking the wheel as Hennecke covered their rear, just in case. Bianca and Francesca hurried to the other vehicle parked down the block. As she walked, Bianca glanced to Kaiser's post and flashed him a quick grin. Helmut flicked the eyepiece closed and disassembled his rifle, preparing his gear for return to the hotel. 'Everyone's in one piece, thank God.' He wondered fleetingly how many times he'd had that thought over the last several years.

Back at the hotel, Ileana and Andy huddled over scattered pages of notes and the photocopies Claude had rescued from his and Aniela's hotel room. Andy fingered Aniela's hair tie with the disk sewn inside. He pressed it to his nostrils, still able to catch a faint smell of her hair.

"You know, I've been thinking, Ileana. Once the newspapers get hold of this, all hell will break loose. I sure hope I'm not in the middle of it."

"What do you mean? Don't you think they'll run with the story? You said it was groundbreaking."

"Don't kid yourself. They all have their separate agendas: this one is allied with that political party; that one is virtually wholly-owned by foreign money who controls Board votes and policy; some are outrageously liberal beyond any parameter of logic and good sense; and others are so conservative that they wouldn't recognize the merit or necessity of positive changes because they are constipated and bound by traditionalism and what has always been.

"Newspapers, radio, TV, and the Internet sites can decide what's newsworthy, and it's their call what they publish, how much, and what spin they put on it. They have no legal responsibility to assess claims made or, conversely, no legal liability by trashing claims made. They can report erroneous views, prejudicial views, outrageously slanted opinions to millions with no liability to themselves. And after the damage is done by their irresponsibility, they don't have to level the playing field by reporting the truth or a correction. That's the way the system works and that's the law. No, it's not going to be an easy road.

"That's one reason I'm being so careful to put together a framework to surround what will be the final translation within an accurate, historical/ political/religious/archaeological/ anthropological context. Whoa, that's a mouthful, isn't it?" he said grinning.

"But you can see why it's so important, can't you? The scrolls can be verified archaeologically, particularly relying on carbon 14. And archaeologists and anthropologists can verify their authenticity referencing the biologic and cultural evolution of man, the development of civilizations, and the study of time periods both through the study of written words and archaeological finds there and elsewhere. Anthropology and ethnology will amplify that verification and place The Message in a class by itself."

He laughed ruefully. "Aniela was always lecturing me about the different aspects of anthropology and how closely aligned it is as a science to archaeology.

"It's subdivided into four main fields: cultural anthropology, which we will definitely need to consider; physical/biological anthropology, which I don't think we need; then prehistoric archaeology; and last, linguistic anthropology. We must present a whole, coherent story."

"Yes, Andy, but I know from many of my associates and from speaking with Bianca, that the most important step in archaeology is interpretation. You know, putting together the bits of data and results of the excavations, background research, and lab analysis to make that coherent, whole story you refer to. I still don't quite understand where the anthropology comes in, except for the linguistic part." Ileana frowned.

"Well, archaeology includes the study of the biologic and cultural evolution of man, the development of civilizations, and the study of time periods both through the study of written words and archaeological finds," Andy explained, "but, as I've said, we also need the anthropological take as a parallel extension of archaeology, if you will. The ethnological and linguistic analyses will help to provide a context in which to interpret the archaeological data.

"By the way, that's where Aniela was such a help, besides listening to me drone on and on as I was thinking aloud. She has this uncanny ability to put her finger on the crux of the matter, or on some obscure point that got buried. She raised really good questions, you know? I can tell you, that's how we spent many an hour: walking and talking, or sitting in our rooms at night, talking until we were exhausted.

"She did more than take me from one place to another, arranging the route, hotels, all of it. Even though she knew we were actors in a play, the ending of which was unknown, she did it all willingly, without complaint. She made it a part of her life, for better or worse. And she gave me so much in the process."

He snorted. "I've never even thanked her properly. I've been too busy trying to stay one step ahead while working on all this." He slammed down the printed manuscript. "And now she's hurt and in a place I can't reach her. There's all of Anton's people, and God knows how many before them, many of them Jews, I'll bet. Then there's you, Ileana, and Aleksandr, and the rest of the team at risk, too. How many more are going to suffer for this? How many more?"

"I know, Andy, I know. I hate that part of this, too. But you know as well as I do, that part of the life we lead is to serve for the greater good. Don't lose that belief, Andy, or you'll lose yourself."

"Yeah, I know, but I'm so tired, and sometimes it gets so hard. When I think of my past . . . my family . . . the carefree, just-plain-normal times . . . I yearn to be able to go back. And then there's Aniela . . ."

"Yes, and the reason you're here, the reason I'm here, and the reason the rest of us are here, is so that those times can continue, survive, and flourish. So let's do what we can do now. We can do our part while the others are doing theirs. Hard work is always a good distraction from the wounds of the soul."

"We've been friends and associates for a long time, but I never realized that you're quite a philosopher, Ileana," he said, giving her a light hug. "You're right. So take a look at what I've been working on, and let me know what you think."

After she had scanned his pages of notes, she said, "Andy, I can't help with the theory end of things, but I'd bet Bianca could. She's a well-respected archaeologist in her own right."

"Yeah, I never considered her. I just figured we'd get someone good once I got to the U.K. But you're right. It would be better to have one of our own team working on this with me. At least, it'd be better for me. Take this down, would you, Ileana?" She reached for a pen and the pad.

"I think the premise needs to be tested against the basic theories of structuralism; ethno archaeology; processual and cognitive archaeology;

and perhaps cultural ecology and evolution. Bianca would be conversant with those basic archaeological theories.

"We'd have to explain this by investigating the whole range of human development and behavior of the time to achieve a total description of the cultural and social phenomena I'll translate. That is, assuming I can successfully translate it."

"I get it now. You're saying that cultural anthropology will support the translation's message because it will speak to this regional group's behavior, origins of religion, social customs, and conventions, right? What about technical developments, and family relationships? Aren't they important, too?"

"Absolutely," Andy nodded enthusiastically. "The better and more comprehensive the framework, the more convincing the argument, and the more readily The Message will be accepted. Then the last step would be to deal with the history and structure of the languages. I'll be able to explain their system of communication and ideas through which they viewed the world."

Ileana was enormously impressed by Andy's wide-ranging and substantial familiarity with scientific approach, particularly with all its subdivisions. His linguistic prowess was well known, but Ileana hadn't realized he was so established with the workings and facets of archaeology and anthropology.

"See, first, I'll have to deal with the major components of language. With phonetics, it's the sounds of languages. With phonology, it's the way those sounds are used in individual languages. Then there's morphology with the structure of the words themselves, and syntax with the structure of phrases and sentences. Semantics concerns the study of meaning. Another major subfield is pragmatics, which studies the interaction between language and the contexts in which it is used.

"All of these are critical aspects of the translation I'm faced with, particularly semantics and pragmatics. But I'll have to consider synchronic and diachronic linguistics too, because synchronics considers a language's form at a fixed time in history—past or present, whereas diachronic—or historical linguistics—investigates the way a language changes over time." As usual, Andy paced as he spoke.

"Now this piece I'm working on, Ileana, is enmeshed with pictograms and logographs against a backdrop of ancient Hebrew and Aramaic, with a smattering of Greek, a kind of codex. So you can see that it's a kind of ancient word jumble puzzle, an early form of encryption. It's not an easy undertaking to be taken lightly, not if I hope to translate and transliterate this stuff with any degree of accuracy.

"That part of it, I understand, Andy. Translation's my middle name. But the rest of it is beyond me, I'm afraid. And even the translation . . . I do many modern languages very well, and old Latin and Greek, but I am out of my league with the ancient ones you have in this antiquity."

"You do yourself an injustice. Everyone knows how good you are, Ileana. Heck, I couldn't do some of the translations you've done. We all have our specialties. Anton's people were only able to piece together a few of the early Hebrew and Aramaic symbols. The Akkadian/Sumerian bits were beyond them, but even from what they were able to reveal, it was plain that the document held specific references, descriptions, phrases, and words which, in their opinion, were the words of Jesus Christ himself, as yet unrevealed. Can you believe it?"

Ileana stared at him, saying nothing.

"Oh my God. I shouldn't have gone into that much detail. I don't know what's wrong with me. I'm going to have to ask you, Ileana, not to repeat a thing I've said, and submit yourself for a debriefing in D.C., even though you're a member of the team." Andy's face looked stricken.

She laughed, "Oh Andy, you're such a by-the-book player. Sillyman, I've got higher clearance than you do! Do you think I'd have been so closely associated with the Vatican all these years if I wasn't? But I respect your concern and admire your loyalties. It's okay, really. Relax. I just wish my translation skills were up to helping you, but they're not. I'm too modern, it seems, even though I speak several languages."

They both laughed together, Andy feeling a bit foolish, but recognizing that the moment of levity eased his inner tension.

"What do you say we take a break and have a drink?" Ileana suggested. They laughed again.

Just as she was passing him a bottle of beer, the door burst open and Hennecke rushed in followed closely by a disheveled Francesca supported by Bianca. Then Morales and D'Orza dragged a now unconscious Noonan through the doorway.

"Claude will be here soon with a doctor," Conrad announced a short time later.

They all turned toward the sound of the door opening once more, and Kaiser strode in loaded down with gear. Ileana ran to hug him, looking questioningly into his eyes.

"Mission accomplished," he said brusquely, hugging her to him. Looking worriedly toward his friend, Jim Noonan, lying on a shower curtain on the couch, he said gruffly, his voice cracking, "How is he?" Bianca looked at him gravely, while Francesca whispered close to Jim's ear.

Andy and Ileana exchanged glances, his words "how many more" echoing in both their minds.

Chapter 51

Birmingham, England

People unfamiliar with the hunter/jumper circuit and related horse shows, might be confused by the class designations of "hunter classes" and "jumper classes".

The former is a subjective process wherein the horse and rider are judged on the degree to which they meet the preset "ideal" standard of style, manners, and way of going. Some of Lars' clients, notably Bernadette and Celia, participated in hunt seat equitation classes, with clothing, equipment, and fence styles resembling hunter classes, but at higher-level technical challenges than hunter classes.

The latter is strictly objective. A numerical score is determined based solely on whether the horse attempts an obstacle, clears it, and finishes the course in the time allotted for the specific class. Jumper courses are usually much more colorful, complex, and technically demanding than hunter courses, because the horses and riders in jumper classes are not judged on style. All of Tommy's classes were jumper classes.

A jumper class course contains obstacles that include verticals, spreads, double and triple combinations, all with several turns and changes of direction. The idea is to jump cleanly over the course within a pre-specified time set for that particular course. Time faults accrue for exceeding the time allowance, and jumping faults are incurred for knockdowns or refusals. Placing is based on the lowest number of faults, with horse and rider clear of faults or penalties scored as having a "clear round". Tied entries have a jump-off over a shortened, timed, raised course. If entries in the jump-off are tied for faults, then the fastest time wins the class.

Here, as with most competitions, Tommy and the other riders were walking the course, giving themselves the chance to walk the lines they would actually ride. Marcy knew he was planning the precise number of strides his horse would need to take, to maximize the angle between the jumps. The course this evening had very tight turns. Some of the jumps clearly had short or unusual distances between the jumps, increasing the technical difficulty. A rider had to carefully plan how to ride the course, based upon knowledge of the horse's size, stride, and athleticism. The standard measure for a canter stride is 12 feet. Thus, with a line with only six and a half strides between jumps, the rider would have to dramatically adjust the horse's stride to make the distance and allow the horse take-off space and time. Each line from fence to fence had to be carefully calculated, planned, and remembered, as riders had to take the best line from fence to fence, save ground, and adjust their horse's stride to promote balance, avoid knockdowns, and be within the time limits.

Tommy had already won the novice class (less than three wins for the horse) with a young and coming gelding from a British barn. He and Demiluna were going to try to win the Accumulator tonight. As they walked the course, Tommy gently stroked the mare. Marcy knew that she was in good condition, but was concerned as Demiluna seemed nervous, particularly with all the music, lights, and the crowd noisily cheering favorites.

Tommy had been daring by choosing two high verticals, a ramped oxer[44], a double combination[45], and several other more standard, but nonetheless challenging, course obstacles for the class, with a triple combination for a jump-off. Marcy watched as rider/horse after rider/horse took the course. There had been two clear rounds so far, but none with the same combinations Tommy had set for Demiluna.

The moment had come, and they trotted in to present themselves before the judges' stand. Tommy removed his derby and bowed. Then he turned to his parents' box, and inclined his head, placing his derby over his heart. Lord Brandon said out loud, "I don't know if that's for you, Madeline, or Marcy." As everyone laughed, Lady Brandon swatted him, then inclined her head to her son. Marcy blew Tommy a kiss. Demiluna pawed the ground, and they trotted to the starting point. Marcy held her breath.

Demiluna was a sight! The mare and Tommy were as one, cutting sharply between jumps, racing for the next, clearing each without a rattle. Demiluna seemed to fly over the course, loving every minute.

Tommy checked her sharply for the oxer, and she slithered over the first, taking two short strides to clear the second jump. One more to go! The double combination required horse and rider to turn on the haunches and double back, taking the jump at an angle. It seemed impossible. How could she get enough torque and power to lift off at such an awkward angle with so little room?

Marcy heard herself screaming encouragement to them both. Before she knew it, the glorious pair were sailing over the jump with room to spare. Tommy bent close to her neck, giving her full rein, and the mare extended her head and neck, galloping for home. The buzzer sounded to uproarious applause and crowd yells and whistles. Tommy and Demiluna had not only won the class, but had achieved the record best time for the most difficult course choice!

"They did it! They won! I can't believe it!" said Marcy, jumping up and down, hugging first Madeline, and then William. "Would you excuse me? I've got to go to them," she said, dashing off, with Madeline waving her away.

When she reached the warm-up area, Tommy was accepting congratulations from a group who had gathered after his go. He spotted Marcy running toward him, and broke away from the well-wishers.

"Darling!" he said. "Wasn't she smashing? Did you see her tuck down and go for the line? I tell you, I had all I could do to hold her at the oxer. She was so full of herself, I was afraid she wouldn't cut her stride enough to make the second rail." He hugged her and spun her around and around.

"You were both magnificent! I'm so proud of the pair of you," said Marcy grinning so broadly, her jaw began to ache. "Let's go see her."

Together they walked with arms around each other toward the stalls chatting animatedly, where Demiluna would be un-tacked, walked and cooled, and then bathed. Watching them go, Veronica gritted her teeth, then swilled down the last of her gin in a temper.

Chapter 52

Munich, Germany

Connections had been arranged, medical attention given, rest taken, secure contact and update to D.C. accomplished, and discussion over the last mission plan completed. The members of the team lounged together in familiar camaraderie. Sofia and Claude had invited the group for a farewell celebration at their much nicer and more spacious hotel accommodation, as moving Aniela was deemed unwise. The team had arrived in dribs and drabs according to plan.

Andy removed his hat, scratching at his face. The mustache and goatee felt odd and looked even odder. He had good-naturedly accepted Francesca's ministrations amid jeers and taunts from the men as she applied kohl pencil to his brows and eyelids. Any humiliation was worth the price of seeing Aniela again, and Helmut had insisted that he be disguised for even their short trip. In consideration of the damage wrought to opposing forces to date, Helmut was taking no chances that Andy might be targeted.

Sofia hugged him. "*Mon cher*! You look so funny!" Andy grumbled and growled.

"If you think he looks funny now, you should have seen him with the makeup before the whiskers. He looked like a bad Omar Sharif imitation!" cackled Rico to everyone's guffaws.

"Where is she, Sofia? Can I see her?" Andy asked tentatively but hopefully.

"*Oui.* Come with me, but be tender with her. Do not upset her. She is better, you will see."

Andy entered the dimly lit bedroom. There she was; the sight of her took his breath away. Reclining on the bed in a shimmering pink dressing gown, with her hair falling loose below her shoulders, Aniela smiled at him, opening her arms.

"My Andrew, it is so good to see you," she said as he covered the several paces from the door to sit on the edge of the bed. She touched his face with her cool hand. "This is new," she said, smiling shyly.

"Oh," he said, smiling, "I forgot I still had it on. Sorry, but it made it possible to come and see you. How are you, sweetheart?" He was shaking slightly from a combination of excitement and concern.

"I am good. Do I not look good?" At the rapid nodding of his head, Aniela laughed. "Oh, my poor Andrew. We have had a bad time of it, *ja*? But now, is good for you to be with your friends. You go to England, I hear, *ja*? When is this? And why do you not kiss me hello, *liebling*?"

They spent the entire evening together, Andy sharing his progress on the scroll Anton had given them, after carefully inquiring about her condition. Except for that one, shocking outburst when she had later collapsed, it was as if they had never been separated.

"I am fine now, my Andrew. I must merely rest up a bit more, and then I shall return to my mountains, *ja*? Sofia has found out for me about Anton. He is all right. Some men tried to beat him, but he told them nothing and played the part of an old professor who cares for nothing but his books. Not so difficult for him, *ja*?" They laughed together, her head comfortably nestled beneath his chin.

"I'm glad he's okay. He's a brave man, and a clever one, too. But I think he's getting too old for this kind of stuff, don't you? Maybe you can convince him to slow down."

"Maybe, *ja*, maybe. But now for you, my Andrew. What will you do when this is finished?"

"Oh, I'll go back to academia, I think. Remember, we talked about that. About me investing all my energies intellectually instead of playing hide and seek with the tough guys?"

"Yes, my Andrew, I remember. It is a good thing for you, I think. Will you tell your Mother and Father about me?" Aniela looked up at him through those amazingly gray eyes, melting his heart.

"Yes, I'll tell them. I'll tell them that I'm in love with the most remarkable woman in the world, and that I'll be returning to Austria to take her to the top of a mountain, a special place she showed me. In that special place, I'm going to kneel in front of her, with only her and me, and the clouds, surrounded by God's mountains. I'll tell them that I'm going to ask her to be with me forever. What do you think she'll say?" Andy feared he had gone too far, misreading Aniela's silence. He whispered, "Aniela?"

"*Ja*, my Andrew, I hear you. If she tells the truth of her heart, the woman will say she will be with you. That she had never left you, not in her heart. That no matter how things will be, you shall always be in her heart. Forever. And forever is not a long enough time."

"Does that mean what I think it means?" asked Andy in a whisper.

"I know that is what I would say. But it must wait until you have finished your job, *ja*? Then come back to me, my Andrew. *Ich werde warten*, I will wait for you, no matter how long it takes." She leaned up to kiss him. Tears rolled gently down their cheeks.

The next morning, Rico Morales and Angel D'Orza accompanied Francesca to the safe house to return the weapons and vehicles. Her people *in situ* would take care of the rest. Jim Noonan was fortunate that Saleh's bullet passed cleanly through his side. While the wound was still tender, and he was recuperating from the damage it had caused, Noonan was as strong as a bull. With the help of several painkillers, he joined Francesca on the plane for Italy, and a well-deserved, granted furlough with Washington's blessings. He would be debriefed at the American Embassy in Rome with a live satellite feed direct to Washington, D.C.

In the afternoon, with Aniela's hair tie around his wrist, Andrew boarded a plane for England accompanied by Bianca Romm. Bound for the help and protection of MI6, he would be taken to a safe house provided and overseen by them to complete his work. Bianca would work a short time with him until he was set up with the group of colleagues arranged by Washington and London. After a quick stop in D.C. for her scheduled debriefing, she would then head for an archaeological dig at the Gault site in central Texas to study new artifacts uncovered from the Clovis culture heralding from 13,300 to 12,800 years ago.

Rico Morales was bound for the States as well, accompanied by Angel "Monkey" D'Orza, Conrad Hennecke, and Helmut Kaiser. All members of the team would undergo debriefing before returning to their "civilian" lives.

Rico had some new ideas for his clubs' décor to provide a European flair. Angel would return to his life as a personal trainer for senators and congressmen. Conrad was eager to return to the Langley computer lab to work on cloaking programs for future missions. The "bad guys" were getting too sophisticated for his liking, and he was determined to outflank them. Helmut was enthusiastic to get back to his passion: marine biology, the research vessel exploring the Biminis, and diving in a fantastically beautiful undersea world, where the odds for survival were considerably better than on missions.

Ileana Muscovici, Sofia Bertrand and Claude Fournier would return to Paris once Aniela was safely home, accompanied by one of Sofia's network. They planned to have a quiet reunion at Colette Franqua's apartment, to which Sofia had a key, in her honor to commemorate her life and courage. They had all been comrades of hers over the years. Her help, her death, and its repercussions, had made the three each other's comrades for life. Ileana would then return to Washington for a debriefing and to collect a promised dinner from Helmut. She would then reassume her interrupted assignment, rejoining Cardinal Monteverdi in Rome, where she would spend some time with Jim Noonan and Francesca Virante, eating mounds of Grandmama Virante's homemade pasta.

Sofia and Claude would pursue unfinished business with Martine. Although Salid's cell had gone quiet, Sofia was tenacious and patient. Claude, her ever-present companion and partner, was content to follow her lead, so long as he had a sufficient supply of good coffee.

Aleksandr Petrov and Lev Rossovskaya had been debriefed via secure satellite link. Aleksandr's leg was still healing, after which he would undergo knee replacement surgery. His faithful partner, Lev, visited him daily in hospital, while keeping a watchful eye out for Martine and contacting other of their operative network, as a special promise to Sofia.

As the Lufthansa Airbus circled for a landing at BHX (Birmingham Airport), Bianca stretched. They had had only an hour and a half's stop in Düsseldorf, and Coventry was only eighteen miles from Birmingham. The flight had been quick and painless, barely giving Andy enough time to replay all the elements of the past weeks in his memory.

His rucksack, returned to him by Francesca after their desperate clash with Al-Mumît—the brother and sister team of Saleh and Fatimah Tariq Khalid Al-Fulan—was his most precious personal possession, and his only piece of luggage. In it were tucked all the special items he had either bought or collected for his family during his assignment abroad. The leather messenger bag between his feet held duplicates of his notes, the papers Anton had given him, and the chip. To anyone's eye, he looked like an innocent professorial type traveling between cities. No one could possibly guess what impact rested within the worn and scratched leather bag. Bianca disturbed his reverie.

"You grew up with horses, didn't you Andy?" she asked. He nodded inattentively. "Well, this travel magazine says there's a race track in Coventry where we're staying, and also a horse show going on at some big exhibition center in Birmingham. Maybe we could take a break and go to one of them. You'd like that, wouldn't you? I'm sure we could arrange it with our guardians, don't you think? We'd be lost in the crowd, as it were."

"Sure, fine, Bianca, it's a good idea. I guess it would be beneficial to brush away the cobwebs. All work and no play makes Andy a dull boy. You take care of it, okay?" He sighed, thinking only of Aniela.

Chapter 53

NEC Arena, Birmingham, England

The day of the Grand Prix dawned brilliantly. Glaring sunshine woke Marcy, as she stretched luxuriantly in the guest bedroom at Wellington. Her body always awakened her shortly after 6:00 AM from habit. She usually fed her horses between 7:00 and 7:30 AM, and was at the clinic no later than 8:00 AM. Old habits are hard to break.

"Yes?" she said in response to a knock at her bedroom door. Tommy entered carrying a tray with a small teapot, steam escaping through its spout, and a plate with buttered toast and jam.

"Would the good doctor care for a spot of tea with toast?" he inquired, grinning. "I thought we could have a lazy morning before going to the grounds. Okay with you?"

"Mmm, wonderful, you're on," said Marcy, plumping her pillows and sitting up to be served. "Warning, warning, I could get used to this, you know," she said giggling.

Later as she, Lord and Lady Brandon, and Tommy made their way to the NEC, Marcy grudgingly decided that she should meet up with Harry and Sandy for an update after talking with Lars. She objected to the case intruding on what had been a wonderful night and following morning of pure bliss. She felt so at ease with the Brandons, and being with Tommy had become as comfortable as her favorite pair of slippers. His dash and mischief added sparkle to her life, like the bubbles that tickled her nose when she sipped from a champagne flute. 'Yes,' she decided, 'I could get very used to this.'

The Grand Prix had the highest prize money because it was the most challenging competition at the show. Historically, the Puissance was the highlight, the *pièce de résistance* of the British Open. It was a high jump competition with a final wall over six feet in height. It was due to start at about 9:30 PM, following various other classes and demonstrations designed to titillate the crowd in preparation for the main event.

Marcy's meeting with Harry and Sandy proved frustrating. They alluded to the fact that they were closing in on the "kingpin," but would tell her none of the details supposedly for her wellbeing. Lars was as jumpy as a cat on a hot tin roof, and Marcy decided to fade into the background, giving him space. It was, after all, the biggest night of the show. She kicked herself for her lack of sensitivity and poor timing. She had had her usual meeting with the other vets in attendance, and all was in order.

Lord and Lady Brandon had arranged a caterer to provide a modest supper in their box. Final checks on all the horses completed, paperwork finished and filed, Marcy collected her bag from the vet clinic and walked to the Ladies Room to wash and change. She had brought her version of a "little black dress," low pumps, and her mother's hand-knitted shawl to celebrate the close of the show. As she struggled with the back zipper, a small, attractive woman walked out of the stall section to the dressing area. She placed a very small shoulder bag on the dressing table, preparing to freshen her makeup. Looking at Marcy, she said, "Can I help?"

"Oh, yes please, that would be great. This dumb thing never gives me trouble, but I'm in a hurry, so naturally, it's sticking." Marcy said.

"I know just what you mean. I always thought zippers were dumb, anyway. Why can't they just make dresses to go over your head and still fit well?" The woman and Marcy commiserated, laughing. "There you are. Well, that looks nice. You going to a party?"

It was then that Marcy noticed the woman was dressed very casually, not at all like the others who tended to "dress up" for the Puissance. It wasn't a "dress down" occasion in general.

"Sort of. My friends have a box, and I've got a friend in the big class tonight. Thanks a lot for your help," Marcy said, attempting to brush the tangles from her mane of auburn hair. "Oh brother, of all nights, my hair has to decide to get wavier," she said, tugging at the brush.

"Do you have a barrette, or an elastic, or something?" asked the woman. "I could French braid it for you, if you'd like. That's always my fallback position when my hair has a mind of its own."

"You would? Oh, that would be great. I think I have something you could use in here," she said, searching through her small valise. "By the way, my name is Marcy. Seeing as you've saved the day for me, it's only right that we introduce ourselves, don't you think? You're an American, aren't you?"

"Oh, yes, sorry. I'm Bianca. And yes, I'm an American. Now let's get to this hair. It's really lovely, you know. All it needs is taming." She worked deftly and quickly, and in a few minutes Marcy's hair looked elegant and refined, the last wisps of hair secured hidden under the braid with her barrette.

"I really appreciate this, Bianca. I hope I haven't kept you too long. Do you have someone waiting?" Bianca nodded, smiling. "Oh dear, I hope I haven't gotten you in hot water. Say, how about you and your friend coming to my friend's box? The least I can do is offer you a glass of wine. After all, we Americans have to stick together, right?" Marcy donned her mother's earrings and locket as a finishing touch.

"What a lovely idea," said Bianca, "are you sure your friends won't mind?"

"No, they're wonderful people. Besides, every Tom, Dick, and Harry stops by all the time. Are you sure your friend won't mind? I wouldn't want to make anyone feel awkward."

"No, I think it'll be fine. Besides, he could use a little cheering up these days. I think your invitation will be just the ticket. Come on, I'll introduce you. He's waiting for me outside." Bianca led the way and Marcy followed.

As they rounded the corner, Bianca walked up to a tall man whose back was to them. She tapped him on the shoulder saying, "I've got a wonderful surprise for you, mister." As he turned around, Marcy nearly fainted.

Andy looked up from Bianca in mid-explanation and, seeing Marcy, said "No way." Bianca looked befuddled from one to the other. Andy's face had the first glorious smile she had seen in days, and Marcy had begun to cry.

"Am I missing something here?" Bianca said, hands on her hips as the two rushed forward to crush each other in an embrace.

After brief explanations, they sat in the Brandon's box together, sipping wine and trading stories, albeit limited in salient detail on both sides. Marcy's face was radiant and her heart was so full, she felt like it would burst. Not surprisingly, Bianca was amusing Lord Brandon, as he had an eye for attractive women. Lady Brandon was busy supervising the caterers. After Marcy had introduced her brother and his friend, Madeline had insisted that they stay the evening in the box and share supper. Both had accepted the invitation for a glass of wine, but had gracefully declined supper, begging the Brandon's pardon because of Bianca's "brother and cousin" who were with them.

"Nonsense, my dear. They are invited, too, of course! After all, this is celebration night, and my son is in the Puissance. I simply could not face him if he learned that Marcy's brother and his friends had been turned away. No, no, my dear, that simply would not do. It would not do at all. You there!"

"Yes, I'm speaking to you. Please, join us. We're about to have a spot of supper before the main event," Lady Madeline Brandon called to the two men hovering near the entry to their box. The two men complied, abashedly moving through the aisles to take seats in the back row.

Lady Brandon, standing and animatedly motioning to them said, "Come now, that's right, don't be shy. You may call me Madeline. And that vagabond over there talking to your relative is my husband, William. And you are?" In a few short moments, Lady Madeline Brandon had two MI6 agents eating out of her hand, behaving like shy schoolboys.

"Oh, Andy, I simply can't believe it. It's like a dream come true." Marcy would not let go of his hand. "You can't know how worried I've been . . . we've been . . . everyone's been. Do Mom and Dad know where you are? Have you called them?"

"No, I haven't, but there's a good reason, honest, Marce. I, uh, have some work to finish up, then a quick trip to Washington, and then I'll be headed for Windward. But for now, no one's supposed to know where I am. Our friends over there are having a fit, if you hadn't noticed. They're my watchdogs, not Bianca's brother and cousin."

At Marcy's questioning look, he said, "Never mind. I can't really say anymore about that. But, who would have guessed that I'd meet up with anyone I knew here? I mean, what are the odds?" "Andy shook his head in astonishment.

"I don't care about the odds, all I care about is that you're here. Oh, Andy, it's so good to see you. If I hadn't had to change and had trouble with my zipper, and your friend, Bianca, hadn't offered to help . . ." Marcy burst into tears and laughter all at once. "It doesn't bear thinking about. It was just a 'meant-to-be' kind of thing. What was it that Gram used to call it? Not a 'co-incidence, but a God-incidence'?" Andy nodded his head, and they both laughed again.

"Listen to us, we sound like giddy school kids. I can't stop smiling," he said, hugging her again. "So, tell me more about this guy. I thought you and Tre were kind of, you know," he said gently.

"Yeah, we were . . . we are . . . well, we are and we're not. It's complicated. Look, this isn't the place to discuss it anyway. Even though I'm dying to ply you with a thousand, million questions, why don't we let that go for later when there's not so much distraction. And besides, I wouldn't want to be rude to the Brandons. I mean, no more than I already have." She hugged him hard, whispering, "Don't you go anywhere tonight without me, not even to the bathroom. I'm too afraid I'll lose you again."

"Deal, sister mine," he said, hugging her back. He looked over her shoulder at Bianca, who gave him a "thumbs up."

"Well now, ladies and gentlemen, if you please," announced Lord Brandon. "My good wife informs me that it is time to take supper. Shall we?" he said to Bianca, offering his arm.

CHAPTER 54

NEC Arena, Birmingham, England

Several entries had finished the course with a wide spectrum of results in overall points, time, and penalties. The international favorite trotted into the ring. The rider had been the past winner of the Puissance for the last two years, and indeed, either he or members of his family, reigned supreme in the British Isles with generations of excellence in the field of show jumping. He was a tall, slender man; not particularly handsome, but very English looking; had an immediately recognizable "light touch" with his horse; and even more surprisingly, a refined grace in the saddle. He had bred the young horse competing in this event. The horse was commanding and bold, suggesting he possessed a tremendous amount of power as yet unleashed. John Harley was two positions before Tommy, and Marcy knew that Tommy would be anxiously watching his every move.

Harley and Motivator took the first three of the six fences easily. With each fence higher than the one before culminating in the wall, the tension in the crowd mounted. Some of the previous contestants had been either penalized or eliminated because of a knockdown or refusal, and there remained only four entries behind Harley with clear rounds. The fourth fence loomed before them, and Motivator tossed his head to the worried reaction of the crowd. He was approaching too fast. The horse acted like someone running downhill, with legs moving faster and faster, slightly out of control. The arena went dead silent.

Motivator leapt over the rail, miraculously clearing it with inches to spare. He charged the next to last fence in the same way, clearing it as well. The crowd emitted an audible sigh of relief and amazement, the

298

low rumble of conversation likely questioning why the famous Harley had not checked his mount in preparation, when he was clearly rushing the fences.

Only the six and a half foot wall remained. Harley did not check his horse at all, merely patted his neck once. Motivator's huge, powerful stride covered the distance from the last fence. Despite his pounding, speedy approach, Motivator hesitated only a second before the wall. With eyes wide, he pushed off his powerful hindquarters and, with Harley leaning his long frame impossibly forward and reaching the reins to the full extent of his long arms, the horse leapt vertically up and over the wall. The crowd erupted! Motivator shook his head again, and dashed for home. Harley had not once broken his focus or composure (except for that one pat before the wall). When the buzzer sounded, his face broke into a wide grin. He removed his hat to acknowledge the judges and thank the uproarious crowd for their applause.

"Wow!" said Andy. "I didn't think he'd make that last jump. Did you see how he paused? I've never seen a horse do that on his own. Amazing, really amazing. It seemed like he was taking its measure, didn't it?"

Marcy nodded breathlessly, too on edge to speak. She knew that Harley and Motivator were the top pair in the competition and, although she had confidence in Obsidian, she was unsure that he could effectively compete against Motivator's obvious strength and ability. Motivator was, after all, a younger horse who had not suffered the injury from which Obsidian had only recently recovered.

The next entry rattled two rails precariously, but also cleared the fences, albeit with significantly more time on the clock than Harley had achieved. If he was lucky enough to have a clear round, Marcy knew that Tommy would have to be competitive on the clock.

He and Obsidian entered the ring. Obsidian was calm, his black coat gleaming. As they trotted the preparation circle for the straight line of jumps, the beginnings of a faint sheen of sweat glistened on Obsidian's flanks. Knowing the horse well, Marcy knew that Obsidian was excited but not frightened. Tommy, too, was perspiring, his mouth set in a line of determination. They paused, and Tommy leaned forward to speak to Obsidian, who flicked an ear back to his rider, listening. Tommy and Obsidian began their run. The horse's hooves pounded the arena footing in perfectly balanced cadence, his muscles bulging.

Just as they cleared the first fence, Lady Brandon leaned backward to Marcy and Andy, saying softly, "My dear, you might like to know that the faint patch of white on his boot top is your handkerchief. Rather medieval, I know, but sweet nonetheless, don't you think?"

She was of course referring to knights of old who carried their lady's handkerchief or scarf in the joust. Marcy paused, frowning slightly. 'My handkerchief?' she thought. Then she remembered. Months ago following his recovery, when Tommy was exercising Obsidian in the arena to test his level of wellness and competency for the horse shows, Marcy had given Tommy her hanky to wipe his perspiring brow. That had been a happy moment for the three of them, full of exclamations and pride. She had forgotten it until now. Obviously, he hadn't.

"Well, that's sweet," Andy said, poking her in the ribs. "The guy seems to have it bad, Marce. I gather you didn't know . . . about the handkerchief, I mean." A smiling Andy, put his arm around his sister.

Bianca quietly witnessed the exchange, pleased to see the closeness between brother and sister. She was even more pleased to see Andy genuinely enjoying himself, free for a time from the overhanging tenseness of the remainder of his mission, and his concerns for Aniela.

Obsidian cleared the remaining fences, approaching the wall. Tommy did something unheard of: he gave Obsidian "spaghetti" reins—completely loosening the reins to their full extent, with no restriction or contact hold on Obsidian's mouth. Although not as large as Motivator, the powerful Obsidian leaped vertically up and over the wall to finish with a clear round! As they galloped for home, Tommy bent forward speaking to his horse while he re-gathered the reins. Their time was just short of Harley and Motivator, but they and the others were through to the jump-off. That in itself was a great accomplishment. Marcy and the rest of the box were on their feet applauding the Herculean effort.

As is the case with jump-offs the world over, fences were raised in height, including the wall. It was put just beneath seven feet. Marcy knew that if there were subsequent rounds, the wall and some of the fences would be raised until there was a winner with either a clean round or the fewest faults. The Puissance had, over the years, boasted a clear winner with a clean round: no faults and top time. Grand live music played behind excited crowd chatter drowning some of its din, as the arena was readied. Marcy's nerves were frazzled to Andy's amusement.

"Anyone would think you were in that saddle, Marce. You should see yourself, moving to the rhythm of the horse. I've never seen you so excited." Andy leaned back happily.

"What? Oh, well, I've spent a lot of time with that horse. I've got a lot invested in him, so I guess you're right. It's kind of like I am going through his paces with him. I don't know, Andy, I keep checking for any sign of weakness in that limb, but I don't see one. Have you?" She looked anxiously at Andy.

"Hey, babe, you're the vet, not me. But he looks solid to me. Kind of hard to tell, though, at this distance. But I'm sure Tom wouldn't take him through if he felt he was off. From all you tell me, he's in love with the horse, right? So, stop worrying. What will be, will be. Just hang tight." Andy rubbed her back, signaling the hovering waiter to refill her wine glass.

Bianca leaned toward Andy. "I suggest you follow your own advice, Andy." Marcy was busy chatting with the Brandons, and Bianca took the opportunity to have a private chat with him.

His head whipped around to her, "What's that? Oh, I get you," he said with a chagrinned nod. "Yeah, you're right, I'll try. But for now, let's put all that behind us and enjoy the show. God knows, it'll be soon enough that we're back on the treadmill. Thanks for suggesting this, Bianca. You'll never know what a shot in the arm it's been to see Marcy."

"An incredible piece of luck, I'd say," said Bianca. "Maybe, there is a God."

"Oh, there is for sure," Andy said, "and if I didn't believe that, I'd have had a much worse time of it than I've had. Think about it," he said, turning around to converse with her. "Aniela and I were lucky against all odds when we were on our own. And linking up with all of you when we did, well, that was also uncanny. All of it tells me we're on the right track, even if it's a difficult road. Nothing worthwhile ever gets achieved without hard work, and sometimes blood, sweat, and tears, my Dad always told us."

"You miss them, don't you?" she said, squeezing his hand.

"That's an understatement. Besides doing what I was sent to do, part of what keeps me going is getting home to Windward. Another component is the thought of getting Aniela and bringing her there. Sometimes, I just wish I could skip to that part, you know? I can tell you, I'm dog tired."

"I know, I know." She paused and then said softly, "After we get you and your group set up, you understand I'll have to leave, right?"

"Sure, I know," Andy said, patting her hand to ease her obvious concern, "but I'm glad you've tagged along at the front end. With your help, I'll be able to have things ready for the head jobs to pick over. I've got the background pretty well set, if only in my head and notes. But we'll have to knock back those glyphs. Are you up for it?"

"Ready, willing, and able, buddy. Since we start first thing tomorrow morning, I suggest we make the most of tonight. How about some more wine? I haven't had a buzz on for weeks, and I'd like to get one started. Do you think it would be rude if I got more of that smoked salmon or curry? I always eat more when I'm relaxed. You should eat too, you've lost too much weight." Andy again flagged the hovering waiter and placed an order. He caught the eye of one of the MI6 agents, who signaled to him.

"Uh oh. Our wardens want me. Hold that thought, Bianca, I'll be right back."

Flaherty told Andy that he and Bianca would have to leave immediately following the last jump-off, foregoing any post-Puissance celebrations. "Make yourselves ready, chum. The party's about to end, at least for you. I want you out of here, so see to your goodbyes, and watch what you say, mate, particularly to your sister." Andy nodded his understanding and agreement.

The jump-off was between the seven riders with clear rounds, albeit four of them with greater times than Harley, Tommy and the entry closing the first round—the only woman in the group. This round eliminated two others: The popular and successful bay mare entry from the United States, and another crowd favorite, a big chestnut Irish hunter, both failing to qualify. That left only John Harley and Thomas Brandon for Britain; Petrik van Hoek for The Netherlands; Fabio Conti from Italy; and Júlia Pereira from Brazil. The final group for the jump-offs was a surprise to everyone.

Brazil was to go first, followed by Harley and Brandon for Britain, Italy, and finally The Netherlands. Júlia Pereira had a clear round, but not impressive time, as she had "played it safe" and was way over in time. Harley and Brandon both had clear rounds, but Harley's time was the quickest by only a hair. Italy, trying to be competitive with the two British entries, had a refusal at the wall that disqualified them. The Netherlands went clear with a time very competitively close to Brandon of Britain, both men still marginally behind Harley of Britain.

Time parameters were decided according to tiebreak rules on an averaged scale of the best and worst achieved time totals, which left Brazil well out of the final jump-off. The crowd gave the tiny woman and her white horse rousing applause, as they took a lap around the arena.

Unseen by the crowd, Tommy shook John Harley's hand in the warm-up area while the staff made adjustments to the course. "Good luck, old man," he said honestly. "He's a great horse. But I'm still going to do my level best to beat you. Either way, let's bring it home for England!" The two men slapped each other's hands, saying, "For England!"

Veronica came forward, looking a bit tipsy and disheveled, dressed in boots and riding britches, her blouse slightly soiled. "Johnny! A kiss for luck," she said, reaching up for Harley.

Embarrassed, John Harley bent to accept the kiss. "Thanks, Vee. See you at the gate, Thomas." He leapt into the saddle, turning his horse toward the arena.

Veronica looked at Tommy saying, "Well, Mr. High and Mighty, you're history!" She walked off arrogantly to Tommy's bewilderment.

Since Petrik van Hoek, John Harley, and Thomas Brandon all scored clear rounds and the competitors were so evenly matched, the judging panel conferred, finally deciding to raise the wall to 7'1" for a final Round 3. Again, the order of go was changed.

Tommy was first to go in the last jump-off between three valiant competitors. Although their horses were fit and well conditioned, the amount of effort required by the horses for a third round was staggering and highly unusual, despite the break in-between. Had not their overall scoring been so close throughout, the trophy would have been awarded after the second round. Marcy shook her head doubtfully, hating that Tommy and Obsidian would have to jump the course again. This was indicative of the war between her veterinarian judgment and competitive spirit.

His sides gleaming with sweat, Obsidian trotted smartly into the ring, showing no sign of labored respiration. The fences for the second and third rounds had been reduced to three. This final round presented two standards at the same height as previously, and the seemingly impossible height of the wall.

Obsidian took the fences cleanly and without effort. Lining up for the wall, Tommy again gave him his head, whispering encouragement. Up, up, up, and over he sailed! Landing hard, he flew for home. The buzzer sounded, posting a time of 52.33, a decrease of four seconds from his last run. The crowd went wild! Obsidian had marshaled such speed for the finish, that it took him several strides to slow. They received a standing ovation.

Petrik went next, but his horse toppled a brick from the top of the wall with a hind foot. His time was .02 seconds better than Tommy's, but the lack of a clear round knocked him out of the competition. Nonetheless, the crowd awarded vigorous applause to horse and rider for their valiant try.

Harley knew that the championship title was between Tommy and him, but either way, they had brought it home "for England," as Tommy had said. He and Motivator covered the course like the devil was after them. The first fences out of the way like child's play, Motivator ran for the wall. Again, he shook his head and almost imperceptibly hesitated before leaping up and over the wall cleanly, much like a deer can leap over a pasture fence from a momentary standstill. His left hind hoof touched a brick on top of the wall. It teetered, and it tottered, and quivered, but held. Unaware, John Harley and Motivator sprinted for the finish line. The crowd was out of control!

The announcer had to call for quiet, announcing the final times:

"For Great Britain: Thomas Brandon   with a time of 52.33
For Great Britain: John Harley   with a time of 52.21"

The times glowed from the digital screens around the arena.

"Ladies and gentlemen," called the announcer, "after a momentous and history-making competition, the winner for Great Britain is John Harley with a record time of 52.21 at seven feet, one inch!" John Harley and Motivator walked to the presentation area, thereafter making a victory circle in the lower quarter of the arena to thunderous applause. When he returned to the presentation area, he was asked to say a few words to the audience.

"Thank you, thank you," he said waving to the throng. "All I have to say is that Motivator is a great, young horse. He's the one who did it. I was just along for the ride." Everyone laughed. "But I want to say also, that my competitors were fantastic and really put us to the test. I think everybody will agree that this has been a competition like no other before it. To think that we had three, very tough courses required to determine a win, and that, only by .12 of a second! Well, it shows the quality of the other competing horse and rider. I think they should come out and reap their fair share of the fanfare."

Having graciously acknowledged his competitor whose name was called out by the announcer, Thomas Brandon for Britain rode into the ring, his gallant Obsidian holding his head high, prancing toward the champion, Motivator.

"Ladies and gentlemen, Great Britain's number one and two riders . . . your Puissance Champion and the runner-up!" blared the audio systems, barely heard over the deafening cheers. Tommy, Obsidian, John, and Motivator trotted around the arena waving to the audience, each clasping the other's hand between the horses above their heads. It truly was a moment for all to remember.

"Now, now, my dear," said Lord Brandon, refusing to hide his tears of pride, "don't be sad. By George, he was magnificent! That's something to be happy about, what? Now, now, stop crying, Madeline," he comforted, patting her.

Lady Brandon swatted his hand away. "For heaven's sake, William! I'm not crying because I'm sad. I'm proud beyond words, you silly old thing." She choked and laughed between sobs.

"Yes, of course. Why, yes! We're all proud beyond words. Isn't that right, Marcia?"

Marcy whispered, "Proud beyond words," holding tightly to Andy's hand and smiling through tears of her own as Tommy rounded the arena to stop before their box. He removed her hanky from his boot and kissed it, looking directly at her. She blew him a kiss.

Andy nudged Bianca and, leaning over to Marcy, kissed her hair whispering, "I've got to go, Marce. Give Tom my congratulations, will you? I'll try to be in touch soon."

She looked at Andy, anxiety in her eyes. "Oh Andy, no! You can't disappear again."

"I have to, sweetheart. Try to understand. But it won't be for long this time, and then we'll be back at Windward again, together with the family. 'Mum's the word,' Marce, promise me."

"Don't give me that look, you big lug. Of course I won't say anything. But you keep your promise, too, okay? I . . . I love you, Andy, don't ever forget that. Oh sugar," she said dissolving into tears again. "It's been so good to see you, Andy, I just . . ." She hugged him with all her strength.

"For me, too, Marce. Now, I've got to go." He rose, taking Bianca's arm as she waved at Marcy, having said their personal goodbyes with thanks earlier to the Brandons. As they slipped away, Andy turned one last time, knowing Marcy would be watching him go.

"Forever," he mouthed.

"Forever," she whispered in response, her heart brimming with love, and her eyes overflowing with tears.

Chapter 55

Birmingham, England

That evening was to be one of the most exciting in Marcy's life. Her heart beat rapidly as she refreshed her makeup. The party was already underway downstairs. The Brandons had arranged a private, catered celebration at Wellington House to celebrate the British win, not solely their son's performance. Many of their friends were in attendance, and the noise from the partygoers sounded through the guest room door. Marcy slipped on the ring Tommy had given to her just before Christmas. She had decided that she would give him her answer tonight. She could envision his smile already, as she smiled at herself in the mirror in anticipation.

She had thought long and hard over the last months, particularly during the Christmas holiday with Tre. His letter had touched her deeply. She recalled how she had felt that day in the tub, rereading it, so aware of his feelings for her, his hurt, and his frustrated apprehension. Then, as now, she wished she could heal his heart. She felt guilty, questioning whether she could have handled things differently to prevent wounding such a fine man and good friend. But she had never intended or suspected that a relationship with Tommy would develop, much less be so overwhelming. She had tried to be fair, time and again.

She cared deeply for them both; she loved them both. The difference was, that despite consistently having reservations or trying to reject it, she was "in love" with Tommy. There was no denying it: she was truly and finally in love. She "knew for sure," just as her father had said she would. She couldn't fully explain it, even to herself.

He aroused reactions in her in ways she never expected. Sometimes, it was only a glance; sometimes it was the feeling of incredibly comfortable, silent togetherness. Other times, it was the sound of his laughter, or how his accent made whispered words so utterly romantic. She loved the way one persistent curly lock of hair fell to his forehead, and the way he orchestrated when listening to opera, his sonorous baritone filling the room. She loved to watch him look at the sea, and listen to his inner thoughts, marveling at the depths of his sensitivity. She loved his sense of fun and impetuosity. She loved "how" he loved: his parents, his horses, nature, his friends, mostly everything. He just "loved." He was full to overflowing with it and a joy for life, in general. Most important, she knew he truly loved her.

As she pondered her reflection in the standing mirror, she thought, "I'm in love!" The person looking back at her was different somehow. She had always seen herself as a tomboy type, only occasionally touching the perimeters of femininity; reasonably attractive, but not pretty; outdoorsy and thus always slightly tousled, not well-groomed and sophisticated; a dedicated professional whose mind was well-trained and whose abilities were practical, as distinct to being steeped in social or cultural graces, although she could "get by" only because of her parents' reinforcements. She realized that the woman she thought she was, was only a portion of the woman she truly was, and the woman she wanted to become.

The woman whose reflection stared back at her as she thought these things was, she recognized, older and wiser, showing the blossom of fulfillment. Her skin was slightly flushed, her hair—for once elegant, thanks to Bianca—shone with glints of gold and bronze. Her figure, atop what her brother always teased her were "impossibly long legs," was slender but shapely . . . possibly even sexy. Her classically simple cobalt blue strapless dress accentuated all her assets, presenting a picture of a young woman of grace and rather uncommon beauty.

'You'll look lovely,' she remembered her mother saying, 'but don't forget to wear a scent . . . here, take this. It's high time you wore something other than that body splash of yours,' tucking a small bottle of her favorite perfume into Marcy's bag. As she applied it, Marcy imagined her mother's beautiful smile, and could feel her father's arms in one of his predictable hugs of pride. She was overcome with love for both her parents. They had always seen the "real Marcy" beneath the surface, and gently nudged it into bud. They had always given her encouragement and gentle advice, confident that she would eventually find the truth of things for herself. They had let her "be" so that she could "become." Now here she was, looking at herself in the mirror, a vision that they had knowingly held in their minds' eye.

"Well, Mom and Dad, I guess we did all right together. Thanks for giving me the wherewithal to get to this moment. It's an important one. I hope you're okay with my decision," she said to herself.

There was a tap at the bedroom door. "Yes?" she answered melodiously.

"Marcy? You all right, darling? Mummy sent me up to fetch you, if you're ready."

"Just coming," she sang out, looking into the mirror one last time, turning fully around. Opening the door, she smiled at him. "You look very handsome, sir." Tommy said nothing in response, but just kept gazing at her. "Thomas Brandon! You could at least say you like my dress."

When he finally spoke, it was a whisper. "You are a vision, my love." He held out his hand.

As she walked with him to the staircase, she asked "Tommy, do we have any champagne? If not, may I borrow the car to go and buy some?" Her eyes twinkled, the surprise bubbling in her chest.

The party had been a raging success. John Harley proved to be a comedian; Lord and Lady Brandon danced an astoundingly flowing but energetic foxtrot around the drawing room to everyone's uproarious applause; the late supper fare was beautifully presented and delicious; and Marcy's toast to John, Tommy, and their hosts, fit the occasion perfectly.

Deciding to leave the party for some privacy, Tommy and Marcy slipped away to the back garden. "Shall we have a drive? I've had enough of people for a bit, how about you?" he had asked her. They left their champagne flutes on the garden wall.

"I've got an idea," she said, "why don't we go visit Obsidian and Demiluna? After all, they're part of the reason we're celebrating, right?" 'And afterward, my knight, I have a surprise to cap off the day.' she thought, smiling to herself. It couldn't be more perfect.

"Capital idea, Marcy! And you're right, they're part of this too. I'll just run and fetch some carrots from the fridge. Won't be a minute," he said, dashing to the back door. He returned with carrots and her mother's shawl. 'Sweet, sweet boy,' she thought.

When they reached the barns, the comforting sounds of quiet nickers, snorts, munching, and occasional stomping reached their ears. Only night-lights illuminated the aisles, except for the office.

"Oh, look Tommy, I think Lars is still here. Funny, I thought he'd be having a few now that the show is over. Want to stop in? We could invite him to come back with us to the party." Tommy agreed, and they walked toward the office at the end of the long aisle. Raised voices reached their ears, then a crash as though something had been dropped onto the floor. Marcy and Tommy looked at each other questioningly.

"You cunning blighter," a female voice yelled venomously, "if you think I'm going to take responsibility for all of this, you're mistaken. I'll take you down all the way to hell with me! You've got to fix this, do you hear me? You've got to either fix this or get me out of it somehow." The woman sounded desperate, shrieking the last phrases.

"Calm down; be reasonable. I told you months ago that I wanted out. But no, you had to go ahead. I told you it was impossible. She's too good, the Feds are on the trail, and things are getting too obvious. Why didn't you listen to me? Did you think you could get around me? Did you think you could fool all of them? Now, we're in an impossible situation thanks to your greed!"

"You bastard," the woman screamed. "Give me that report . . ." Then there was a pause followed by a loud bang. Tommy stopped dead a short way from the office, grabbing Marcy's arm.

"Go and get someone, the police, anyone in authority. Go!" he ordered, trotting backwards, motioning for her to skedaddle.

Marcy kicked off her heels, running for all she was worth. At the opposite end of the aisle, she turned sharply to bound across the warm-up ring for the main show office, relieved to see lights still burning. Dashing through the door, she yelled "Help! Someone . . . anyone . . . come quick. And call the police!"

A constable came from the inner office holding a coffee cup. "What's the matter, miss?"

After a hurried explanation, the constable, one of his mates, and two people from the show office were running with her to Lars' office. They arrived in time to see Veronica backing out of the office, a smoking pistol in her hands.

"Hold on there, miss. Stop right where you are! What's going on here?"

Roused by the commotion, other people—grooms, some of the owners, etc.—were running toward the office from all directions. Flustered, Veronica stood still, dropping the weapon, crying. "It's not my fault! They tried to attack me. I . . . I . . ." The policemen took her into custody, retrieving the pistol. Marcy dashed into the office.

Lars sat in the desk chair staring vacantly, a circular wound in his throat just below the Adam's Apple, another just below. Tommy was sprawled awkwardly on the couch, lying on his side, clutching his chest. A red stain was spreading rapidly on his white tuxedo shirt.

"Tommy! My God, no . . ." wailed Marcy, running to him.

"Seems I got in the way of a bullet, my darling. Aagghh," he moaned. Marcy removed her half-slip, gently prying Tommy's hands away, pressing the wound with her slip.

"Lie still, sweetheart, help will be here soon," she soothed. Then to the policemen just entering, she yelled, "Get an ambulance and a doctor. Quickly, it's an emergency!" Turning back to Tommy, she said, "Why oh why did you have to play hero?"

"I didn't, love, I . . . tried to . . . talk to her. She was . . . crazy. She . . . shot Lars." Tommy winced.

"Oh darling, hush now. Save your strength. The police have her." Marcy said weeping.

"No, Marcy, you must know. It was . . . her . . . Vee . . . she was behind it all. Her connections here . . . aagghh . . . she and Lars. But he wanted to stop . . . she wouldn't let him . . . she went on . . . but . . . because you were . . . so good, my love . . . Lars had stopped, and . . ." his voice fell to a feeble whisper. His eyes widened with the pain, mouth working, but emitting no sound, his breathing raspy.

"Hold on, Tommy, hold on. Don't you pass out on me, do you hear me? Damn you, hold on. I love you! Do you hear me? I love you!" She spoke firmly, feverishly trying to stop the blood flow.

In what were only moments but seemed hours, an emergency crew appeared and took charge of Tommy. Marcy hurried after the stretcher, distractedly glancing at a group of British policemen questioning Veronica, who sat bent over, sobbing pitifully. She grabbed one of them as she passed, ordering, "You! Come with me. I've got information given to me by that man on the stretcher. I'm Dr. Stanton."

Later in the hospital waiting room accompanied by a distraught Madeline Brandon, Marcy waited for news. Tommy had been in surgery for over four hours.

Earlier, she had been debriefed by the constable, and Tommy had been sufficiently lucid in the ambulance to insist that he speak to the policeman or he would refuse further treatment. Although against procedure, he haltingly confirmed what Marcy had conveyed to the constable in greater detail. By the time they had arrived at the hospital, he was struggling to maintain a semblance of consciousness. As they wheeled him away, tubes in his arms, an oxygen mask on his face, he reached for her. She bent close.

"I love you, doctor," he had said weakly, his words muffled by the mask.

"I love you, too . . . see you in a little while, darling," she had said, tears spilling down her face, blurring her vision. Despite her medical qualifications and personal relationship, she had been prevented from accompanying him to the treatment area. The last thing she saw of him was his outstretched hand, reaching for her. She had fainted.

"Marcia, dear, would you like some coffee?" Lord Brandon inquired, standing before her. His stoic, benign demeanor was a comfort of a sort.

Marcy shook her head. "No thanks," she said. She rose and paced the room, dissolving into frantic sobs at the window. Lord Brandon walked over to her, placing his arm around her shoulders.

"He shall come through, Marcia. I believe that. You must try to believe it, too."

She turned to look at him, searching his face for some substantiation of his words. Had he perhaps heard something? How could he be so stolid when his son lay with a gaping hole in his chest, his life perhaps slipping away? "Promise me, promise me," she murmured distraughtly.

"My dear, you know I cannot. What I can do is tell you that Thomas is of good stock. He has a strong will, Marcia, and he has potency, physical stamina, and strength of character. Those all bode well for him. And, dear heart, he has one thing more . . . he has you, and his love for you.

"You must believe that he will gather together all of it to overcome this. A man who never quits, is never defeated, and Thomas is not a quitter, Marcia. The only thing we can do now, is to believe and to pray."

With those last words, Lord William Brandon's voice cracked, and he brushed away an errant tear.

"Come, Marcia," said Lady Brandon. "Come and sit here by me. It always falls to women to wait. Wait we shall, my dear, but with strength of spirit from each other, giving our hope some teeth." Marcy walked ghostlike to the chair. Together, the three sat, waited, and prayed.

The surgeon walked toward them. All three rose simultaneously. He introduced himself and told Tommy's parents that they had done as much as possible, and the outcome would be revealed with time. Madeline collapsed into a chair, with William standing silent like a tree rooted in stone.

Marcy introduced herself, giving indication of her medical affiliation, and questioned the surgeon further. The single gunshot wound had missed the heart, but had torn through adjacent organs, muscle, and tissue. There had been massive bleeding and trauma, which they had been able to relatively control with internal massage and intracardiac epinephrine. Tommy had been administered many units of plasma, platelets, and associated fluids required to stabilize him when he had "coded." Marcy shook uncontrollably when she heard that word, but urged the doctor to continue. She had to know all of it.

He had sustained cavitation injuries to the right lung and diaphragm, right lobe of the liver, gallbladder, right colon, and right kidney, as well as a small area of the stomach and small bowel. They had surgically resected the lung and diaphragm; performed a partial hepatectomy; a cholecystectomy on the gallbladder; a colectomy on only the right portion of the colon; and fortunately managed to repair the damage to the kidney, stomach, and small bowel.

"The most important wounding characteristic of a projectile is its kinetic energy," said the surgeon. "The terminal energy—the amount of impact the bullet exerts on the body—can be anywhere from 1100 to 2000 feet per second. One tiny bullet wreaks an incredible amount of damage.

"The good news is that the high elasticity of lung tissue helps to protect it somewhat from the damaging effects. The bad news is that the liver is very similar to water in density, and has almost no elasticity. Fortunately, this seems to have been a low-velocity pistol bullet, so it had little flight alteration from its angle of entry. In other words, internal injuries sustained were to tissue along a wound tract with no deviation or tumbling. If those things had happened, we would have been looking at a cavity wound up to thirty times greater than the actual bullet. And," the trauma surgeon continued, "we would not be having this conversation. But we have sustained life here, miss . . . weak and holding by a thread, but sustained. I'm afraid that's the best I can give you just now. Courage." he said, wearily turning away.

There it was, completely out in the open. Marcy knew that Tommy's condition was dire. She walked as if in a bad dream, not thinking about where she was going. Someone grabbed her arm. It was Harry Lochmere with Sandra Dunne standing beside him. She looked at them blankly.

"We came as soon as we could. How is he?" asked Harry. Marcy collapsed into his arms, her last thought the sight of Tommy's hand reaching out to her, hearing his muffled whisper, "I love you, doctor."

Chapter 56

Coventry, England

Andy was more than satisfied with the group of colleagues gathered in their safe house. They had had benefit of some of the finest research tomes available, and each participant brought stellar qualifications to the group. Although he was the designated head of the team, in his heart of hearts he felt mediocre in comparison to such learned, venerable people.

So it was that he began to submit his findings rather tentatively, having completed the presentation on historical and political background, religious factors, and elements of linguistic considerations.

"As we are all aware, gentlemen . . . and lady," Andy nodded to the woman with a traditional crimson *bindi* on her forehead, marking her heritage, "the document is a mixture of languages both ancient and obsolete, as it were."

He continued, but his attention was drawn to the Indian woman drawing symbols on her pad. "There have been, and will continue to be, detailed tests beyond carbon 14, pollen analysis, DNA, infrared photography, and electron microscopy carried out on the original documents. These further tests will, of course, be under the control, protection, and scrutiny of Israel, albeit attended by a team of several international scientists. Some are from the countries each of us represents. I have assurances that we will be notified of all results."

The exotic woman was lovely, the part in her hair exhibiting *sindoor*, in the Hindu tradition signifying strength, love, and that she was a married woman. Her skin was a rich coffee color, and her slight build was clad in a richly hued sari. She bade Andrew pause by lifting a long, slender finger.

"We are all, gentlemen, in a millennial scavenger hunt, are we not? Thus, we must place ourselves almost meditatively in the frame of mind of our conjoint ancestors. If you will give me a moment," she said, finishing a few symbols on her pad. "Ah, yes, there." She rose and approached the series of white boards covering the room's far wall opposite the table at which they all sat.

"As Andy has kindly reminded us, the cuneiform writing system originated perhaps around 3000 BC. It underwent considerable modification over the next 2000 years in the form of rotation, abstracted glyphs, and simplifications made primarily by Assyrian scribes in the 1st millennium. In the interim, writing direction changed from left to right in horizontal rows, which rotated pictograms 90° counter-clockwise in the process.

"Pictograms offered certain signs to indicate names of gods, countries, birds, trees, vessels, etc., that looked much like these Andy has drawn for you." She used a grade school pointer to indicate the symbols on Andy's first white board to be used as a comparison to the images on a second board, duplicative of those in the scroll from Anton.

"Those 'determinants' served as a guide for the reader, but began to lose their function because a sign could have various meanings depending on context. Thus, the sign inventory was reduced from some 1500 to only about 600, and a simple word underwent the changes indicated as with this word." Again, she pointed to Andy's illustration board showing progressive changes in common signs.

"Remembering that we began with the Sumerian archaic cuneiform adopted by the Akkadians, we then move to its evolution into Old Assyrian cuneiform. Then, as we all know, writing became increasingly phonological, using a sound system with determinative signs to avoid ambiguity, because ultimately, Semitic language needs and equivalents for many signs became distorted. Agreed?" Everyone's head nodded.

"But," interrupted Andy, "then they were abbreviated to form new phonetic values because the syllabic nature of the Sumerian/Akkadian script was neither instinctive nor perceptive to Semitic speakers. The Akkadian didn't account for pharyngeals,[46] emphatic consonants, or glottal stops."[47]

"Exactly, Andy, I see you already get my point. Very good!" She smiled at Andy, looking at her other colleagues. "I see everything from question marks to empty gazes, professors. Please, bear with me." The petite woman took up a marker and began to write images on the board.

"Former pictograms like that one," she said, pointing to one of the images that Andy had reproduced for their consideration, "were further reduced to a higher level of abstraction," she said, linking an original sign to an image from the scroll reproduced on Andy's board. As she spoke, her drawings demonstrated her words.

"They were composed of only five basic wedge shapes: horizontal, vertical, two diagonals, and the vertical impression created by the tip of the stylus used in that time. Are you there yet, professors? As Andy has drawn for us, we must consider the tenû,[48] because a vertical wedge sign with tenû becomes a diagonal one. Then we are faced with gunû[49] and šešig,[50] also." Anjali Mukherjee paused, then continued, slightly frustrated by her colleagues' slowness at grasping her point.

"The images Andy has reproduced from the scroll are examples of the progression in the evolution of the original cuneiform, which would be correct for those who formed the scrolls. By the time the scrolls were written, only a very few possessed knowledge of ancient cuneiform, and those scribes who did, would have written with tenû, gunû, and šešig influence!

"We have been struggling to translate these images on the basis of the first known examples of ancient cuneiform, my friends, as distinct to evolved, modified cuneiform. We failed to consider the implications of our long, dead scribes being Semitic not only in culture and religion, but in language and phonological influence as well!" Satisfied, she took her seat to allow the impact of her theory to germinate in their minds.

An energized Andy took the floor, quickly diagramming for their conjoint consideration. "I can't believe I didn't see it before. Look . . . typical signs have about five to ten wedges, right? But complex ligatures, still distinct signs, can have twenty or more. If we isolate the tenû, gunû, and šešig images, and combine them with the logograms that read as whole words and representational thoughts, we'll have cracked it! Watch . . ." Andy made his point through illustration of commonly known signs.

"The Hebrew and Aramaic is a cinch from there, because the entire scroll becomes merely a mixed method containing ideographic and phonetic writing. Some of us are conversant with the Aramaic alphabet, and others are experts in ancient Hebrew. So we will end up with a semi-alphabetic syllabary, using far fewer wedge strokes than Assyrian used, with a bunch of logograms for frequently occurring words like this one for 'God,' or this one for 'king.' Although some of the symbols like these," he said pointing to figures, an obelisk, and geometric shapes of a triangle or pyramid, "resemble Greek characters. They represent words and syllables. And they must be read from left to right, do you see? This is definitely decipherable, my friends!

One of the men queried, "Yes, but logograms represent words, do they not? Can we be sure that the modifications that came with the influences presented are correct word references?"

"If you'll forgive me, Professor Zoran, logograms are both graphemes[51] and morphemes[52]. Please, at the risk of sounding pedantic, understand that these logograms provide us with words, speech sounds, and determinatives or ideograms, as we've discussed. We can establish definitive symbols for divinities, people, animals, plants, parts of the body, etc. Although they helped in reading, and will clearly help us in translating, they were not pronounced. But they will be critical in the transliteration once we have deciphered and translated all the signs and letters, because ideograms represent ideas rather than words and morphemes.

"Understand, we have a combination system in these scrolls: logo grammatical and alphabetic language. From there, we will have the semantics. And the semantics will provide the interpretation of the signs used by this community within their specific circumstances and context."

Aharon Rozen, the Israeli doyen, who had years of study at and free access to the enviable library collection and archives of Ecole Biblique et Archéologique Française de Jérusalem, said, "Cuneiform was a syllabary writing system with a consonant and a vowel making one writing unit. That would have been inappropriate for a Semitic language which required triconsonantal roots, or three consonants minus any vowels, no?"

"Yes, Dr. Rozen," said Anjali, "which is precisely why the signs underwent such evolution . . . in an attempt to be used and understood by the development of the peoples. It was only the trend toward spelling out each word with alphabetic symbols that caused it to become extinct, because as you and Andy have said, it was not compatible with the Semites and their language needs as they developed."

The brilliant Professor Mukherjee continued, "It was not until I studied Andy's drawings from a different perspective, that I realized our efforts had become entrapped by our very expertise in deciphering ancient languages. We approached it as academicians, not scholars, and we did not consider the history, the evolution of the language. By then, cuneiform was more or less extinct, having been supplanted by Aramaic. Our 'scroll scribes' had a lingering knowledge of Akkadian, but theirs was of the 'evolved' version," offered the Indian woman, "though they cleverly included some symbols from their ancestors to create a 'coded' document."

"It should be relatively easy to ascertain the sound of alphabetic written words and remember them, and even easier to remember the meaning of the ideographs. If what you tell us proves true," said Aharon, "the message should be made very clear."

"Yes, so let's get started. Aharon, together with Professor Zoran and Dr. P, work on the ancient Hebrew, Aramaic and Greek. I will join Anjali and Dr. Amun al-Misri on the Sumerian/Akkadian. We can reconvene together as we get breakthroughs, and then trade places and do a second round of analyses on the alternate languages. Agreeable to everyone?"

"But first, let's break for lunch. I don't know about you, but I'm starving." Andy smiled at the group, giving a thankful nod to Anjali, relieved that they were all excited and eager to get to work. The air rippled with excitement. He was convinced that the combined brainpower in the safe house would reveal the message of the scrolls in a relatively short time.

As he walked toward the dining room, noting the excited buzz between his colleagues, he thought 'What do I do when we're done?' The plan was to unveil the message properly couched in statesmanship from an alliance of nations. How would they be able to prevent the message from leaking and stirring even greater trouble prematurely? 'What will be done with us? Will we be kept under lock and key?' He shook those thoughts away, lest they cause him to lose his exuberance and succumb to the black clouds that hovered at the edges of his mind.

When he saw the small vase of daisies on the table, a familiar warmth spread through his chest as he recalled his beautiful Aniela skipping through a meadow gathering her favorite flower—daisies—just before they made their climb. That was just before they were shot at, and just before they had to feel their way through that dark, slippery, musty cavern. And it was before his sweet Aniela had acted without thinking to protect him. It was before she had collapsed from the weight of the burden he had placed upon her, and the danger into which he had led her.

A wracking heartache resurfaced, assuaged only a little by the memory of a sweet and spirited, sometimes sassy, Austrian beauty who wore a filigreed locket around her neck. 'If only . . .' he ruminated.

He sighed, wishing . . . wishing what? That he could rewrite history? The impact of his personal reflections made him chuckle to himself. Wasn't that what they were all attempting to do together?

CHAPTER 57

Coventry, England

After several days of work and meetings together, the group convened in the drawing room. Andy opened several bottles of wine, motioning to some of the men to pour and serve.

"Now that we have completed all we can do to the best of our ability, I would like to take this opportunity to say a few words to all of you. We've worked hard together; we've put our hearts, minds, and bodies to the task. And we have, I believe, done a good job.

"We know that collectors are keeping precious items far more secreted and taking incredibly circumspect measures for their transactions these days. As much as it may be unwelcome to acknowledge, some Middle Eastern countries have tried to eliminate all evidence of Jewish presence within their state, destroying or keeping all such evidence hidden. As we all recognize, most things are smuggled out of those countries with sufficiently sound documentation to be later sold to collectors.

"How these scrolls came to our hands is irrelevant, but suffice it to say that many good and honorable people like yourselves sacrificed much to deliver copies of them into our hands. The copies of the documents we've been analyzing together present a source of religious authority never before comprehended since antiquity. As I understand it, our role as scientists, historians, linguists, translators, and investigators is not to advocate any side, but to explore the evidence.

"Clearly, the words as revealed from our conjoint project will sharpen the world's awareness of the major issue. Two of the world's largest and most prevalent religions have been at war with each other for centuries. Another . . . my own . . . has unwillingly become a target.

This has evolved into political warfare, in the least, and latterly into terrorist activity all over the globe, with hovering cataclysmic potential involving sponsor countries.

"Certainly, had these words been understood 1000 years earlier, they would have been burned and destroyed as heresy or all of humankind's history might have been changed. But they remained hidden. Now, our own cultural and political experiences give us a new perspective on the issues the translation raises. It will take greater minds than ours, greater powers than ours, greater combined spirit than ours to determine exactly what shall be done with it, and in what way.

"Because of your help and cooperation, and thanks to the support and protection of the UK's Secret Intelligent Service, MI6, we've been able to safely conclude our work. Copies of the final translation will be presented to all the allied nations, which, I pray, will once and for all end much of the bitterness that has evolved with mankind's development and competition for world rule.

"Now, it is my responsibility to inform you of the latest agreements between our governments. I learned of them only this morning.

"Each of you will be sequestered for a time with a delegation from your country of origin, already agreed by the allied nations involved. This is for your protection, and will last only a short time."

As expected, there were exasperated remarks, shocked expressions, and grumblings from the group of scientists. Andy held his hands out to them.

"Thereafter, we shall meet again together in one of the following countries, all neutral: Norway, Sweden, Finland, Ireland, Switzerland, Liechtenstein, Austria, or Costa Rica. Although Turkmenistan and Malta are also neutral, those countries have been so for a significantly shorter time, and are therefore outside consideration. However, it should be noted that the neutrality of some countries now in the European Union is under dispute, as the EU now operates a common foreign policy. I can't say when this meeting will take place. Ultimately, its date and venue will be up to the countries in the alliance."

Dr. Maahes Amun al-Misri (Egypt) asked, "And what of our families? When our names are released, how will they be kept safe?"

Dr. Nikos Papadopoulos (Greece) complained, "We all have lives, Andrew, and work to be completed. Yes, of course, we were on loan for this project, but unfinished business awaits. How long are we to be kept as virtual prisoners?"

Dr. Aharon Rozen (Israel) opined, "This reminds me of the days before the Holocaust. Can you promise me it will be different with us?"

Professor Anjali Mukherjee (India) quietly wept. "It seems a poor reward for so great a task and so insightful and powerful a message to the world. One wonders, will any of us ever be safe?"

Professor Albrecht Zoran (Germany) laughed until he made himself cough. "All of you, listen to yourselves. We are all in the same boat together. Have you forgotten the words, 'Never Again,' the words the world ashamedly recites because so many looked the other way?

"This is not the time of the Holocaust, my friends. Our boat will not be sunk with all of us in it, as might have been done then, except then it was gas chambers and holes in the ground. But I digress. No, world governments will not risk such a thing because too many know about our little journey together.

"Be sensible; be calm; be patient. The Message has lingered for thousands of years in the care of this one or that. It is powerful, and through us has come again to life.

"Perhaps, its power is what makes you think of yourselves as individuals, with concerns about the trappings of everyday life? We all surrendered our reputations, the definitions of who we were, when we agreed to this undertaking. We are those people no longer. We are changed. We are the people who unlocked the greatest secret in mankind's history.

"We all know that The Message bodes change to the entire world. Impossible? Maybe. But your lives and mine will be irrevocably changed once it is released, that is certain. And the lives of your family and friends, your governments, and your work will also be changed. So, I ask you, would you prefer to face those changes alone and unassisted, knowing what may lie ahead? For me, for my puny part in this big thing, I want all the help, support, and protection the world has to offer."

Heads nodded contemplatively, and Andy unabashedly allowed tears to roll down his cheeks. "Thank you, professor. Your remarks have helped clarify our position and our great accomplishment.

"My friends, I know this is an unexpected development, and therefore a shock. However, please do not let it dampen your spirits or cheat you of hard-won elation over completion of this project. Conjointly, you've succeeded where others have failed. Likewise, in uncharacteristic fashion, results of your work will be published for all the world to benefit, as distinct to being mired in individual group discussion and testing for years, like many other finds.

"Remember, this time it's been different. We've had the best the world has to offer in all of you. We've had unlimited scientific support from our allied governments to accomplish the required testing and verification. You will all receive the credit you richly deserve, but we must be wise about the way in which this is handled for reasons of your personal safety and the safety of the countries you represent.

"When all of this is unveiled to the world, our work will come under close scrutiny which may mean strong criticism and, potentially, you may be placed in danger. Each involved country has agreed to deal with that eventuality to the best of its ability. However, if any of you wish to remain anonymous, it will not be regarded negatively by any of your colleagues, nor of your sponsor nation. The decision is, and shall remain, yours and yours alone.

"For myself, I thank each and every one of you for your considerable help and expertise. You know, I'm not as learned a man as compared to most of you. But as I worked with you, I found I was inspired to reach beyond my limits. I think we all did that for each other. So I'd like to close with a quote by Johann Wolfgang von Goethe: 'True excellence is rarely found, even more rarely is it cherished.'

"My friends, we have found true excellence in our combined midst, and I want you all to know I cherish it and you. God bless and keep you all safe until next we meet."

Professor Anjali Mukherjee wiped away tears; Dr. Maahes Amun al-Misri looked at no one, but stared contemplatively; Professor Albrecht Zoran lit a cigar; Dr. Aharon Rozen grinned, rising to shake everyone's hand; and Dr. Nikos Papadopoulos raised a glass and made toast after toast after toast.

They had all become friends in their endeavor to translate and transliterate the scrolls that had so long ago been buried for safekeeping, hidden for millennia from the rest of the world, then journeyed from hand to hand, country to country, after their rediscovery. Now, treated with the reverence and respect they were due, the documents were safe, and their words and message would be revealed to the world. What the world would make of it, remained to be seen. What forces would attempt to exert influence could only be speculated. What result would come would be in the omniscient hands of God.

After brief, quiet conversation, each left for his/her room to pack. Vehicles were scheduled to collect them in less than two hours. The burden, complexity, and astonishment of their achievement rested heavily on their shoulders.

As they mounted the stairs, one behind the other, Aharon quoted Shakespeare.

"How far that little candle throws his beams! So shines a good deed in a weary world."

CHAPTER 58

The Message

"**M**y Brothers, I walk with you in your steps in this place. I have come among you as I must go among others, to bring you a message from the Father.

"There shall come a time when I shall be no more; when the closed hearts of men will turn against the Son of Yahweh born in Nazareth, and take me from our people. There shall come a time when the skies shall shudder and moan and lash with the Father's sorrow and anger. There shall come a time when many shall turn their face from me and hide in fear of what is to come.

But you, my Brothers, shall not be among them. You shall be safe. if you remain steadfast and true to the Father. You shall be as seeds scattered in a fertile field, which shall bloom and bloom again, to send seeds on the winds of Time to far places, so that the Father's Message will be planted beyond the Great Sea in the time beyond memory.

Fear not for me, my Brothers, for while I am with you, I share the blessing and gird my loins for what is to come, by sharing your purity untouched by those who would revile, seek to destroy, and live by the sword. You are truly my Brothers, in heart, mind, and soul, and it is the will of the Father that I, Eashoa, the child of Joseph and Mary, the Son of Yahweh, share with you His great blessing.

1. It is not I, the Teacher of Righteousness, who should be remembered and revered. The Son of God is but a mast to take the breath of God, to capture the wind of the destiny the Father

has chosen for you. I tell you these things as your teacher of righteousness, the son of God, so that you will know the true Way to the Father, as Sons of God. Do not forget the way to the kingdom of heaven. To turn your face or to close your heart is the greatest vice.

2. You must bring forth that which is within you. It will save you, for it is that part of you which is divine, like that part of me which is divine. If you do not bring forth that which is within you, it shall be as fertile seeds cast upon a fallow field that are scattered by the winds.

3. I am the first, but I shall not be the last. I am the honored one, but I shall also be the scorned one. I shall also be the sacrificed one, the first-born lamb, in the way of our people.

4. There are those who will come teaching heresy. My life and my words I give to you to show you the truth, and so that you may see the falsity of the ones who come after me.

5. I do this, I give you my words unto safekeeping, to spread among all the peoples both near and far, so that you may urge all those with whom you are connected to run from the abyss, to stay strong in the faith, to shun the madness of blasphemy against me. For when I am blasphemed, the Father is also.

6. For whosoever denies me as the Son of God, denies himself, and forsakes his place with God the Father, as his rightful Son and true heir.

7. We move toward our rebirth with every breath. How do we know what rebirth is? By taking ourselves from ourselves to our very starting point. From whence comes this spark? From God the Father. Learn whom it is within you, safely waiting for the time when you shall search. Learn who it is that says 'everything is mine.' Learn the beginning and the end, the alpha and the omega, the source of all joy and sorrow, all love and hate. In these opposites will you find what you seek. You will find the Father inside of yourself.

8. Do not call me Master. I am not your Master. Only God the Father is your Master. You are in me, and I am in you. You are you, and I am I, but you are also me, and I am also you. Together and apart, we are also God the Father, because He dwells within us if we seek His voice.

9. You feel that you are drunk because you have drunk of the stream
    of life I have poured out for you and will pour out for many. Soon
    that stream will turn to vermilion with the blood I shall shed for
    you and for many, to mark you for the Father. He who drinks of
    this stream will become as I will become, will become one with
    the Father.

10. When you drink, you shall see me in all things, as you shall see
    the Father in all things. I will be one with the birds of the airs and
    the clouds of the skies, and the fishes of the seas and the plants of
    the earth. You shall become one with the birds of the airs and the
    clouds of the skies, and the fishes of the seas and the plants of the
    earth. Just as the Father, who says 'everything is mine,' you will
    be His, and you will be one with all that is His, just as I am His,
    and just as I am one with all that is His.

11. There will be those who call you false believers and treat you
    with scorn and hate and revile you, just as they will treat me with
    scorn and hate and revile me. Do not be afraid. Though I will not
    always be here with you, our Father has sent me to give you my
    words, which shall be with you always.

12. My words are His words. My life is His life. My life is your life.
    Your life is His life. Those who call you false believers because
    you see the Father in all things and call yourselves His will try
    to frighten you. They will war with you and drive you from your
    lands. They may kill you. But hear me, they cannot kill you, for
    you belong to the Father, and everything is His to do what He
    wishes. If you drink of the stream I pour out for you, none can
    hurt you, for you will always be His, and you will always be me,
    and you will always be in all things that are His.

13. You know there are those who rule over you. There are those
    who rule over all the tribes, and the tribes of the gentiles. There
    are those who rule over the peoples of the rest of the world. They
    are but as an eagle who soars above all for as long as it pleases
    the Father to allow the eagle to soar. One day, the eagle shall fall,
    as they too shall fall. For all things belong to Him who owns
    everything.

14. It shall not be so among you, for you will always be you, and you
    will always be me, and you will always be one with the Father.
    But those among you who would lead the peoples in the mission
    for the Father for all of the world, must be the least. For as the

least, you shall be great. Just as I am your servant, you must be the servant. Just as the least is the first, whoever among you would be the leader, must first be the servant.

15. To you I give the greatest secret: the way to the kingdom of God. There are those who are outside everything, outside where they cannot hear, outside where they do not see, outside where they do not perceive the things that I give to you. Yet, they are your brothers. You must follow the Father's will for all the world and bring them inside so that they will hear and understand. You must bring them inside so that they can see my power in you, and the Father's power in you. You must bring them inside so that they will be able to perceive the things that I have told you, else they shall turn away from the Father's will.

16. There will be those who only feel, and by feeling, believe that the things that happen to them are part of the divine will of the Father. But this is not the will of the Father, for they do not know the Father, because they do not know me, and they do not know you. They do not love the Father above all things, and they do not love me, and they do not love you, and they do not love themselves with the love of the Father. They must be as you, just as you must be as me, just as you and I must be as the Father. These heretics and strangers cannot advance or receive by the power of their own will. You must follow the will of the Father that is in you, that is in me, and make known to them that there is no God but God the Father, who claims everything as His own. It is the Father who says, 'everything is mine,' because He alone is the root of all, not begotten, He is the one who begot and created all.

17. Beware of those who stand with you and say the things you say, and do the things you do. If they do not search for the start of all things within, they are not you, they are not me, they are not one with the Father of all, but are as wolves in sheep's clothing. In time, they may claim to have power beyond every power. They may claim they may do what they please to do, and have no fear in anything. They may claim they are beyond the power of any judge, or any tribe, or any land. But I tell you, they are no better than the eagle, and they shall fall.

18. Anyone who speaks against God can be recognized by all who truly worship God. All of these who speak against God, speak

also against me, and will speak against you. All of these have fallen from the truth or have corrupted the truth, or have never seen the light of the truth within them. They are not the ones who speak the truth, because only the Father speaks the truth. God is the voice within every creature. He is the real voice, He is the seed within. He is the first and the last and the holy one. The only truth is that the Father is the only Father, and there are no other Gods by any name but His. And the only truth spoken by men is the truth of God that speaks through them as Sons of God who do His will.

19. He sent me to tell you my words, words that He put in my mouth so that you would hear and understand, perceive and know, look and see. When you see my suffering, you will understand that it is your suffering, but you shall not have to suffer it. You must learn how to suffer by seeing my suffering, so you shall be able not to suffer. Then you shall understand suffering. And when I speak, you must listen to what I speak so that you will understand. With the power of my words in you, you shall speak to all the others so that they will understand. With the Father's light within you, you will perceive and know that I am He, and He is I, and I am you, and you are me, and He is in me and He is in you. You shall know from the beginning to the end, and no one shall be able to take this from you. And you shall be as one with the Father and give this secret to all the people, so that they may be one with the Father. And the Father shall say again and again, 'everything is mine.'

20. There shall come a time when you will have been the servant of all for ages of time as the Father's mission tells you to do. Many of you shall pass away, as I shall pass away, but the Father shall never pass away. There shall come a time when you will be persecuted for the light within you, for the words you speak that I have given you, the words that the Father has given to me. Your faith will be tried, you shall burn with fire, you shall fall by the sword, you shall be tormented by your brothers, and all over the world, many will rise against you. Do not be afraid, for the Father shall see that when you pass away, you shall yet live, just as I shall live, because the Father is in us, and the Father is, and always shall be.

21. But there shall be brothers from among who will raise this one or that one. They shall rise and become great among their peoples. Yet they are your brothers, even if they are not yet the Father's sons. You shall be in the midst of very great heat, the fire of persecution, and the fire and the sword will try you, as the beasts of the forests try each other. You shall be like the hares of the field and the hounds shall hunt you. But do not be afraid.

22. The Father is of the same nature as we ourselves, because He is in us and He is in me. He offers me up as the first fruits of the tribulation, His own Son, His own humanity, so that you will not be discouraged and will confess your faith and live your faith and give your faith to others, so that you shall walk with me, because what the Father grants to His Son, he grants to all His Sons. But this love that the Father sends forth to every place throughout all time is given only to those that bear love for God and confess their faith. If you are oppressed or persecuted, you must do the Father's will and I tell you that He will love you and make you the same as me in spirit, just as I am the same as you in life. You shall know that my words are true when you hear that I walk the earth in spirit after I die. I shall walk in spirit to show you and all my followers that my words are true, and that the Father's words are true that spill from my mouth. So shall it be for you after you die. Just as I am the same as you in life, I am the same as you after death. You are the same as me in life, and you shall be the same as me after death.

23. The Kingdom of God waits for those who find the Father as the seed within, and see themselves in others, and in all things that the Father made, just as I see myself in you. I will pass away, but I have already put myself to death to be one with the Father. So too you must put yourself to death to be one with me and the Father, for none who fear death will be saved, for the Kingdom belongs only to those who put themselves to death to be as one. This is how great the love of God is for everything that he owns.

24. But you must follow the will of the Father in all things to receive this great love and walk with me in the Kingdom of God which is beyond death, after you pass away, and all things pass away, according to the Father's will for all things. You must go to those who revile you, who persecute you, who say all manner of things against you, and confess the name of the Father. You must

show them by the light that shines within you the power of the Father, so that they shall look and truly see; hear and understand; perceive and know. For if you do not spread the Father's love to those brothers in other lands, they shall rise up against you and false ones who come after me will tell the people false things. But these people will not know that the teachings are not the teachings I give you from the Father, and they will believe, and they will not be under the Father's will, and the Father's love will not live in them as it lives in you.

25. If you war with your brothers, if you forsake your brothers in faraway lands and do not share the light of the Father as I have shared it with you, the Father will not pour His love out to you, for you will have forsaken your brothers who are also His children. Would you forsake me? Then you must not forsake them. Would you forsake the Father now that you know His light and His power and His love? Then you must not forsake them. For if you forsake them, you forsake yourselves, and you forsake me, and you forsake the Father. You cannot share in the love God pours out for you without sharing with your brothers. For just as I am in you, and you are in me, you are also in your brother, and your brother is also in you.

26. So you must go beyond the Great Sea to the lands of Cilicia, Cappadocia, Galatia, Bithynia, and Pontus. You must go to Asia and Macedonia, Thrace and Achaia. You must journey to Syria, Arabia, Egypt, and Cyrenaica. You must go beyond Judea to all the lands beyond so that the Father's love may be a light unto all the peoples. You are the chosen people. The chosen people receive the blessings of the Father because they have the light of the Father within them and do His will. You were chosen to do more than to be brought to the Promised Land, to be restored. Hear O Israel, the Promised Land is His, you are His, and destiny is His.

27. If you do these things and follow the will of the Father, you shall share in the Kingdom of God, and God will look upon you with love and pleasure, and God will continue to live within you for all your days, and for all the days to come after you shall pass away, and you shall be one with me and all the things that God has made, for the Father says, 'everything is mine.'

28. But if you do not do these things, if you do not serve your brother, you forsake yourselves and the light that is within you, and the wrath of the world shall fall around your heads, and my words shall pass away just as I shall pass away. The Father's wrath will be poured out among you and your brethren, and on all the peoples of the world, and the world shall come to terrible tribulation, until it has been purified by the fire of God's power and will.

29. If your brothers do not hear the word of the Father, and turn from the father's light and his will, they shall become as wolves. They shall tear at the very fabric of the world which is not the Father's will for all his people. They must see you as brothers as you see them as brothers. Brothers must not resist brothers, or both shall fall, and both shall be outside the kingdom of God, the Father of all. Both shall be outside the cup of righteousness and the water of life everlasting. Both shall be separated from me and therefore from the Father. Both shall be sacrificed, as the lambs who remain outside the fold are devoured.

30. But I shall live with the Father, because I shall be one with the Father. You can be one with the Father only if you think as the Father, not as a man. If you separate from your brother in any of the places I have told you, or in any of the places beyond, then you separate yourself from God the Father and from me, the Son, and you deny the destiny God has made for you, and you shall continue to suffer, and you and the children of Israel shall suffer a terrible tribulation.

31. Just as he who made the outside of the cup also made the inside of the cup, both sides must be washed. Those outside must be made like those inside. My words are given to you to unite them in that place. My words will give them a new heart, just as I have given you a new heart, and the Father will put a new spirit in them, just as He has put a new spirit in you. To God belongs all the earth and all things it holds, and all the people who live on it.

32. This law is implanted in brotherhood to enlighten the hearts of men and to make straight the way of true righteousness. You must love the Father above all things in life. So you must know that all things exist by the Father and there is none beside His law. You must love God above all things and love others. Just as God loves you, God is in you, and you must love the God within you and

the God within your brothers, and bring to them the light of the Father according to His will, so that they like you may become true Sons of God. You belong to no country as I belong to no country. I belong to the brotherhood, as you must belong to the brotherhood as God's children of light.

33. And the vast brotherhood of the earth shall raise their voices as one and sing to the Father. And He shall sing to them, 'I am the "Alpha and the Omega, the beginning and the end, which was, which is, and which is to come. I shall make all things new, and he that overcomes shall inherit all things, and I will be your God, and you shall be my Sons.

34. And so my brothers, write the things you have seen and the things you have heard and the things which are, and the things which shall be hereafter, all of the mysteries of the earth and of heaven. Let the voices of the Holy Brotherhood raise in song. 'Come ye, and let us walk in the light of the law and the truth of the Father in brotherhood.' And so brothers, reach for the inner vision, and through the spirit in me hear the wondrous secret. Through mystic insight will come a spring of knowledge to well within you, a fountain of power pouring forth living waters, and a flood of love and wisdom and eternal light.

35. Let us give thanks together, for I will be saved, and I will save; you will be saved, and you will save. I will be born, and I will bear; you will be born, and you will bear. I have heard, and I will be heard. You will hear, and you will be heard. I will be understood, being wholly understanding. You will be understood, being wholly understanding. I am a lamp to you who see me. You shall be a lamp to those who see you. I am a mirror to you who perceive. You shall be a mirror to those who perceive.

36. Those who do the Father's will are my brothers and shall enter the Kingdom of God. Be in harmony. I go to prepare a place for you. Those who have ears, let them hear. Be vigilant and allow no one to mislead you by saying, 'Here it is!' or 'There it is!' Remember, it is within you, as I am in you, as the Father's light is in you. Those who seek him, find him. Walk forth, my brothers, and announce the gospel of the Kingdom of God. Be well, children of love and peace, and keep my words safe among you, for they are the Father's words and belong to His world,

to be spread near and far, that all men shall come to the Father through me and through you. May the Father of glory and of every perfect gift of strength and grace be with your spirit now and in the days to come."

ChAPTER 59

Washington, D.C., Summer 2008

"Yes, sir, insofar as my part goes, that's all of it," said Andy to Liam Corruthers, having finished a morning's recitation of his European assignment. "The rest, concerning details of the team's op, will have to come from them, Helmut Kaiser, in particular. He did a helluva job, sir. They all did." Corruthers was silent for a few moments, contemplating the entirety of Andy's narration.

"Okay, Andy, that's a fairly thorough report in my book. Of course, you'll have to work with the official debriefing unit and go over it again for the record, you realize." Andy signaled his understanding.

Corruthers went on, "You'll also have to appear before a specially appointed Senate Committee on Foreign Relations with a bevy of other participants and attendees. I've had preliminary discussions with the President, and he'll choose the members carefully. They will, of course, require special clearance and cloaking for this meeting. The President himself will be there, as shall I.

"We've got to have people from both sides of the aisle, Andy, and the going will get rough, I can assure you. But something of this gravity that will necessarily affect elements of our existing and future foreign policy aims and posture will have to be handled sensitively, with all hands on deck in support. So your report had better be good . . . and convincing. Get me?"

"Sir, I can assure you I'll do my level best. But the message is The Message. There's no changing it to soften the implications, and with respect, I don't view my role as being persuasive. I have done what was asked of me, and I will report on the results. As to what our government chooses to do with it, how far they'll go, what actions they deem prudent to take or not to take, is not my concern.

"What is my concern, sir, is the immediate future of that handful of brave people who joined with me in this. It was my understanding that we already had an alliance of sorts in place. Those good folks are still in seclusion, and their future is uncertain. It's only because the documents were passed to me that I got to brief my government first. I assured them, based on what you advised, that their governments would receive a copy of the completed manuscript. It's not something that belongs exclusively to the United States, sir, if you'll pardon my outspokenness. It belongs to the world. And besides, I gave them my word and the word of my country, sir. If at the outset we don't keep our word, then as far as I see it, anything we do afterward will not be trustworthy, either, sir."

"I know, son, I know. I admire your sense of loyalty and your wish to do what's right, but the decisions aren't mine to take, understand that. Ultimately, it'll be up to State, and they will confer with the leaders of the alliance. Together, they will decide what to do, when, and how."

"Yes, sir, I know that. But what about my team's future? They're not in our business, sir, but they risked themselves to join up with me in England. And how long do you think this thing can be kept secret? The longer they're kept under wraps, the more suspicion will grow, the more they'll get frustrated and worried."

"Andy, I get it, okay? I'll speak to the President about that element of it, today. All he'll have to do is make a few calls, and then the countries can decide what they'll do with their own people. I promise you, I'll bring it to his attention. I can't, however, make any promises as to what he will do, but I'll make your case. You have my word on that."

"And me, sir? What are you going to do with me?" Andy sat forward in his chair, a worried look plainly on his face.

"Well, once you've made your case before the Committee, I expect you'll be due a furlough. That suit you? After all, it'll be completely out of your hands then, and mine. Of course, you'll be sworn to secrecy until this thing is public."

"That's a given," said Andy without hesitation. "When is the meeting, sir? I'd kind of like to phone my folks to let them know I'm okay, and that I'll be coming home. They've been on tenterhooks for a long time now."

"Day after tomorrow. Until then, you'll have to remain with us and, of course, under protection. But we've planned a good, old-fashioned American dinner for you, at least. You're to be holed up in a pretty nice suite, so relax, and enjoy it. I'll be in touch. Thanks, Andy. You've done well. Your country thanks you, and I thank you. You're a credit to the Service."

"Thank you sir. Is there anything else, sir?" Andy stood, waiting at attention for his dismissal.

"No, now go on, get out of here. And Andy? I suggest you tie one on. You've certainly earned it." Corruthers watched Andy salute, turn, and walk toward the door. 'Thank God that fine young man came home whole. I wonder if he really knows how lucky he was,' he thought broodingly.

Once he was settled in his "pretty nice suite," as Corruthers had described it, Andy removed his clothes and took a long, hot shower. As the water pounded his body, he couldn't help but make comparisons to recent weeks. During their European travels, he and Aniela rarely had showers. If they were fortunate enough to have their own bathroom, it was usually equipped with a basin, or a tub, if they were lucky. The safe house in England did have a shower, but the pressure there was via gravity feed from a large tank in the attic, and the flowing water felt less like the showers he had taken for granted, and more like standing under a gentle waterfall. He had forgotten how wonderfully cleansing American showers were.

As the therapeutic pulse of the showerhead kneaded his tense muscles, his thoughts inevitably turned to Aniela. The piped music he had unconsciously flicked on to drown out the sound of the television watched by his assigned companion, was a public broadcasting station featuring classical music. The familiar strains of the third movement of Haydn's Cello Concerto in D filled the steamy bathroom. He recalled Matthew struggling with it years ago. The memory of his mother's patient piano accompaniment going over a challenging section time after time until Matthew "got it," brought a tender smile to Andy's face that melted into tears, swept away by the shower.

'Could it have been any other piece of music?' he thought wryly. The parallel memories of Aniela and of his family were bitter-sweetly augmented by the Austrian composer's cello concerto. 'Soon, soon . . .' he promised himself.

Cbapter 60

Windward Farm, Maine, Summer 2008

As Marcy ambled aimlessly through the garden, she hesitated under the pergola near the stone wall overlooking the west pasture. A shoot of her mother's coveted American Bittersweet vine gracefully arched from the side of the pergola to cover a portion of the stonewall. 'Bittersweet,' thought Marcy glumly, 'how appropriate.' As she fingered the smooth vine, she recalled how fanatically her mother had tended the young plant, explaining to Marcy that one day it would be vigorous and reward her care by providing berries for the birds, particularly bluebirds, and turn the back garden into a halo of gold.

During her childhood, this had become one of her favorite, "private" places, and she had loved to read and sketch in the nestled comfort of the pergola. As a teenager, she could recall that she had received her first kiss under the boughs of the bittersweet vine. Now, as an adult, she had once again come to the place that held so many memories and had restored her confidence in so many ways through the years. "It's the little things that are important, Marcy, because they help us live through the big things in life," her mother had said.

Although the vine had been different, she recalled that last night with Tommy by the stone wall at Wellington. When they left the party for the privacy of the garden, she had intended announcing that she was in love with him and would accept his proposal. As the conversation evolved, she had been the one to propose that Tommy's suggestion of a drive take them to the show grounds to celebrate with the horses. If only she had followed her original plan. Instead, she had prolonged the surprise, thinking that a visit to his two, favorite champion horses would be a perfect backdrop to her declaration of love. Had she not tried to be clever, Tommy would not be lying in a hospital bed now, with an uncertain future. All of it was her fault. Yes, the bittersweet vine was all too appropriate.

"You thinking about Tommy?" Her father's voice had always had a soothing effect on her. He walked toward her, extending a cup of steaming tea. "Your mother thought you might like this."

"Chamomile," smiled Marcy. "it's supposed to relax you, right?" Her father smiled and nodded. "I haven't heard anything more this week, Dad. Don't get me wrong, the Brandons have been terrific, but I so hoped that he would have come out of the coma before this. The doctors thought that once his wounds healed sufficiently . . ." Marcy's voice broke, and she forced back tears.

"No one can predict how much time the body requires to heal, Marcy. You of all people know that. Every person and every animal is different. Everything God made is unique, even within a species, and each one has its own rhythm and its own sense of time." He said it so simply and surely, that Marcy marveled at the depth and confidence of his faith.

"I could just use something to hold on to, you know?" she said to him in a small voice.

"Well, I know I'm a poor substitute, but how about your old Dad?" She moved into his outstretched arms.

Elizabeth came running from the house calling to them.

"Liz, what's the matter?" Jeremy broke their embrace and turned toward his wife, who was crying and laughing at the same time.

"It's Andy! Oh, Jeremy, it's Andy. He just phoned. He's coming home!"

Elizabeth shared every word of her telephone conversation with Andy, slightly miffed and temporarily frustrated at the limited amount of information supplied by her son. Nonetheless, father, mother, and daughter all hugged each other, thrilled that a long absent son and brother would soon be among them.

"Home! Home! Oh, Liz honey, that's the best news we could have had. Come on, girls, we'll round up the boys and go celebrate. What do you say?" A grinning Jeremy hugged them both again.

Although she, too, was happy, Marcy looked at her parents, not wanting to dampen their high spirits, but finding it difficult to match their lightheartedness. "Sure, let's celebrate." The moment she uttered the words with their flat intonation, she regretted it deeply, particularly when she saw her parents' faces lose their beam. "Oh, I'm sorry . . . I . . . it's just that . . ."

"Honey, forgive me," said her father. "I didn't mean to make light of your feelings. I shouldn't have said 'best news.' I was just so happy; I wasn't thinking."

"Daddy, please. You know how I adore Andy. Of course, I'm thrilled that he's coming home. I'm the one who's at fault. I am happy, and we should all celebrate. It's just that I can't get Tommy out of my mind. I never got to tell him, not really. I mean, he was in such pain, I'm not even sure he heard me or remembers. If anything happens to him, well, I'd just like him to know that I love him. No, that's not all of it, either. I realize I don't know what I'll do if I lose him. It scares me to death every minute," she said. As much as she tried, she could not hide the anguish that marred her lovely face.

"Honey, it doesn't bear thinking about. You get those thoughts right out of your head, hear me?" said her mother. "You're no defeatist, Marcy. Think of all the times you beat the odds with this horse or that. Think of Obsidian. When things looked bleak, you kept going, never giving up. You've just got to find the strength to recapture that attitude now. If not for your own sake, then do it for Tommy, and in honor of Andy's coming home. Now come on, the best place for you is with your family, not out here brooding all by yourself. We love you, honey. And we'll stand with you, no matter what happens." Elizabeth hugged her daughter comfortingly.

Marcy allowed herself to be drawn into the bosom of her family's joy. Over the ensuing hours, little by little, the depth, comfort, and reassuring familiarity of their family bond eased her despondency, restoring her strength. Walking back to the house after her usual night check at the barn, she called back to Rex in answer to his following whinny.

"It's okay, boy, I'm okay. Settle down now, I'll see you in the morning." Dear, dear Rex, her closest friend, always knew when she was troubled, and never failed to let her know he loved her and would be there for her. She hesitated for only a moment, then turned and walked back to the barn. She entered his stall, and he looked expectantly at her.

"I love you, Rex. I just wanted to tell you, to make sure you knew," she said, stroking the beautiful horse. He snuffled contentedly and went back to munching his hay.

"I love you, I love you."

ChAPTER 61

Washington, D.C., Summer 2008

"Gentlemen, I appreciate the latitude extended to me today. I confess unfamiliarity with politics, senate hearings, procedural matters, indeed, all matters of statesmanship. You've been briefed on my professional, academic, and scientific qualifications by my superiors. You have before you a summary of my journey to retrieve the scrolls and the period of work with other international representatives of the alliance, all highly esteemed individuals in their respective fields; a general background of historical, cultural, and political data against which stands the final document; a summarized list of the detailed tests to which portions of the original documents have been subjected; and a transcript of the completed manuscript taken from verified copies of the original, which remains in secure hands abroad.

"Before discussion commences, I would appreciate the opportunity to clarify some aspects of today's deliberations that, in my view, are critically relevant to your understanding."

Andy waited for the Chairman to counsel with the members of the hearing panel. Although representation was balanced between the two prevailing political parties, the President of the United States, his Vice President, members of the Supreme Court, and one representative head of the mainstream religions were also present, by special invitation. The vetting process for this assemblage had been not only thorough, but steeped in security and previously sworn testimony by all participants and auditors.

"You may proceed, Dr. Stanton," said the Chairman. The atmosphere in the room was heavy with anticipation.

342

Andy smiled. "Thank you, Mr. Chairman. I want to assure all of you that I shall answer your questions to the best of my ability from the perspective of unbiased comment, in honor of my professional ethics and the central task of providing you with sufficient peripheral information to make an informed decision. I know we have much to discuss, as there is much to digest. So, I will begin by outlining some of the fundamental considerations I believe are important.

"Please understand that I'm unable to respond to any questions regarding the location of the original documents. That decision remains between the President, his security advisors, other leaders of the alliance, and the principals in possession of the scrolls. Last, I would ask that all questions be put only following my concluding comments."

"You have the floor, Dr. Stanton, and we will honor your requests. Proceed." The Chairman removed his glasses, sitting back in his chair. The other members of the special committee sat poised, pens and pads at the ready.

"As concerns this issue, we have to consider essentially three main bodies of religious writing: the Torah, the Holy Qur'an, and the Holy Bible.

"To fully understand the scope of this issue, let me break it down for you a bit. The Hebrew Bible, the Tanakh, is a Hebrew acronym incorporating the initial letters of its three main divisions.

"'T' for Torah, or teaching, comprised of the five books of Moses known as the Pentateuch. In English, you know those books as Genesis, Exodus, Leviticus, Numbers, and Deuteronomy. The corresponding names in Hebrew are Bereshit, Shemot, Vayikra, Bamidbar, and Devarim.

"Next is 'N' for Nevi'im, eight books of the prophets, containing familiar books like Jeremiah, Ezekiel, and Isaiah.

"Finally is 'K' for Ketuvim, writings or scriptures, containing eleven books like Psalms, Proverbs, Ecclesiastes, and others.

"Hence, T-N-K, or Tanakh. We'll concern ourselves with only the first of the Tanakh's three sections, the Torah, the most holy of all the sacred writings in Judaism. The word literally means teaching or instruction, although it is sometimes translated as law.

"In rabbinic tradition, the word Torah signifies both written text: Torah Shebichtav or Torah that is written; and oral tradition: Shebe'al Peh or Torah that is oral. The oral segment contains the interpretations and clarifications handed down by word of mouth from generation to generation, embodied in the Talmud and the Midrash.

"Now before you all give me a glazed look," said Andy with a sheepish grin, "it's not that difficult. The Talmud is an historical record of rabbinic discussion relating to Jewish law, ethics, custom, and history that is the central text of all Rabbinic Judaism. The Midrash is a Hebrew term for interpretation or exposition, much like the concordances and commentaries available in the Christian faith. Both are outgrowths of Torah, and as such, are designed to clarify the holy writings, an exegesis, if you will.

"While you needed to be reminded of the breakdown of Hebrew religious writing from the perspective of the complexity of challenge, the most important thing you need to remember is that the Torah contains the commandments of God, 613 Mitzvot, that form the basis for Jewish religious law called the Halakha.

"Orthodox rabbis date the revelation of the Torah through a process of divine inspiration to Moses as occurring on Mount Sinai in 1280 BCE, although there is some dispute as to whether it was written down as complete in one event, or over the forty years in the wilderness." He received affirming nods from the rabbi. "That's only a synopsis, gentlemen, of Judaism represented by only its writings.

"Now we come to the Muslim world. The central religious text of Islam is the Qur'an, literally the 'recitation', or 'al-qur'an' in Arabic. According to Islamic belief, the Qur'an is the book of divine guidance for the direction of mankind, and the original Arabic text is considered to be the final revelation of God, or Allah, in Arabic.

"The Qur'an is represented as the final word, in the prophetic tradition of Abraham, Moses, and Jesus, although it is approached in an entirely different way than the Torah or the Christian Bible. Whereas most Jews and Christians admit that Biblical texts may have been written by a significant variety of authors over time, their position is that each book or text was under divine inspiration.

"Muslim consensus views the Qur'an as a direct revelation by the angel Gabriel, Jibrīl, to their prophet, Muhammad, over the last twenty-three years of his life. Although it was written down by his companions, Muhammad is believed to be the first to recite the entirety of the Qur'an over that time period.

"Nothing was seen of the Qur'an before 610 AD, nor after Muhammad's death in 632 AD. The earliest surviving fragment, written in Kufic script, is from the eighth century AD. That said, it is important to recognize that orthodox Islam regards the Qur'an as Allah's book of guidance, not as Muhammad's book, and refers to it as nothing other than God's book. The Qur'an does recognize and refers to the Torah, Christian Scriptures, and their respective prophets, but it retells various stories and events in a distinctly different way with differing emphasis than is found in the Torah and the Holy Bible.

"Last in the trilogy, we come to that portion of the world under the umbrella of Christianity. The Christian Bible recognizes and includes the Hebrew Scriptures—the Old Testament—and later writings, known as the New Testament, in its compilation of scripture, the Holy Bible.

"To be fair to all, I must remark that some Christian groups include additional books as part of their sacred writings. I refer to the biblical apocrypha, meaning 'hidden', which includes books omitted when Protestant and Catholic versions were canonized; and deuterocanonical books, used to describe books and passages that were not contained in the Jewish Bible, as distinct from the protocanonical books which were coextensive with the Hebrew Bible and accepted by most Christians.

"As most of you are familiar, the New Testament is a collection of twenty-seven books with Jesus Christ as its central figure. Written during the early Christian period primarily in Koine Greek, many continue to argue for Aramaic primacy, on the basis that the language of Jesus, his apostles, and most if not all the writers of the New Testament, was Aramaic, not Greek. However, it is relatively certain that some of the Pauline Epistles were written in Greek for Greek-speaking audiences, indicated by Paul's missions.

"That aside, the earliest surviving complete manuscript of the entire Bible is the Codex Amiatinus, a Latin Vulgate edition produced in England in the eighth century. However, the discovery of older manuscripts, notably the Alexandrian and Byzantine text types, date from the fourth century.

"There exist disputes between theologians and camps of belief because of differences that occur in the writings of some of the authors of New Testament books. Some believe that the Bible was written by a variety of men over many years, yet inspired by God; others believe the Bible to be the undisputed word of God.

"That, gentlemen, is an encapsulated history of the prevailing historic religious texts. We know unequivocally, that the Hebrew documents and religion preceded Christianity and Jesus Christ. We also know that organized Islam occurred well after the emergence of Jesus Christ and the established religion of Christianity, therefore also considerably after the establishment of Judaism. You have also been made conversant with the relative content of the Dead Sea Scrolls and other ancient documents and their dates.

"The manuscript in question is in addition to all of these. Its authenticity is attested by carbon 14, ultraviolet, and other reliable dating methodologies, as well as by the conclusions set forth by our scientific and academic team. This, of course, includes the background justification for the encryption using Sumerian/Akkadian cuneiform embedded into the ancient Hebrew, Aramaic, and Greek to form a protection of sorts. It is the conjoint conclusion of my scientific team that the scrolls were thus protected because of the prevailing political, cultural, and religious times during which it was formed.

"Only as a side note, it is interesting that Psalm 83 from Hebrew Scripture and included in Christian Scripture, both of which originated before Islam, contains a prophecy about Arabs surrounding Israel with a view to destroying it. There are probably many other references, but this is just further evidence that this 'war,' so full of vitriol, has been alive and well for a very, very, long time. And equally interesting is the third chapter of the Old Testament book of Zephaniah that speaks to the future of Jerusalem and the restoration of the Hebrews.

"Now, I can't speak to the verity of the words of The Message. Its rhythm, overall tone, and language clearly fits the time. I can tell you that the scrolls themselves are legitimate, from linguistic, scientifically archaeological, and scientifically anthropological perspectives.

"I would also remind you that the New Testament's eye-witness recording of Jesus Christ's words from strictly intellectual and logical perspectives, do not disagree theologically with The Message, in the main. Given the lapse of time over which all religious, political, philosophical or historical writings are silent in mention of Jesus Christ, the manuscript offers an explanation for the missing years of Jesus Christ, until his re-emergence shortly before his crucifixion and subsequent death.

"One last point: The Message is a series of sermons, the individual themes of each pertinent to the following. It will help you to think of a college professor's lectures on a subject that has been divided into digestible segments. At the end of the course, the student will have grasped the content of the entire course." With a broad grin, he continued, "At least that is the intended aim."

The audience chuckled briefly.

"It was clear to all of us on the investigative team that the lessons or themes that comprise the entirety of The Message, were delivered over a significant period of time. Perhaps each session occurred only once every few weeks or so, and was followed by discussion; perhaps it was deemed too laborious to record all of it at one time; perhaps they ran out of prepared hides."

Again, the audience responded to Andy's light humor.

"We shall never know. What we do believe with certainty based upon scientific evidence and conclusion, is that more than one scribe recorded the text on the leather scrolls.

"Gentlemen, and ladies," Andy smiled at the handful of females present, "that concludes the presentation of my introductory remarks. You have before you Section I's background and evolutional analysis, the results of our scientific investigation with the complete translation in Section II, and Section III is an up-to-date clarification of current world politics. The closing statements to Section III that cover speculation as to how current affairs might relate to The Message itself, are designed to serve only as assistance in your discussions. I will now take questions at your pleasure. Thank you."

The Chairman recognized the elder Senator from the South.

"Dr. Stanton, I thank you for a comprehensive picture. I have scrutinized everything you have provided, and more than once, I might add. My compliments: it is a significant body of work. You folks seem to know what you're talking about."

"On behalf of the entire team who worked so hard and sacrificed so much, I thank you, Senator," said Andy evenly.

Continuing in disregard of Andy's response, the Senator said, "Now, we all know that the Middle East is a tinderbox for more than one reason. As I understand all this, you are asking us to believe that this Message, excuse me, *The* Message, is a gospel of Jesus? That's my first question.

"My second question is this: how in the world do you expect us, with the delicate balance of things over there already strained, to publish The Message to the world?

"And last, if you'll forgive an old man for going on a bit, what do you believe our chances are of getting the Islamic world to listen, much

348   Callie McFarlane

less accept a message that goes against thousands of years of cultural, political, and religious rejection of everything non-Muslim, based on the Islamic faith?

"Before you answer, I would ask my learned colleagues and all present to bear in mind the many times throughout history that Arab hatred and destruction of anything other than the Muslim religion and way of life has been perpetuated against many . . . all with dire consequences.

"Now I know our Muslim clerics will jump all over me by saying that Islam is a religion of love and peace. But we cannot forget the Muslims who were motivated by the Islamic religion and their concept of Allah's will in their Jihad in the recent 9/11 attacks, now can we?" He paused deliberately, looking slowly around the assembly, allowing the import of his comments to sink in.

"I can't wait to hear your erudite responses. Thank you, Dr. Stanton," he said caustically. "I relinquish the floor, Mr. Chairman, thank you." The Senator sat back in his chair, folding his hands in satisfaction, looking expectantly at Andy with a acid smile.

Andy sat for a few moments in deep thought.

"Senator, my function has been and remains one of a simple man whose task it was to secure the artifacts or rather as it turned out, a legitimate copy; translate and transliterate, and bring it to the relative safety of the free world. That, sir, was my mission. With all due respect, that mission was completed.

"However, to answer your first question: The referential term of the Teacher of Righteousness fits the profile of Jesus Christ chronologically, theologically, archaeologically, anthropologically, linguistically, geographically, and ethnically. Taken in context, sir, The Message is astounding. That is all I can confirm which is, if you'll forgive me, a great deal in this field.

"Your second question presupposes that I possess the understanding and judgment to make such a determination. I do not. With respect, we must also be cognizant of the fact that other members of the alliance who were involved in the final phase, are all aware of The Message's essence, and their loyalties are first with their own people, countries, and governments. Therefore, I don't believe it's practical to attempt to keep it secret.

"And last, to your third question, Senator. All I know as a citizen of my country and of the world, is that such a sterling find belongs exclusively to no man and no country.

"The United States is known as a country that champions every man's intrinsic right to self-determination. The best course, in my view, would be to release it in a coordinated fashion with the members of the alliance, retaining control of the background presentation as an introduction. If we present this manuscript for all the world to see and consider, knowing it is irrefutable in terms of its legitimacy, then it remains open for each man and each country to either accept or reject the essence of The Message.

"I'm a practical man, Senator. I'm well aware that our government and others in the alliance must consider the reaction of Arab League[53] nations, organizations like the PLO,[54] Fatah,[55] and certainly Hamas.[56], certainly Al-Qaeda[57], and perhaps other organizations of like nature. Thus, whatever decisions are taken, must be thoughtful, comprehensive compromises that consider points of view that may be antithetical to our own preferences. In my view, it is realism that must adjudicate, sir.

"Last, I believe, and let me repeat that, I *believe*, as distinct to any intellectual or scientific conclusion, that The Message is indeed a gospel of Jesus. What remains outside the parameters of belief is if the conclusions of the world's best science and great minds are accepted. If those findings are rejected for whatever reason, or if The Message itself is tarnished or suppressed in other places of the world, then the matter is truly in the hands of God, not in ours. And if all findings are accepted, but for private or political reasons The Message itself is rejected, then again I say to you . . . the matter is truly in the hands of God, not in ours.

"But one thing is clear to me, Senator. The Message offers something that mankind has been unable to master since the beginning of recorded history: peaceful co-existence through the knowledge that all people are brothers, because all of us were created by the same God, even though we may refer to God by different names.

"If things like man's injustice to man, war, and all of the baser sides of humanity could be altered by the potential for change The Message advocates, then I think we ought to give it a chance. Personally, I'd much rather be on the side of God, than of men. One has a great record; the others are sadly deficient."

Amazingly, the room remained silent for several minutes. The clapping began sporadically, sweeping the audience like a tidal wave, people rising to their feet, whistling, and calling out "Hear, hear!"

Although he had been prepared and committed to do his duty, as well as to honor the sacrifice of all those connected with the scrolls, Andy just wanted it to be over so he could leave. He felt tired from the inside out; he felt a pervading sense of sadness; he felt doubt as to the ability of mankind to address its own prejudices, cruelties, and wounds. He longed for the peace of Windward Farm. He ached for Aniela. He felt completely drained and powerless to influence the auditors to do what his scientific mind believed was the right course.

Andy endured and responded to further questions from other panel members for the remainder of the morning, when it was decided that the most productive course would be for all auditors to fully familiarize themselves with the thick binder containing the report Andy presented.

"Thank you, Dr. Stanton," said the Chairman. "For the moment, that will be all. You are excused until further notice, although we will require more testimony from you tomorrow. You'll be notified. Thank you, son, now go and get some rest. I suspect you need it after all you've been through." The Chairman gave him a kind smile.

A surge of relief swept over him. Andy stood, nodded his head to the panel, left the meeting room, checked through the various security points, and walked out of the building into the sunshine. He took in a deep breath to cleanse his troubled heart, all the while imagining the crisp smell of Austrian mountain air many miles away, and the lilting sound of the laughter of a tall and beautiful woman with hair of spun silver and gold.

ChApter 62

Washington, D.C.

The following day wore on with questions from every member of the panel, as well as from the President himself. Representatives of mainstream religion were given the floor for both questions and statements. The counsel of members of the Supreme Court in attendance was sought. The hearing, insofar as Andy was involved, concluded at 11:00 PM after twelve hours' duration on the second day, with an hour's break for a "brown bag" snack served *in situ*, and no break for the dinner meal.

Anyone who left the meeting room for rest room needs was accompanied by a member of the Secret Service. No ingoing or outgoing telephone calls occurred, as all cellular phones, 2-way pagers, personal organizers, and other palm devices, briefcases and laptop computers had been disallowed. Everyone had been subjected to metal detector and X-Ray inspection as a requirement, had been issued valid DOD passes, and were given escorts.

For one special interval in the life of modern man, no one complained because everyone recognized the importance, the immediacy, and the staggering implications of the task at hand. For one special moment in time, everyone present worked together.

After a brief conference with the President, the Chairman suggested that everyone "sleep on everything we have heard." Sleeping arrangements had been made through the Protective Services Unit of the PPD (Pentagon Police Department under the auspices of the Department of Defense) and FPCON Normal (Force Protection Condition Normal, as distinct to increasingly elevated like Alpha, Bravo, Charlie, and Delta) conditions had been assigned. Thus, all security issues for participants had been addressed. They would reconvene for a working breakfast at 7:00 AM.

The next morning, as the exhausted group was busy downing as much caffeine as possible, the President arrived, and everyone rapidly took their seats.

The room immediately quieted as the President stood before the podium.

"Good morning to you all. I suspect that few of you slept much last night. I know I did not. At the outset, I'd like to thank all of you for your valuable input over the last two days. Your comments were truly thought provoking. I know we all have pressing business at hand. I also recognize that it is unfair of me to expect you to make a recommendation for a decision of this magnitude beyond comments and statements already presented.

"Therefore, the final responsibility for the position taken by the United States of America, given the likely geo-political fall-out, and the danger that The Message will ignite further unrest between Muslim Fundamentalists and the Judeo-Christian world, must rest ultimately with me.

"Friends, all things considered, there is only one decision a country with our heritage can make. The Message must be released and cannot be suppressed, hidden, or altered in any way. Such a step would be unforgivable before God and man.

"I will personally inform the members of the alliance of the position of our government. Thereafter, I will coordinate release arrangements with members of the alliance, providing the salient background to The Message, as well as The Message itself . . . in its entirety. Two days following the receipt of all materials by the other members of the alliance, assuming they concur, global release under the auspices and complete agreement of the alliance will be effected.

"Now I recognize that this is an ambitious schedule. It is possible, of course, that we may encounter some snags or delays, depending upon the reaction of other alliance members. But I am going to trust that, with God's help, we can move forward with prudence. I shall do my utmost in this regard. I would ask that all of you pray for success in our upcoming international discussions.

"The Chairman will adjourn and provide directions and closure arrangements for this meeting. Thank you." With that, the President was hustled from the room by a bevy of Secret Service agents, but not before he gave Andy a salute.

A quiet buzz slowly filled the large meeting room. As Andy looked around, he could see obvious relief on the faces of all delegates. Corruthers squeezed his shoulder, sitting back in his chair with a faint smile on his face.

"Well, Andy, it's over. Dare I say, 'dismissed with honor'? Now, I expect you'll be wanting to get out of here. Go on, go!"

"Yes, sir. Thank you, thanks very much." He didn't need to be told a second time. His thoughts turned to home and he was overwhelmed by a desire to see Windward and soak in his family's love.

Bianca's comment replayed in Andy's mind, "Maybe there is a God."

Chapter 63

Windward Farm, Maine,
Late Summer 2008

As they played a special edition of Maine Monopoly, Jeremy could not get enough of looking at Andy. 'Thank you, God, for bringing my boy home safe,' he thought, just as he had thought it earlier, and the day before that, and the day before that.

"Andy, you stink!" pouted Luke, as he counted out the tariff for landing on one of Andy's properties with a hotel. "You've got more houses and hotels than any of us."

"Luke, stop being a baby," chided Marcy. "You'd be just as unbearably smug if they were your hotels. Besides, you've got all the utilities and . . . darn . . . I've just landed on one!"

The sound of their children's squabbling and laughter was music to Jeremy's ears. It sang "normal," a lacking ingredient of the past many months. He glanced over to the kitchen area where Liz was rolling a piecrust for the evening's dessert. Her humming drew his attention,. Jeremy leaned back in his chair lighting his pipe and smiled. He was the luckiest man in the world. 'Thank you, God.' He picked up the newspaper, and absently joined his wife in humming the chorus, "Rejoice in the Lord always, and again I say rejoice!"

The following afternoon, Marcy and Andy went for a ride. They had packed a picnic lunch and relaxed on the promontory looking out at a calm sea. It had been an idyllic, sunny afternoon reminiscent of years gone by. Marcy had shared her angst about Tre, her love for Tommy, continuing concern for him and their future, and her mounting restlessness. Despite an increasing practice, Marcy was less and less invigorated by her job, although her nature made her meet the daily challenges with nothing less than her usual excellence.

Andy told Marcy about Aniela, their trip through Austria and Germany, the things he had seen, and the wonderful moments they had shared.

"Wow, you're in love, too! Typical, we always seem to do things at the same time," she said. "Aren't we just the pair? Both of us in love, and both our partners are in Europe."

"Yeah, kind of takes the twin thing to extremes, don't you think? But I'm going to go back there and get her, Marce. I'm going to bring her home to Windward so you can all meet her. You'll love her."

"Are you two going to get married, Andy? I mean, have you asked her?"

He frowned. "No, not yet. At least I haven't asked her formally, but we've talked about it."

"Where would you live? Giving up her home country and her profession is a lot to ask, don't you think?" After a pause and Andy's silence, she exclaimed, "Oh, no! Don't tell me you're going to live there," worry lines etching her brow and punctuating her remark.

"Hold your horses, babe. We haven't gotten that far yet. Actually, no, I don't want to live there. I don't want to live anywhere over there for a number of reasons. I want to be close to home. That's one thing I learned about myself over the last few months. I'm going to make some changes in my life. I want to be close to home and the people I love, and I want to be somewhere relatively safe and normal."

Marcy looked at her brother, at once thrilled with his decision, but cognizant of something hidden imprinted in his face. Was it worry, or was it the memory of harrowing experiences? She knew all too well about the ravaging effects of atypical events.

"So, Andy," Marcy began hesitantly, "now that you're done with all that stuff in Europe . . ." She sighed, visibly struggling with how to continue.

"My last assignment, you mean?" he interrupted, amused at how she was tiptoeing around the subject. "It's okay, Marce, I can talk about it now. At least, the parts of it that are public info."

"Good, okay, so now that it's over . . . it is over, right?" He nodded, knowing she had more questions. "Good, right. I just wondered, seeing as there's all this hoopla and posturing in the news. What's it really all about? They haven't released much, except that some ancient documents were found that seem to be a missing gospel of Jesus, and that several heads of state had a big meeting about it because it has some kind of potential effect on international relations. Is that right? I never know how much to believe of what's said in the news."

"Yes, that's about it," he said wistfully.

"And? If you think you're going to get away with stopping there, Andrew Vale Stanton, I've got news for you!" She punched him playfully in the shoulder.

"Ouch! Is that any way to treat your long, lost brother who loves you, and who brought that special, oh, never mind." Andy tried to act hurt, but he chuckled to himself.

"Special what?" He made a zipping motion to his lips. "Andy! Special what? Come on, that's not fair, tell me. You brought me a present, didn't you?" The two wrestled just as they had done when they were children.

"Okay, okay," he said to Marcy, "stop the tickling and maybe I'll tell you. Which is it to be . . . the documents or the special something? You can have only one."

"You know, sometimes you're the most frustrating, the most . . . ooh!" Marcy said in exasperation. "Hmm, let me see. If I know you, you might tell me about the special thing, but not let me have it because it's probably a birthday or Christmas present, so I'd have to wait anyway. So, my choice is the documents. Now, give!"

Marcy poured them some more tea from the thermos, tucking her long legs. Andy's smile dissolved and his face turned serious . . . not unhappy, but contemplative.

"I won't bore you with the difficult details surrounding their retrieval and translation, but they are verified, authentic documents, Marcy, and perhaps the most exciting find in two centuries. I feel privileged just to have worked with them."

"Where are they now?" she inquired.

"Oh, the originals are with the Mossad. I have no idea what they did with them, but I presume the Israel Antiquities Authority has them somewhere safe under the auspices of a Mossad detachment. By now, a team of scientists will have seen to appropriate preservation and handling. Since the horse is out of the barn, so to speak, I think they'll be safe for posterity.

"The scrolls not only theirs by right, but I think they regard them as a kind of insurance or leverage in the summit talks. If they can make the group of Arabs who want to wipe Israel from the face of the earth look like they're going against the will of God, even as foretold by Jesus, well, that'll take a lot of wind out of their sails. Best case, maybe it'll cause them to reign in Al Qaida and similar terrorist groups. Anything that puts the brakes on those lunatics is fine by me. But it's not going to be easy, that's for sure."

"Agreed, but you still haven't told me the nitty gritty. Why is everyone making such a flap about it? There's all this secrecy with talks and such between nations, summit conferences . . . you hear it all over the news. And the pundits say we've got to handle things carefully so as to avoid inflaming an already tenuous relationship with some of the Arab countries. How come? That's nothing new, but why do these ancient documents have the power to stir things up worse than they are? What do they say, Andy?"

Andy breathed deeply and exhaled loudly. "What do they say? That's a huge question, Marce, and would really take much more time than the sun will let us have today. But, in short, the man whose words were recorded—the Teacher of Righteousness, later identified by the scribes who made the scrolls as Jesus of Nazareth—foretells in his message of love and access to God, that the Father of all things and all peoples wants them to live a life of brotherly love and understanding.

"They say that the responsibility of those who have come to know God and chosen to follow His will, have the corresponding responsibility to spread the message throughout the world to all people, to teach the way of access to God, so all people can be under God's Will and exist in His pleasure.

"They say that if the people so blessed with light fail to do God's Will in this respect, despite leading pious, religious lives paying homage to God, they forfeit God's pleasure, incur his wrath, and lock themselves out of the Kingdom of Paradise. In other words, they give up the promise of eternal life, and guarantee themselves a life of hell on earth, and perhaps thereafter. That's it in a nutshell."

"Are you serious?" Andy frowned at her. "No, I know you're serious, Andy, you know that's just an expression, and a stupid one at that. It's just that, well, that's not how things happened, historically speaking, is it?

"I mean, all kinds of religions developed over the centuries. Granted, most of them have at their center that goodness, peacefulness, and honoring God is the right way to go, but the methods, tenets, cultures, practices, and the rest of it . . . they're all very different. Heck, even the Arabs and Christians had and have infighting in their own midst, like the warfare between Sunni and Shia, or the Crusades, and the Reformation years, to name only a few. Lord, the Message could literally topple religions and societies, to say nothing of governments. Hmm, that is, if it's accepted. Somehow I don't think that's going to be an overnight proposition, if it has any success at all, given the nature of the human."

Andy stretched, leaning back to look at the sky. "Yes, Marce, it could, but only if it's accepted, as distinct to being rejected *in toto*. That's why it's been hidden all these years, why those bad guys were trying to get it to prevent it from becoming public information, why the initial panel was international in scope, and why the talks are international. It's a very delicate situation and not one that's going to get resolved quickly or without hiccups. I just hope it can get settled without more violence."

"Yeah," said Marcy thoughtfully, "I can see that. No wonder you had to stay under cover for so long with a hot ticket like that one."

"Marce, the trick is going to be finding a commonality based upon this undeniable message of the scrolls. It's a path to a clear destiny, Marcy, a way for all of mankind to live in peaceful co-existence by recognizing their same root.

"Remember, it's a clear and definitive prophecy from the time of Jesus that the Jews would face persistent turmoil and, sadly, attempts at murder or worse. Well, we know that's happened times over. But the most riveting portion deals with the Jewish people being the children of God, the chosen people.

"While I'm sure they're fed up with being called that, given their history, the Message tells them that they'll receive the outpouring of God only if they act as servants to the rest of mankind. They're given a mandate of sorts to be missionaries to share the message of the love of the Father. They're told by Jesus, a Jew, that they have to share and show the rest of God's children how to reach God; that theirs is the task to spread the message that all are one . . . brothers . . . made by the same God." Marcy could see and feel Andy's passion.

"The catch is, if they don't follow the Message's instruction, they lose out on everything. They lose the promise of the Kingdom and they lose God's favor. Early Christians were Jews as well, so the Message applies to them equally. And those early Christians grew into us, so we're on the hook, too.

"We know from history that the Jews have already experienced terrible persecution from ancient times to today. We also know that they haven't followed the words of The Message. Neither have we as Christians, although some would argue that point on the basis of Christianity's worldwide missionary program and other things. But one has to remember that they've been hidden for centuries. So mankind's development has taken place without benefit of The Message. Now that it's out, there's no excuse for anyone anymore.

"The fly in the ointment is that if the Jews—and presumably the Christians who evolved from Jewish roots—fail, everyone loses. The Teacher of Righteousness, Jesus, says that God won't accept one without the other. So, both are doomed, but for the power and persistence of God's chosen people to bring all the world into God's fold."

Marcy shook her head, shocked at the breadth of his words.

"Whew! I can't imagine all of the Islamic countries just throwing up all their culture, history, and beliefs and falling into line, can you? Then there's us, the Christian faith, I mean. We're very close to Judaism. Heck, we base all our religious record and history on Jewish scripture, and trace our roots from Judaism. Christ was a Jew, after all, followed Jewish law, and was a product of its culture and genealogy, right?" As the seriousness and scope of the issue settled in on her, Marcy began to quiver, and Andy reached out to hold her hand in his.

"Correct on all counts, sweetie. As to whether civilized man will be able to swallow the direction and put aside self-serving interests, vendettas, differences, desire for world superiority, and the rest of it, well, that remains to be seen.

"But one thing is certain: the scrolls are legit, and can't be denied or refuted. So it follows that if we want to avoid all the prophecies about the tribulation and global unrest that leads to cataclysmic war and perhaps total destruction, we've got to find a way to reach out to our resistant human brothers and convince them.

"It wouldn't mean abolishing a way of life, or destroying things like culture and language for a common one. But it would mean the acceptance of God as God, the same God, despite being referred to by different names because of culture, language, history, geography, things like that. And it would mean setting aside ethnic, religious, and political hatred.

"It all hinges on everyone's acceptance of Jesus as the singularly chosen Deliverer of God's Word for all people, for all time. And it would mean that, oh, babe, it would mean a lot of changes in hundreds of ways that would affect international relations, governments, global attitudes, resources, industries, and personal, everyday attitudes. It's a tall order, huh?"

Marcy sat silent, quietly and thoughtfully nodding her head. She pulled his hand to her cheek, kissing it. "You said it outlined a clear destiny, didn't you, Andy? Clear but complicated destiny seems more like it, because it sure sounds like it's going to get very, very complicated in the weeks and months ahead. Global guilt on the one hand; global resistance on the other. No matter how you slice it, it looks like a pretty impossible situation."

Andy heaved a sigh, shifting to sit close to her, slinging an arm around her waist as they looked out at the endless power of the sea. "If only we'd found them sooner," he whispered, "but now that we have them, I only hope it's not too late. If humankind rejects The Message, even though the majority profess a belief in God, they guarantee the wrath and disdain of the God in whom they have based their history, their beliefs, and their future. I'd hate to be on the receiving end of that unknown."

She stroked his face, wishing she could erase what were clearly painful memories made more poignant by current worry and speculation. "My poor Andy. You've had a rough time of it, haven't you?"

Andy lay back on the blanket, chewing on a piece of grass. "Rough... hmm... no, what I had, Marce, was the worst time of my life. I exposed the love of my life to unwarranted stress and danger; I put some very good people at risk because they tried to help me; because I couldn't shake my tails and get to England safely under the circumstances, a team had to come and rescue my butt, possibly jeopardizing my country; I became the courier of a message that puts our world in flux and risks our very future; and I... became a killer... I killed men, Marce. I took away lives," he choked.

He looked at her, unsurprised at the myriad of emotions revealed by her expression. "Guess you don't think I'm such a great brother now, do you?" His eyes overflowed and, although he was annoyed by it, he felt too depressed to brush the tears away.

Marcy lay down next to him, snuggling close. "Oh, Andy, I'm so sorry. I didn't know. How you must be suffering, and how you must have suffered for all those weeks. But you had to go on, and go on, you did. You didn't give in, and you didn't give up, because you knew deep down that what you had to do was for something bigger than yourself, no matter the cost. That took selfless courage, brother mine, and a hell of a lot of guts and discipline, too."

They were quiet for several minutes. The few clouds overhead danced slowly and lazily toward the far horizon, leaving a stunning, azure blue, clear sky above them. The sun warmed them; the soft breeze washed over them; the sea gently rolled against the rocky shoreline, rhythmically cleansing them of troubled thoughts and calming their spirits.

"Andy, you need to know something," Marcy whispered against his shoulder.

"Hmm? What is it, Marce? Nothing can be as bad as my confession," he said dourly. "And remember, what I told you is between us only. Leave the rest of the family out of it, okay? I don't think I could stand Mom and Dad knowing, or the twins."

"Of course, I never thought it would be otherwise . . . things between us stay between just us, like always. No, what I wanted to tell you is that someone tried to kill me, too."

Andy sat erect, pulling Marcy up to face him, looking sternly at her. "What?"

"Yeah, it was over the horse thing I told you about. But that's not the important bit, because I was really in no ultimate danger. The two undercover FBI agents were within running distance. I suppose he could have snapped my neck before they got there, but he didn't. He just kept strangling me. Sounds funny to talk about it now, you know?"

"Go on," he said patiently, all the while his heart beat frantically at the news.

"Well, it was the guy who killed one of the grooms. Hosea was his name . . . the groom . . . he was a sweet guy. Now he's gone, and all because of greed. When I caught Phil and his accomplice implanting another mare, he didn't like it, and was trying to cover their tracks. Anyhow, that's not the important part.

"What I wanted to tell you was that when I was so scared, choking, not able to breathe and all . . . the only thing I could think of was fighting back, you know? I finally remembered that I had a used syringe in my pocket, because the sharps container was in the office. I had been walking toward the office when I heard them in the stall.

"My brain said, 'stab him with the needle in the eye', and I was just about to do that when Harry and Sandy stopped him. So, if there'd been just another minute, I'd have killed someone too. The point is, Andy, when you find yourself in that kind of situation, all of us just react for our own survival, no matter who we are, or the kind of person we are under normal circumstances. We fight to stay alive. It's no different with war. It's just that things like this are a personal kind of warfare.

"Okay, you killed someone. I'm not making light of it, and I know that's a horrible thing to have to live with. But it's not something you deliberately set out to do, for Heaven's sake. The whole point of lollygagging around Europe was to take the high road and avoid confrontation, wasn't it? So what you did, you did because you were forced to do it. Think how you'd feel if you'd done nothing. Then you'd have lost the copy of the scrolls, and someone you love . . . someone innocent could have been killed because of your inaction. From all you've told me, Aniela was in danger too, wasn't she?

"So, I think you need to take a different perspective on all of it. Seriously, Andy, you'll never learn to deal with it otherwise. I know you, and you're thinking about what you did in terms of the essence of the Message—brotherhood. But don't forget, soldiers for God have died before in war and in persecution. You didn't die, Andy. God kept you alive for a reason: to fulfill His mission, get the copy of the scrolls to safety, and translate the Message. You killed, yes, but you killed for the reason that you were acting as a soldier of God, to keep God's Message for the world secure. You need to hold tight to that justification."

After a short time, he hugged her, nodding his assent. "You're a pretty smart cookie, Dr. Stanton. Thanks." 'Thank you, God,' he thought, 'thank you a thousand times over for keeping her safe, and for giving her to me as a sister.'

"It's going to take awhile, but I'm going to try to follow your advice. I never considered . . . never thought of it in that way. Thanks, Marce, you've always been able to soothe my soul." After a few moments, he laughed out loud.

"What? What's so funny?" she demanded, smiling at his change in mood.

"Oh, something just occurred to me. Of all the people in the world, only you, Mom, and Aniela have that effect on me—relieving my concerns and calming my spirit. And in this case, I can't tell Mom, and I can't speak with Aniela about it for a ton of reasons. Maybe someday we'll be able to sort it all out, but not just now. I wanted to give her time to heal. So that leaves you, sister mine, and yet again, you've come through.

"Here we are in our favorite place under God's sky next to the sea, all of it working its magic. Oh, Marce, I've been so sick inside, and I've felt tired beyond belief. But today, well, it's been good for me. Kind of makes me think it's another 'meant-to-be' time. It seems like forever since I could even think about the future. The past has been dragging me down and down. But now, after our time together, I find myself actually wondering what lies in store for me next, you know?"

"Well, brother mine, let me know when you're planning your little Austrian excursion, will you? If we keep paralleling each other, I'd like advance warning as to when I'll get to see Tommy again."

It felt good to laugh together, as they packed up their knapsacks, tacked the horses, and headed for home. They both felt free. The magic of their special place had performed its enchantment once again, empowered by their loyalty and love for each other.

"Mom's got another really good dinner tonight. I peeked," said Andy mischievously, as they neared the barn.

"You big baby! You always peek," said Marcy, laughing. "Hey, who's that with Dad?"

Andy looked toward the house and, in a flash, leapt out of the saddle, tossing the reins to Marcy. He ran to the driveway and hugged a tall, blonde woman, swinging her around and around.

Marcy said to Rex, "I've no idea how it happened, but that must be the famous Aniela, so I know it's going to be a really, good day. Come on, you two, let's get you into the barn." Rex nickered in reply.

"Aniela, oh, Aniela! How did you . . . oh, who cares, you're here!" Andy was ecstatic.

"*Liebling*, your papa came to meet me. Is a surprise, *ja*? I am so happy to see you!" She hugged him fiercely, laughing with him.

"My Andrew, here," she said, handing him an envelope. "I am to give you this at once," she said. "You are to open it as soon as you see me, but I do not think one kiss is a bad reason to disobey the order, do you? It will not make you in trouble?"

"No, sweetheart, it'll be fine. But I'll claim the right for another kiss after I deal with this," he said smiling at her, beyond excitement at her arrival. He looked at the official envelope bearing Liam Corruthers name and division. Andy's face fell, his heart thumping as he opened the envelope.

'Not now, please God, not now,' he prayed silently. Inside was a single sheet of paper with Liam's meticulous handwriting. It read:

Andy—

"Well done, good and faithful servant." Bull and I thought this was the least your country could do. Bianca tipped us off. Enjoy!

Liam Corruthers

Andy read and reread the note, his smile and happiness growing more expansive, looking suspiciously at his father.

"Ayeh, I knew," answered Jeremy to the unspoken question, "but I was sworn to secrecy. You're not the only one the government trusts, you know. This has been in the works awhile. That's why your mother's been outdoing herself lately. We weren't sure exactly when it would happen, and she wanted to make the day really special for you."

Jeremy collected Aniela's bags and walked toward the house. "Come on in, now, honey," he called over his shoulder. "You're sure to be wanting to get refreshed after that long haul."

But Aniela didn't hear him. She was too busy kissing his son.

Chapter 64

London, England, Winter 2009

"Hullo, yes, this is Lord Brandon. What? Oh my God, are you sure? Yes, yes of course, we shall be there presently. Thank you . . . thank you very much."

Placing the phone in its cradle, Lord Brandon collapsed into his leather desk chair, holding his head in his shaking hands. 'Wake up from your sleep, rise from the dead, and Christ will shine on you,[58]' he whispered through his tears.

Having composed himself, he hurried into the central hall, calling "Madeline! Madeline! Come quickly, my dear, I've had the most wonderful news!"

"Findley, I've no idea how long we shall be," said Lord Brandon as the chauffeur helped Lady Brandon from the Bentley under the hospital's portico. "I expect our visit will be only a short one, so perhaps you had better wait in the Reception Area for us to come down. There's a good man."

As they reached the fourth floor, an impressive group of doctors awaited them. Mr. Barker, the specialist heading the team of doctors overseeing all aspects of Tommy's case, approached with a wide grin.

"My Lord, how good of you to get here so quickly." Then to Madeline, he inclined his head. "Lady Brandon."

"Of course, Mr. Barker. Now then, tell us everything, and be sure to start at the very beginning, else Lady Brandon shall pounce on us all."

With a dismissive gesture to her husband, Lady Madeline Brandon took a seat in the Waiting Area and entreated Barker to begin.

"Do sit down, William," she commanded.

"Well, M'Lord . . . M'Lady . . ." the specialist began, deferentially inclining his head to each in turn, "your son has given us a sign that he has overcome the coma. His eyes opened, um, only momentarily and unfocused, understand, but they opened. And even better, he had a reaction to a sensitivity test on the fingers of both hands. We called you at once, of course. I've ordered that nothing further be done until we conferred with you."

"Wonderful news, Mr. Barker, wonderful! Now what do the other doctors say about his overall condition?" inquired Lord Brandon.

"It seems that the wound tract is healing nicely, sir, and all the major organs are functioning normally. His vitals are reasonably good overall. Of course, he's lost considerable weight and muscle tone, but that can be addressed if he fully regains consciousness and, uh, has no, uh . . ."

"You mean when he fully regains consciousness," Madeline interjected firmly. "I simply will not entertain 'ifs,' Mr. Barker."

"Now, now, my dear," soothed Lord Brandon.

"And do you mean to say that you lack confidence that Thomas will regain full use of his limbs, Mr. Barker? Let's not pussyfoot around this matter, shall we? I assume you have tested his legs and feet, as well as his arms and hands?" Lady Brandon held Mr. Barker's gaze with a determined stare.

"Well, M'Lady, we have of course done some preliminary sensitivity tests on several sites. But Mr. Brandon's reactions have been, shall we say, in a range from zero to only partial to date. But it is early on, remember that. And today was the first time he opened his eyes."

"I see," said Lady Brandon, pursing her lips. "Mr. Barker, thank you for being straightforward, and please thank the remainder of the team for me. I shall speak with them all in a few moments after consulting with Lord Brandon, assuming they can spare me the time." She nodded her dismissal, and Mr. Barker flashed a worried glance at Lord Brandon before departing.

"Madeline, really, my dear . . . let's not . . . well, let's just be grateful and take this one step at a time, shall we?" Lord Brandon took her hand, stroking it.

"William, I want your full backing on this," she said in a determined but soft tone. "Thomas is all we have, and we've almost lost him twice . . .

first to that mad woman who shot him, and then to this wretched coma. That he has held on and on, is a tribute to the man he is. I believe we must fully support the man we know him to be, even though he cannot speak for himself.

"Therefore, that is precisely what we are going to do. I am certain it is what he would wish of us. He has given us a sign, William. That said, it is up to us to marshal the forces full steam ahead!

"Now, while I go and speak with the doctors to set up a constant watch and program of physical therapy to encourage and repair his body, you place a call to Marcia. If there is a tonic for our boy, William, it is Marcia. Her love for him will call him back, now that he can hear. If he will respond to anything, he will respond to her.

"We are going to have a victory, William. A victory, I say! Never doubt that, my love."

As she rose, he kissed her hand, silently weeping, nodding his head. She bent toward him, cradling his head against her ample bosom, whispering, "My darling William, you've been very brave and strong. Our son has those qualities too. Have faith, William. I'll be just a few moments, and then we shall return to Eaton Place for a quiet celebration."

Across the Atlantic, Marcy was just returning from a winter ride. Rex had faithfully followed their routine without so much as a nudge from her the entire time. Now back at the barn, she distractedly went through the motions of removing his tack and rubbing him down, and feeding all the horses. As she walked toward the barn door to leave, she noticed that Rex was standing at his stall door totally ignoring his full feed trough.

"What's the matter, boy?" she crooned. "Have I been neglecting you?" She walked into his stall to pat and scratch him in atonement. He nickered softly and hung his head over her shoulder in contentment.

"Oh, Rex, you're such a sweetheart. You know my mind's been elsewhere, don't you, boy?" Sighing, she hugged her horse affectionately, and closed the stall door. The intercom buzzed.

"Darling, it's Lord Brandon from England," her mother's voice informed excitedly. "Come quickly!"

Marcy flicked off the intercom and, turning toward the door, spied Rex still standing at the stall door, looking anxiously toward her.

"It's Tommy, Rex. You knew, didn't you?"

As she ran up the hill from the barn, Rex craned his beautiful head and neck over the stall bars watching her. He whinnied his approval, encouragement, and love. She turned and waved at him, a glorious smile beautifying her lovely face.

Endnotes

1   Psalm 23: Song of David: Adonai is my shepherd, I lack nothing. He has me lie down in grassy pasture, He leads me by quiet water, and He restores my inner person. He guides me in the right paths for the sake of His own Name. Even if I pass through death-dark ravines, I will fear no disaster, for you are with me; Your rod and staff reassure me. You prepare a table for me, even as my enemies watch; You anoint my head with oil from an overflowing cup. Goodness and grace will pursue me every day of my life; And I will live in the house of Adonai for years and years to come.

2   Thank you in Hebrew and Arabic, respectively.

3   All praise and thanks is for Allah

4   Someone who knows better or best and who does not hesitate to inform others about. it; loosely to "know-it-all."

5   Idiot, literally "dumb-head."

6   Thank God!

7   An extension of the Dominican Order in Jerusalem at the time; for over a century the pre-eminent research center and school for biblical and archaeological studies in the Holy Land.

8   Earthen jars used for storage of relics, important documents (usually in the form of Papyri or leather scrolls), etc.

9   Russian nesting doll created in 1890 In Abramtsevo estate in new Moscow. Called "matryoshka" to symbolize image of a healthy, portly-figured mother of a big, peasant family.

10   Arabic for Noah

11   Arabic for Moses

12   Arabic for Jesus

13   Mossad—Institute for Intelligence and Special Operations, Israel

14   The die is cast. May God's will be done.

15   A warm, comfortable, convivial atmosphere, often associated with drinking.

16   "God is with us"

17 Literally, "greet God"—a traditional passing form of hello in Bavaria and Austria

18 Leather shorts, the wearing of which is associated with Bavarian culture

19 Beer originally brewed by monks

20 Direction Centrale des Renseignements Généraux—France.

21 Abdullah Ahmed Abdullah—identified terrorist.

22 Mujahedin-e Khalq Organization.

23 BND—Federal Intelligence Service, Germany.

24 While I breathe, I hope.

25 Where there is life, there is hope!

26 Now I know what love is—from *Virgil, Eclogues* VIII.

27 Pliny the Elder—a geographer whose writing was after the fall of Jerusalem in 70 AD, who described a group of Essenes living in a desert community close to the ruined town of Ein Gedi, seen by some scholars as evidence that Khirbet Qumran was in fact an Essene settlement.

28 According to ancient Arabic belief, caves were sources of power.

29 Sweetheart

30 A segment or unit of prayer consisting of standing and reciting a chapter from the Qur'an, bowing at the waist and glorifying God, and then prostrating twice on the ground while extolling God's power.

31 A headscarf or veil Muslim women wear over their hair, a requirement for women to wear in the presence of men to whom they are not married or related.

32 A veil over the face.

33 The ritual Islamic prayers performed five times daily.

34 A gemstone believed to give power and influence to its owner; these particular stones were mined in the eastern lava fields of Saudi Arabia.

35 Qur'an 6:164

36 *Tasbihs* or *masbahas* (from the Arabic word for glorify) are beads on a string, sometimes carried by Muslims much in the same way as Catholics carry rosary beads.

37 A person who has committed the entire Qur'an to memory; the name reference means a '*guardian*' literally.

38 A fresh tomato salad with chopped parsley, fresh mint, and crushed wheat.

39 Stuffed grapevine leaves containing rice, lemon, and (usually) lamb.

40 "Here you go, bastards. I just hate men who treat women badly!"

41 "Hi, boys. Like what you see? Yes? Well, I don't like what I see.

42 "Sisters... my closest friend...always, in everything."

43 How you must suffer! I regret asking for your help. It must bring everything back. Will you forgive me?

44 Two verticals close together to make the jump wider, with the furthest pole higher than the first.

45 A double combination: Two jumps in a row with two strides between; a triple combination: Three jumps in a row with two or three strides between.

46 A type of consonant articulated with the root of the tongue against the phalanx.

47 The sound made when the vocal cords are drawn together by muscular action to interrupt the flow of air expelled from the lungs, *e.g.*, the break separating the syllables of the word "uh-oh."

48 Signs tilted by 45 degrees.

49 Signs modified with additional wedges.

50 Crosshatched signs.

51 A fundamental unit in written language including alphabetic letters, characters, numerals, punctuation marks, and other individual symbols of writing systems.

52 The smallest unit that has semantic meaning: spoken morphemes are composed of distinctive units of sound called "phonemes," and in written language have the smallest written units called "graphemes."

53 Currently 22 nations: Egypt, Iraq, Jordan, Lebanon, Saudi Arabia, Syria, Yemen, Libya, Sudan, Morocco, Tunisia, Kuwait, Algeria, UAE, Bahrain/ Qatar, Oman, Mauritania, Somalia, Palestine, Dijibouti, Comoros, Eritrea (observer since '03), Venezuela (observer since '06), and India (observer since '07). Its goal is to draw relations between members closer and coordinate collaboration to safeguard independence and sovereignty through political, economic, cultural, and social programs to promote member interests.

54 *Munazzamat al-Tahrir al-Filastiniyyah* or "Palestine Liberation Organization," a political and paramilitary organization regarded by the Arab League as the legitimate representative of the Palestinian people. Its goal is the liberation of Palestine through armed struggle, calling for a right of return and self-determination for Palestinians.

55 A reverse acronym of *Harakat al-Tahrir al-Watani al-Filastini*— Palestinian National Liberation Movement," *Fatah* is a major political party and the largest division of the PLO, a multi-party coalition with center-left bias in Palestinian politics. Unlike its rival, *Hamas*, *Fatah* is not recognized as a terrorist organization.

[56] An acronym for the Arabic phrase *Harakat al-M*
or "Islamic Resistance Movement," a Palestinian
terrorist organization, and political party that hol
in the legislative council of the Palestinian Nation
calls for the destruction of the State of Israel, recla
known as Israel, the West Bank, and the Gaza Stri
Palestinian Islamic State. Its charter asserts that th
Palestinian issue except through *Jihad*.

[57] Al-Qaeda, alternatively spelled al-Qaida and
(meaning *The Base*) is an international Su
movement founded sometime between August 19
1990. Characteristic techniques include suicide
and simultaneous bombings of different targets, a
terrorist organization. Its objectives include the e
Muslim countries, and the creation of a new Isla
beliefs include that a Christian-Jewish alliance i
Islam, and that the killing of bystanders and civilia
in jihad.

[58] Ephesians 5:14, Holy Bible

Character Information And Family Timeline

rr Stanton   Residence: Windward Farm
Anne Grey Vale [Stanton]   coastal Maine

le Stanton   } fraternal
ne Stanton   } twins

arr Stanton   } identical
Stanton   } twins

le marriage   Jeremy (23); Liz (22)
e)

vins born   Jeremy (27); Liz (26)

vins born   Jeremy (35); Liz (34); Andy/Marcy (8)

Jeremy (41); Liz (40); Andy/Marcy (14); Matthew/Luke (6)

summer   Jeremy (53); Liz (52); Andy/Marcy (27)—post college, grad school, and internships; pre-college Matthew/ Luke (18)

t al
nn   Jeremy (55); Liz (54); Andy/Marc (29; Matthew/Luke (20)

cter entries: *Trevois Hattingley Swift* ("Tre"), Cmdr - (32 - Marcia's boyfriend *Thomas Brandon* ("Tommy"), E barrister and equestrian showin US and Europe - (33 - acquaint and client of equine clinic)

43 How you must suffer! I regret asking for your help. It must bring everything back. Will you forgive me?

44 Two verticals close together to make the jump wider, with the furthest pole higher than the first.

45 A double combination: Two jumps in a row with two strides between; a triple combination: Three jumps in a row with two or three strides between.

46 A type of consonant articulated with the root of the tongue against the phalanx.

47 The sound made when the vocal cords are drawn together by muscular action to interrupt the flow of air expelled from the lungs, *e.g.*, the break separating the syllables of the word "uh-oh."

48 Signs tilted by 45 degrees.

49 Signs modified with additional wedges.

50 Crosshatched signs.

51 A fundamental unit in written language including alphabetic letters, characters, numerals, punctuation marks, and other individual symbols of writing systems.

52 The smallest unit that has semantic meaning: spoken morphemes are composed of distinctive units of sound called "phonemes," and in written language have the smallest written units called "graphemes."

53 Currently 22 nations: Egypt, Iraq, Jordan, Lebanon, Saudi Arabia, Syria, Yemen, Libya, Sudan, Morocco, Tunisia, Kuwait, Algeria, UAE, Bahrain/Qatar, Oman, Mauritania, Somalia, Palestine, Dijibouti, Comoros, Eritrea (observer since '03), Venezuela (observer since '06), and India (observer since '07). Its goal is to draw relations between members closer and coordinate collaboration to safeguard independence and sovereignty through political, economic, cultural, and social programs to promote member interests.

54 *Munazzamat al-Tahrir al-Filastiniyyah* or "Palestine Liberation Organization," a political and paramilitary organization regarded by the Arab League as the legitimate representative of the Palestinian people. Its goal is the liberation of Palestine through armed struggle, calling for a right of return and self-determination for Palestinians.

55 A reverse acronym of *Harakat al-Tahrir al-Watani al-Filastini*— Palestinian National Liberation Movement," *Fatah* is a major political party and the largest division of the PLO, a multi-party coalition with center-left bias in Palestinian politics. Unlike its rival, *Hamas*, *Fatah* is not recognized as a terrorist organization.

[56] An acronym for the Arabic phrase *Harakat al-Muqāwama al-Islāmiyya* or "Islamic Resistance Movement," a Palestinian Sunni paramilitary and terrorist organization, and political party that holds as majority of seats in the legislative council of the Palestinian National Authority. Its charter calls for the destruction of the State of Israel, reclamation of all land areas known as Israel, the West Bank, and the Gaza Strip, to be replaced with a Palestinian Islamic State. Its charter asserts that there is no solution to the Palestinian issue except through *Jihad*.

[57] Al-Qaeda, alternatively spelled al-Qaida and sometimes al-Qa'ida, (meaning *The Base*) is an international Sunni Islamist extremist movement founded sometime between August 1988 and late 1989/early 1990. Characteristic techniques include suicide attacks suicide attacks and simultaneous bombings of different targets, and it has been labeled a terrorist organization. Its objectives include the end of foreign influence in Muslim countries, and the creation of a new Islamic caliphate. Reported beliefs include that a Christian-Jewish alliance is conspiring to destroy Islam, and that the killing of bystanders and civilians is Islamically justified in jihad.

[58] Ephesians 5:14, Holy Bible

Character Information
And Family Timeline

Father:	Jeremy Carr Stanton	Residence:	Windward Farm
Mother:	Elizabeth Anne Grey Vale [Stanton]		coastal Maine

Children: Andrew Vale Stanton   } fraternal
                  Marcia Anne Stanton   } twins

                  Matthew Carr Stanton   } identical
                  Luke Grey Stanton   } twins

1972	Stanton/Vale marriage (post college)	Jeremy (23); Liz (22)
1976	Fraternal twins born	Jeremy (27); Liz (26)
1984	Identical twins born	Jeremy (35); Liz (34); Andy/Marcy (8)
1990	Chapter 1	Jeremy (41); Liz (40); Andy/Marcy (14); Matthew/Luke (6)
2002	Chapter 2 Maine late summer	Jeremy (53); Liz (52); Andy/Marcy (27)—post college, grad school, and internships; pre-college Matthew/Luke (18)
2004	Chapter 3 *et al* Maine autumn	Jeremy (55); Liz (54); Andy/Marcy (29; Matthew/Luke (20)
	Main Character entries:	*Trevois Hattingley Swift* ("Tre"), USN Cmdr - (32 - Marcia's boyfriend) *Thomas Brandon* ("Tommy"), English barrister and equestrian showing in US and Europe - (33 - acquaintance and client of equine clinic)

Lord William   } Tommy's visiting
Brandon
Lady Madeline   } English parents
Brandon
Dr. Rawlings ("Doc")—established
equine veterinarian, Marcia's boss
and owner of equine clinic for which
Marcia works
Aniela—Austrian undercover
contact in Austria and Germany,
paleoanthropologist by profession
(30)
Anton—Retired Austrian professor,
respected European author and
academician